LOINCLOTH
MURDER BY MEDIA

by Rick Paiva

LOINCLOTH
MURDER BY MEDIA

by Rick Paiva

First bound edition published 2024

ISBN 979-8-9919265-0-8 (print)

Published by Rick Paiva

Cover photos, treatment and design by D. H. Robbins
Book design by D.H. Robbins—Typeface: Times New Roman 11.5/13

23456

This book is dedicated to my parents, Ray and Julie, who worked so hard to put all their children through college. And to Bob Turner and Dr. Jim Tiedge at Marquette University who both challenged me to pursue my potential.

Many thanks to my patient wife, Linda and our son Jeremy. Special thanks to our daughter Amy who educated me on the lingo unique to a teenage girl.

Thanks to Belinda, Norm and Brad. And a huge thank you to Dave, who has patiently slow-walked me through this process.

Chapter 1

It was the aching cold on the soles of his feet that roused him. Of course, it always felt cold in San Francisco at night, no matter the season. His next sensation was the cool splattering of water on his ankles. His eyes fluttered open and he was shocked to find himself standing in a dark, damp corner.

"Holy shit, I'm naked!" He looked down, confused then horrified, to see himself urinating on the concrete floor. "Dammit Ray!"

Chapter 2

TWO HOURS EARLIER

Ray Pernell's cheeks hurt from laughing so hard. Leaning back in the limo, he saw his reflection in the mirrored ceiling. His hair was now mostly gray, his beard following suit. His normally hazel eyes were red. Ray tried to focus on his three companions. His partner, Carlos Madrigan, and Sol Korman and Les Santarelli, representatives from ThickBrickk Design in LA.

The buttons on Korman's splashy Hawaiian shirt strained to contain his ample midsection. His bald head, gripped by his horned-rimmed glasses, seemed attached directly to his shoulders, as if someone had stolen his neck. Santarelli, short and thin with a mop of bleached blonde hair over dark eyes, was in his traditional suit coat over t-shirt and jeans.

ThickBrickk's expertise in sound design had been instrumental in the completion of the movie trailer. Korman and Santarelli were currently happy captives of the story being spun by Ray's partner, Carlos. He and Ray had worked together at Tucker Entertainment for more than a decade. Madrigan, who topped six-foot-two, with curly dark hair, matching dark eyes, and a neatly trimmed goatee, sipped from a sake bottle while sharing his favorite New Orleans story about the time he and Ray went out on Bourbon Street and drank too many rum-filled "Hurricanes".

"We woke up in our hotel room the next morning, surrounded by dozens of shucked oysters, scattered all over the damn place. They had 'ripened' overnight. Damn, that shit stunk! It cost us a small fortune to bribe the maids to clean that room." Carlos laughed. "It smelled like the inside of a whale."

"Here's to oysters!" Sol held his glass high.

"Here's to maids!" added Les.

Two days earlier, Ray and Carlos had come to San Francisco, from Tucker Entertainment Media headquarters in New York City. Ray, the VP of Creative Services at TEM, never approached an important project without the brilliant creative input of Carlos, his top Senior Creative Director. Tucker's latest big-budget movie, targeting their usual demographic of children and tweens, was due to launch in two months. Ray's department was charged with delivering a trailer to generate nationwide interest. After weeks of developing the video edit, Ray partnered with ThickBrickk on the sound design. Les, Sol, Carlos and Ray had spent the last forty-eight hours perfecting the trailer in a world-class audio production suite.

Ray was anxious to get back to Connecticut, to Mia, his wife of 18 years, and their three kids. It bothered Ray that Mia had to be a single parent during his many business trips. She had given up so much for their family, including her career as a Producer in the Graphic Design business.

Ray's thoughts were interrupted. "Earth to Ray, come in Ray!" It was his buddy Sol, who was holding a nearly full glass of brown liquid, which sloshed around in his unsteady grip. "We're doing shots".

Ray grabbed the glass and downed the liquid in one quick gulp. The whiskey felt like red hot razor blades as it scraped down his throat.

"Holy shit!" said Ray. "That was smooth….not!" The others laughed and went back to pouring another round. Ray leaned back, transfixed by the LED lights chasing each other around the ceiling of the limo.

The limo arrived in front of the boutique Smythville Hotel. There were handshakes and goodbyes all around as Ray and Carlos clumsily exited the vehicle with Ray now holding the half-empty sake bottle. The limo sped away, taking Les and Sol to their downtown hotel.

The elegant Smythville Hotel lobby could have been airlifted in from the 1950's. Hanging from the two-story high ceiling were giant, oversized ceiling fans, turning lazily, casting soft, slowly migrating shadows on the stucco walls. The walls featured ghostly images of San Francisco cable cars. Overstuffed rolled-arm sofas served as anchors to small clusters of period furniture scattered around the generous space. The thick, soft carpeting, featured a splashy green and gold geometric pattern.

Leaning on a tall, leather wingback chair, Ray gulped another mouthful of sake. "Damn, I love this place. One of my favorite hotels in the whole world."

"Well good, cuz you're gonna see it again in about three hours. We are 'wheels up' at six am. Flight's at eight-something"

The desk clerk spoke from behind the desk. "Morning, gentlemen. May I be of any assistance? A wake-up call, perhaps?"

Carlos quelled the urge to laugh at the center stripe of purple hair on the clerk's head. "No need for old-fashioned analog solutions. We come armed with multiple digital devices which shall awaken us from our slumber! Now on to our chambers!"

The two friends entered the elevator. Ray fumbled with his iPhone. "I know I'm on four because I put it in my phone before we left".

"Veteran move. I know I'm on the top floor, whatever number that is."

The door slid open. Ray stumbled as he exited the elevator, falling to one knee, the sake bottle spinning across the floor, spewing its contents like a lawn sprinkler.

"Have that rug removed!" ordered Ray to no one. Struggling to his feet, he grabbed the bottle and weaved toward his room.

"You okay, Ray? Need any help?"

"All good. See you in the lobby in a few hours."

Chapter 3

"Mom, do you have choir practice tonight?"

"Yes, Phoebe. Why?" answered Mia Pernell, scooping oatmeal into the three bowls on the countertop. The school bus for Phoebe and Karl would soon arrive, followed 10 minutes later by the Grant Prep van for Ricky.

"Because I really need to go to Amy's house after school. It's really, really important."

"I'm sure it is, but you'll have to wait until Ricky gets home after wrestling practice."

Karl was shoveling raisins onto his oatmeal. "Gee Mom, I'm seven years old. I can stay home alone for a little while until Ricky gets here. Phoebe's always on her phone, anyway."

Mia was pouring orange juice into three glasses. "I know. Maybe we'll try that soon, but not today."

"C'mon Mom, I'm big now."

"We've been over this before. Since you and Phoebe ride the same bus, she can wait until Ricky gets home after wrestling practice. She'll probably be FaceTiming with Amy the whole time anyway."

Karl grabbed a handful of bacon strips.

"Karl!" admonished Mia, "Leave some for everyone else."

"Not me," said Phoebe. "I'm trying to get skinny. Junior Prom is next month."

"Me neither," said Ricky. "Coach wants me to make weight at least two days before the freshman meet next week. Can you and Dad come?"

"We'll have to check with your father when he gets back from San Francisco. But I'm planning on it."

"Oh yay. I get all the bacon!" said Karl.

"Please leave me a strip or two," said Mia. "Dishes in the sink before you leave. Don't forget your backpacks."

———————

Mia flopped on the soft couch, her tiny frame sprawled across the cool leather. She had promised to call Debbie Slater today. She hadn't seen her best friend since last week and was looking forward to catching up.

After a sip of her Earl Grey tea, Mia headed to the den to grab her laptop. Pausing in front of the hallway mirror, she saw a pretty Asian woman with shoulder length dark hair, almond eyes, and porcelain skin. "Gotta do something about those crow's feet!"

She opened her laptop journal entry from last night. She found it relaxing and sometimes helpful to recount the events of each day. It was usually the last thing she did before going to sleep.

Last night's journal entry included "Mom and Dad anniversary next month," "Gotta get Carlos and Debbie together," and "Hope your project is going well, Ray. Love you and miss you."

———————

At 6 am Pacific Time, a hungover Carlos Madrigan arrived in the Smythville Hotel lobby, surprised that Ray Pernell wasn't already there. Carlos parked his luggage next to the front desk, nodding at the overnight clerk who Carlos would not have recognized, except for the very memorable stripe of purple hair.

"Good morning sir," said the clerk, sounding a bit too perky for 6am. "We have coffee right there by the elevator. Do you need any assistance with transportation this morning?"

"No thanks. We'll be calling an Uber."

"Absolutely sir. Please let me know if you need any help with your luggage or anything else."

"Will do." Carlos hit Ray's number on his cellphone.

"You've reached Ray Pernell, please leave a message and I'll get back to you as soon as possible. Thanks for your call."

"Hey, Ray. This is a first. I'm in the lobby before you. We gotta get going. I won't order the Uber until I see you down here. Call me back."

Ten minutes later, another attempt to reach Ray went unanswered. Carlos asked the desk clerk "Do you have a house phone in the lobby? I can't seem to reach my buddy on his cell. I wanna try his room phone."

"Yessir, we do. It's that white phone over there next to the elevator. May I have his name please?"

"Ray Pernell. I think he's on the fourth floor."

"Got it. I'll connect you. Just pick it up when it rings."

Carlos hustled over and picked up the already ringing white phone, but there was no answer. "Damn, Ray. You still sleeping? Or in the shower?"

He asked the desk clerk. "Can you watch my bag while I run back upstairs to get my friend? He may have forgotten to set his alarm."

"Of course, sir. And please call me Bernie."

"I think that Ray said he was staying in room 407. Can you confirm that for me?

"Last name?"

"Pernell! C'mon, man. We're gonna miss our flight."

"I can confirm that your friend gave you the correct room number."

"Thanks." Carlos, hurried to the elevator. Getting off on the 4th floor, he trotted to room 407 and pounded on the door. "Ray! Ray! It's Carlos. C'mon, get up Ray. We're gonna miss our flight!" There was no response from within. Putting his ear to the door, Carlos thought he could hear the beeping of an iPhone alarm.

Suddenly no longer concerned about making their flight, Carlos shouted "You okay Ray?" Still no response. Carlos rushed back to the elevator and headed down to the lobby.

"Bernie! Ray's not answering. I think I can hear his alarm going off. Do you have a master key that we can use to unlock his door?"

"Yessir," said Bernie, as a uniformed Security Officer approached the desk. "This is Freddie Smith. Matt Smith, no relation, should be arriving in a moment. Hotel rules dictate that two security officers need to be present when we key the room of an unresponsive hotel patron."

"Look Bernie, my friend may be in trouble. This ain't like him. Can we please open his room right now?"

"Yes, we can!" said Bernie, as he pointed at Matt Smith walking into the lobby.

"What's up?" asked Matt.

Grabbing the key from Bernie, Freddie Smith said "We have a non-responsive guest on the 4th floor. Let's go."

While on the elevator, Matt spoke to Carlos. "Sir, please remain in the hallway while we open the door to the room. You are not allowed access to the room of another hotel guest, even though he's your friend."

"Yeah, sure. I just want to know that he's alright."

After pounding on the door for a few seconds, Matt keyed the door and shouted "Security! Mr. Pernell, are you in here?" Matt and Freddie carefully opened the door. They all heard the beeping of an alarm. The two Smiths entered the room. They quickly realized that Ray was not there.

"What the hell? Where's Ray?" shouted Carlos.

"Sir! Please do not enter the room!" said one of the Smiths. "We need to report this."

Carlos felt paralyzed. Ray was gone.

Chapter 4

SFPD Detective Devante James Harland was staring into his coffee while listening to his wife Liz from across the kitchen.

"The thought of being pregnant again is making me a little crazy. Every time I allow myself to be excited about it, I go to that dark place. I just cannot go through that again."

"Heard that, me too," said DJ, remembering the pain of their miscarriage four years ago. "You know the Doctor said we were good to go. We still want a family, right?" *Please say yes!*

"Yes we do Sugar," said Liz. "Are we ready? There's so much to think about. Money, education, religion, culture..... DJ, are you listening?"

"Yes, Baby. I feel you." DJ had learned long ago to be a good listener. His parents, both high school teachers, had taught him the importance of being attentive. Growing up middle class wasn't always a wonderful experience for DJ. As a child, it seemed that his parents were his sole cultural connection to his history as a black man in America. They had decided that young Devante would benefit most from attending the more prominent private schools, despite their lack of diversity. By the time DJ was a senior, he had grown into his full six-foot, well-muscled frame. A three-year starter in football, he'd received inquiries from some small colleges. DJ recognized that he didn't possess the talent necessary to make a living playing ball, so he put his efforts into academics and enjoying high school.

DJ developed an interest in law enforcement after losing a close friend to an overdose and seeing no repercussions for any dealer. It had been a long road, but after spending 2 years in Junior College to acquire an associate's degree in criminology, followed by 7 years as a San Francisco police officer, he finally made Detective last year.

DJ looked lovingly at Liz, who was whisking scrambled eggs. *Damn, still just as sexy and beautiful as the day we met!* Her Portuguese / French Canadian heritage was evident in her striking combination of dark eyes, olive skin, and deep auburn hair. They'd met in college where she was studying to become a paralegal. DJ loved Liz's no-nonsense personality, although he'd been surprised when she asked him out for their first date. It was just after he graduated from the Police Academy that DJ gathered enough nerve to propose marriage. Her answer was typical of what he had come to expect from Liz Drouin, "Yes, Sugar. It's about time. I thought I might need to ask you."

Except for several very dark months following Liz's miscarriage, their marriage had been everything they wanted for nearly 8 years. Liz's gig as a paralegal kept her challenged and professionally engaged. DJ's years as an officer seemed to fly by, although he was unhappy about not making Detective on his first try. Their first pregnancy had been a surprise. The pain and depression brought on by the miscarriage was deep. Once Liz had healed physically, the emotional baggage lingered. That was four years ago and now they were getting excited about the prospect of starting a new family.

Scooping the scrambled eggs, Liz said "Tomorrow is your turn to cook breakfast. I gotta be at work early."

"I will Baby. Tall stacks of hotcakes, bacon, sausage, biscuits, butter, and syrup!"

"Gross. I'll take a bowl of fruit and some juice. Can't go to work full of meat and fat. I wonder if they'll let me work from home after the baby comes."

DJ wrapped his arms around Liz. "Slow down Mrs. Harland. You can't be skipping over the good parts. First, we gotta make the baby! It may take many, many tries over multiple months to get pregnant." *We need to try every day, just to be sure.*

"Not judging by the first time. Should we get busy? I could be ovulating right now" she said with a sly smile.

"Oh Damn, so tempting. Unfortunately Baby, that's gotta wait. I got someplace to be real soon." *Rain check?*

"You're working so many hours these days, do I need to book a reservation to make a baby?"

"You know it ain't like that. I do it for us."

"And I appreciate you Sugar. Are you putting yourself in danger today? I worry about you every minute that you're gone."

"No, just some bad kids that need a spanking." *And maybe a few years behind bars.*

Liz hugged him tightly. "Well, be careful. You know I love you. Stay Safe."

———

"Officers are in place, the target bus is arriving," crackled the police radio.

"I'm about 2 minutes out, don't wait for me" answered DJ Harland, feeling the usual pre-bust nervous energy. He found it disgusting that gangs used their younger members to blend with students to push their oxy and heroin on school buses, playgrounds, parking lots, and athletic fields. There was always an appetite for drugs in the schools.

Not my kid thought DJ, recalling his discussion with Liz over breakfast. Just thinking about having a baby was so exciting.

DJ parked his unmarked car on the edge of campus and started walking quickly through the parking lot of Gurtin High School, where the buses dropped off their students. His plain clothes allowed him to blend in with any arriving teachers and staff members.

DJ spotted the target bus. Next to the bus, three uniformed officers had detained two young men. One of the youths suddenly spun around, knocking over one officer, and broke into a sprint, running between rows of parked cars with two of the uniforms in pursuit. DJ bolted quickly to his right and started running at full speed. The suspect then slid across the hood of a car and jumped into the next row.

Oh shit, you can't lose me that easily! DJ grabbed the side view mirror of a pickup truck and yanked himself into the new direction without breaking stride. The suspect kept weaving between rows, causing DJ to jump between cars, nearly being run over by a student driving a Mustang who leaned on his horn yelling "What the fuck, dude!"

The sprinting suspect was glancing back at the pursuing officers, when he was suddenly knocked off his feet and slammed into the side of a Jeep. DJ had launched his muscular 205-pound frame directly at the midsection of the suspect while running at full speed. The suspect's body provided a cushion for DJ as they smashed into the vehicle. *Damn, that felt good!*

"Fuck! Asshole, my shoulder!" screamed the young man, while trying to reach across his body to grasp something on his right side. DJ stepped on the suspect's hand and reached down to remove a small handgun from the suspect's right-side pocket.

"Motherfucker! My shoulder is broken. Get me a Doctor."

"They got doctors in the penitentiary," said DJ, brushing off his jeans and jacket. *You'll have 5-7 years to get better.*

The suspect tried a different approach, as the two uniformed officers were closing in on them.

"Look, brother, how 'bout you cut a black man a break. I won't come around here no more. You know how it is."

DJ stared at him. "Let me put this into words that even you can understand. Yeah, we're both black. But only one of us is a man. Any asshole who deals death to teenagers is a fucking embarrassment to his family and his race. The world is a better place with your punk ass off the street."

"Fucking Uncle Tom."

DJ shot back, "Do me a favor while your ass is in prison, read 'Uncle Tom's Cabin' and find out something about the type of pain suffered by your black family. Now shut the fuck up while these nice officers read you your rights." *Assholes like you really piss me off!*

Chapter 5

Arriving at his cramped little cubicle, Detective Harland began leafing through his tall stack of cases. The office was quiet, but soon the daily cascade of commotion would be flowing over the low dividers that marked the territory of each detective.

DJ's ancient phone intercom buzzed. "What's up, Kahuna?"

Kahuna, officially known as police Captain Tehaki Kekoa, head of Narcotics and Vice, had been DJ's only captain since his promotion to Detective. A native of Hawaii, the usually good-natured Captain Kekoa was given the nickname "Kahuna" early in his tenure at SFPD. It took DJ a few months to understand when he could address the captain as Kahuna, and when to use his proper title of Captain. That was generally dependent on Kekoa's mood at any given time.

"DJ, get your ass in here. I got a missing person complaint to chase down."

"Yes, Cap'n". DJ slowly made his way to Kekoa's office. *Damn it. I've got a ton of cases....this is probably just another teenager with Daddy issues who'll turn up in a day or two....a damn waste of my time!*

"Good morning mighty Kahuna! How goes the battle?"

"Take a seat DJ. I hear you did a terrific Ronnie Lott impersonation at Gurtin High this morning."

Ronnie Lott, aka the Human Missile, was one of the hardest hitters the San Francisco 49ers ever produced. "It ain't nothing any other super athletic, speedy, brave, handsome Detective wouldn't have done."

"Don't rip your arm out of the socket patting yourself on the back. We've got a few million more cases to handle. But good job on nailing those assholes."

"Thanks Cap'n".

"I'm sure you're not thrilled at the prospect of another missing person case on your desk, but this one feels different. The subject is a senior executive at TEM."

"Tucker? Loved their movies when I was a kid. Had my first kiss at a Tucker movie!" *Didn't get a second date.*

"Very touching," said Kekoa, glancing down at his monitor. "Ray Pernell. In from New York. Went out last night with some business associates, and returned to the hotel, but didn't show up in the lobby this morning. Hotel security opened his room and he is gone."

"Gone, gone?"

"Yes, gone DJ. As in no longer there."

"They file a missing person report yet?"

"They will, as soon as you show them how."

Aw shit! "C'mon Captain, he's probably shacked up with a different type of business associate and missed his wake-up call. These guys usually turn up."

Kekoa's voice got a bit more serious. "This is different. His clothes, wallet, and phone were left in his room. Who goes out looking for anything without those items?"

"Someone who is probably very fucked up."

"That's up to you to figure out, Devante. Get your ass down to the Smythville. They're waiting for you at the front desk".

"Your wish is my command," said DJ through clenched teeth. Whenever the Captain addressed him by his proper first name, DJ knew there was no room for debate. He thought about the boutique Smythville Hotel. *Those Tucker executives certainly know how to live large!*

Chapter 6

Entering the opulent Smythville lobby, DJ briefly entertained the notion of removing his shoes to fully enjoy the deep, luxurious carpeting.

Spotting a group of people at the front desk, DJ zeroed in on the desk clerk, a handsome dark-haired young man, with a bright purple strip that split his head like a mohawk. *Nice fashion choice!*

"I'm Detective Harland with San Francisco PD."

The hotel clerk responded. "Hi, Detective. I'm Tim Bernard, everyone calls me Bernie." He gestured at a cluster of three men standing nearby and singled out Carlos Madrigan. "That fellow was with Mr. Pernell, he's the missing person, when they returned last night." Then pointing at the two uniformed security officers standing nearby: "And these two guards went to check on Mr. Pernell, and discovered that he was not there."

"Thanks, Mr. Bernard. Stick around." Turning to the group of three men, DJ handed each of them a form used for missing person complaints. "I need to know all of your names, contact details, and a description of your interaction with the missing person since his arrival in San Francisco. That includes everywhere Mr. Pernell has been, who he has been with, and any interactions he may have had with other people."

Carlos spoke with a tired voice, "My name is Carlos Madrigan. I work with Ray Pernell at Tucker."

"OK, Mr. Madrigan. How about you give me a quick explanation of what's going on here."

"Ray and I came out here from New York a couple of days ago to do some work at Eustachian Sound Works. This is Les Santarelli and Sol Korman, from ThickBrickk Productions in LA. We were working together on finishing the sound design for a movie trailer."

DJ nodded at Les and Sol saying, "Stick around fellas. Mr. Madrigan, I'll need you to provide information about Mr. Pernell, including family and work contacts".

"Yes, of course."

DJ removed a digital recorder from his jacket. "I'm notifying all of you that I am now recording our conversations." *Mainly because I hate taking notes.* "Everybody good with that?" Seeing nods all around, DJ turned to Carlos. "So tell me what happened."

"After we wrapped our project yesterday afternoon, we went out for dinner and drinks."

"Who is 'we' Mr. Madrigan?"

"All four of us, Detective." Carlos pointed at Korman and Santarelli. "Les, Sol, Ray, and me. ThickBrickk rented a limo. We hit a couple of bars, and then went to dinner at Le Meillure."

DJ was familiar with Le Meillure. Despite the French name, the cuisine was Vietnamese and very pricey. *Damn, these guys are on some serious expense accounts!*

Carlos continued, "After dinner, we hit a couple more bars and then ended the night since Ray and I had an early flight. At around 2 am, we came back to the Smythville."

"All four of you returned here?"

"No. Les and Sol went on to their hotel. Ray and I came into this lobby and took the elevator up to our rooms. He got off on four and I was on seven."

"Was that the last time you saw him?"

"Yeah. We agreed to meet in the lobby at 6 am. But Ray wasn't here. He's never late for anything. I waited a while but he didn't show up."

"And…?"

"I tried his cell phone, but got no answer. We tried his room phone, no luck. I went to his door and pounded on it. Nothing."

"Did you see or hear anyone else when you went up there?"

"No, but I could hear the beeping of an alarm through the door. So I came back down here and asked Bernie if he could have Security open Ray's door."

Bernie spoke from behind the front desk. "I gave Freddie and Matt the key and they went upstairs with Mr. Madrigan".

"OK Bernie," said DJ. "Write that down for me. Make sure that Mr. Pernell's room remains locked and untouched until I tell you otherwise. And I'll need all hotel security footage from the last 24 hours."

"Absolutely Detective. We have cameras here in the lobby, the bar, and the public stairwell. I'll get that footage to you."

DJ didn't have to ask why there were no cameras in the hallways on each floor. He was very aware of the much-celebrated case currently before the California Supreme Court concerning the privacy of hotel patrons. It was filed after one hotel guest had been captured on a security camera while "misbehaving" in the hallway outside of his room. That footage had found its way to the internet. The issue of personal privacy within the confines of a hotel was now being litigated in a very public trial.

DJ turned back to Carlos. "Mr. Madrigan, Would you say that you and Mr. Pernell were under the influence of alcohol when you returned to the room?"

"Well, yes. We were celebrating, but no one was driving."

"Good to know. Did you walk Mr. Pernell to his room?"

"No. Guess I should have. He got off on the 4th floor. Last time I saw him."

"When you went upstairs with Security to unlock his door, what did you guys find in the room?"

"Ray was gone", said Carlos. "The Security guards wouldn't let me in. But even from the doorway, I could see a bunch of his stuff on the bedside table."

"What kinda 'stuff did you see?" *Booze, syringes, hookers?*

"I saw some money, his phone, and his CPAP machine. There were some folded clothes on the floor. Why would he leave that stuff there if he was going somewhere in the middle of the freakin' night? I don't get it."

"We can't assume anything at this point", said DJ, handing Carlos his business card. *But this doesn't sound good.* "You need to call 311 and tell them you want to file a documented missing person report. They'll send you an email with the appropriate form. If you have a photo of Mr. Pernell, include it in your response."

"Okay, Detective."

"List me as the investigating officer so I will be copied on all their responses. And remember to fill out this form for me before I leave."

Turning to the "Smith Brothers" security team, DJ asked, "Do you guys remember seeing anything else in the room?" *Like maybe a body?*

Matt Smith answered. "That's about it, Detective. We didn't touch anything. The alarm is probably still beeping. Once we were sure that the room was empty, we got the hell outta there."

"Exactly" added Freddie Smith. "We left everything just as we found it."

"Thanks for your diligence." Turning back to Carlos, DJ said "Now tell me more about Mr. Pernell, his family, and your relationship."

Carlos told Detective Harland all that he could think of concerning Ray's job, their close relationship, and Mia and the kids.

"Thanks, Mr. Madrigan." DJ motioned to Les and Sol. "I'm gonna have a quick chat with your associates here. But there's one more thing you can help me with."

"What's that, Detective?"

"We need to reach out to Mrs. Pernell to see if she has heard from her husband in the last few hours. After we speak to her, I will need to take a look at Pernell's room."

Carlos suddenly felt sick to his stomach. He knew this news would scare the hell out of Mia.

Chapter 7

Mia Pernell, sitting at her vanity surrounded by an array of cosmetics, was chatting on FaceTime with Debbie Slater, her best friend and former business partner.

"I never understood what you saw in him. He must've been good in the rack."

"That was never an issue," said Debbie. "It was everything else. Frank sunk all his money into his damn law firm, then borrowed more to keep the dream alive. Then he started going to the casino to try to make ends meet."

"That had to suck".

"Hell yes. It was tough. But, not everyone hits a home run on their first try like you and Ray did."

"We were lucky," said Mia, looking into her propped-up cellphone. "We've had our ups and downs, but it's been a good marriage."

They'd been discussing Frank Dorrington, Debbie's ex-husband. His dream of creating a successful law firm flopped soon after law school. Frank was soon leaning on Debbie's income from her graphic design job to help them stay solvent. Their divorce had not surprised Mia.

"I know I've mentioned this before, but Ray works with a guy who is perfect for you," said Mia. She knew that Carlos' good looks and pleasant demeanor would appeal to Debbie. And what man wouldn't be attracted to her best friend? Mia had always thought Debbie was gorgeous….Tall, brunette, athletic with sparkling green eyes and a confident attitude. Mia knew some men may be put off by Debbie's confidence and intelligence, but she'd always thought that Carlos seemed to be the type of man who would be a perfect fit. And, they both worked in the design industry. Ray had warned Mia about playing Cupid, but she just knew this match was perfect.

"Oh yeah" replied Debbie. "Carlos right? I've just been so busy with trying to keep ZTA afloat that I haven't had the time to date." Mia had heard this excuse before. She and Debbie had formed ZTA Design together, choosing the name to honor their college sorority: Zeta Tau Alpha. But seven years ago, Mia withdrew from ZTA Design upon the birth of her third child, Karl. There just weren't enough hours in the day.

Debbie continued: "The thought of dating makes me sick to my stomach. I just can't do all that superficial crap again."

Mia's cellphone vibrated. She saw "Carlos Madrigan" appear on the screen. Mia exclaimed, "Speak of the devil! Carlos is calling me. Must be fate! Wonder what he wants. I'll tell him you said hello".

"Please Mia, don't embarrass me! Talk to you later."

Mia tapped her phone and brought it to her ear. "Hi, Carlos. How's the trailer coming? Is Ray behaving?"

Carlos sounded tired. "Mia. Have you heard from Ray since yesterday?"

"No, I haven't. Why?"

"I have some bad news".

Mia felt a rush of fear. "You're scaring me, Carlos. Is Ray alright?"

"I don't know. He's not in his room. We can't find him."

"What the hell are you talking about? Where's Ray?"

"The police are here. We are looking for him."

"Carlos! What happened? Carlos!"

A different voice came from the phone. "Mrs Pernell. Mrs. Pernell! Are you there? This is Detective Harland from the San Francisco Police Department. Mrs. Pernell!"

"The police! Oh my God! What happened to Ray? Where is he?"

DJ answered in an even voice: "Mrs. Pernell, your husband and Mr. Madrigan, returned to the hotel together last night. But this morning, your husband was not in his room and we have yet to locate him".

"I don't understand. Carlos should know. Oh my God! I'm coming out there. Ray needs me. He might be hurt."

"Listen to me Mrs. Pernell," said DJ firmly. "You can best help your husband by staying where you are. He may contact you there, or even show up, at home."

"I can't believe this! Where is he?"

"Mrs. Pernell! Let us spend a few hours looking into this and I will contact you later today with whatever we've learned."

"Oh dear God."

"Is there someone who can stay with you for a bit? Mrs. Pernell? Mrs. Pernell?"

Carlos grabbed the phone. "Mia! Talk to me!"

Mia collapsed to the floor, leaning against the vanity, sobbing uncontrollably, her phone staring up at her from the rug. She reached over and pounded the phone to end the call.

Chapter 8

Following her chat with Mia, Debbie Slater sat down at her Mac and fired up her After Effects design program. ZTA Design had a solid reputation in the local design community for its 3D logo treatments. Most of Debbie's clients didn't know that ZTA's studio was actually her spare bedroom.

Her mind drifted. Maybe she should meet Carlos. It's not that she didn't want to, it's just that she didn't have enough time. Or, maybe it was because her marriage to Frank had been such a mess. But she knew that Mia wouldn't steer her wrong.

"Yipes!" The sound of Debbie's cell phone yanked her back to reality.

"ZTA Design. How may I help you?"

"Is this Debbie Slater?"

"Speaking. How can we be of service?"

"Hi Debbie, my name is Carlos Madrigan."

Debbie could not believe it. Mia had gone too far. It's one thing to suggest a possible date for her, but another altogether to encourage him to call her unannounced like this. She suddenly felt like a nervous schoolgirl, as she answered with "Hi Carlos. Don't you work at Tucker with Ray Pernell?"

"Yes, I do. I'm calling about Ray and Mia." Debbie thought those words were certainly an odd way to start to get to know someone."I have some bad news. We're in San Francisco and Ray has gone missing. He didn't show up in the hotel lobby this morning and when we checked his room he wasn't there. The police are involved."

"Oh my God!" blurted Debbie, as she silently chastised herself for thinking this call had been arranged by Mia. "Where is he? What happened? Does Mia know?"

Carlos provided a brief description of what little they knew. "We had to call Mia to see if she had heard from Ray. I know that you two are best friends and I was hoping you could stop by….."

"Oh my God, Mia!" shouted Debbie, grabbing her keys and running for the door. "I'm on my way right now!"

Chapter 9

"Thanks, guys. Hang in the hallway." Detective Harland didn't want the "Smith Brothers" security team to re-enter Ray's fourth-floor room.

The room seemed unruffled. Putting on rubber gloves he reached down to the iPhone on the bedside table and turned off the still-beeping alarm, using just one gloved fingertip. He started snapping photos with his department-issued digital camera. An empty suitcase sat open on a folding luggage stand. Draped on the side of the stand was a leather jacket. The bed was unmade on one side as if it had been slept in. The TV remote control was lying on the unused half of the bed. On top of the nightstand next to the bed was a wallet, some folded cash, an expensive-looking watch, the iPhone, and a CPAP machine with the hose draped over the top of it. DJ knew that some of those machines had removable chips that tracked their time of operation. *That'd be some valuable knowledge to have if this guy doesn't turn up soon.* In the bathroom, DJ noticed the neck of a bottle protruding from under some crumpled tissue in the waste basket. He used his gloved fingertip to push the tissue aside revealing what appeared to be an empty sake bottle, the label covered with Asian characters. *Sake! Tastes like paint thinner. I don't get the attraction.*

DJ noted the neatly folded clothes on the floor next to the bed. He saw jeans, dark socks, dark men's briefs, and an off-white collared shirt that had a TEM logo on the left breast area. A pair of shoes sat next to the clothes. *Either this guy is a neat freak, or we've got an exceedingly tidy kidnapper.*

Exiting the room, DJ said, "Let's go take a look at the guest stairwell". Freddie locked Ray's room and then joined DJ and Matt as they climbed the three carpeted flights up to the top floor and then retraced all seven flights down to the lobby. They saw nothing unusual.

Rejoining the rest of the group in the lobby, DJ collected their written statements. He swapped business cards with Santarelli and Korman and told them to "stay available". ThickBrickk's executives departed to catch their flight back to LA.

Carlos, on the phone, handed his written statement to DJ.

"Detective Harland!" In this short time, DJ had come to recognize Bernie's voice. *Could that nasal tone be more annoying?*

"Yes, Mr. Bernard?"

"My boss and I just did a quick review of the security video for both the lobby and the guest stairwell last night. Nothing unusual. It was precisely 2:32 am when Mr. Madrigan and Mr. Pernell came through the lobby."

"Good info, Mr. Bernard."

"I offered a wake-up call, but they both declined…..hardly anyone takes those anymore. They got on the elevator and that's the last I saw of them until Mr. Madrigan came into the lobby this morning at around 6." Bernie handed DJ a small removable drive saying "Here's all the video from midnight to 6 am. Both the lobby and stairwell cameras".

DJ pocketed the small drive. "Thanks. I'll look at this as soon as I can. But maybe you can help me now. Did you notice what Mr. Pernell was wearing when he and Mr. Madrigan passed through the lobby?"

Bernie seemed excited to be helpful. "I remember seeing a TEM logo on one of their shirts. The other guy was wearing a leather jacket but appeared to have the same color shirt on. Tucker really does a tasteful job of outfitting their team, don't they?"

"Yes they do, Mr. Bernard." *Unlike the 'tasteful' choice you made with that purple mohawk.* "Are there any other elevators, stairwells, or exits that I've not visited?"

"Please call me Bernie……and yes, we have a freight elevator. It's locked from 10p to 7a. There's also a service stairwell at the back of the hotel that is used by our maintenance staff."

"Thanks…uh…Bernie. Can you have someone take me to that stairwell please?"

"Of course," said Bernie, pleased that the Detective had called him by his preferred moniker. "Matt will provide whatever you need."

"Sure. Let's go Matt."

DJ and Matt walked through a storage area, adjacent to the kitchen, then passed through a locking metal door that slammed behind them as they stepped onto a damp concrete landing. Looking up into the dim stairwell, DJ saw nothing but dull concrete steps, lined by heavily oxidized metal handrails covered with splotches of corrosion. Dim bulbs cast yellowish light at each landing. Lowering his eyes, DJ found himself staring directly at a somewhat distressed metal door. The locking bar on the door included a faded metal sign which read "Do not touch. Alarm will sound".

Matt said "This is it, in all her glory, our fabulous service stairwell. Kinda stinks in here, doesn't it?"

"No argument. The hotel might want to invest in a dehumidifier." *Smells like a Turkish prison!*

"Preaching to the choir, Detective".

"What's on the other side of this door?"

"That's the alley where many dumpsters and rats reside. Check it out." Matt hit the locking bar on the center of the door with his forearm and it opened, squealing loudly on its rusty hinges.

"No alarm?"

Matt laughed. "Never heard it, and I've been working here for more than four years. Only employees use this door and the lock still works."

DJ stepped outside. The smell of rotting garbage filled his nostrils. "Holy shit!" *Putrid' would be a compliment!*

"You should check this out on a hot afternoon" crowed Matt.

DJ surveyed the alley, seeing a row of rusty dumpsters and garbage strewn everywhere. Stepping inside, he tried to clear his nose. "Let's take a look up these stairs."

On each level, DJ tried the door to the interior of the hotel. They were all locked.

Matt offered, "Only the maintenance team and cleaning folks use these stairs. I have a master key if you'd like me to open any of these doors". When they reached level 4, DJ asked Matt to key the door. They walked through it and into a dim hallway.

"Where are the guest rooms?" asked DJ.

"You gotta go down to the end and bang a left through another door to get to the guest rooms. These areas are all storage for the cleaning crews and event people. The freight elevator's around that corner".

"Who's responsible for locking that freight elevator?"

"We are. The Security guard on duty locks it at 10 pm and leaves the key at the front desk until we unlock it at 7 am."

DJ climbed through the next two levels of stairs, cursing when he stepped into a shallow puddle on the 6th-floor landing. Turning to Matt, he said, "You oughtta have maintenance fix these damn holes before somebody breaks an ankle." *Or catches the plague.*

"I hear you. I'm guessing our service stairwell is not a high priority on the hotel budget."

"Shocking," said DJ, as they reached level seven, the top floor. On that landing sat a well-worn janitor's cart loaded with spray bottles, duct tape, rags, and various cleaning items. DJ was struck by how a high-end hotel like the Smythville, still had its low-end areas like this disgusting stairwell. *Don't look behind the curtain Mr. and Mrs. wealthy guests!*

Beyond the cart was a doorway secured with a metal bar and padlock. DJ asked "Roof?".

Matt nodded. "Never had reason to go up there."

DJ perused the items in the janitor's cart. "OK we're done here. Can you key this door and take me to the passenger elevators?"

"No prob". Matt unlocked the 7th-floor door and led DJ down the hall, past the freight elevator and through the doors into the hallway lined by numbered hotel rooms, finally arriving at the guest elevators.

Carlos and Bernie were still in the lobby. DJ collected all the written statements. Carlos spoke in a tired voice, "Detective Harland. I tried to reach our boss at Tucker. She was in a meeting, but I should be speaking to her in a few minutes."

"Great. Let me know when that happens."

"But then what? Our project is finished here, Les and Sol have gone back to LA, but I can't just go back to NY. I can't leave here without Ray. Do you think he's alright?"

Highly doubtful my friend. "No idea. Sometimes a missing person simply shows up. Other times, it takes a few days before someone wanders back with some type of medical issue. I recommend that you head home and keep your phone on."

"Then what?"

"Be sure to reach me with anything at all that you forgot to write down. I'll be reaching out to Tucker soon."

"Thanks, Detective," said Carlos, staring at his roller bag that had been sitting in the lobby since his arrival at 6 am. It seemed like a lifetime had passed since then.

As DJ headed for the door, he considered two other scenarios that he didn't mention to Carlos. *Sometimes these cases go unsolved. And sometimes, they result in a DOA.*

Chapter 10

After a morning filled with meetings, Sharon Dillard returned from the Tucker cafeteria where she'd purchased a salad and Diet Coke. She grabbed a handful of wheat crackers from the box she kept in a file drawer and began to gobble down her lunch while listening to the rain slamming against the windows of her 8th-floor office at Tucker Entertainment Media headquarters in Lower Manhattan.

Pulling a thick shock of gray hair back behind her head and securing it with a hair tie, Sharon scanned the photos arrayed on her desk. The memories of a long, successful career were on display. Her thoughts were interrupted when Patti Nazzo, her assistant, buzzed her intercom.

"What is it, Patti?"

"Sorry to bother you, Sharon. It's Carlos Madrigan calling from San Francisco. He says he needs to talk to you right away."

"I'm trying to grab 15 minutes of peace here. Tell Carlos that he should take it up with Ray. Or he can text me like he usually does."

"I'll let him know."

Sharon appreciated how Patti kept her schedule so beautifully organized and still managed to preserve these few precious minutes for a lunch break on most days. The life of a TEM Executive Vice President, while very rewarding, felt like an endless loop of meetings, only to be interrupted by other unplanned meetings.

Twenty seconds later, Patti buzzed Sharon again. "What is it?"

"Carlos says he can't talk to Ray because he can't find him."

"Whaaat? Let me talk to him!".

Patti transferred the call.

"What is it Carlos?" asked Sharon. "What the hell are you talking about? Where's Ray?"

Sharon thought that Carlos' voice sounded tired. "Sharon, we've got a problem here. Ray has gone missing. The police are involved now."

A chill shook Sharon. "Carlos, slow down and tell me everything." As Carlos related the details of the previous couple of days, Sharon messaged Patti, telling her to reach out to Tucker's Legal and HR departments requesting an immediate priority meeting.

"I gave the San Francisco police your name as Ray's supervisor, so you'll probably be hearing from Detective Harland."

"OK, good to know".

"He'll be requesting all security information on Ray from TEM, including his fingerprints and travel history".

"We'll have that information ready for the police. Carlos, get on the next plane home. Don't share this with anyone else. HR will reach out to his family".

"Uhhh, no need for that Sharon. The Detective and I called Mia this morning."

"What'd she say?"

"She hasn't heard from him, and now she's scared as hell and fearing the worst."

Sharon tried to use her calmest voice. "No need to jump to conclusions, Carlos. I'll brief HR and Legal. They'll reach out to the San Francisco police and provide any necessary information."

"Okay, thanks, Sharon."

"You need to get back here and we'll talk as soon as you arrive. Ray will probably turn up, with a very logical explanation, before you even land at LaGuardia."

Sharon wished she had shown a little more conviction in her last statement. She couldn't imagine what might constitute a logical explanation for this type of disappearance.

Patti buzzed Sharon again. "HR and Legal will join you on a video conference call in five minutes."

Chapter 11

Debbie's car skidded to a stop in the Pernell's driveway. Jumping out, she ran through the rain and opened the front door shouting "Mia! Mia! You here?? It's Debbie!" Hearing nothing, she walked through the living room and glanced into the kitchen, den, and bathroom. Ducking her head into the glass-enclosed sunroom filled with greenery and flowers, she shouted again. "Mia! You here?"

Debbie bounded up the stairs and into the master bedroom where she found Mia, still sitting on the floor, slumped against her vanity. Her face was soaked with tears and streaked with what was left of this morning's makeup.

"Oh my God, honey." Debbie put her arms around Mia and lifted her up to the edge of the bed. "I just heard about Ray from Carlos. Are you okay?" Under any other circumstance, Mia would've been ecstatic that Carlos and Debbie had spoken, but that irony was completely lost on her.

"Did they find him?" asked Mia in a low voice that seemed devoid of hope.

Debbie hugged her tight. "I don't know any more than you do. I just heard."

Mia pushed Debbie away to arm's length. "What could it possibly be? Ray is never late for anything. We get to church early every freaking week!"

"I know honey. But we shouldn't assume….."

"When he's home, he always gets the kids to their stuff on time….Oh God, what am I gonna tell the kids? They'll be home soon. I don't want them to worry."

Checking her watch, Debbie said "I'll take care of it. We've got some time until they get home. Why don't you lie down?"

"I can't lie down. I'm just so worried."

"Me too. I'll go greet the kids and tell them you've got a major headache, and I'll take care of dinner. Hopefully, we'll hear something from San Francisco soon, and this'll all just be a misunderstanding."

Mia wanted to believe that last statement, but she felt something undeniably awful in her heart. "Thanks, but no. I need to be with my children. I don't want them worrying about their Dad.....oh my God Ray, where are you?" Mia's voice trailed off as she sank into Debbie's arms.

Twenty minutes later, Debbie was helping Mia clean up when they heard the unmistakable squeal of the school bus brakes in front of the house. She handed Mia the tissues. "I'll go meet them and tell 'em about your headache. Take your time."

Running downstairs, Debbie grabbed an umbrella from the stand next to the front door and stepped outside just in time to see Phoebe, then little Karl, exit the bus. Ricky's van, from Grant Prep, wouldn't arrive until later, after wrestling practice. Debbie nodded at a couple of neighbors who were also meeting their kids.

Debbie saw Phoebe's slender figure appear in the bus doorway. She had grown into a beautiful young woman, a combination of her Mom's Asian beauty and her Dad's height and hair color. Her thick brown hair reached to her shoulders, framing a pert nose and lovely almond eyes.

"Hi Aunt Debbie!" said Phoebe, bounding off the bus and joining Debbie under the umbrella. "How cool to see you. Where's Mom?"

"She's got a headache. Resting right now" Debbie felt Karl hug her around the waist. She looked down to see his round cheeks, brown eyes, and curly dark hair as he looked up at her.

"Hi, Aunt Debbie. Do you want to play Minecraft? I just got the new update. It's awesome!"

Before Debbie could answer, Phoebe asked "Are you and Mom going to choir practice tonight? If you're not, I need to go to Amy's house to work on our school project." Debbie understood that "school project" was code for "talk about boys". She remembered those days well.

"I'm not sure about that yet. We'll see how your Mom feels".

Phoebe's mention of choir practice grabbed Debbie's attention. Rehearsal at St. Joseph's Church was tonight. Debbie and Mia enjoyed singing together, even though it was clear neither of them had a future as a professional vocalist. They usually joined a few choir members at DacMintons for a glass of wine after practice. It was something to look forward to each week.

But tonight just wasn't going to happen. She would have to phone Lynette Elmer, the Choir Director. Debbie was pretty sure the ancient Mrs. Elmer was not yet and never would be, making use of texting technology.

While hustling Phoebe and Karl along the curved brick walkway leading to the front door, Debbie said "You guys leave your Mom alone for now. I think she may be sleeping". Phoebe headed for the den to plug in her laptop and Karl sprinted into the kitchen, in search of the cookie jar. Following Karl into the kitchen, Debbie said "You know your parents don't want you to eat a bunch of junk before dinner. No more cookies after those two."

"OK Aunt Debbie, but I'm hungry. What's for dinner? Mom usually makes dinner before she goes to choir practice."

"How about pizza? This'll be special pizza night."

"Yay pizza!"

Overhearing Karl's excitement, Phoebe yelled from the den, "No meat!"

Karl could hardly control himself, "Extra cheese! No green stuff."

As Debbie was dictating her credit card number to the pizzeria, she was shocked to see a refreshed Mia walk into the kitchen. Her hair was neatly pulled back, her makeup looked refreshed, and she was dressed like she was going out. "Hi Mom," said Karl. "We just ordered pizza because we thought you were sick." He backed out of the kitchen, cookies behind his back.

Debbie stared at Mia. "What the heck? I told you I would take care of the kids."

Mia looked into Debbie's eyes. "Love you, Debbie. But I'm so scared. The only way I can stay anywhere near sane is to try and act 'normal', and that means being with my kids, and then going to choir practice."

"Understood. I just ordered pizza for them."

"Thanks for that." Lowering her voice, Mia said "I just know something is wrong with Ray. I feel the need for some alone time in the church. And since you've already ordered dinner, I want to get there early."

Debbie knew that any disagreement would not be welcome.

Mia added, "I just told Phoebe that her Dad might be staying in San Francisco for an extra day or two and that she should text me if she hears from him". Tears were starting to crowd Mia's eyes.

"You sure you want to do this? I can call Lynette and tell her we are both sick."

"Yes, I need this. Let's go, now. I want to pray before practice."

————

Mia immediately silenced the radio when Debbie started the car. They began the 10-minute drive to St. Joe's accompanied only by the rattling of the driving rain and the pounding rhythm of the windshield wipers. Mia stared straight ahead, stone-faced.

Debbie spoke. "We really don't have to…"

"Yes I do!" interrupted Mia. "I need to light a candle for Ray. And then I want to sing." As a lifelong Catholic, Debbie knew that it was customary to light a candle to pray for a specific person, living or deceased. She hoped that Mia wasn't already thinking about the latter possibility.

Almost as if she was reading Debbie's mind, Mia said, "I just know something awful has happened to Ray. I just feel it in my heart, and it hurts."

They rode on in silence.

Debbie pulled up in front of St. Joseph's Church, a modestly sized, but lavishly appointed flagstone edifice. St. Joseph's had been the home church of Debbie's family since she was a kid. Mia and Ray began attending St. Joe's shortly after they were married. It was part of a compromise with Mia's parents, Hiroshi and Miyoko, who had raised Mia in the traditional religion of Okinawa. But that religion was wrapped around ancestor worship and local Okinawan geography, which made it difficult to practice in Connecticut. The Higorus loved Ray and were confident that their grandchildren would stay connected with their Okinawan ancestry.

Mia pulled the collar of her raincoat up around her neck and opened her door. "I'm going into the church to light a candle. Meet you in the basement for practice." Mia walked down the center aisle, genuflected in front of the altar, and then knelt in front of the stand where a few candles were already flickering, each in their own little red glass vessel. Grasping a long-handled match, she got fire from one of the other candles, and proceeded to light her own. "I love you, Ray. Why do I feel like we will never see you again?"

Shaking off the rain as she entered the main lobby of St. Joe's, Debbie again marveled at the beauty of the carved depictions of the 14 Stations of the Cross that were displayed in order around the space. Resisting the urge to walk to the altar and check on Mia, Debbie headed downstairs to the church basement where the choir would soon be assembling for practice. The basement was not nearly as ornate as the church above. Dull blue walls surrounded a grey-tiled floor. The floor was populated by at least a dozen red metal poles, neatly spaced out in a matrix pattern, which Debbie assumed were necessary to support the church above. The only person in the basement was the ageless Lynette Elmer, who had been the Choir Director here for as long as Debbie could remember. "Hi Lynette!" yelled Debbie from across the room. Lynette, sitting at the piano, with her back to Debbie did not respond.

Debbie stepped closer. "Yoohoo! Mrs. Elmer. It's me, Debbie Slater."

Lynette Elmer turned around and greeted Debbie with a big smile. She was very proud of her new dentures. "Well hello, young lady. Have you been standing there long? I didn't hear you." Debbie thought it ironic that their Choir Director was so hard of hearing. She struggled with the average conversation, but as soon as the singing started, she could pick out one singer's off-key mistake when a group of 20 voices were singing in unison, while she was playing piano. Amazing.

The remainder of the choir, including Mia, began to filter in. Debbie started to approach her, but Mia waved her off. Debbie could see some puffiness around Mia's red-rimmed eyes. Father Keenan walked into the basement and took his usual seat along the wall. Debbie was not a fan of Father Keenan. She thought that his sermons were often archaic, sexist, and totally out of touch with today's world.

Mia and Debbie were standing in their usual side-by-side position on the second tier of the rickety choir riser. They had started with a rousing version of "City of God", a hymn that everyone enjoyed singing because of its up-tempo pace and its strong message. Mrs. Elmer was pleased with that initial effort, so they moved on to the next hymn, "Be Not Afraid". As they sang the refrain, "Be not afraid, I go before you always, Come follow me and I will give you rest", Debbie felt Mia slouch against her shoulder and then drop to her knee, nearly tumbling off of the riser.

Gasps and shouts arose from the choir members closest to Mia. Mrs Elmer stopped playing. Debbie was perched precariously, straddling the riser and holding Mia tightly to keep her from tumbling. Speaking directly into Mia's ear, Debbie asked "Mia, honey, you ok? Can you you hear me?"

Mia turned toward Debbie, her face a mask of tears and grief, and quietly said "I thought I could do this. I can't. Please take me home".

Father Keenan rushed over to see if he could help. "Mrs. Pernell, are you ok? Should I call 911?"

Debbie answered. "No thank you, Father. Mia has been a bit under the weather today. I'll take her home. She'll be fine."

"If you are absolutely certain Miss Slater, then at least allow me to help you get her upstairs. And please let me know if there is anything else we can do."

"Of course, thanks Father."

The choir members were voicing their support with "Feel better Mia, take it easy, see you next week".

Mia couldn't wait to get out of there and go home.

———

Debbie made them each a decaf coffee with a shot of Kahlua. They were chatting at the kitchen table while Debbie munched on the lone remaining slice of cold pizza.

Mia read a note from Phoebe. "No news from Dad, I'm at Amy's."

She jumped as her phone emitted the chirp of an incoming text. "Nothing new. Talk tomorrow. Text me if you hear from your husband. - Detective Harland"

Mia started crying. "Why hasn't Ray called? I have such a horrible feeling. I just know we'll never see him again."

Debbie tried to exhale some of her fear. "Listen, we don't know anything yet. Let's hope and pray that there is some kind of explanation to this that we just can't think of right now".

"Thanks so much, Debbie", said Mia as firmly as she could muster, "I love you. But I just want to be with my kids now."

"You sure?" asked Debbie.

"If I hear anything, you'll be the first to know."

"Okay. Call me if you hear anything at all. Love you."

"Love you too," said Mia.

Chapter 12

Peeking through little Karl's bedroom doorway, Mia could see that he was snoozing, curled up with "Fuzzy", his favorite stuffed bear. She remembered the moment that Ray first placed Fuzzy in Karl's crib, more than seven years ago.

After dabbing her eyes, Mia then knocked on Ricky's door.

"Come in". Ricky was sitting up in bed, writing in a notebook on his lap. "Hi Mom. You feeling ok? Phoebs said you were sick".

"I'm fine. Thanks for getting Karl to bed. What are you working on?"

"Geometry. Do you know how to figure the volume of a cylinder? Why do I need to know that? This is so stupid."

Mia almost chuckled. She felt comforted by Ricky's voice. "I hear you. Maybe this isn't only about finding the volume of a cylinder. Solving a problem this tough might make it easier for you to figure out other solutions later in life."

Ricky made a face that conveyed his confusion over her answer. "Great, Mom. Not helpful."

"Just make your best effort. And sorry, no, I don't remember how to determine the volume of a cylinder."

Ricky grunted his acknowledgment.

Mia thought it best to change the subject. "How was wrestling practice?"

"These guys are really good. I think I'm doing ok for a freshman."

"That's great, we are so proud of you."

"Thanks. I've never had such a tough coach. Are you and Dad coming to Tuesday's meet?"

The mention of Ray nearly knocked the breath from her chest. Ricky's brown hair, hazel eyes, and strong nose evoked images of a young Ray. But Ricky was more compact and muscular, although he had yet to experience his growth spurt.

"I'll be there. You know that Dad's schedule is always up in the air. But he sure does love watching you wrestle. Don't ever forget that."

Ricky looked at her, and for a fleeting moment, Mia felt like her emotions were fully exposed. "Of course I won't Mom, why would I forget that? I like it when you guys come to my meets."

"That's great. We love it too. Don't stay up too late, the bus comes early. Goodnight. Love you."

"Goodnight Mom." Mia walked away, feeling so proud of their son, but wondering how old Ricky would be before he would give her a verbal "love you too".

After doing her best to wipe the day's miseries from her face, Mia zipped into her favorite one-piece flannel pajamas and fell into bed. Ray had given her these pajamas for Christmas last year. When she wore them, she felt his warm embrace, now more than ever.

Knowing that sleep wouldn't come easily, she grabbed her laptop and started to type her nightly entry into her journal. "Please, Ray. Call me and tell me you are alright. I need to hear your voice." Tears were rolling down her face again. She heard the front door slam downstairs. Phoebe was home. She quickly grabbed a couple tissues from the bedside box and started to wipe away the tears.

Phoebe tromped up the stairs and went directly into the bathroom. Mia continued to furiously wipe her face. She then heard Phoebe's low voice outside her partially closed door. "Hi, Mom. How was choir practice? You feeling ok?"

"Hi Phoebs. Practice was good. I'm fine. What's going on?"

Mia could hear excitement in Phoebe's voice. "I've got the most exciting news. But first I've got to talk to Amy."

Mia thought it useless to point out to Phoebe that she just came from Amy's house. "That sounds great. Can't wait to hear it." She heard Phoebe go into her room and close the door. 10 seconds later, Mia could hear excited chattering coming from Phoebe's room. She went back to typing in her journal.

"Please Ray, call me. Whatever happened to you, we can fix it together."

She closed her eyes for what seemed like only a second before hearing, "Mom. Mom! You still awake?" Phoebe rushed into the room and sat on the edge of the king-sized bed. "I've got the best news ever!"

Mia's sluggish brain slowly started to reboot. "What is it, honey?"

"Justin Flowers asked me to go to the Junior Prom. Me! I was hoping, but I never thought he'd ask. Today, he texted me and asked if I would go with him. How cool is that?"

Despite being appalled at the thought of being invited to a prom via text, Mia attempted some enthusiasm. "That's awesome Phoebs! Is this the football player that you've told me about?"

"Duh, yes Mom! He is THE football star. Dad said he's good enough to play in college. We're gonna double-date for the prom with Amy and Ed. Oh my God, we gotta go dress shopping soon!"

Mia sucked in her breath. "We've got some time. You need to think about what type of dress you want to wear. Then, we'll go shopping."

Mia wanted to ask more questions about young Mr. Flowers, but Phoebe had already popped up saying "I gotta talk to Amy" and sprinted out of the room. Mia couldn't possibly imagine what else needed to be said between those two, but it felt good to see Phoebe's joy.

Then it all came down on her again. She hoped Ray would be home to see his daughter go to the prom. She started to enter that thought into her journal and soon succumbed to her fatigue, falling into a restless slumber.

Chapter 13

While driving to work, DJ was mulling over yet another stressful breakfast conversation with Liz. *Hope we get pregnant soon and get on with it.* He understood Liz's concern about his long hours. But now that he had made Detective, this wasn't the time to slow down his career path. Of course, the baby would be his top priority when that time came.

His police radio snapped him back to reality. The call indicated a DOS in the Hollis section of town. *Another junkie wastes their life.* The Hollis area was known for drugs, violence, and prostitution. The radio then barked that the "DOS displays a GSW." The mention of a gunshot wound grabbed DJ's attention. *Might as well check this out before Kahuna sends me back here.*

- - - -

Detective Harland approached the officers on the scene.

"Hey DJ, how goes the luxurious life of a Detective? Didn't expect to see you here, at this hour" said Officer Jeremy Cumberland. DJ had a good relationship with Cumberland from their days together in uniform.

"Just passing by, thought I'd save a return trip by checking this out now. How you been? What's up with Jen and the little Cumberlands?"

"You know, things never change at our house. The bedlam just recycles, every 24 hours".

Better you than me. "So, who's the stiff?"

"Unknown, no ID. But he ain't the usual OD we see in this neighborhood. That hole in his forehead says that somebody wanted him dead."

"Local?"

"Doubtful. He's clearly a fish out of water. White, looks to be 50ish, nice haircut, wedding band, no tats, manicured nails, and no obvious tracks."

"Thanks, Jeremy. Anything else before I take a look?"

"Some weird shit here, Deej. He ain't exactly fully dressed. He's naked except for a small towel front and back, held by duct tape. The word 'FREAK" is written on his chest in what is probably his own blood. Forensics is on the way".

"Thorough as always, my friend. I'll take a look while we wait for them".

As soon as he pulled the sheet off, DJ was nearly certain who this was. "Aw shit." *He fits the description in every way.*

"What's up Deej? You know this guy?"

"Not personally. But I've got a real strong idea of who this is."

It had been roughly 48 hours since Ray Pernell's disappearance. This body certainly seemed to check most of the boxes. *What was he looking for on the streets? Drugs? Sex? How'd he earn a bullet in the head? What's with this weird outfit?*

DJ asked the forensics team to forward their full report ASAP. He felt certain the fingerprints, which he had requested from TEM, would identify the victim as Ray Pernell.

Then the Pernell family would need to be notified.

––––––––––

"C'mon, C'mon, move out of the way" muttered Wes Bell, better known online as "SecretEye233". He was wedged between a collapsed fence and a cascade of crumpled bricks while peering down at the cops who were standing around the victim. From his vantage point, he could only see a portion of the dead person, who was white and nearly naked.

Bell listened daily to police scanners, hoping that he might someday capture that one sensational photo that could launch his career as a "true crime" photographer. Knowing his Mom could never afford to pay for college, Wes was trying to make a name for himself with his photos. He hoped that his recent purchase of a $20 zoom lens for his precious iPhone would help him get some better shots. He didn't feel safe in this Hollis neighborhood, always looking over his shoulder for the next junkie or thief who wanted to mess with him. But, this area was always ripe with police activity. And bad guys made for "good" pictures, and hopefully profitable ones.

Wes couldn't get a clean look at the victim. He started recording rolling video instead of still photos, hoping that there may be a quick moment when he got a clean look at the body. He'd then lift that single image from the video to try to promote his photographic expertise online at CoCriRev.com, an online repository for crime-related photos.

Seeing the body covered with a sheet, Wes was about to turn off his camera. A plainclothes cop removed the sheet. For a quick second, the entire body was exposed. Wes stopped recording and checked the video, and there, for just the briefest moment was a clear image of a mostly naked white man, body propped against an old tire, with blood on his forehead, a silver belt around his waist, a piece of filthy cloth on his lap, and something drawn on his chest. As Wes zoomed in on the photo, he saw "FREAK" scrawled on the victim's chest. Excited by the prospect of a great photo, he jumped on his bike and headed home to the safety of his Mom's basement, where he would post this new image. This photo might be the one that would make him famous on social media!

Chapter 14

Mia was crashed on the soft leather couch, waiting for Debbie to stop by. It'd been almost 48 hours since Ray's disappearance and the San Francisco police were now texting her every few hours. So far, there was nothing new.

She just couldn't keep the charade going any longer and had decided to tell the kids about their Dad this afternoon. They probably thought she was going nuts based on her constant sobbing the last couple of days.

The doorbell emitted its familiar ding-dong. "Come in Debbie. The door's open." Another ding-dong. "Who the hell locked the door?" Mia dragged herself off the couch and shuffled to the door. Standing there was a uniformed Hudson Police Officer and a woman in a business suit. Mia started to shiver.

"Mia Pernell?" inquired the officer. Mia nodded. "My name is Officer Nathaniel McKane. This is Vera Eden. May we come in? It's about your husband."

Mia didn't hear those last few words because she already knew. "No, no. Not my Ray!" Falling to her knees, she vomited on the doorstep. Officer McKane and Mrs. Eden, the Hudson Police Department grief counselor, assisted Mia into the house and onto the couch.

Debbie's lanky body appeared in the open doorway and her voice filled the room. "Mia! Oh no, Mia!" She turned to the visitors and asked "What's going on?"

Officer McKane asked Debbie "Are you family?"

"Just about. We're close friends. Is this about Ray?"

"We need to talk to Mrs. Pernell first. You may listen so long as she approves."

Mia, still facedown on the couch, yelled "It doesn't matter. I already know what you're gonna say!"

All Mia heard was "Mrs. Pernell, the Hudson Police Department regrets to inform you…" She heard nothing else as she curled up on the couch, making a guttural groaning sound. Debbie had her arms wrapped tightly around Mia as they sobbed together.

Officer McKane finished with "While foul play is suspected, no determination on cause of death will be made until all forensic tests are complete. If an autopsy is required, the San Francisco Police Department will seek your approval. Mrs. Pernell, I am truly so very sorry for your loss."

Officer McKane departed, but Vera Eden stayed behind to help Mia, and now Debbie, come to grips with what they had just heard. A career Psychiatrist, she'd been working at the Hudson Police Department as a grief counselor for the last few years. Eden gave Mia a mild sedative and offered a few comforting words that went unheard. Mia was curled up on the couch drawing short, sharp breaths.

"Mia's lucky to have a friend like you" Eden said to Debbie.

"Huh? Oh yeah" said Debbie glumly. "I still don't understand what happened to Ray. What do they mean by 'foul play'? Was he robbed? Attacked? Hit by a car? Why can't you tell us that?"

"I honestly don't know those details. Those questions are for the San Francisco Police Department. They'll be in touch, likely later today. I've just notified them that Mrs. Pernell has been informed about her husband's passing."

Debbie burst into tears again at the mention of the word "passing". While cradling Mia's head and stroking her hair, Debbie looked at Eden. "So what are we supposed to do now? Do we bring him home? How does he get here? I remember that the three of us once agreed that we all wanted to be cremated."

Eden handed Debbie her HPD business card and placed a second card on the coffee table. "I can help you with all of those questions. Our priority is to notify her immediate family."

Debbie knew that Ray, like Mia, was an only child, and that his mom, Juliette, lived in a local nursing home. Better known as Grammy, she had lived with Ray and Mia's family until her Alzheimer's required more daily care than they could provide. Then there are Mia's parents. And the kids.

After checking on Mia, who was alternately groaning and grunting "no, no, no" Debbie asked Vera Eden "Do you call all of the family members?"

"If Mia's not up to it, then either you or I need to make those calls before word gets out. And with social media, that time frame can be very short."

"That's for damn sure. Mia's kids will be home in a couple of hours. They didn't even know he was missing."

"No time to waste. Can you please fill me in on Ray and Mia's immediate family?"

As Debbie began to describe the family tree, her phone buzzed showing "Carlos Madrigan".

"Just a second. I need to take this." Debbie spoke only one word, "Carlos?"

"Hi Debbie. So sorry to bother you. Are you with Mia? Is she ok? I'm in Sharon Dillard's office. She said the police had requested fingerprints and we…."

Debbie interrupted "Carlos! Stop! Yes, I'm with Mia." Debbie walked quickly into the den away from Mia's ears. "He's gone, Carlos. Ray's gone."

"Oh dear God, you mean he's gone….dead? He can't be. He was fine when I left him. This just can't be real!"

Across the desk from Carlos, Sharon Dillard's face welled up and she burst into tears.

Through sobs, Debbie said. "We don't know for sure. Only that Ray is, uh, gone and that foul play is suspected. We're supposed to hear more from the police soon."

"I don't get it. Was someone waiting for him in his room? I should've walked him to his door. Oh my God, is Mia ok? Should I come over when I get home?"

"Thanks Carlos, but the police counselor is here and we're about to contact Mia's parents and maybe Grammy Pernell. And the kids will be home soon. Right now, Mia is struggling"

"Oh my God. I just can't believe it. I'm leaving New York right away. Back home in a couple of hours. Let me know if I can do anything."

"Thanks, Carlos, gotta go." Debbie walked back into the living room. Looking at Vera Eden, she said "TEM is now aware of Ray's….uh….situation". Debbie just couldn't bring herself to say the word, as if maybe it wouldn't be true if she never spoke it. "We need to call Mia's parents. Maybe they can be here before the kids come home".

———

Mia had told Debbie to "do whatever you have to do". Debbie managed to convey the basic facts to Hiroshi and Myoko Higoru, who rushed to the Pernell home.

Myoko, her four-foot eleven-inch frame topped by grey hair, ruddy cheeks, and silver-framed circular glasses, rushed in the door and went directly to a curled-up Mia who was sobbing on the couch. "Oh, my poor baby" was all Myoko said in her thick Okinawan accent while hugging her daughter.

"Mr. and Mrs Higoru, my name is Vera Eden. I'm a counselor with the Hudson Police Department. Thank you for coming right over."

Hiroshi was standing erect, his neatly trimmed hair combed to one side above steely Asian eyes, his slim body clothed in a collared shirt and pressed slacks. In an accent that was now more New York than Okinawan, he asked "What happened to my son-in-law? Heart attack? Was there an accident? Could there have been some mistake?"

"No sir," answered Eden. "The identification has been verified. All we've been told is that foul play is suspected. The San Francisco police will be in touch with Mrs. Pernell as further information becomes available."

Hiroshi shook his head. "Foul play? Damn that San Francisco. Dangerous place." Looking at his wife holding Mia, Hiroshi asked Eden "How's Mia?"

"I've given her a mild sedative. She may be a bit out of it for a while."

Mia's face was buried in a pillow. "This has to be a mistake! You cannot be ......gone!"

Myoko was hugging Mia and rocking back and forth. "Oh, my poor baby".

Debbie wiped away tears. "Phoebe and Karl's school bus should be here soon. Ricky gets home later after wrestling practice."

Eden spoke to the Higorus. "Thanks again for running over so quickly. Miss Slater mentioned earlier that Mr. Pernell's mom lives locally. We should reach out to her."

Myoko looked up from the couch. "I'm not sure that would matter much to Julie. I work at her care facility. Her Alzheimers is pretty bad. She probably wouldn't understand this at all."

"Good to know," said Eden.

"I'll tell her tomorrow at work. She needs to hear about this, whether or not she understands."

The squeal of the school bus brakes interrupted the conversation.

"That's the kids' bus", said Debbie.

Mia suddenly sat up straight and tried to wipe her eyes. "Oh my God. The children."

Debbie started toward the door, but it opened before she got there. Phoebe and little Karl entered.

"Hi Aunt Debbie," said Phoebe. Seeing her grandparents, she exclaimed "Oba and Oji! What are you guys doing here?" Her eyes then settled on Mia. "What's wrong Mom? You look awful. What are you crying about"

Hiroshi scooped up Karl and held him close. Mia dabbed her eyes. "I have some bad news kids. Your Dad….your Dad….has had an accident in San Francisco. He's, he's….I just can't say it!"

"What!" yelled Phoebe. "Dad is what? Is he ok?"

Debbie started to speak, but Mia waved her off and finally managed to say "No Phoebe. He's gone."

"What do you mean gone? How bad was this accident? Is he still in San Francisco?"

Debbie reached out to hug Phoebe, who pushed her away with "What the hell is going on?"

Hiroshi spoke in an even tone. "Your father has passed away. We don't know the details of what happened, but we do know that he is gone."

"I don't believe you!" yelled Phoebe. "We just texted a couple days ago. He was fine. This has to be a lie!"

Karl wriggled free from his grandfather's grip, jumped down, and ran to his bedroom.

Debbie said "This is Vera Eden, of the Hudson Police Department. She was sent here by the San Francisco Police."

Glaring at Eden, Phoebe said "I suggest you get the hell out of here right now and take your vicious lie with you. My Dad cannot be dead!" Bursting into tears, she ran up the stairs to her bedroom and slammed the door.

Debbie started to follow Phoebe up the stairs. Eden grabbed Debbie's arm. "Give her some space. She needs some alone time to deal with the shock. There'll be plenty of time to talk with her later on".

Mia was sobbing. "They need me. I gotta be strong"

"Yes they will," said Eden. "Your love and support is essential. They need a little time right now, to begin to process this news."

Mia groaned, emitting a burst of emotion.

Hiroshi asked Eden. "Do you suppose Karl could use a little grandfather time?"

"Given his age, a hug from his Granddad could be very reassuring right now. Just let him talk and try not to lead him to feel a certain way. He has got to work through that himself."

"Understood," said Hiroshi, as he headed towards Karl's bedroom.

Finding the door open, Hiroshi stepped through into Karl's heavily decorated bedroom, his love of Marvel comics in full evidence.

Karl was lying on his bed, clutching his Fuzzy Bear.

Hiroshi asked "Are there any questions I can answer for you?"

"When will I see my Daddy again, Oji?"

"Any time you want, Karl. You can always see him in photos and videos. But more importantly, you will see him, and hear him, and always feel his love for you, in your head and in your heart. He was very proud of you."

"I taught him Minecraft"

"He thought that was cool. Every time you play Minecraft, you can hear your Daddy's voice playing along with you, learning from you and loving you."

"I think I'll play Minecraft right now. I want to talk to my Daddy."

"Good idea, my grandson. Keep him close."

Twenty minutes later, the Grant Prep van dropped Ricky at home. He walked through the front door, backpack over his shoulder, and looked at the adults in the living room. "You don't have to tell me anything. I already know. Phoebe texted me. I didn't believe it, but looking at you guys, I know it's real." Ricky walked to his Mom, who was still in Myoko's embrace and put his arms around both of them. "Don't worry. We're gonna be ok." A look of rage swept over Ricky's face as he growled "But if I ever find out who did this to my Dad, I will make them suffer before I fucking kill them with my bare hands."

He stomped up the stairs and disappeared into his bedroom.

"Oh God!" cried Mia.

Chapter 15

"Damn Baby, you trying to wear me out?" DJ was holding his lovely, sweat-covered wife in his arms, both still breathing heavily from their heated lovemaking. "Geez Liz, don't you think it's healthier for the baby if we conceive more slowly…over time?" *With many tries!*

Liz laughed. "Listen stud. I'm not sure about that. We have to strike while the iron is hot. Some people try for months or years before they get pregnant."

DJ began to extricate himself from their sweaty embrace. "My iron and I need to jump in the shower for some rejuvenation. Can we plan on round two tonight?"

"I'll think about it." Tossing her mane of dark auburn hair over her shoulders, Liz started to giggle. "Damn, I forgot how wonderful it is to make love with a purpose."

"No argument from me!" *There's the wild child I married!*

DJ always did his best thinking in a hot shower. He considered the Pernell case. The ME's report confirmed that Ray Pernell had died of a close-range gunshot wound to the forehead. He also had some bruising along the right side of his face and eye socket, but those bruises were not considered life-threatening. The silver duct tape and shredded rags needed further investigation. The word "freak" had been scrawled on his chest in what appeared to be Pernell's blood. It would be a few days before the full blood and toxicology results were available. The Medical Examiner noted that "an autopsy is not required relative to the cause of death".

The forensic team's examination of Pernell's hotel room didn't reveal much more. There was no evidence of anyone else having been present in his bed or room. No tearing or damage to his clothes. The hotel phone in his room had received no calls until Carlos called in the morning. Ray's cell phone revealed no late-night communications with anyone. The only new messages were the frantic morning calls from Carlos and then Mia. Curiously, the chip in his CPAP machine revealed that it had been utilized for exactly 18 minutes, from 2:50 am to 3:08 am.

DJ was holding his head under the steamy stream of water. *If no one reached out to him on his phone, then his departure from his room must've been pre-planned, maybe with a hooker or dealer. But why would he sleep only 18 minutes, and then get up? Or did someone knock on his door and force him to leave? And why the bizarre outfit?*

DJ dried off, wrapping a towel around his waist. As he stepped back into the bedroom to get dressed, he was accosted from behind by his feisty wife who whispered in his ear. "I think we need to try again. I'm feeling very fertile this morning."

"Your wish is my command" answered DJ, as they tumbled back into the bed.

Chapter 16

Mia stared at the mahogany urn containing Ray's ashes, perched on a low table in front of the shiny marble wall of vaults. Most of the funeral mass attendees also made the short trek to the cemetery for the internment of Ray's ashes.

Mia's parents and Debbie Slater handled the arrangements for the memorial service, helped take care of the kids, and even helped select the urn for Ray's ashes. Vera Eden had collaborated with the SFPD on expediting Ray's cremation and the delivery of his ashes to Connecticut. She'd also become a regular visitor to the Pernell home.

The funeral mass had been a blur to Mia. So many people, all expressing their condolences, and expressing their love and respect for Ray. Carlos Madrigan had delivered a thoughtful, emotional tribute to his friend and mentor. The St. Joseph's choir provided a moving performance of Amazing Grace.

Suddenly, the mass had ended and Mia now found herself at the cemetery.

Father Keenan was saying some final words before the placement of the urn inside the small vault. The inscription on the engraved marble vault cover read: "Father - Husband - Friend". Mia remembered how pleased they'd been when the Catholic Church began to allow for cremation, as long as the ashes were wholly contained in one urn and laid to rest in a Catholic cemetery.

Debbie Slater had a firm grip on Mia's right arm. "You okay honey?" whispered Debbie, from behind her sunglasses.

"I love you, Debbie. Thank you."

Myoko was holding Mia's left arm. She and Hiroshi had been constantly present in the Pernell home since Ray's death.

Turning to her left, Mia whispered, "Thank you so much, Mom, for all you've done."

Standing ramrod straight in the bright sunlight, Hiroshi had one arm around a sobbing Phoebe and the other was holding a restless little Karl to his hip. Ricky stood stoically off to the side, staring at the urn, with one hand resting on Grammy Pernell's wheelchair. Grammy Juliette appeared to be blissfully unaware of the events unfolding around her.

Father Keenan read from the 23rd Psalm. "Yea, though I walk through the valley of the shadow of death, I will fear no evil."

Debbie surveyed the large group of mourners. She saw Vera Eden, from the Hudson PD. In addition to Carlos, a large contingent of Ray's co-workers from Tucker were present, led by his boss, Sharon Dillard. Sol Korman and Les Santarelli had made the trip from Los Angeles, joining dozens of friends and neighbors from the Hudson area. Glancing again at Carlos, Debbie couldn't help but note that he was every bit as stylish and handsome as Mia had suggested. His emotional eulogy had touched her heart.

Those thoughts quickly disappeared when Debbie spotted Frank Dorrington, her ex-husband, among the group of mourners. She briefly thought back on better times. Frank had been so handsome in college, a young man with big dreams which she had bought into. It was clear he had fallen on hard times since their divorce. His six-foot frame now wrestled with an ill-fitted suit. The sparkle seemed gone from his eyes, his face was ruddy and a bit puffy, and his thick, beautiful brown hair had thinned to the point of comb-over status. Debbie was surprised to see Frank here, but she no longer had the time or energy to invest in him.

After a final prayer, Ray's urn was ceremoniously placed into the vault by Hiroshi.

As the crowd started to disperse, Mia clutched Ray's wedding band, now on a chain around her neck. She whispered, "Love you, Ray".

Chapter 17

The police scanner was barking out its usual litany of Monday morning domestic violence, assaults, auto accidents, and robberies. Frank Dorrington always listened to the scanners, searching for new clients. He preferred to think of himself as a hero to the oppressed, as opposed to the more demeaning label of "ambulance chaser". He had never once, physically, chased an ambulance.

Frank also perused local newspapers, TV news, radio broadcasts, and the occasional podcast. Finding paying clients was his number one priority.

Following graduation from law school, Frank had envisioned himself as the senior partner at a huge firm, with a 20th-floor corner office in Manhattan, a full slate of wealthy clients, a beautiful wife, and a loving family to come home to each night. Aside from marrying the beautiful Debbie Slater, none of those visions had become reality. Frank's inflated ego and grandiose plans soon had him overextended financially. After the local banks denied his request for additional funds, he extrapolated the problem by trying to solve it in the Connecticut casinos. His desperation led him to seek a loan from an "unconventional" source to keep his law firm solvent. His marriage to Debbie Slater quickly crumbled after she fielded a call from "Stanley", who was not shy about Frank's indebtedness to him, or the serious physical ramifications of Frank's failure to pay.

Frank's thoughts were interrupted by the local Hartford newscast on his small flatscreen TV. "San Francisco police are continuing to investigate the apparent homicide of TEM executive Ray Pernell, a resident of Hudson, who was found dead two weeks ago in the Bay Area. Police have classified this case as a homicide."

Since Debbie and Mia were best friends, Frank and Ray had met a few times, but never seemed to click. Their socially forced conversations were uncomfortable. The one time they played golf together seemed ok to Frank, but Ray was never again "available" to play another round with him.

Frank said to the TV screen "Ya poor bastard…… You had it all, and now, nothing."

Chapter 18

Food containers of every conceivable shape and size were piled high on Mia's kitchen counter, with little or no chance of ever finding their rightful owners. That was one constant about Catholic post-funeral gatherings, everyone brought food for the victim's family.

This morning, the kids had polished off some eggplant lasagna, before returning to school for their first day in class since their Dad's services. Mia had been serving them "silly breakfast" for the last few days in an effort to empty some of the casserole dishes.

Mia studied herself in the hallway mirror. She thought that she looked 100 years old. Her tired eyes were puffy and her nose was red.

Her cellphone chimed with a FaceTime call. Stepping into the living room, Mia grabbed her phone and saw "Detective Harland".

"Hello Detective".

"Hello Mrs. Pernell." DJ saw a tired-looking Mia on his iPhone screen. "Did I get you at a bad time?" *Have you slept at all?*

Running her hands through her hair, Mia anxiously responded. "No, Detective. Any progress on the investigation?"

"Working on it. Have you got time for a couple of questions?"

"Go ahead, Detective".

"Great. You gotta understand that there are things we need to know, even if only to eliminate possibilities from the equation." *You're not gonna like some of these questions.*

"Such as?"

"First, Mrs. Pernell, did your husband have any close friends in San Francisco that he might've wanted to visit?"

"At 3 am?? I don't think so, Detective. I believe his social time there was spent mostly with business partners."

"Understood. So no close friends, business associates or college pals that he might have wanted to visit?"

Mia stared at DJ's image, "If you are asking me about Ray having a lady friend in San Francisco, my answer is absolutely not!"

Probably not something he'd share with you…"Not at all, Mrs. Pernell. I'm only trying to track down any and all possible leads. There's something about your husband's homicide that we've yet to share with you." *So sorry to have to do this.*

"Oh God, what is it?"

"When your husband's body was found, he was wearing only a…uhh… what could be described as a sort of homemade modesty lap covering. It was made outta duct tape and a couple of shredded washcloths."

"What do you mean? Where were his clothes?"

"His clothes, money, wallet, and phone were all still in his hotel room. The only other item on him was his wedding band."

Mia fingered Ray's wedding band, permanently hung on the chain around her neck. "This has to be a mistake."

I wish it was. "Unfortunately, no. I was at the scene myself. The Department sometimes doesn't share certain details about some of the more graphic crimes to spare the families involved from further grief."

"So why are you telling me this?"

"Sometimes, these types of details become essential to the investigation. We've arrived at that point now, with your husband's case."

"I don't understand."

"Mrs. Pernell, knowing why your husband was wearing only rags may be essential to understanding what happened to him." *He wasn't going to midnight mass!*

"No idea. Someone else must've forced him to wear that stuff! He would never go out in public like that!"

"Definite possibility. Mrs Pernell, did your husband have a habit of folding his clothes before going to bed?"

"Yes, he always did that. Why would that matter?"

"At this point, everything matters."

"Ray was neat like that. I think he slept better feeling organized."

"OK, thanks. Has your husband mentioned any disagreements or problems at Tucker?" *Corporate Execs have many agendas.*

"No. Ray loved his job. He sometimes complained about too much travel, but he rarely said anything negative about his work."

"How well do you know Mr. Madrigan?"

"I love Carlos. He and Ray were close."

"No professional rivalry there?"

"No, Detective. They were best pals with tons of mutual respect."

"Understood. What about finances? Are you guys ok?"

"Yes. I handle the finances. We're good in that area."

"Any recent withdrawals that might've gotten your attention?"

"Trust me, Detective, I would notice something like that."

"Did Mr. Pernell gamble? I know there are casinos out there in Connecticut." *Gamblers only brag about their wins, never their losses.*

Mia almost laughed. "Ray gambled a little when we would go to a concert or show at the casino. But he was pretty frugal. Unless Ray was living a double life, he was not a gambler at all."

They stared at each other on their little smartphone screens, three thousand miles apart, both silently speculating on the phrase "double life".

DJ broke the silence. "Has Mr. Pernell ever sought counseling?"

"For what?"

"Drugs, alcohol, depression, marital counseling?"

"Not that I know of. I can tell you that we never needed marriage counseling. Ours has been a very solid marriage."

"Did he use any drugs besides alcohol? Maybe sedatives or painkillers. Perhaps after a surgery or injury of some kind."

"The only major surgery Ray had was on his knee after he tore his ACL during a ski trip to New Hampshire."

"When was that?"

"A couple years ago" answered Mia, feeling a bit guilty for not sharing the complete truth about Ray's New Hampshire knee injury.

Uh-oh. She held something back just now. "Was he given painkillers following the surgery?"

"Yes, he was. Oxy-something. But he didn't like the way they made him feel. I think he flushed them."

"What about recreational drugs?"

"Well Detective, recreational drugs were part of our lifestyle in college and maybe a bit beyond, but we have left those days way behind."

"Understood."

" And before you ask, yes we drink socially, but I don't think we are any different than anyone else in our social circles."

DJ nodded. *If I had a nickel for every time I've heard that.*

Mia had felt a twinge on that last statement. She knew they'd drank too much on more than a few occasions. She and Ray had once or twice discussed "cutting back".

"Mrs. Pernell, your husband was inebriated at the time that he and Mr. Madrigan returned to the hotel. Have you ever seen him in that condition, or is that something he only did with his buddies on the road?" *And whoever else he was looking for at 3 am.*

Mia spoke defensively. "Did Ray make a habit of staggering around drunk? No! I know he enjoyed celebrating when his projects were done. But they were always careful."

"Thanks for that, Mrs. Pernell. I'm more interested in your husband's mindset when he got to the hotel. Can you think of any reason that he might want to go back out?"

"No".

"Or any reason for him to dress like that?" *The library is closed at that hour….*

"No".

"I need you to think hard about this. It could be anything: Cigarettes, ice cream, a newspaper, drugs, or even more alcohol. Drunk people can become focused on just one thing that they think will bring them some satisfaction, and they'll sometimes act upon those urges, no matter what it takes."

"I suppose something like that is possible, Detective. But I just don't know what Ray was looking for."

"Understood."

"I've been wracking my brain ever since this happened. Why would someone want to hurt Ray?" Mia began crying.

DJ sucked in his breath and asked one last question. "Mrs. Pernell, does the word 'freak' have any significance to you or Ray?."

"No, why?"

"That word was written on Ray's body." *In his own blood!*

"Oh God. This just keeps getting worse." Mia dabbed her eyes with a tissue. "I don't want this stuff getting out. Can we keep these latest details between us?"

"That's the plan," said DJ. "Please reach out to me if you think of anything else." *Like whatever you held back a couple of minutes ago.*

"Yes, of course"

"Again, I'm sorry for your loss. I'll be in touch."

Mia stared into the phone. "Thanks, Detective. Bye."

This news about Ray's clothing was bringing a whole new level of angst to Mia's speculation about the horrors Ray may have had to endure.

She buried her face in the couch pillow and screamed.

Chapter 19

Sitting in his cubicle, feet on his desk, DJ was on the phone with Liz. "Yes, Baby. This is a big decision. You sure you don't wanna know our baby's gender?" *Cuz I sure as hell do.* "We've got at least 9 months and a day to decide. We ain't pregnant yet."

Captain Kekoa walked by and motioned DJ to come to his office. DJ said to Liz, "Sorry baby, gotta go, Captain wants to see me." He paused, listening to Liz for a second. Then added, "You know I do. Love you baby".

Arriving in Captain Kekoa's office, DJ was greeted with one of the Captain's deep belly laughs that only a man of his size and South-Pacific origin, could generate. "I see the marriage is going well. Don't worry, it'll all be over in about 60 years".

"Thanks, Kahuna. You're giving me so much to look forward to." DJ knew that the Captain was just yanking his chain. The mighty Kahuna was happily married and had his own posse of five children whose pictures were proudly displayed across the credenza behind his desk.

"Heard from the D.A. today about those bangers you took down at Gurtin High," said the Captain.

"No way they're talking." *Snitches get stitches!*

"Correct. They'll both likely be guests of the state of California for a long time."

"No one gives a damn about those two kids. Those shithead dealers will just reload with new recruits and keep pushing their poison on those school kids." *Goddamn child abuse.*

Kekoa agreed. "I never cease to be amazed by the crap these assholes will try, just to get over. What's next on their list, kindergartens?"

"Heard that."

"There's no freakin' honor among criminals anymore. Drug dealers are a different breed."

"Sure are, Kahuna".

"So where are you on the Pernell case?"

"I FaceTimed with Pernell's widow yesterday. She was shocked to hear about his outfit. If her husband had a kinky side, she didn't know about it."

"How'd she look? What'd you see in her eyes?"

DJ knew that Kahuna was old school when it came to interviews. He thought you could see all the way to a person's soul by looking into their eyes. While DJ agreed with that, he'd also met some pretty damn convincing liars. "I saw a pretty lady who looked depressed and tired. She wasn't exactly at the top of her game."

"What'd your cop instinct tell you?"

"That she was being defensive."

"About her husband?"

"Yeah. And she clammed up when I asked about alcohol and drugs. She said they were 'social drinkers like everyone else'."

"Of course. That all?"

DJ sighed, "Look Captain, I'll get more from her when she chills out. We know that Pernell and his pals were shitfaced. The security footage shows Pernell and Madrigan weaving through the Smythville lobby. The desk clerk confirmed that."

"Shitfaced people tend to seek the shortest path to self-gratification. Maybe he had a regular out here unknown to his missus."

"Or he could've met someone that night while they were out, and promised to hook up later." *Wouldn't be the first "businessman" to seek that kind of business.*

Kahuna countered. "It was likely either sex or drugs. But why the outfit?"

"Hell if I know. It takes all kinds. I'm stopping by the Smythville today for some follow-up."

"Good luck. You gotta keep me tightly in the loop on this one.

The Captain's desktop phone buzzed. He glanced down, his face scrunching into a quick flash of anxiety. "Gotta take this. Alone. Bye DJ" snapped Kekoa.

"Aye, aye sir. Your wish is my command."

————

On his way to The Smythville, DJ was organizing his thoughts. He suspected that the shredded rags and duct tape Ray was wearing may have come from the janitor's cart in the service stairwell.

Mia might be right. Pernell could've been forced into those rags. Where was he going dressed like that? How did he exit the building? Who felt the need to kill him?

Arriving in front of the hotel, DJ exited his unmarked car and showed the valet his Police ID.

He again enjoyed the walk across the thick lobby carpeting. Arriving at the desk, DJ leaned forward to read the clerk's name tag and said "Hello Samantha Cabner". "I'm Detective Harland. I called your manager and….."

"All set for you Detective. Security will assist you. This is Officer Matt Smith"

"No need for introductions, Samantha. Matt and I go way back".

"What's up, Detective?" asked Matt.

"Wanna see the freight elevator. Then, since I enjoyed it so much the first time, let's hit the back stairs and that fragrant alley."

"Nothing but the best for you, Detective."

Per standard hotel procedure, the freight elevator had been locked the night of Pernell' disappearance. But, DJ wanted to be as thorough as possible.

"Here we are," said Matt.

It looked like a standard freight elevator. Furniture padding hung on all three walls. The heavy-duty metal buttons protruded from the wall and were well-worn. The number three button was broken off. *Guess the third floor won't be receiving any freight.*

DJ looked around inside the elevator for a few seconds. "OK, let's head to our alley door."

The moist, musty smell of the service stairwell filled DJ's nostrils as they passed through the security door to the ground floor landing. Matt asked, "Wanna look outside again Detective?"

"Of course. I love ripe garbage as much as the next guy." Matt struck the bar with the heel of his hand and the alley door swung open. DJ exited into the alley, the odor assaulting his nostrils. *Damn, this is some rancid shit out here!* "Keep the door open, I won't be long."

"Suit yourself, Detective. Watch out for rats."

"Damn straight." *I ain't down with no rats.*

Turning right, DJ started walking along the heavily patched concrete and brick alley wall. He passed the two graffiti-covered dumpsters and then spotted a messy, cramped little space that looked like it had recently been occupied. There were newspapers on the ground, along with styrofoam containers, cans, and bottles scattered around, and a sawed-off trash can in the middle of the tiny space between dumpsters. DJ reached out to feel the heat from a still-smoldering fire in the can.

He walked toward the end of the alley, which emptied into Lund Avenue, a four-lane thoroughfare that supports significant traffic. A car, parked at the end of the alley, started up and sped out before DJ arrived there. *Wonder what you were up to?*

After reaching Lund Ave, DJ reversed direction, walking back to the doorway where Matt was dutifully standing by.

"Any luck Detective"?

"Not sure. I'm gonna take a quick look in the other direction. Hang tight." Two more dumpsters lined the wall in this direction. Beyond those, the alley narrowed, then ended where two buildings were connected by a chain link fence. *Damn, dead end.*

Returning to the stairwell, DJ said to Matt "Gotta get the Health Department to take a look back here. It's freakin' disgusting."

Matt chuckled and slammed the door. "Where to next, boss?"

"Up the stairs"

DJ repeated his journey up the poorly lit, damp stairwell. The doors accessing the hotel interior remained locked on every landing. As he and Matt arrived at the 7th floor, DJ again spotted the janitor's cart loaded with spray bottles, rags, brushes, duct tape, and a few other maintenance essentials. Crouching on one knee, next to the cart, was a balding man in a one-piece janitorial outfit, busying himself with one of the cart's wheels.

"I'm Detective Harland with San Francisco PD."

The man looked up at DJ through his thick peepers, and said "Jack Clinton, building maintenance."

"Jack, can you spare a minute?"

"Sure Detective. But please hurry, I've got a ton of stuff to get to."

"Have you ever been up on the roof?"

"Yes, of course. Why?"

Ignoring Clinton's question, DJ asked "What's up there?"

"Just two huge HVAC units that take up all the space"

"Is there any other way down from the roof besides these stairs"?

"I suppose you could jump seven stories, but otherwise no."

Gotta love a funny maintenance man! "Who else has access to this roof door?"

"The other key is in the Manager's office downstairs."

"Thanks, Jack. Does this cart get parked on the seventh floor every night?"

Jack looked at DJ quizzically. "Yeah, it's usually here overnight, near my supply closet. Every morning, I resupply it and take it down to the first floor to start my day. Which is what I'm about to do, as soon as I replace this goddamn wheel."

"I see that you have black duct tape in your cart. Do you ever use other colors?" *Please say yes!*

"Sure. The hotel buys whatever is on sale. The whole world is held together by duct tape."

"What other colors have they bought?"

"Well, we just got these black rolls in. We've had red and blue. Our last batch was silver, which I like best. It blends in better on pipes and ductwork."

Bingo...silver! "Where do you get those blue cleaning rags I see in your cart?"

Jack looked at DJ quizzically. "Those are just old hand towels that are no longer suitable for our guests." *Bingo again!*

"Thanks a lot, Jack. OK, Matt. I'm good to go."

Chapter 20

Mia was tucking in young Karl. "Goodnight sweetheart, I love you and you know your Daddy's love will always be in your heart."

"I miss him Mom," said Karl, his arms wrapped tightly around his Fuzzy Bear.

"So do I honey. But you know that Dad loved us very much and would want us to be strong." Mia heard herself saying those words, but her mind was racing with questions about what Ray was doing when he was killed. The latest news from Detective Harland had created an entirely new layer of angst in her mind.

"OK, Mom. Maybe I'll see him when I get to heaven."

"No doubt you will."She hugged Karl tightly. "Love you, Karl. Goodnight"

"Goodnight Mom."

Mia headed for the kitchen where she had some dirty dishes waiting. Passing the den, she saw Ricky at the computer, deeply engaged in a video game. Mia never considered video games as intellectually stimulating, but she thought it was great that Ricky had something apart from schoolwork and wrestling to occupy his mind during his idle time.

Mia entered the kitchen. "Hi Phoebs. What's up?"

Phoebe looked pensive, picking at a cup of yogurt. "Mom, Is it okay for me to go to the prom, I mean, so soon....you know....after Dad?"

Mia felt an emotional surge. She turned on the faucet and began to rinse dishes while staring straight ahead. "Of course, it's ok. Why wouldn't it be?"

"I don't want to seem like it doesn't matter to me that Dad is gone. I want to be sure to do the right thing. I'm not even sure that I could have much fun."

Mia turned off the water and spun around to face Phoebe. "You know your Dad loved you very much, right?"

"Yes, I know."

"Do you think your Dad would have been proud of you on prom night?"

"I hope so."

"I know so. He wouldn't be happy to know that you didn't go to your junior prom because of him. And neither would I."

"I get it Mom, but I just feel a little bit weird about it."

Mia leaned in closer to Phoebe. "Listen, honey. I completely understand. My whole life feels like that right now. But we both know that your father would be disappointed if we chose to punish ourselves because he is gone. We just gotta keep him in our hearts."

Tears were trickling down Phoebe's face. "Thanks, Mom. I just miss him so much. I want to do the right thing."

"I know you do." Mia hugged her daughter. "It's still a month away, but even if it were tomorrow, going to the prom is the right thing. Plus you don't want to disappoint that handsome Justin!"

Wiping her tears, Phoebe showed a slight smile of embarrassment, "Aw, geez Mom…."

Entering her nightly thoughts into her laptop journal, Mia reread her entry from the first night of Ray's trip. "Hope your project is going well Ray. Love you and miss you." That night seemed so very long ago. The pain of his death came rushing back to her.

The revelation about Ray's clothing and the probing questions from Detective Harland had sent her mind spinning.

"I'm confused, Ray. Were you involved in something weird at 3 am? I can't believe that. Just wish I knew."

Mia slammed her laptop shut, her mind awash with confusion.

Chapter 21

While listening to the local police scanners, Frank Dorrington was searching local websites including "Community Crime Map" and "SpotCrime" in search of potential clients.

Frank's voyeuristic urges sometimes steered him to CoCriRev, otherwise known in long form as 'Covert Crimes Revealed', a website for dramatic "insider" crime-related videos and photos. Frank knew the postings weren't all authentic, but he was often fascinated, nonetheless.

He navigated to California, his favorite state for the most fascinating images. After viewing several disappointing and likely Photoshopped images, Frank's noted a photo labeled "Bizarre San Francisco Murder". He clicked on the link and saw what appeared to be a naked murder victim. He zoomed in on the image and spotted a silver belt and a small raggedy blue cloth across the victim's lap. He zoomed further to get a better look at the word "Freak" scrawled on the victim's chest. As he did, the face of the victim was magnified. Frank could not believe his eyes.

"No! It can't be! Holy shit, is that you Ray? What the hell?"

Frank immediately grabbed a still frame of the photo. The photo credit was posted as someone named "SecretEye233".

Frank examined the photo. Despite it becoming more digitized as he zoomed in, he was certain that he was looking at Ray Pernell. The face and hair were unmistakable. Frank wondered how the hell Ray had wound up dead, with 'freak' written on his chest, and nearly naked.

His thoughts were interrupted by his doorbell. He walked to his apartment door and immediately regretted opening it, uttering "Oh fuck!"

A large man with pale skin and slicked hair, in a black suit, pushed his way in and shoved Frank into a chair. Leaning over Frank and placing his strong hands on Frank's shoulders, the man said: "I'm running out of patience with you, asshole."

Frank searched for a confident voice. "Hi, Stanley. Long time, no see."

"Fuck that crap, Frank. Your window is closing. You owe me 150 grand. And I ain't waiting much longer."

"C'mon, Stanley. I only borrowed a hundred thousand."

"You knew what you were getting into. Not my fault that you fucked shit up. I want my money."

"I'm a little short on cash right now, but I have a huge opportunity to make a ton of money" lied Frank. "I just need a little more time."

Stanley was tightening his grip on Frank's throat. "You better put that big lawyer brain of yours to work my friend. If I don't see my cash very soon, well.....It's time for consequences."

"Alright, alright. I'll get it" gasped Frank.

"I ain't kidding Frank. I'll be watching you. And don't try to go nowhere." Stanley released his grip on Frank's neck.

Frank sucked in a deep breath, "OK. No problem. I'll have the money soon."

As Stanley headed for the door, he said "It wouldn't be a good idea to fuck me on this Frank."

"I'll get it," said Frank, closing the door and dropping to his knees, shaking.

Rubbing his throat, Frank grabbed his cell phone and hit "Ex".

"What the hell could you possibly want? Are you broke at the casino again?" snapped Debbie, "And no, I don't need an ambulance chaser."

Ignoring Debbie's insult, Frank said "This is important. It's about Ray."

"I'm sure. Let me guess. You've identified the killer and obtained a full confession. Am I right?"

"Look, I just learned something that Mia might not know. She's gonna need an attorney. Someone exactly like me who is familiar with the….."

Debbie cut him off. "No chance in hell, Frank. This is so like you to try to backdoor your way into representing Mia by claiming you have some "important" information. Have you no shame? Never mind, I know the answer."

"Look, this info is legit. I called you because I didn't want to freak out Mia. Just ask her if she is aware of what Ray was wearing on the night of his murder."

Debbie followed a derisive laugh with "Of course, I won't. Are we done here? Never mind, I am. Bye Frank".

Frank understood that his ex-wife had multiple reasons to be angry with him. But this was important. This photo was definitely Ray. He was sure of it. Sitting at his laptop, Frank spoke to the captured image.

"Damn Ray, what kinda kinky shit were you into?"

It occurred to Frank that if he properly utilized this new information, he just might be able to generate some income for himself.

The seed of a potentially profitable idea was sprouting somewhere deep in his desperate brain.

Chapter 22

Arriving at his desk, DJ found an interoffice envelope from Officer Amal Ahmadi in the Digital Forensics Department. He removed an 8x10 glossy photo. DJ couldn't believe his eyes. *Holy shit!* He was staring at a photo of Ray Pernell's body. It was unlike any of the police photos. The details were clear enough to identify the victim and read the "Freak" on his chest. DJ quickly dialed Ahmadi's extension.

"Hello Detective. Thought I might hear from you."

"Damn, Amal. Where the hell did you get this?"

"Found it on a dark website called CoCriRev. Do you think it's authentic?"

"Hell yes! See those those blue jeans in the background? Those are my legs. Who took this? I've never heard of CoCriRev."

"It's a website populated by wanna-be crime photographers. I thought this looked a lot like your photos of Ray Pernell."

"This is definitely the real thing."

"The photo credit is 'SecretEye233'. We are working on identifying that person. I should have something soon."

"Can anyone see this?"

"Right now, yes."

"Incredible work, Amal. This photographer could be a witness." *Or a murderer.*

"Thanks, Detective. I'll give you a buzz as soon as we learn more."

DJ considered this new development. *Gotta inform Mia Pernell about this photo in case it gets out.*

Two minutes later DJ's phone rang. "Yes, Amal?"

"Hey, Detective. I opened the CoCriRev website right after we spoke. The photo has been taken down, probably because of my inquiry."

"That's good." *We don't need that getting out.*

"Agreed," answered Ahmadi. "But I saw it. Undoubtedly, others did too." I'll keep working on IDing the photographer."

"Thanks Amal. Keep me posted." *Uh oh. This has a chance to get ugly!*

———

"I really do need your help." Debbie Slater was chatting with Mia in the Pernell's living room.

"I appreciate it, Debbie. I know you're just trying to help me. But I had to leave ZTA because I didn't have the time. And now with Ray gone, I am just too busy."

"Look, I'm not offering any charity here. The business is growing. I need your writing and marketing skills. Remember those?"

"Yes, I do."

"We're a great team. Don't make me hire some stranger who doesn't get me like you do."

Mia slowly shook her head from side to side. "I'm just not ready yet."

"How about just a part-time commitment? Maybe 10 hours a week. You can do the work from home. C'mon, I need you."

"You know how much I love writing a creative brief and pitching it to a client, but…" Mia was interrupted by the chiming of her cell phone. She looked down and saw "Detective Harland" on the screen.

"What's up, Detective?" said Mia, walking into the privacy of the den.

"You know how we had hoped to keep the exact circumstances of your husband's death to ourselves? That may not be possible now." More likely, impossible.

"Why not?"

"Someone managed to snap a photograph of your husband before we were able to completely secure the crime scene."

"I don't understand."

DJ took a deep breath and plunged in. "A photo of Mr. Pernell's body has surfaced on the internet. It's not one of the photos from the police forensics team. It was taken by someone else."

"Oh my God. Is it really Ray?"

"Yes. It was taken down shortly after we inquired. It was on a website called CoCriRev."

"What the hell is that?"

"It's a dark site for crime photographer wannabe's."

"Who took the photo?"

"We're chasing down some leads…..should know soon."

"Maybe this photographer saw Ray's killer? Can't you talk to the CoCri-whatever people?"

"We're pursuing every possible scenario. I just wanted you to know that this photo was posted for a relatively short period, but there's always a chance that somebody may have seen and copied it." *Probably a very good chance.*

Mia answered in a flat voice. "Oh, dear God. Hopefully, nobody else saw it."

"We hope so too. That's all I've got for now. I'll be in touch."

"Okay, thanks, Detective."

Mia was deep in thought as she walked back into the living room and jumped when she heard Debbie's voice. "You ok honey? What was that all about?"

"There's something about Ray's death that I haven't shared with you."

Debbie nodded.

"Detective Harland recently told me something about Ray that I didn't want anyone to know because I was afraid it might embarrass my family."

"You don't have to tell me if you don't want to."

"No, I want to." Mia, grabbed a tissue to dab her eyes. "When Ray was found, he wasn't dressed in his normal clothes. He was naked except for an old cloth on his lap, held on by duct tape. The word 'freak' was written on his chest."

"Oh my God" uttered Debbie.

"I didn't want anyone to know about this because I had no clue what he was doing. I mean, why was he almost naked?"

"There's got to be a logical explanation."

"I believe that his killer put him in those rags. I didn't want this stuff to get out. I wanted to protect my family."

"Oh no," said Debbie, recalling Frank's phone call.

"Somehow, this picture of Ray showed up on the internet for a while but then disappeared. The cops wanted me to know just in case it somehow got out."

"Holy shit!" said Debbie.

"I know. What the hell could've happened to Ray?"

"I didn't think it could be true. No way. How did he know?"

Mia stared at her best friend. "What the hell are you talking about?"

"I got a call from Frank."

"So? Did he want money again?"

"No. But I completely dismissed everything he said. And now I'm not so sure."

"Debbie! What are you talking about?"

"Frank was being his usual dirtbag self, trying to see if you needed a lawyer. I shut him down."

"Thanks for that. So what's the big deal?"

"He said that he had some information that the police might not have shared with you."

"What information? Frank? No way!"

"He said to ask you about what Ray was wearing when he was found. That son-of-a-bitch must've somehow seen that photo online."

"No doubt! Have you seen it?" asked Mia.

"No, I haven't. I'm so sorry I didn't tell you right away. I never believe anything that asshole says."

Mia's eyes moistened. "Oh my God, if Frank has seen it, other people have too. It's gonna get out. I can't imagine why Ray was dressed like that."

Debbie hugged Mia tightly. "Don't worry honey. Ray was a wonderful husband and father. Everyone close to you knows that. And we don't care what anyone else thinks."

———

"Hey Kahuna, got a second?" asked DJ, leaning into Captain Kekoa's office.

"No, but since you're already here, you got two seconds to tell me what you want."

"Amal Ahmadi has identified the shooter of that Ray Pernell photo. Uniforms have picked him up. Should be here soon."

"Damn, Amal is good. But this guy won't know much."

"How can you possibly know that?" *What are you, omniscient?*

"I don't 'know' it, Detective," said the Captain, holding his fingers up in air quotes. "But the people who post photos on those crime sites will always post their most provocative images."

"This one is pretty damn provocative."

"Exactly. If he had seen anything more interesting at the murder scene, we'd be seeing it. But that's just my opinion. It's up to you to get him to talk."

"Yes sir. I'll let you know what we get from SecretEye233."

Kekoa laughed. "Sounds like a Bond character. Remember: shaken, not stirred."

"Thanks, Kahuna, I'll be on the lookout." *For secret weapons!*

Outside the interview room, DJ was approached by Officer Anna Kamsky. Smallish in physical stature, the feisty Kamsky was known for her big personality.

"What's up, DJ? How goes the detective business?"

"I'm up to my ass in felonies. How you been? How's the old man?"

Anna sighed, shaking her head. "Got divorced about a year ago. Thanks for keeping up."

"Aw shit, sorry. I think I knew that." *Open mouth, insert foot!* DJ, quickly changed the subject. "Tell me about SecretEye233."

"Clean pick up. Teenager. His name is Wes Bell. Lives with his Mom. We put the cuffs on to ensure his cooperation, but you don't need 'em".

"Thanks, Anna. And sorry about that other thing." *I'm an idiot.*

"Don't sweat it. At least you're not behaving like some of these trolls around here who believe that marital fidelity is optional."

DJ chuckled. "Hell no! Liz would have me neutered if she ever thought that."

"Always liked her," said Anna, walking away.

Inside the interview room, DJ observed a pale young man, sitting at the table, his handcuffs looped through the restraining ring. His roundish body was topped by tousled dark hair tipped with blonde highlights. Multiple piercings decorated his left ear. His hazel eyes looked frightened.

"Hello, Wes Bell. I'm Detective Harland. Do you have any idea why you're here?"

"No. They only said I was wanted for questioning. Am I under arrest? Why the handcuffs?"

"You are not under arrest. You're here for questioning relative to a felony. The cuffs are just a precaution. Mr. Bell, do you post photos online under the name of SecretEye233?"

"That's what this is about? asked Bell. "Yes, I use that name, along with several others. There's no law against that is there?"

Ignoring his question, DJ moved on. "Do you use that name when posting material on a site called CoCriRev?"

"Yeah, so? It's not a porn site or anything like that. Why would it be a felony?"

"Wes, I'm interested in a photo that you posted recently showing a nearly naked white man propped up against a tire, with the word 'freak' written on his chest."

Wes straightened a little. "That's one of my best shots."

"So, how did you come to be in a position to take that photo? And what else did you see?" *Like maybe a murder being committed?*

"Oh, I get it. You think I have something to do with that dead guy? Didn't seem like an OD. I thought that was a bullet wound on his forehead. It was a murder, wasn't it?

"We're still investigating. You need to tell me everything you know." *Damn it, Kahuna was right. This kid's got nothing.*

"I'm a crime photographer. I listen to police scanners and check a couple of local websites, looking for something that might make for a good picture. When I hear something interesting, I go and try to get some pictures."

"When did you arrive at that location? What did you see?"

"I didn't see any crime, if that's what you mean."

"Just tell me about it from the beginning."

"I heard the call on my scanner. I just bought a new zoom attachment for my iPhone and I was dying to try it out. Rode my bike down to Hollis, even though it's not my favorite part of town. The flashing lights made it easy to find. I found a spot where I could see the body without being seen, and I started taking pictures."

"Of what?" asked DJ.

"There were a couple of cops standing around. I could see a sheet over a body on the ground. I kinda thought that I'd missed my chance when a dude in plain clothes walked up and pulled the sheet off. That's when I got that photo. Then I got the hell out of there. Don't love that neighborhood."

"Did you see anyone else lingering in that area?"

"Just cops."

DJ reached over and unlocked the handcuffs. "Look Wes, I know that you are proud of that photo. But it's not smart to be posting photos about ongoing police investigations. You follow me?"

Rubbing his wrists, Bell said, "Yes, I get it."

"Your photo has been removed from the CoCriRev website. Have you posted that photo, or any others from that particular event, on any additional websites?"

"No sir," said Wes. "That was my only decent shot. I thought CoCriRev was a good place to post it. I guess not."

"Are you sure that you haven't saved any other shots from that day?"

"No sir. I erased the other pics and video. They weren't worth shit. I only have just so much memory."

"That photo is not to be posted anywhere else. Understand?"

"Yeah, sure," said Wes, sounding annoyed.

"Do you have the phone with you?"

"In my pocket."

"Just to be sure, Officer Ahmadi from our Digital Forensics Department will sit with you and go through your phone and also talk to you about any other drives you may have used to store these images."

"This is bull….baloney, Detective. I don't have any other pictures."

"Great, then it shouldn't be a problem." DJ placed a legal pad and pen in front of Bell. "I need you to write down a full description of what you saw that day. Start with when you heard the call on your scanner and take us through the moment you posted your photo on CoCriRev."

Bell grunted his agreement.

"Don't leave anything out, no matter how trivial it may seem to you. And make sure we have all your contact information."

"Geez, I didn't do shit, and now I'm here."

"Listen, Wes," said DJ. "You're a smart kid. You're messing around in police business with this hobby. Someday, you'll piss off a bad guy and he'll come after your ass. You need to find a safer way to use your interest in photography." *Or we'll be investigating your murder.*

"Damn, you sound like my mother," said Wes. "It ain't that easy. I just wanna get the hell outta here." Grabbing the pen, he began to write.

"Thanks, Wes. Officer Ahmadi will join you shortly. We'll contact you if we need anything more." *Damn, just a dead end.*

Chapter 23

Frank Dorrington was adding a caption to the photo of Ray Pernell's body he had grabbed from the CoCriRev website. After trying various phrases, he settled on "TuckerExecFreak – Hate Crime?" He then posted the newly captioned photo to an anonymous image upload service called 'noTrace' to protect his identity. Now it was time to get the local media involved.

Using his recently purchased burner phone, Frank called a local Connecticut news-talk radio show. "May I speak to a Producer, please? I have some news they may find very interesting"

"Sir, what does this pertain to? I can have a show Producer call you back or reach you by email if they have an interest in your story."

"I can't do that right now. But I promise that if you let me talk to someone who is a decision-maker, they won't regret it."

"Sir, have you considered using our online news submission site? Anything you submit will be kept in strictest confidence."

Frustrated, Frank said, "You'll be sorry that you missed out on this huge story."

Subsequent calls to another radio station and two local TV newsrooms were met with similar responses. Searching for other local news outlets, Frank spotted a pop-up ad for a local live call-in podcast.

Thirty minutes later, he was monitoring the podcast. The current caller was regaling the two hosts with a complaint about methane gas "spewing" from the local dairy farms.

Frank called. "You've reached the 'Hudson Hears You' podcast. What do you wish to discuss with Bruce and Sarah?"

"Uh hello?" said Frank. "I'd like to talk about the lack of properly designated crosswalks in front of Fairgrounds Elementary School."

"Terrific," said the young voice. "You'll be on next with Bruce and Sarah."

The wait was only about 2 minutes.

"Greetings citizen. I'm Sarah, he's Bruce. Welcome to 'Hudson Hears You'. We're ready to listen to your concerns about crosswalks at Fairgrounds Elementary."

"Uh yes, Thank you," said Frank. "there is a definite lack of clear markings on those crosswalks. They need new paint badly."

"That's very important," said Bruce.

Frank then changed the subject. "I also wanted to add my condolences to the Pernell family of Hudson on the recent passing of Ray Pernell. He was a huge asset to TEM and such a pillar of the community. He will be missed."

"Well yes, he was a fine man," said Sarah. "We discussed his legacy a few days ago with Father Keenan of St. Joseph's Church. If you didn't hear that discussion, it might bring you some comfort. You can find it on our website's podcast list."

"Thank you, I will," said Frank. "It's a shame that he was the victim of such a hideous hate crime. You would think that a huge company like Tucker would throw their full support into investigating such an abhorrent crime."

Bruce answered with surprise in his voice. "I'm sorry. What did you say about a hate crime?"

"There will soon be some information coming out indicating that Ray's murder was a hate crime. I cannot elaborate any further than that."

After a few seconds of silence, Sarah answered. "Well sir, if that is true, the Connecticut news stations will be on top of that. Of course, they will seek confirmation before airing any news of that sort. May I ask how you know this to be true?"

"I'm a very close friend of Ray's. I'm aware of some things that the public has yet to learn. Thank you for your time. And, I hope those crosswalks do get repainted."

After a few moments of self-congratulation, Frank sent messages to the news-submission sites for all four local TV stations and two news-radio outlets which read: "TEM Executive Ray Pernell, of Hudson CT, was the victim of a vicious hate crime in San Francisco. Listen to today's 'Hudson Hears You' podcast for further info."

Frank had to get to the courthouse for a bail hearing. Two hours later, and $175 richer, Frank hurried back to his 12-year-old Honda Civic and flipped on a local news radio station, hoping to hear speculation about Ray Pernell. He tried the other Connecticut news station and heard only a discussion about the budget issues facing the state.

At home, Frank popped open a beer and excitedly opened his laptop to check for responses to his news submissions. He was disappointed with what he saw.

All of the news outlets showed some interest in his information, but no one would air his "speculation" without corroboration. He thought about sending the news outlets a link to the "noTrace" posting of Ray's photo with the new caption, but he didn't want his name associated with that posting.

Frank yelled at his laptop. "Dammit. I gotta find news outlets with fewer scruples!"

Chapter 24

Frank Dorrington tossed a couple of grocery store tabloids onto his stained coffee table and grabbed his laptop. All local media outlets had refused to run his Pernell hate-crime murder story without legitimate corroboration from a credible source.

Frank eyed the tabloids. Those publications never let facts get in the way of a juicy story. Staring up at him were cover stories about alien invaders, foolproof diet plans, and Hollywood secret romances. The possibly kinky behavior and murder of a TEM executive would be a huge story.

It occurred to Frank that high school kids had the best, and fastest, command of moving social media information. Ten minutes later, Frank used his new burner phone, with a prepaid SIM card, to leave a message in the voicemail in-box of the Hudson High School student newspaper with an instruction. "Check out the "noTrace" website for a photo of Hudson's Ray Pernell in a scandalous outfit that was undoubtedly related to his recent homicide."

Frank had just lit the fuse.

Within 20 minutes, that photo link had been shared among many of the students at Hudson High and was rapidly spreading throughout multiple social media outlets.

———

Mia was preparing green peppers, carrots, celery, and onion dip for Phoebe and Karl when they got off the bus.

Her phone rang.

"Hi, Debbie. What's going on?"

Debbie's tone of voice brought Mia right back to her dark place. "I take it you haven't seen what's trending on social media."

"What the hell are you talking about?"

"I don't know if it's real, but that photo of Ray that the Detective warned you about is now on the internet."

"Oh my God. Should I see it? No, I don't wanna see it."

"I'm so sorry honey. It's captioned "TuckerExecFreak – Hate Crime?".

"Freak? What hate crime? I have to see it. I'll know if it's my Ray".

"It's Ray, and it's very graphic. You don't need to see it."

Mia started to answer but was interrupted as the front door flew open and Phoebe burst in.

"Mom! Where are you? Have you seen this? Oh my God, this sucks! Where are you?"

With a quick "gotta go", Mia disconnected Debbie and rushed into the living room.

Karl went racing off to his room as Phoebe continued wailing. "Oh my God! Mom, Dad's body is on the internet! He's almost naked! Now it's all over Instagram, Snap, and TikTok! It's gone viral!"

"Slow down Phoebs!"

"It says 'TuckerExecFreak – Hate Crime'. People are leaving comments about Dad being some kind of freak. What hate crime are they talking about? Why would someone hate him? This is so fucked up!"

"Phoebe stop! I can hear you!" yelled Mia. "I just found out about it. I haven't seen it yet."

"Don't Mom. It's gross."

"Are you sure it's your Dad?"

"Yes. Mom. It's him. Now everyone at school thinks Dad was a weirdo who was roaming the streets of San Francisco naked! Was he looking for sex or drugs? Did you know about this side of him?"

"You shut your mouth, young lady! You don't know what you're talking about."

"I know that I'm the laughingstock of Hudson High. Why did he have to ruin my life?"

Phoebe stormed off to her bedroom, slamming the door, cursing the world.

Mia opened her laptop. It only took a few seconds to find the photo. She burst into tears at the sight of her husband. "Oh God, why did I look?"

Chapter 25

DJ peeked inside the door to Captain Kekoa's office. Seeing the Captain on the phone, DJ slipped in and quietly sat on a chair directly in front of the Captain's desk. Kekoa motioned for him to remain.

DJ couldn't help but overhear the Captain. "Understood sir. Unfortunately, anything that is posted, for even a minute, can be captured by somebody else. We can't put the toothpaste back in the tube."

Oh shit. He's getting reamed.

"Yes, sir. PR will need to address the media, but we'll share whatever we can with the Tucker people. Yes, could've been a hate crime." After another pause. "Of course sir. We will allocate all available resources and update you daily. Thank you, sir."

Kekoa hung up and stared straight at DJ. "I'm guessing that my discussion with Commissioner Francis is directly related to why you're here. Am I right?"

"The Commissioner? Wow! What did he want?" *Police royalty!*

"Right now, he wants our heads on a platter. That damn Pernell photo has gone viral. The Commissioner's pal, who sits on the board at Tucker, is mighty interested in how that photo became public."

"Makes sense," said DJ. "They gotta protect their reputation. That pic doesn't exactly reflect Tucker's values."

"Tell me something I don't know!"

"That's why I came in here Captain." *Not a good time to use "Kahuna".*

"Why, what you got?"

"That caption about a 'TuckerExecFreak' and 'a hate crime' was not there on the first version posted by Wes Bell. His original posting had no text at all. Someone, who likely has an issue with Tucker or maybe with Ray Pernell, must have added that text and pushed it out to the world."

"Interesting, but why should I give a shit?"

"It had to be someone who knew the identity of the victim and the victim's employer."

"Whoever did that certainly wanted to stir up some negative publicity. Coulda been one of those weekly tabloids trying to create publicity around this story."

"Possibly. I've asked Amal Ahmadi if he could trace this new version of the photo."

"Fine Detective," said Captain Kekoa, rubbing his temples. "Anything else?"

"Hell, yes. What do you want me to do with the press inquiries?" *Could I please tell them all to go to hell?*

"Who've you heard from?"

"We've heard from TV and radio in Connecticut, and also from CNN. They want confirmation on the identity of the victim in the photograph."

"What are you telling them?"

"We ain't confirming anything at this time, but we all know the photo is genuine. Wes Bell confirmed that for us." *Hello….my freaking legs are in the background!*

"From now on, all inquiries from the press go to Marty Penderson in Public Relations," said Kekoa. "We can expect that new version of the photo, with those damning words, to be everywhere within 24 hours. Where you at?"

"This is all gonna take a minute to unravel." *Drunk people do drunk shit!*

"What've you got?"

"I'm certain that the stuff used to make Pernell's raggedy outfit came from a janitor's cart, which was parked in the hotel service stairwell, 3 flights above his floor. The rags and tape match."

"Good to know. But why go up three stories for some duct tape and rags?"

"Maybe he didn't" said DJ. "Maybe the killer grabbed that stuff."

"And then went to his room and forced him into those rags?"

"Could be. But there ain't a damn thing to indicate that, at least not yet."

"Stay on it!"

"Aye aye, Captain."

Kekoa's frustration surfaced. "Look, I don't need the Commissioner, or his pals at Tucker, riding my ass. You gotta put everything else on the back burner and focus on this mess. I'll get you some help." Pointing at the door, Kekoa growled: "Get your ass outta here! And keep me in the loop."

With a tight-lipped "Yes sir", DJ scooted out the door. *Happy to still have my nuts!*

———

Scanning the tabloids at the corner store, Frank Dorrington spotted the latest edition of "Dishing Dirt". On the cover was the photo of Ray's body, his face slightly shaded in a transparent "effort to protect" his unconfirmed identity. The giant headline screamed: "Loincloth Murder…TEM Exec Freak - Hate Crime Victim?" Frank suddenly wished that he'd thought of the "loincloth" label. He whistled that whistle of admiration. "Loincloth! Damn these guys are good!"

Buying two copies, Frank returned to his apartment. He knew it only took one "publication" to print something like this, before other media, including the "mainstream media", also chose to run the story, while citing the Dishing Dirt's "unsubstantiated" article. This bit of trickery allowed some of the more legitimate press outlets to publicize stories that were not properly corroborated.

Frank checked his laptop. The online reaction to the "loincloth murder" was already going viral. The kid-friendly profile of media-giant TEM, along with the bizarre nature of Ray's appearance, was proving to be jet fuel for emotion-filled postings. Many of the posts assumed that the victim was leading some sort of double life that included dressing in bizarre outfits and cruising the streets of San Francisco looking for sex, drugs, or both.

Frank reviewed some of the reactions:

-"This dude was clearly a freak, just like it says on his chest. Who walks around SanFran dressed like that? Freaks, that's who"

-"How can a huge company like Tucker Entertainment Media allow someone like this to create material aimed at our kids? Done with them."

-"Hate crimes are awful. This man was killed because of how he was dressed, or who he was hanging out with. That's wrong, no matter how you feel about alternate lifestyles."

-"How dumb do you have to be? Who wanders the streets of San Francisco in an f-ing loincloth? Got what he deserved."

Frank could see a possible path to profitability in defending his "close pal".

Chapter 26

Sharon Dillard surveyed the five Managers seated in her office. "There has been a lot of speculation about Ray's death. Our CEO has asked that we refrain from sharing any public opinions about Ray's passing. And that includes any discussion of the distasteful photo that has been making the rounds on the internet. Is that clear?"

Sharon saw five heads nodding assent.

"And be sure to push that message down to your teams. Now, let's talk about covering Ray's duties. He had a lot on his plate. Until we fill his position, I'm asking each of you to assume more responsibility."

Sharon surveyed the faces.

Leigh Grayson, Senior Creative Design Director, is highly respected among her peers, and she'd be a fine replacement for Ray.

Bill Grayson, Leigh's husband, had done a wonderful job of growing and managing the Animation Design Department. Ray had been the Best Man at Bill and Leigh's wedding.

Tim O'Shea had made a huge impression during his 2 years as the head of Graphic Design. He was destined for amazing things.

Mitchell Claudino, TEM's wonderfully talented Chief Video Editor, had the extraordinary ability to make a so-so movie look spectacular in a 60-second trailer.

And there was Carlos Madrigan. He had developed and directed nearly all TEM location shoots for the last few years, mostly working with very young actors.

Looking at his co-workers, Bill Grayson spoke. "Maybe we could get together at O'Finsky's after work to kick around some ideas. Sharon, you care to join us?"

Before Sharon was able to answer, Patti's voice came through the intercom. "Detective Harland on line two for you Sharon."

"Thanks, Patti. Sorry gang, you guys gotta go, I need to take this. We'll discuss it later."

Drawing a deep breath, she picked up the phone. "Hello Detective, this is Sharon Dillard."

"Hello" replied DJ. "Got a minute?"

"Good timing Detective. I was just meeting with my staff about Ray. Do you have anything new?"

"Again, my thanks to Tucker for sending us Mr. Pernell's prints and info."

"Tucker Media is always ready and willing to help. Our people are our number one resource" said Sharon.

"Glad to hear that," said DJ. *Clearly a corporate mission statement.* "Have you seen the photograph that claims Ray is the victim of a hate crime?"

"Yes. Is it real, Detective?"

"Off the record, yes."

A gasp escaped Sharon's lips. "Oh my God. What was he doing? Why is he naked?"

"Not sure yet. I've got a couple questions for TEM. Are you the appropriate person?"

Sharon knew that all questions should be directed to Human Resources, but her curiosity got the best of her. "If I can't answer your questions appropriately, I'll redirect them to HR."

"Great. Who did Mr. Pernell hang out with at Tucker?"

"Ray's closest friends were probably my other five direct reports. Carlos Madrigan was probably his tightest work buddy."

"I'll need a list of those names." *Send them now before HR gets involved!*

"Sure detective."

"Are you aware of any odd behavior by Mr. Pernell that seemed contrary to his character?"

"Not really. Ray liked to have fun as much as the next guy, but he was not a lampshade drunk." Sharon immediately regretted her choice of words.

"Of course not." *So what kind of drunk was he?* "It's clear that he and Mr. Madrigan were inebriated when they returned to the hotel. Was that type of behavior a regular thing for Mr. Pernell?"

"Not to my knowledge" answered Sharon, a bit defensively.

"Great. Are you aware of any groups or organizations that Mr. Pernell may have belonged to which might encourage unusual attire?" *Churches, Boy Scouts, Shriners?*

"I don't think so."

"Did you know Mr. Pernell to frequent the casinos there in Connecticut?"

"I know that he and Mia attended a concert or two at Mohegan Sun. Don't know about any gambling. Ray was very solid financially. People at his level are well-compensated."

I'm sure they are. "Does Tucker provide any counseling services for employees?"

Sharon answered proudly. "Yes. Counseling services are available to all full-time employees."

"Did Mr. Pernell utilize that counseling?"

"No idea. Those services are offered with full anonymity, and the company covers the costs."

"Can you at least tell me what areas of employee distress these counselors might cover?"

"Stuff like drug addiction, alcoholism, marriage counseling, financial counseling, work-related stress….pretty much anything and everything."

"Thanks. That's it for now. If you think of anything at all that might help explain Mr. Pernell's actions, please give me a call."

"Will do, Detective."

After hanging up, Sharon sighed and said, "Damn Ray, what the hell was going on with you?"

Chapter 27

Debbie Slater wanted to run something by Mia before they arrived at St. Joseph's for choir practice. But Mia spoke first.

"That awful picture of Ray is freaking me out. I have no clue what he was doing. But everyone seems to have an opinion. And none of them are good."

"You know how shitty people can be," said Debbie. "We need to be prepared for more of that crap. Even tonight."

"From the choir? Geez, I hope not. Phoebe is already getting shit about her Dad at school. High-school kids can be so damn mean."

Debbie agreed. "I feel for Phoebe. High school is tough enough without that bullshit. You know, we can skip choir practice if you'd like. Everyone will understand."

"Absolutely not! Then everyone will think that Ray and I had something to hide."

Pulling up in front of St. Joe's, they saw a group of choir members on the front steps, engaged in the usual pre-rehearsal chit-chat. After parking the car, Debbie and Mia started walking toward the church entrance, the front steps now empty.

"Where'd everybody go?" asked Debbie.

The church door opened and they were greeted by Lynette Elmer. "Hi Mrs. Elmer," said Mia. "Nice to see you."

"Hello, girls. I'd like to have a quick word with you before we begin practice."

Feeling a bit tense, Debbie said "What's going on?"

Lynette Elmer shook her head slowly from side to side. "I feel I should warn you. I'm hearing a lot of chit-chat about that awful photo of Mr. Pernell."

Mia blurted out. "So?"

"Well, I'm afraid you might find some uncomfortable conversation inside the church. I wouldn't blame you for skipping practice this week, just until things settle down a bit."

Mia's voice was tense. "Lynette, I appreciate you trying to protect my feelings, but I'm a big girl. I'm not afraid of the choir. C'mon Debbie." Mia marched by Mrs. Elmer and into the church.

Arriving in the basement, Mia saw a few of her fellow choir members clustered around Father Keenan, engaged in an animated conversation, which ceased as Mia approached the group.

"Good evening Mrs. Pernell," said Father Keenan. The group around the priest quickly dispersed. "So nice to see you and Miss Slater."

"Evening Father. Everything okay here?"

"Yes, of course. We were just reviewing the rehearsal list for tonight. We're gonna have a terrific service on Sunday."

Debbie almost broke out laughing. She found it amusing when Father Keenan tried to disguise the truth.

Mia raised her voice. "If anyone has any opinions they want to share about that awful photo of my husband, I'd love to hear them now!"

The awkward silence was broken by Mrs. Elmer playing a gentle melody on the piano. The ensuing rehearsal was charged with tension. The silence between songs was deafening. Father Keenan spent the entire time sitting uncomfortably in his chair, trying desperately not to make eye contact with Mia.

Exiting the church, Debbie put her arm around Mia. "To hell with those gossiping bitches. They got nothing better to do than to amuse themselves with someone else's troubles. I'm not interested in stopping at DacMinton's tonight"

Mia stopped walking and looked into Debbie's eyes. "I get that Debbie. What scares me is that I don't know any more about what the hell happened to Ray than they do. Some of their crazy bullshit might be right."

30 minutes later, Mia was in bed, chardonnay on her nightstand, entering her thoughts into her laptop journal. It had become a nightly one-way conversation with Ray.

"Honey, people are saying awful things about you. Phoebe is getting a ton of grief at school. The choir nearly froze me out tonight. Only our family and our closest friends are being supportive. I wish I could understand what happened to you."

Mia gently closed her laptop, chugged her remaining wine, and laid her exhausted head back upon her pillow, eyes wide open.

Chapter 28

Frank Dorrington began his morning ritual. Powering up his coffee machine, police scanner, television, and radio, Frank tossed a bagel in the toaster oven and reached for his laptop.

The radio conversation, on the Dave & David show, immediately grabbed his attention. The hosts were discussing Ray's photo, but carefully referring to the person in the photo as the "alleged Tucker Executive".

Frank listened carefully.

Dave was in mid-sentence. "….because we don't know exactly what happened to this guy, or why. But he might have had some specific agenda in mind that night. Probably something that most of us might find a bit out of the ordinary."

"I'll say what everybody out there already knows" chimed in David. "The San Francisco police have confirmed that Hudson native, Ray Pernell, who was a TEM executive, was the victim of a homicide during a recent trip to the Bay Area. Then this picture pops up on the internet describing a Tucker Executive Freak as being the victim of a hate crime in San Francisco. It doesn't take a genius to put the two together."

Dave did his legal due diligence as he interrupted David. "Of course David, that is only speculation. There has been no official confirmation that the internet photo is actually Mr. Pernell."

"Of course" answered David. "However, it appears that the dude was looking for companionship, or maybe drugs. What else can you find on the streets of San Francisco at that hour? And he was dressed for action, or should I say undressed?"

Dave interrupted. "We don't know how or why he was dressed that way."

"Sure," said David. "But this is not a good look for an executive of a company like TEM. They must be going crazy in the boardroom. Their reputation will take a huge hit with this."

"No doubt," said Dave. "Let's give our listeners a chance to weigh in. We're opening our phone lines. Give us a call on the Dave & David hotline, or you can send your questions to the Dave & David website. We'll be right back."

As the commercial break rolled, Frank grabbed his phone and dialed the number.

The screening Producer greeted Frank. She asked the usual question: "What do you wish to discuss with Dave & David?"

"I want to talk about the Tucker executive."

"What's your name?"

"My name is Frank. The victim was a friend of mine and I think he is being misrepresented by your hosts."

The Producer replied, "A friend, really? Hold for Dave & David. You'll be next in line."

Coming back from commercial, David said "Welcome back to Dave and David. We have Frank on the line. He claims to have personal knowledge of this incident. Hello Frank. Please tell us what you know"

"Hello. I don't have any knowledge of the incident, but I do know the victim. He was a dear friend of mine."

Dave jumped in. "Would your friend's name be Ray Pernell? Can you confirm for us that he is the unfortunate victim seen in that photo?"

"I can neither confirm nor deny that," said Frank, gently leading the two hosts down his intended path.

"Fair enough. We'll play that game for now. Tell us something about 'your friend', Frank."

"Well, he has a beautiful family and was active in his church. Something very awful happened to him in San Francisco, but we shouldn't be assuming anything about his behavior. Yes, he may have had a few quirks, but he was not the weirdo that he is being made out to be online and in the media."

David went right for the bait. "Tell me, Frank, what did you mean by 'a few quirks'? Would those quirks explain why he was on the streets of San Francisco that night wearing only what amounted to a loincloth?

Frank was working hard, trying to elicit his intended responses from these two. "I'm not at liberty to discuss his personality traits. And I have no personal knowledge of him ever choosing to dress like that."

That comment left the door cracked open a bit and Dave stepped through. "Well Frank, while you aren't confirming any personal knowledge of your friend's behavioral quirks, you aren't denying them either.

Pleased to hear those words, Frank answered in a serious tone. "Maybe you should think about this event as a hate crime. My friend could've been murdered because of the color of his skin, or maybe some sort of social profiling."

David jumped in."Or because he was wandering around, dressed in a freaking loincloth, in a neighborhood known for its sexual opportunities, drugs, and violence. Why was he there, Frank? What do you know about him that would help us make sense of all of this?"

"That's not right," said Frank sternly. "I thought you guys would want to understand what a good dude my friend was, not try to destroy his reputation."

Dave took the good cop route. "Fair enough, Frank. If this is a hate crime, it needs to be identified as a hate crime. Then maybe we can make some progress on battling those types of crimes."

"Wouldn't that be great" stated Frank. "I've said enough. Gotta go. Please assume nothing about my pal."

David shouted, "Wait, Frank!"

Hanging up the phone, Frank congratulated himself as he reached for his now cold bagel. "Always leave them wanting more!"

―――――――

"Damn, this stuff is so long-winded….." Mia was muttering to herself as she was finally taking the time to go through the paperwork from Tucker regarding Ray's benefits. The entire document was wrapped in legalese intended to limit Tucker's potential legal exposure.

Mia learned that her benefits from Tucker would include Ray's life insurance, unused vacation time, and accrued pension. Money was not going to be a problem.

Mia heard the familiar squeal of the school bus brakes out front. She headed out the door to greet Phoebe and Karl. The neighbors were also out there to meet their children, but Mia's neighborly 'hellos' were met with only cool nods of recognition.

Karl exited the bus and ran to his Mom, hugging her around the waist.

"Phoebe's crazy!" exclaimed Karl.

"What are you talking about?"

Karl didn't have a chance to answer before Phoebe stormed off the bus, rushed by her mother yelling "I hate my life and everyone in it!", and stalked angrily into the house.

"Uh oh," said Mia, while feeling the eyes of her neighbors upon her. "C'mon Karl."

Sending Karl into the kitchen to grab a snack, Mia entered Phoebe's room and closed the door behind her.

"Ok, what's up?"

An agitated Phoebe was pacing back and forth across her room. Her face was covered with tears. "Why the hell did I have to get parents like you? My life is ruined! I might as well die today!"

"What the hell are you talking about? Can you please slow down and tell me what happened? Is this about your Dad?"

"Damn it, Mom! Everything is about Dad! Why didn't you tell me he was a freak….with quirks! Was he a drug addict? Was he gay? Was Dad some kind of sexual predator?"

"Shut your mouth!"

"Why? Why should I ever listen to you again? You and Dad have lied to me all my life."

Mia tried to take it down a few decibels. "Listen, honey, I don't know where you got these crazy ideas, but you shouldn't believe everything that is on social media."

"Social Media? You gotta be shitting me! How about everyone in the world knows that my Dad was some sort of freak…..good God, it even said so on his chest!"

Mia swallowed her anger and tried again in a lower voice. "Please slow down and tell me what happened."

"What happened? The whole world knows that Dad was into something kinky that night. That's why he was killed. It's all over the internet."

"What are you talking about?"

"Everyone at school knows, and they are saying terrible things about Dad and our family." Phoebe was flailing her arms and yelling. "Except for Amy, almost no one even will talk to me, and I think she's only being nice because she feels sorry for me."

Tossing a crumpled piece of paper at her Mom, Phoebe continued yelling through her tears. "Here! This is the kind of shit I'm getting at school! And I don't blame them!"

Mia unfolded the wrinkled paper. Her heart sank as she read it. "Phoebe, what shoes will you be wearing with your loincloth to the prom?"

"That's just cruel jealousy from some kid who has no life."

"Just leave me alone!"

Mia's anger boiled over. "You listen to me, young lady! Your Dad was not a freak. There are no secrets that we kept from you. The bullshit you are hearing about your Dad is all lies. Did it ever occur to you that whoever killed your Dad forced him into that awful outfit?"

"All bullshit?" snapped Phoebe. "Maybe you should check with Dad's friend who went on the radio and said that Dad had quirks! Everyone in school has heard it by now."

"Who? What the hell are you talking about? What friend? Who would tell lies like that about your Dad?"

"I don't remember his name. Don't you think that if Dad's friends know about his weird stuff, his own family should know too? Why did you guys do this to me? My life is over."

Mia tried to tone things down. "Listen, honey, things are never as bad as they seem. Your life is not over. There has to be an explanation for all of this."

Phoebe was sobbing, face down on her bed. "This will never get better. I cannot go back to school. My life is over."

"Stop saying that!" yelled Mia. "Your life is not over. Your Dad would hate to hear you say that."

"Who cares? You guys have been lying to me my whole life."

Mia started to cry. "That's not true! I promise you, honey, that things will get better. Please give it some time."

"Whatever," said Phoebe dismissively, as she pulled her pillows over her head.

Chapter 29

Peering across the breakfast table from behind her newspaper, Liz Harland saw that her husband was deep in thought. "You ok Sugar?"

"Huh? Oh yeah. Sorry. Just getting geared up for the day. Got a lot on my mind."

"Anything I can do to help?"

DJ stared into his coffee cup. "No thanks, Baby. Just police business, you know how I'm not down with talking about work. Gotta keep things straight." *Except this case is fully scrambled.*

"I hear you. They are trying to get every last bit of work out of me at the firm. You'd think I was taking my pregnancy leave starting tomorrow."

DJ nodded, but his eyes were far away.

Liz asked "How about some more oatmeal? Gotta keep you strong so we make a healthy baby."

"Damn, girl," said DJ, snapping back to reality. "I love it when we are making a baby. I hope it takes a long time so we can enjoy the process for a while!" *Repeatedly!*

As they both laughed, DJ's phone vibrated on the table. He saw 'Marty Penderson' displayed on his phone. DJ knew Marty well. A journalism major in college who never quite made it in that field, Marty eventually became a police officer. He had found his niche with the SFPD Public Relations group a few years back and had become an outstanding representative for the department.

"Gotta take this, Baby. PR Department. Hey Marty. What's up?"

"Hi, Detective. Just wanted to check with you on the Pernell case. That photo has gone viral and the inquiries are off the hook. What's the department's official stance on the photo?

"You might want to run this by Captain Kekoa, but we have not officially confirmed the ID of the person in the rogue photo."

"Do you think it is Ray Pernell?"

"I know for a fact it is." *Don't you recognize my jeans in the background?* "And we've interviewed the photographer."

"Oh wow," said Marty. "Can I release that info to the press?"

"That's above my pay grade. There's always plausible doubt about photographs." *Except this one.* "And I don't want the media trying to track down the photographer. Off the record: he's just a kid looking to make a splash with his photos, but he has no knowledge of this crime."

"OK, thanks DJ," said Penderson. "It doesn't matter, the entire internet is already identifying that photo as Mr. Pernell, and they'll keep doing it without our confirmation. They're calling it the loincloth murder".

"Of course. They never miss a chance to sensationalize a big story. Anything else I can do for you, Marty?"

"No. I'll talk to the Captain. Tucker is all over us for details, but they want everything kept out of the limelight. Apparently, Commissioner Francis agrees with them."

"Heard that," said DJ "Tucker's gotta protect that sparkling image". *Truth be damned!*

"Roger that. Thanks, DJ."

DJ saw Liz grab her car keys and purse. "Gotta go. So much work to do. I don't know how they will ever survive without me. Love you. Bye."

"Love you too Baby," said DJ to Liz's back as she headed out the door. *Thanks for leaving me the dishes!*

Soon DJ's hands were busy rinsing out bowls, but his mind was far away, trying to put together the pieces of the loincloth puzzle.

Chapter 30

Following yesterday's appearance on Dave & David's radio show, Frank Dorrington was quickly booked to guest on today's 7 pm TV broadcast of "Nutmeg State Newsmakers".

Frank was ushered into the studio and seated on the familiar talk show set. He could see four cameras, a few crew members, numerous cables, and dozens of unpowered lights hanging from the lighting grid high above.

"Mr. Dorrington?" Frank looked into the face of an attractive young lady.

"Yes. I'm Frank."

"Hi," said the young lady. "I'm Doreen. May I put some makeup on you? These HD cameras show every detail, and sometimes we need a little makeup to soften our image."

"Of course. Have at it."

Doreen turned and yelled, "Can we get the lights please?"

A voice from across the studio yelled. "Lights coming. Watch your eyes!" The entire light grid suddenly bloomed with bright lights, causing Frank to raise his hands to shade his eyes.

"First time in a TV studio?" asked Doreen, as she applied some pancake makeup.

"Yes," said Frank. "Damn, the lights are bright."

"You'll get used to it," said a male voice from just over Doreen's shoulder. "Try not to look directly at them. I'm Bill, the Stage Manager. Mr. Woodley should be here in a second. If you need anything, just let me know."

"Thanks, Bill," said Frank. "Maybe a bottle of water."

"No prob. Here comes Mr. Woodley now."

Woodley, a tall, broad-shouldered black man, with a full head of silver hair, and a signature baritone voice, had been a local TV icon for decades.

"Mr. Dorrington!" boomed Woodley. "What a pleasure to have you join us today. We're looking forward to any light you can shed on the unfortunate case of your friend."

"Pleasure to meet you, Mr. Woodley."

Bill handed Frank a bottle of water which he opened, taking a quick sip to quench his dry mouth.

"30 seconds" yelled Bill.

"All set Frank?" asked Woodley. "Just relax and let everyone know what a great guy Ray was".

Frank tried to gather his thoughts, but music was already playing and Bill was counting backward from ten.

"Good evening Connecticut. Welcome to Nutmeg State Newsmakers. I'm Calvin Woodley. My first guest today is Frank Dorrington, a local attorney and close friend of Ray Pernell, the Tucker executive from Hudson who, unfortunately, lost his life during a recent business trip to San Francisco."

"Welcome Mr. Dorrington."

"Thanks for having me."

"So sorry for your loss, Frank. I understand that you and Mr. Pernell were close friends."

"Yes, we were" lied Frank.

"Tell us something about him."

"Ray was a good man, very active in his church and community, and a valuable asset to Tucker. Ray was also a great husband and father. My heart goes out to his wife Mia, and their three beautiful children." Frank wanted to name the kids but wasn't sure he'd even get two out of three names correct.

"He sounds like a great guy Frank. I gotta ask you. Are you legally representing the Pernell family relating to this case?"

"No. If Mrs. Pernell requested my legal services, I would've declined. I'm too emotionally close to this situation to provide Mrs. Pernell with the dispassionate legal advice she requires."

"Good to know. Frank, we've all seen the photo that is alleged to be of Mr. Pernell on the night he was killed. It has gone viral. But we find it disturbing and we won't air it on this show."

"I appreciate that".

Woodley leaned in a bit. "Frank, you knew Mr. Pernell very well. Do you have any idea what he was doing so late at night, on the streets of San Francisco, dressed like he was?"

Frank was surprised with the directness of the question, but pleased with the direction of the conversation.

"That's the million-dollar question, Calvin. The short answer is 'No, I don't'. Ray was a smart guy. We've shared a few beers after work and on the golf course. I always enjoyed our conversations."

Woodley dug a little deeper. "You said yesterday on the radio that Mr. Pernell had some quirks. Could you describe any of those quirks, Frank?"

Frank ran his hand through his thinning hair. "What I meant Calvin, is that Ray's sense of humor sometimes tended toward the outrageous. Nothing too weird. But some folks might consider that quirky behavior."

Woodley locked eyes with Frank. "Would Mr. Pernell's quirks include dressing in bizarre outfits and roaming the streets at night?"

Frank carefully considered his answer. "I've certainly never seen him dress like that before. And we should remember, Calvin, that we don't know that Ray was roaming any streets. His killers may well have dictated his clothing and his ultimate location."

As Frank had expected, Woodley reshaped the question. "What specific behavior do you know about, Frank? What might Mr. Pernell have been seeking, alone, in the middle of the night, dressed only in rags? There's nothing on the streets at that time, except trouble."

Frank had rehearsed his next line. "I'm sorry Calvin, I cannot betray the trust of my friend. No one deserves to have their innermost secrets broadcast to the public."

"So you know what he might have been looking for?"

Frank summoned up all his phony conviction. "Perhaps, Calvin. But it's not my right to share anything that my friend had told me in confidence. I cannot go there."

"Spoken like the attorney you are. But don't you think it's important for our viewers to have the opportunity to learn from Mr. Pernell's misfortune? Maybe a little good could come from this awful tragedy."

Frank then steered the conversation in his desired direction, "Well, there's speculation that this could have been a hate crime. Those types of crimes are growing exponentially in this country."

"What type of hate crime, Frank?"

"As you know, Calvin, hate crimes are usually violent and always motivated by some type of prejudice. Ray could have been killed for the color of his skin or the way he was dressed. There is no lack of racist violence or gay-bashing these days."

Woodley followed Frank's lead. "Are you saying that Ray was killed for being gay?"

"Absolutely not!" said Frank, with just the right amount of planned indignation. "I'm suggesting that he might've been killed simply for being white, or in the wrong neighborhood, or for the way he was dressed. Perhaps some hateful gay-basher thought that he was gay because of the loincloth."

"That doesn't answer the question of why he was dressed like that, but I recognize that hate crimes are becoming all too prevalent these days."

"You're right Calvin. That's why I will soon bring a proposal to the Connecticut Legislature designed to set tougher mandatory penalties for hate crimes. I want to call it Ray's Rules, in honor of my dear friend."

"That's terrific Frank," said Woodley. "Good luck with that and we'll be sure to follow any proposed legislation. Do you know if Mr. Pernell was using any prescription drugs? It's been reported that he was out celebrating with friends that night. Maybe the combination of alcohol and a prescription drug might've contributed to his behavior."

Frank was relieved to see the "30 seconds" cue card from Bill.

"I don't know about that. As I've said before, Ray and I enjoyed a few beers together from time to time. But, as far as I know, prescription drugs were not part of the equation."

"Understood, Frank. I've got 15 seconds left. Is there anything else you can add to help us understand what happened to one of Connecticut's finest citizens?"

"Well" offered Frank in his humblest tone, "I would just ask your viewers not to jump to any conclusions about Ray Pernell's lifestyle, no matter what they may hear or see in the media."

"Fair enough," said Woodley. "My thanks to Frank Dorrington for joining us today. We'll be right back with this week's winner of our Top Teacher award, chosen from your viewer nominations. Stay with us."

"Back in two minutes!" yelled Bill.

"Thanks, Frank. Appreciate your time."

"Nice to meet you, Calvin," said Frank, as his mic was being removed. He was hustled off the set and escorted into the station lobby.

In her Hudson apartment, Debbie Slater was yelling at the TV. "Goddam it Frank! What the hell are you doing? You hardly knew Ray Pernell....and he was not a fan of yours!"

———

Mia was propped up in bed, laptop in hand, chardonnay on the nightstand, typing her nightly note to Ray in her journal.

"Phoebe's getting harassed at school and on her stupid social media. Everyone is guessing about how and why you wound up dressed like that. They don't seem to care about why someone saw fit to take you away from us......"

Mia's phone buzzed with a FaceTime call.

"Hi Debbie," said Mia, seeing what looked like rage on Debbie's face. "Something on your mind?"

"I take it you didn't see Frank's appearance on TV this evening."

"Frank who?"

Debbie's voice was strained. "Frank fucking Dorrington, that's who! I can't believe I was ever attracted to that pile of shit!"

"Your Frank? What was he doing on TV?"

"That jerk was talking about his close relationship with Ray. And how they shared secrets. And how Ray had quirks."

"Quirks! That's the word Phoebe used. It must've been Frank who said that crap about Ray on the radio. Why would he do that?"

"Because he's an asshole!"

Mia's rage quickly matched Debbie's. "What quirks is he talking about? What secrets? He and Ray only met a few times. Ray didn't much care for him."

"I know that. I always thought Frank was jealous of Ray's success. But Frank's making it sound like they had a close relationship and Ray shared some personal secrets with him."

Doubt briefly crept into Mia's mind as she considered that possibility, but she brushed it off. "Impossible. What's Frank trying to prove?"

"He's always got an angle," said Debbie. "He said that Ray's murder could've been a hate crime."

"Hate crime? Hated for what?" Mia took a full swallow from her wine glass.

"For being white, or for being dressed like that, or maybe a wrongful victim of gay-bashing."

Mia started to cry. "Frank's saying Ray was gay? Sweet Jesus, when will this nightmare end?"

Debbie tried to tone it down. "He's not saying those exact words. In fact, he's not saying anything about Ray, exactly. But a lot of possibilities were raised and none were ruled out."

"I will sue him for this bullshit!"

"Doubt that you can. Frank may be a horseshit lawyer, but he understands the law. He didn't make any specific claims about Ray. Just a lot of innuendo and speculation."

"I wanna hear everything he said about Ray," said Mia.

"It's on the 'Nutmeg State Newsmakers" website. Easy enough to find."

"Geez Debbie. Why would Frank need to stick his nose into this? They sure never seemed to hit it off. They only played golf once, that I know of."

"It's all bullshit," said Debbie. "When you watch that video, you'll hear Frank saying something about proposing some new hate crime legislation, in honor of Ray. No way that's true."

"But we don't know that he was the victim of a hate crime!" shouted Mia.

"Truth has never been Frank's strong suit."

"That's for sure. I gotta watch this now. I'm sure everyone's gonna see it! Damn you Frank!"

Debbie shouted. "Yes. Goddam you Frank!" Then lowered her volume. "Mia, you know I'm here whenever you need me. Call me back after you watch the video or just call me tomorrow morning. Love you."

"OK. Thanks, love you, bye."

Mia navigated directly to the website and watched the interview twice, her anger rising. After watching it a third time, she nearly threw her laptop across the room.

Mia blurted out "You're an asshole Frank. Why are you doing this?"

After gulping down the remaining half-glass of wine, Mia returned to writing her journal entry for the night. "Ray, I wish you could tell me what the hell happened. I will always defend you and our family, but I'm feeling completely lost."

Chapter 31

DJ sat up in bed, his clock showing 1:03 am. His mind was buzzing with the Pernell case. He rose, dressed, and left a note for Liz on the fridge.

Driving to the Smythville Hotel, DJ was hoping that he might find something significant. *If I can trace his steps at the same late hour that he walked them, maybe I'll better understand what the hell happened to him.*

After parking his car on Lund Ave, DJ entered the alley and headed toward the familiar back door of the Smythville. Smelling smoke, he crept down the alley until coming upon the space between dumpsters where a fire was smoldering in the same sawed-off trash can he had seen on his previous visit. Sleeping next to the fire was a man dressed in filthy clothes.

DJ was startled when a voice came from the shadows, between the dumpsters. "Whadda ya want, mister? We ain't got no money."

"Easy my friend," said DJ. "I'm a cop." *With an itchy trigger finger!*

"Bullshit," said the voice. "I'm the fucking Queen of England."

DJ retrieved his badge from his jacket pocket. "Not screwing with you pal. You need to come out here, and have your hands where I can see them."

A stooped-over man shuffled out from the shadows. He was dressed in a filthy green sweatsuit and a dark blue knit hat, with bloodshot eyes and a wild beard that seemed to crawl up his face to join his eyebrows. The nauseating stench around him assaulted DJ's nostrils. "What the hell could you possibly want?"

Before DJ could answer, the fellow snoozing by the fire rolled over onto one elbow, a tattered San Francisco Giants baseball cap hiding most of his face. His words were slurred. "A cop? Please take me to jail. Could use a decent meal."

"It ain't about that," said DJ. "You got names?"

"I'm Ernie," said the standing man, who then gestured at his buddy lying next to the fire. "And this human liver-spot here is Doc."

"OK, Ernie. You guys here every night?"

"Only when we can't get into the Four Seasons" mumbled Doc.

DJ stared at Doc. "You can see I'm not dying of laughter here." *But that was a pretty good one!*

Ernie spoke. "Every night, no. But this place is good. We don't usually get bothered by the cops, until now."

Everyone's a comedian! "Do you recall seeing a white man come through this alley, late at night wearing only some rags, like a loincloth, maybe drunk or confused."

Still lying on the ground, Doc burst into laughter. "Loincloth! That's a good one. This is San Francisco man, we're all drunk and confused!"

No argument there! DJ unfolded the now infamous photo of Ray's body and showed it to both men. "This is the guy I'm talking about. He may have come down this alley, late at night, a couple of weeks ago. Then turned up dead."

"Whoa!" said Ernie. "We don't know nothing about no dead guys. We just keep to ourselves."

"He must've been cold" slurred Doc.

"That all you got?" said DJ. *Another damn dead end.*

"Got nothin' else. We see all kinds of shit. I don't remember seeing that guy, but we ain't here every night. Lots of guys flop here. Talk to them."

"I intend to," said DJ. "Thanks, fellas. Stay warm."

"See ya cop," said Ernie. Doc was already snoring his goodbye.

DJ walked away, frustrated at his lack of progress, but feeling a pang of sympathy for Ernie and Doc. *Man, that's gotta be a tough life.*

Chapter 32

Mia was sharing tea with her parents. "It seems like the collection of media vultures outside is growing every day," said Hiroshi.

"I know, Dad," said Mia. "They are driving us crazy, and the neighbors are complaining too. I've asked Ken Samantis, our attorney, if there is anything we can do about it. He said the streets and sidewalks are public property. And he wants us to ignore all questions."

Hiroshi chuckled. "Easy for me. I just look at them quizzically and speak in Japanese. They don't know what the heck to do with that."

"Good one, Dad!" said Mia. "But be careful what you say. No doubt you are being recorded and your words might get translated."

"Well, then, they will soon find out that I think they are America's equivalent of bottom-feeding sea urchins!"

Mia laughed. It occurred to her that she hadn't laughed in a long time.

Turning to her mother, Mia asked "Mom, have you seen Grammy Pernell this week? Does she fully understand that Ray is gone?"

"Julie is doing great, physically," said Myoko. "She might outlive us all. But her Alzheimer's is really bad. I'm not sure that she understands Ray's passing. Most of the time, she doesn't recognize any of us."

"That's probably for the best. I love that you get to see her a couple of times a week."

"I love working there," said Myoko. "Some of those people never have any visitors. They need someone to talk to."

"You're an angel Mom."

Mia's Dad spoke. "Look honey, it's you and the kids that we are concerned about. We want to help in any way we can."

"You've been great, Dad. I don't know how I could have made it this far without you guys and Debbie."

"So how are the kids doing honey?" asked Myoko. "Is Phoebe still struggling?"

"Yes. High school kids can be so awful. It's such a difficult age."

"Very true," said Hiroshi, who'd spent the last nineteen years working as a Japanese / English two-way teacher at the International High School in New York City. "Kids that age are mostly only interested in being as selfish as possible. It's the ones who decide to give of themselves who become special."

"Yes Dad," said Mia, fighting back the urge to remind her Dad that he'd said that line to her a couple thousand times throughout her life. "The boys seem relatively okay, but Phoebe is overreacting to social media.".

"Worst thing ever invented," said Hiroshi.

Mia's phone buzzed on the table. She didn't recognize the number, but she'd been expecting a call back from Vera Eden, the police grief counselor.

"Excuse me. Gotta grab this."

"Hello?"

"Is this Mia Pernell?"

"Speaking" answered Mia. "Who's calling please?"

"Hello, Mrs. Pernell. This is Richard Weller, VP from Tucker Human Resources."

"Oh yes Richard, hi." Mia had met Weller at a few TEM social functions. He was a short, humorless, round man with a military-style crew cut and an ever-present pair of reading glasses perched on the end of his stubby nose. Mia remembered Ray telling her that Richard Weller had never once cracked a smile in his entire life.

"How can I help you? Did I mess up on those forms for Ray's benefits?"

"No, Mrs. Pernell. You did a wonderful job. Everything was properly filled out. I very much appreciate when our employees and their families are so efficient with paperwork of this nature. It doesn't happen very often."

"Thanks."

"But there is one detail that is holding up the processing of any of these benefits."

"What's the problem?"

"Every employee signs a morals clause when they are initially employed by Tucker. This clause allows the company to take punitive action against any employee that engages in reprehensible behavior or conduct that may negatively impact the company."

Mia's anger immediately rose. "Which part of being murdered, while traveling on behalf of the company, violates that clause, Mr. Weller?"

"I understand your surprise, Mrs. Pernell."

Mia momentarily lost her cool. "Oh, I'm not surprised Richard. May I call you Dick? I'm upset! Tucker not only owes us a ton of money, but I want my husband back. Can you please do that for me? He died working for you."

The unflappable Richard Weller stuck to his script. "This temporary hold on the distribution of benefits is pending the conclusion of the San Francisco PD investigation. Tucker Entertainment Media will then make a determination as to whether or not Mr. Pernell has violated the terms of our morals clause and thus voided all benefits due upon his departure from the company. Do you understand this, Mrs. Pernell?"

"Departure from the company?" mocked Mia. "That's rich! What I understand is that Tucker is trying to withhold benefits from my husband, who has done absolutely nothing wrong, except DIE while in the service of Tucker."

"Once we get the results from the investigation…"

"You're not from HR Mr. Weller, you're from the 'cover your ass' department. How dare you try to avoid paying my husband's benefits. It's the very least TEM can do! I will expect full payment of all monies owed to Ray's estate after the police investigation. And so will my attorney!"

Mia disconnected the call before Weller could respond.

"Damn!" she screamed to no one in particular. "I cannot believe the gall of those chicken-shit corporate assholes!"

Mia quickly regained her senses and opened her eyes to see her parents sitting across from her, eyes frightened and mouths hanging open. Her Mom was crying.

Chapter 33

Frank Dorrington surveyed the orchestrated chaos of Grand Central Station. This cavernous, bustling place always thrilled him.

During the train ride from New Haven, Frank reviewed the media inquiries he'd received in the last 24 hours. His conversation with Calvin Woodley was all over the internet. It was amazing how popular he'd become, just because he claimed to know the innermost secrets of Ray Pernell. He'd been contacted by newspapers, cable news networks, tabloids, talk shows, fringe websites, and a couple of influential bloggers.

It was the inquiry from the nationally syndicated Hammy Bogdon show that caught his eye. Frank had been a Hammy fan for a few years. He loved watching the wiry, slicked-haired dude in the tattered sports coat dart around the stage as he fired up his studio audience. Bogdon was always passionately defending those who were the victims of some perceived mistreatment or abuse. Plus, they were the first media outlet that accepted Frank's request to be paid his fee of three thousand dollars, in cash, at the time of the interview.

"Oh honey, let's get some foundation on your face and some product in your hair," said the makeup woman. "I'm Kathleen".

"Thanks, Kathleen," said Frank. "Long train ride from Connecticut."

"No worries. I've made up everyone from A to Z and some non-humans as well."

As Frank contemplated Kathleen's comment, a short, casually-dressed woman with brilliant green hair, rushed into the make-up room.

"Hi, Frank! I'm Jungle Jane, Hammy's Producer. Thanks so much for joining us."

"Pleasure to meet you," said Frank. Hammy often interacted with Jungle Jane on his show.

Jungle Jane was all business. "You understand that we tape delay this show for forty-eight hours to allow us time to promote it nationally…..correct?"

"I didn't know that. Smart."

"And it is you we hope to promote. We've put you in the 'Hammy Rant' segment, which is the biggest segment of our show."

"That's my favorite part of the show! I love the Hammy Rant."

"Good to hear," said Jungle Jane, "Then you'll be pleased to know today's subject is the increase of hate crimes in America. Hammy is tying that to the Ray Pernell murder. Then he will introduce you and you'll walk out onto the set."

"Great. Looking forward to it."

"Warning, the lights will seem very bright. You'll already be wearing a wireless mic. Just sit in the blue chair to your left. And don't look for the cameras, they'll find you. Other than that, it's up to you guys to make TV magic. Got all that?"

"Got it," said Frank "Blue chair. Ignore the cameras."

"OK great. Break a leg and we'll catch you on the flip side."

Frank wasn't exactly dialed into Jane's lingo, but he answered with "roger, flip side."

Standing next to a monitor behind the set, Frank was watching and listening to Hammy Bogdon who was whipping the studio audience into a frenzy with his rant. It sounded like a stadium full of rabid fans out there who were now chanting "Hammy B! Hammy B!" Frank always enjoyed watching all that crazy energy on TV.

The Stage Manager tugged on his sleeve, "Let's go, Mr. Dorrington, you're on!" Frank walked around the end of the scenery and out into the bright lights of the studio.

Temporarily blinded, he stopped for a second to get his bearings. He was shocked by the modest size of the studio. The small set, with two chairs, seemed to occupy half of the floor space. The other half was lined with some low bleachers that were packed with maybe 40 to 50 people, who were hooting and applauding. Frank couldn't believe that this was where Hammy B did his wild show every day. It always seemed like a full arena on TV.

"Welcome Frank' said Hammy as Frank found the blue chair. "That's terrible, what happened to your friend."

"Thanks for having me. Yes, Ray Pernell was a good man. A family man. A good..."

Hammy interrupted. "Do you know why anyone would want to kill such a well-loved man? A high-profile executive at Tucker, no less! Hate crimes are a bitch!"

"The police have not yet designated this as a hate crime," said Frank, doing his best to play the prudent attorney. "But I am planning on advancing hate crime legislation in the...."

Hammy jumped up and put one foot on the seat of his chair. "Let me ask you something, Frank. Do you think this was a hate crime?"

"It certainly has the earmarks of a hate crime. No one had a valid reason to kill Ray other than some misguided prejudice."

Hammy started to respond while walking toward the audience with his arms spread wide. Turning suddenly toward Frank, he said. "So Frank, you're telling me that Mr. Pernell was killed because he was white?"

"That's a possibility" Frank then lit the fuse he had come to ignite. "But prejudice can also be about religion, sexual orientation, or pretty much anything else."

With some help from the Stage Manager, the audience started chanting "End Hate, End Hate, End Hate!"

Hammy waved at the audience and they stopped chanting. He sat on the arm of his chair. "Well Frank, what religion was Mr Pernell?"

"Catholic" answered Frank.

Suddenly contemplative, Hammy asked, "Would you say he was killed because he was Catholic?"

"There's no indication of that."

Hammy paused dramatically. "So it's not religion, and if it's not race, what's left, Frank? Was there anything else about your friend that might've motivated someone to want to kill him?"

"Not sure what you mean" answered Frank innocently.

"No need to be coy, Frank. Take a look at the monitor. We've all seen this awful picture. Did your friend normally dress in a loincloth to go out for a couple beers with his pals? Or was he nearly naked to seek some other type of attention?"

"I can't explain how he was dressed. His killers may have dressed him like that."

Hammy stood again, facing the audience. "So what do you think he was looking for on the streets of San Francisco, at three in the morning, dressed in only a shredded loincloth? Companionship? Drugs? What Frank?"

As Frank started to answer, Hammy jumped in.

"We're all aware of gay-bashing Frank. It is a hideous, heinous crime. But we can't be trying to hide what Mr. Pernell was doing if we're ever going to make any progress on dealing with these awful attacks and murders."

Frank's answer was obliterated by the audience chanting "End Hate, End Hate!".

After ten seconds of basking in the frothing frenzy that he had created, Hammy again brought his adoring audience to silence with a wave of his arm.

Frank spoke. "Ray never shared anything like that with me."

Hammy kept drilling. "Tell me Frank, what DID he share with you? You must've known something about his freaky side. No one just dresses up like that and hits the streets in the middle of the night without having given it some thought."

"Again, we don't know for sure that Ray chose to dress like that," said Frank, playing the prudent attorney. Then he expanded his self-serving narrative. "But to answer your question, I can only say that Ray was not without issues. But if he had any inclination for that kind of behavior, he didn't share it with me. He may have shared it with his family, or perhaps a counselor."

Frank knew that Hammy couldn't let that little nugget slide by. "So Mr. Pernell was seeing a counselor? Can you tell us what his issue was? Did it have anything, perhaps, to do with a conflicted sexual identity or maybe a substance abuse problem?"

"I can neither confirm nor deny that Ray was seeing a counselor. However, I can say that seeking the input of a company-provided counselor is not uncommon among corporate executives these days. There's a lot of pressure at that level."

"I'm sure there is" responded Hammy, "especially in a corporate environment like Tucker." He then leaned in closer to Frank. "Listen, Frank, we want to help you in your battle against hate crimes, but we've first gotta understand why your buddy was killed. Maybe it was because of one of those quirks you've mentioned. Exactly what are those quirks, Frank?"

Before Frank could answer, the studio was filled with chants of "Hate sucks! Hate sucks! Hate sucks!" Looking to his right, Frank could see Jungle Jane holding up a "hate sucks" cue card. The Stage Manager was next to her, flailing his arms, as he conducted the symphony of chants from the bleachers.

Again, a wave of the hand from Hammy quieted the crowd.

Frank tried again. "Well, Ray was a bit of an adrenaline junkie. He liked things like fast cars, zip lines, bungee jumping, and skydiving. As challenging as his job was, creating media content for kids didn't provide that adrenaline rush that he needed."

Hammy started pacing, playing to the bleachers. "Would dressing in a loincloth and walking the streets of San Francisco in the middle of the night have satisfied his need for adrenaline? Or was he looking for something else to give him that rush that he needed? Like a sexual hookup or drugs?"

Frank was hoping that he sounded appropriately defensive of Ray's reputation. "I don't know about any of that. Again, he may not have chosen that clothing."

Hammy whipped off his jacket and tossed it to the floor. Standing directly in front of his audience, he preached his message like a Sunday sermon. "Mr. Dorrington, we all grieve for the loss of your friend. And we endorse your efforts to pass new legislation to battle hate crime. But there's a bigger issue here. An elephant in the room."

The entire studio audience was now standing, hanging on Hammy's every word.

"Is it appropriate for a media giant like Tucker Entertainment Media, a company that prides itself on entertaining and educating our young people, to employ a senior executive who partakes in this kind of behavior?"

The audience yelled "NO!"

"Does Tucker want its young consumers to learn about right and wrong through the eyes of this man who was running nearly naked through the streets of San Francisco at 3 am?"

"NO!"

"I ask you America, do you want this loincloth-wearing man teaching his questionable morals to your children? I say no!"

The audience again repeated "NO!"

Kicking his jacket across the studio floor, Hammy, in full froth, delivered his message. "Good grief people! This man had FREAK written on his chest. He was wearing a damn loincloth for God's sake! What else do you need to know? How did Tucker, with all their money and resources, not know this troubled man was lurking in their midst? Big mistake T-E-M! You really screwed this one up!"

He then suddenly delivered his signature daily sign-off: "I'm Hammy B. Talk later".

The crowd was standing, clapping in unison, as the stage manager led them in chanting: "Tucker Sucks! Tucker Sucks!"

Hammy quickly disappeared, never thanking Frank. Removing Frank's microphone, Jungle Jane hooked his arm and ushered him toward the exit. She placed an envelope in Frank's hands and said "You were great Frank. Good luck."

Frank got in a waiting cab. "Grand Central Station, please".

He closed his eyes, and patted the envelope in his pocket, imagining the tons of cash that he would earn with future media appearances.

Chapter 34

Slumped at his desk, holding his head in his hands, DJ was exhausted after three consecutive nights of walking the back alley behind the Smythville Hotel. While he had met several colorful characters, none of them recalled seeing a man who might have been Ray Pernell. Captain Kekoa wanted an update on the case this morning.

"Hey, Devante."

DJ turned around and saw the broad nose, brown eyes, and shaved head of Levi Sharpe peering over the top of his cubicle partition. Sharpe, the senior Detective in Captain Kekoa's group, had helped DJ navigate some of the unique challenges they'd both experienced as black detectives.

"What's up Levi? When the hell are you gonna retire?"

"Just as soon as every last asshole has been sent to the penitentiary, or I become fully vested in our pension fund."

"So, never?"

"You got that right my man. Gotta look at the upside, though. Working all these long hours has saved my marriage. The less time we spend together, the better we are."

"Heard that."

"So this probably ain't shit, but I've got a low-life in room three who claims that he knows something about the loincloth murder. You interested?"

"Hell yeah. What's his angle?"

"John Gandolf. Street name: 'Johnny G'. Late 20's, three-time offender, meth. He's a street surfer, carries his belongings around in a guitar case. Yesterday, those belongings included a kilo of Mexican crank. He's looking at a long bid, but he wants to trade some information on the loincloth homicide in return for a break on his case."

"What's the DA say?"

Sharpe laughed. "The DA says we got no deal without first verifying whatever crap he's trying to sell us."

"You got some kind of impression?"

Sharpe snorted. "I think this piece of shit would sell his mother for a line of blow. But he is a career snitch, and snitches don't have much of a future behind bars."

"Truth," said DJ. *They tend to die quickly from unnatural causes!*

"He's very motivated to share anything that could help keep him out of prison. Why not hear him out?"

"Let's go. Got nothing to lose."

The two detectives entered interview room three, nodding to the uniformed officer who'd been watching the prisoner.

Sharpe spoke first. "Johnny, this is Detective Harland. He's gonna ask you some questions about the loincloth case. And remember that you're still being recorded."

Johnny G was rocking back and forth in his chair. He nodded nervously toward DJ who carefully looked him over. Johnny was dressed in filthy jeans, tattered laceless sneakers, and a faux leather jacket that appeared to have been shredded by lions. Underneath was a faded t-shirt that may have once had a skull and crossbones on the front. His pale, almost transparent, skin was shiny with perspiration, and his chin featured a few scraggly hairs. His greasy hair had been chopped to form bangs in the front but hung over both ears. The stench around him was so bad that DJ thought he could see a purple funk.

"Geezus!" exclaimed DJ. "I'm supposed to believe anything this fucking picture of health has to say? You shittin' me? Just throw him in jail." *And delouse his ass!*

"Hey, wait a minute," said Johnny. "I know I haven't washed up in a while, but you gotta hear me out."

DJ noted Johnny's rotten teeth, common among meth addicts. "Damn brother, I'm guessing it's been more than a while since you've seen a bar of soap or a toothbrush." *Or a toilet!* "I can't imagine that you'd have anything to say that could matter to me."

"I promise I'll be straight with you," said Johnny. "I can't go to prison."

Detective Sharpe interjected. "Just pick up your story where I stopped you, Johnny."

"I want the DA here so we can make a deal."

"Doesn't work that way, Junior" said Sharpe. "If what you tell us is worth anything, then we'll share it with the DA."

"How long I gotta wait?" asked Johnny, fidgeting with his hair.

"Depends what you got." Levi then pointed at the mirror directly in front of Johnny. "And, you never know who is behind that mirror, Johnny."

DJ almost laughed out loud. He knew the observation room was empty. Levi loved screwing with suspects. DJ said "I have actual police work to do. Enough with the chit-chat. Let's hear what Johnny here has to say, or let's get his greasy ass down to booking." *Let them deal with the stench.*

"Whatever, just don't screw me on this," said Johnny G., seemingly in perpetual motion in his chair.

"So?" said DJ. *This oughtta be good....*

"Ok, Detective. As I was telling Detective Sharpe here, I was, uh, socializing with some friends at someone's home."

"Translation" interrupted Sharpe. "He was shooting up with some strangers at a crank house."

"Shocking," said DJ." Where was this party taking place?"

"Down in Hollis."

"Shocked again."

Johnny continued. "One of these dudes was a scary gang-banger who just did 8 years in Solano. From his tats, I could tell he was hooked with the Aryans. Man, this dude had some kinda jailhouse wrong that needed to be settled out in the world. He was gonna kill a couple dudes in Oakland the very next day. He scared the shit outta me."

"Still listening, but barely," said DJ. "This guy have a name?"

"He called himself 'Capone'."

"And?" said Detective Sharpe.

"Well," said Johnny, "While he was bragging about how he was gonna off two dudes the next day, he also said that he had really enjoyed killing some gay freak who just ran right into his hands."

"How could that happen?"

"I don't know, man. This scary dude was raging and he was bragging about offing a gay guy. I wasn't about to question a damn thing."

"What else?" asked Sharpe.

"Capone talked about how he made this faggot beg for his life. He said the freak was crying about how he 'woke up naked, pissing in a corner'."

DJ nodded. "I'm losing interest, Johnny." *This ain't going anywhere.* "What else you got?"

"Capone laughed when he told us that the last thing that went through this gay dude's mind was his bullet. He was waving his 9-mil while he was talking. I was pretty fucking scared right then."

DJ said "I came here for this? Anyone who's seen that photo could make up some shit like that. It's all over the internet, and so is the kind of bullshit you just spewed. The word 'freak' was written on his body. I'll look into this Capone dude, but you need to tell me something I don't already know or your ass is grass, my friend."

"But that's what I'm talkin' about!" said Johnny. "You don't have to look for him. Capone was shot up the next day."

"Say what?" *You gotta be fucking kidding me!*

"Those Oakland dudes he was out to get were ready for his ass and he was ambushed by some waiting AKs. Never even got out of his car"

"Oh that's precious!" laughed DJ. "That Oakland massacre has been all over the news. We go to the DA to ask them to believe this shit? You just fingered a conveniently dead murderer. Are you enjoying fucking me, Johnny?" *But I give you points for creativity!*

"Hell no!"

"A lying snitch like you should be able to conjure up something more believable. Like maybe an alien came down from the sky and put that meth in your guitar case! Get the hell outta here with that bullshit!"

"It's the truth! Ain't my fault he got himself killed. Check it out for yourself."

DJ stared at Johnny G. "Look asshole, here's what I think I'll find. Maybe this Capone actually existed, and maybe he was the dude that was ambushed in Oakland. Then a smart little pecker like you decides that you can score some points with the DA. You attribute your fake info to a guy who just conveniently turned up dead. And boom! Bulletproof bullshit. No way to verify!"

"No that ain't it," yelled Johnny. "You gotta believe me!"

"You got any corroborating witnesses to that conversation Johnny?" asked DJ. *Meth heads have such great memories!*

"C'mon, you know what we were doing. The other dudes in the room wouldn't remember, and if they did, they wouldn't talk. And, no, I ain't got no idea who they were."

"Of course you don't" mocked DJ. *No guest book at the crank house!*

Throwing a notepad and pen at Johnny, DJ said "Write down everything you just told us and anything else that you may have left out of your colorful story. You do know how to write don't you?"

"Very funny," said Johnny.

"The DA will split a gut laughing at this. Hope you're ready for 10-15 upstate."

"C'mon, man. I gave you all I know. That's how it went down!"

"I'll tell the DA you said that." *While they're rolling on the floor in laughter!*

Johnny started to slowly print out his testimony.

The detectives left the room and motioned the uniform to keep Johnny company.

Once down the hall, Levi put his arm around DJ and said: "I taught you well. That was some great entertainment! That kid was ready to tell you anything just to keep his ass outta jail."

"Whadda ya think?" asked DJ. "Anything he said true?"

"Hell yes. When we look into the Oakland ambush, I'm guessing we'll discover that Capone is the shredded victim."

"Probably, but everyone knows about that slaughter, including young Johnny there."

Sharpe continued. "I'll check it out. If it's Capone, I'll get his real name and we'll pull his jacket."

"Thanks, Levi. That'll be good info. But it doesn't help me unless we choose to believe what this twitchy little bastard had to say. It's just too damn convenient to finger a dead man for a murder."

"For sure." Sharpe continued, "What about that phrase 'woke up naked, pissing in a corner'?"

DJ shook his head. "Sounds like a meth-head's imagination run wild. Doesn't even make sense."

"Probably not."

"And it's not like this Capone guy couldn't have made up the story about killing the 'gay freak'. That photo is everywhere. There's probably a hundred assholes taking credit for that murder."

"That's true" offered Sharpe. "But…"

"Don't say it" interrupted DJ. "That's why we're called Detectives. I know. I know."

"Spoken like my number one student!"

Chapter 35

Frank Dorrington's appearance on the Hammy B. show brought him instant notoriety. The requests for interviews were flowing in. While legitimate news operations at the mainstream networks don't generally pay for "news" interviews, Frank knew that many other "media" outlets often paid for guests to share their "truth". He decided to raise his appearance fee to a minimum of five thousand dollars.

Frank had become very adept at insinuating things about Ray and then allowing the media to extrapolate whatever sensational elements they wanted from his comments. Since his actual relationship with Ray was minimal, Frank had to be vague. He'd developed a statement that he felt was legally safe, but would still serve to fan the flames of public interest: "We all have that one special person in whom we confide our innermost secrets, and those conversations are not meant to be shared."

Sifting through numerous inquiries, Frank was thrilled to see that this story was developing a national profile. It was now commonly known as the "loincloth murder" and most media outlets were also calling it a hate crime. His "TuckerExecFreak – Hate Crime?" graphic had gone viral and was drawing thousands of comments. Most of the comments were critical of Ray Pernell and Tucker. The nation seemed increasingly fascinated by the idea that a Tucker Senior Executive may have had a secret, kinky lifestyle.

Frank tapped his vibrating phone. "You've reached the law offices of Frank Dorrington. How may I direct your call?"

"What the hell do you think you're doing? Have you lost your goddam mind?"

Frank recognized that voice and the attitude that came with it. "Oh, hi Debbie."

"Frank! Why are you telling the world that you knew Ray so well? You hardly knew him."

"You have no idea how often Ray and I got together."

Debbie let out a terse laugh. "Oh really? Let me guess. How about never? It was easy to see that you two didn't hit it off. Mia and I both knew it."

"Ray and I played golf."

"Once!"

"Once that you know of. We started to talk occasionally over a few beers."

"Sure you did. Is that when he told you that he went skydiving Frank? Ray never went skydiving. You're a fucking liar!"

"Check the tape, Debbie. I never said that he went skydiving. I said that he had an interest in it. He liked to talk about his dreams. Ray was a conflicted guy who needed a confidant."

"Save that news-baiting bullshit for the media. You're doing this crap to make money. And you don't care who you hurt. You're an asshole Frank. This baloney about Ray having a freaky side is hurting his family. You need to stop this bullshit right now, or…."

"Or what?" asked Frank. "Go back and check any media I've done. I've never said anything bad about Ray. Any negativity is coming from the media."

"You're not that clever Frank. It's obvious what you are doing."

"I've done nothing illegal."

"That remains to be seen, but does the word 'immoral' ring a bell? Your public bullshit about Ray is killing Mia and the kids. Doesn't that bother you, even a little bit?"

Frank shot back "How do you know that he didn't have some secrets? What do you think he was doing that night, in a fucking loincloth, on the streets of San Francisco? He wasn't going down to the corner for a pack of gum!"

"I don't know Frank. But neither do you."

"That may or may not be true. But I do know that Ray was a troubled man."

"Bullshit! Go sell your phantom relationship to the tabloids Frank!"

"Look Debbie, no one is happy that Ray was killed. I'm trying to make something good come from this awful situation."

"By something good, do you mean making dirty money on the fact that my best friend's husband was murdered? That kind of money dries up once the media moves on to the next big story. Your 15 minutes of fame will be up and you'll be broke and alone again."

Frank winced. The word "alone" had been delivered with full vitriol, and he felt it. Debbie sure knew how to hit him where it hurts. She'd always been good at that. Swallowing his anger, Frank then answered in his lawyerly voice. "The something good I'm trying to derive from this situation is the new hate crime bill I hope to put in front of the Connecticut legislature. We need tougher penalties for hate crimes. It's a good cause. How can you be against that?"

"C'mon Frank. Don't play saint with me. If you cared about that stuff, you would've done something by now. This is just you, seeking fame and cash. And you don't care who you screw in the process. You are, and always have been a selfish asshole!"

"Love you too, Debbie," said Frank, ending the call. It occurred to him that this conversation ended with the same acrid exchange that had signaled the end of their marriage.

Chapter 36

Detectives Harland and Sharpe were summoned to Captain Kekoa's office.

"I'll get right to it. DJ, I'm assigning Levi to partner with you full-time on the Pernell homicide, or should I call it the Loincloth Murder? You're already sharing info, I'm just making your partnership official."

Both detectives nodded.

"The full power of the department is now at your disposal. Use it wisely!"

"We will. Thanks, Captain" said DJ.

"Commissioner Francis and his pal at TEM are now well up my ass. Social media has gone crazy. PR is bugging me for more 'public-facing' statements, whatever those are. I need you guys to close this case as soon as possible."

"Roger that, Captain," said DJ.

"Works for me" added Sharpe. "We're a good team."

"You better be," said Kekoa. "Walk me through what you know, from the very beginning."

"OK, here's what we know for sure," said DJ. "The victim was Ray Pernell, Vice President of Creative Services at TEM. A resident of Hudson, Connecticut, he worked out of Tucker's New York City office. He and his co-worker, Carlos Madrigan, were here to finish the trailer for an upcoming kids' movie. They spent two days working with Sol Korman and Les Santarelli, both from ThickBrickk Design in Los Angeles. After finishing their project, ThickBrickk rented a limo to go out to dinner and a couple of bars before returning to the hotel at around 2 am. We've confirmed those destinations through credit card receipts and the limo driver's log"

"Anything happen at any of those stops?" asked Kekoa. "Any interaction with strangers or perhaps professionals?"

"Not that we know." *Hookers and dealers don't leave business cards!* "These guys kept the party to themselves. The waiter at Le Meillure remembers that they drank three bottles of wine on top of their cocktails, and tipped him well. Both of the bars they went to after dinner were of no help to us. Mr. Korman's credit card shows that he not only bought the limo and dinner, but he also picked up the bar tabs, as is customary in their vendor-client relationship."

"Anything there with these two guys from LA?" asked Kekoa.

"We've done our due diligence on them," said DJ. "ThickBrickk Design is a regular vendor for Tucker. They've worked with Ray Pernell at least 6 times in the last decade."

Captain Kekoa sat on the front edge of his desk. "Ok. We know that the two Tucker guys were dropped at the Smythville and the two LA guys went on to a different hotel, correct?"

"That's right, Kahuna," said DJ. "Pernell was last seen alive when he and Madrigan, returned to the Smythville Hotel at 2:32 am. They were clearly drunk. They interacted with Tim Bernard, the hotel clerk, and got on the elevator. The hotel lobby security video confirms exactly that."

"Anyone else in the lobby?"

"Negative. Pernell's room was on the 4th floor, Madrigan's on the 7th. They were gonna meet at 6 am in the lobby. Madrigan was there at 6, but Pernell was a no-show. Madrigan tried Pernell's cellphone, then his room phone, but obviously, no answer. That's when he reached out to the desk clerk about keying the room"

"Anything else useful on the hotel video?" asked Sharpe.

DJ responded. "As we all know, there are currently no security cameras in hotel hallways while the California Supreme Court is deciding whether or not they can do that without violating anyone's privacy. But the cameras in the lobby and the public stairwell were functioning."

"But no Pernell sightings on those cameras after 2:32 am," said Kekoa.

"True," said DJ. "So Pernell didn't use the stairs or pass through the lobby to exit the hotel. There are only two other options. The service stairwell exit into the rear alley and the roof, which doesn't seem like a viable option. The access door to the roof is locked, and even if Pernell somehow got up there, there's no way down without a parachute."

Sharpe chuckled. "I'm guessing he didn't have the space in his loincloth to pack a chute."

"Not likely," said DJ. *Good one Levi!* "That leaves only the exit at the bottom of the service stairwell. To access the stairwell, Pernell would've had to walk through a door labeled 'employees only', down a hallway, and around a corner. The stairwell door would've locked behind him unless he propped it open."

"Where was he going?" asked Kekoa.

"Not sure, but at the bottom of the service stairwell, the exit door to the alley is triggered by a pressure bar and it opens into a world of dumpsters, rats, and stank that'll knock your socks off. That's gotta be how he exited the building."

"Makes sense," said Kekoa. "Probably didn't want anyone to see that he was leaving or how he was dressed. Any other solids before we launch into speculation?"

"We know he left all his belongings in his room. Forensics found nothing special in there, but we still own the room. His phone record shows no calls or texts at that hour. His cellphone alarm went off at 5:15 am. It was still beeping when Security entered his room. We know he used his CPAP machine for 18 minutes, from 2:50 to 3:08 am. The chip in the machine provided that info to us"

The Captain asked "How do we know that he utilized the machine? Maybe he turned it on but got busy doing something else. Like making a loincloth."

"I got this one," said Sharpe, "Pernell was using an AirFlaire CPAP machine. The AirFlaires are pressure-sensitive. If the user doesn't have the mask on, the machine will turn off within 30 seconds. It won't run long without a wearer."

"Damn Levi," said Kekoa. "That's some next-level info."

"Naw man. I use an AirFlaire at home. Louise got tired of my snoring. Works great."

"She's a saint," said Kekoa. "So we know that Pernell, at least, tried to sleep for 18 minutes. So why did he stop?"

"Million-dollar question, Chief." *If I had the answer, we wouldn't be having this discussion!*

"Maybe someone was in there with him? Or someone came to his door? Why did he need to undress, put on a loincloth, and exit through the alley door? Or did he maybe, just lock himself out of his room?"

"Good questions," said DJ. "It's hard to believe that someone was waiting for him in his room. Tough to imagine a scenario where he would neatly fold his clothes, then try to sleep for 18 minutes before being accosted by someone who was already there."

"OK. Back-burner that idea," said Kekoa.

"That leaves us three scenarios," said DJ. "Scenario one: He left the room of his own volition. Either naked or already dressed in the rags he would've found in the janitor's cart."

"Makes sense, all his clothes were still in the room," said Sharpe.

"He might've been looking for alcohol, drugs, or companionship," said DJ. "But it's not likely that he was keeping an appointment that he made with a professional earlier in the evening. I mean, who goes to bed for 18 minutes before going out to get with a hooker or a dealer?"

"Fair point, especially un-dressed like that and carrying no cash," said Kekoa.

DJ continued. "Scenario number two. Someone came to his door, awakened him from his 18-minute nap, and forced him to leave the room, maybe forcing him to wear the rags."

"Sounds more likely," said the Captain.

"Agreed," said DJ. "But that person would've had to be hanging out, undetected, somewhere in the hotel for at least several hours. The hotel video of the stairs and lobby has been carefully reviewed, beginning at 6 pm that evening. Together with the hotel staff, we've been able to identify everyone who came and went through those areas. To the best of our knowledge, no one other than employees, registered patrons, and a few identified visitors are seen on those recordings."

Kekoa spoke. "Our killer could've been staying at the hotel, or hiding in the service stairwell, or is a hotel employee."

"Always a possibility Captain." said DJ "

"And scenario three?" asked Sharpe

"Well, maybe he locked himself out of his room. But that theory just doesn't make sense."

"Why?" asked Kekoa

DJ nodded. "Well, why would you sleep 18 minutes and then get up and leave your room with no key, wallet, or clothes? And, if you lock yourself out of your room, wouldn't you go down to the lobby to get another key?"

"Makes sense," said Kekoa.

"Why would you choose, instead, to walk through doors labeled 'employees only', down a long hallway, and through a locking door into that musty service stairwell? That gains you nothing."

Sharpe answered. "So the only means he had to leave the hotel without camera detection was through the service stairwell and out into the alley?"

"Right". *Unless he pulled some Houdini shit.*

"Yet, he probably wouldn't have gone that way if he had locked himself out of the room. So he must've had another reason for taking that route."

"That's what I got so far, brother," said DJ.

Kekoa clasped his hands in thought. "That seems to make sense concerning Pernell's departure from the hotel. But then what happened to him? How the hell did he wind up in that empty lot in Hollis? Someone felt very strongly that Pernell needed to die."

"No doubt," said DJ. "I'm sure that the rags and duct tape used to make the loincloth came from the janitor's cart on the seventh floor of the service stairwell, three flights above Pernell's room."

Sharpe added, "We need to know when he put the loincloth on."

"Agreed," said DJ. "Did he bring those items to his room earlier so that he could change into them before going out in the middle of the night? Or, did someone bring that stuff to his door and force him to wear it?

Kekoa interjected. "And that alley outside the stairwell is where you've been hanging out on recent nights?"

"Yeah. There's a cozy spot on that alley that hosts some of our finest homeless folks. I'm hoping to find someone who may have seen Pernell come through there in his loincloth. So far, no luck." *But I've made some cool new friends.*

"That's some needle-in-a-haystack shit right there," said Sharpe.

"Right again, partner," said DJ.

"What's the latest on the photograph of the victim that leaked out to the world?" asked Kekoa.

"The photo is authentic. As you know, the shooter was just a scanner-chasing kid trying to get famous on social media. He's a non-factor."

"But his photo lives on," said Kekoa.

"Roger that," said DJ. "And we'd like to know who added the "TuckerExecFreak – Hate Crime?" caption to that photo and pushed it out to the world. The folks at Tucker wanna know that too. Amal Ahmadi is working on it for us."

"If anyone can figure that out, it's Amal," said Kekoa. "Anything new from the crime scene?"

"We know he died of a 9-mil gunshot wound to the forehead. Had some bruising on the side of his head. And of course, the word 'FREAK' written on his chest in his blood. Toxicology showed that he was likely still legally drunk at the time of his death."

"Drugs?"

"None."

Sharpe spoke. "No way he walked all the way to Hollis."

"Agreed," said DJ. "We've checked with taxis, Uber, Lyft, and livery services. Nothing. The quickest way from the hotel to Hollis is straight down Lund Ave to Shorter Street. We've checked all traffic security cameras along the way. No sign of Ray on foot."

"So his killer transported him?" asked Kekoa.

"Seems like it," said DJ. *Ain't no way he walked.....*

"Which brings us back to our theories. Do you think he was looking for drugs?" asked the Captain.

"There's always a chance, I guess," said DJ. "But it doesn't feel right to me. No drugs in his system. And his wife didn't react much when I asked her about drugs."

"Companionship?" asked Sharpe.

"That seems to be the national opinion at the moment," said DJ. *And the leader in my clubhouse.*

"Which makes Tucker crazy," said Sharpe. "This ain't good for their image."

"Tell me something I don't know," said Kekoa.

DJ shook his head. "There's gotta be more to this story." *There better be, or we're screwed.*

Kekoa asked, "What's the deal from our snitch who claimed to have info on this case?"

"Oh yeah, Johnny G." said DJ "That punk would say anything to save his ass. We believe that he was shooting up with Lester Hollowell, street-name Capone, the night before Hollowell was ambushed over in Oakland."

"And?" asked Kekoa.

"And not much else," said DJ. "Johnny's claims that Hollowell bragged about killing a 'gay freak', who might have been Pernell, are pretty thin."

"How thin?"

"We don't know if Hollowell did any such thing. We don't know if Hollowell even said any such thing. Without corroboration, it's just a line of bullshit from a professional bullshitter, who saw the word 'freak' on the victim, and is trying to save his ass." *And he's playing us for fools!*

"Captain", Sharpe interrupted. "Johnny G did say that Hollowell was waving a 9-mil when he was bragging about killing the gay man. It was a 9-mil slug in Pernell's head."

"Any match?"

"Nah, Oakland PD didn't recover Hollowell's weapon. His executioners probably snatched his weapon. Gotta have their scalp."

"I know there are millions of 9-mils in America, but it might be more than a coincidence," said Kekoa. "Your snitch might have made that shit up, but don't rule anything out."

Both detectives nodded.

DJ added, "For what it's worth, our snitch claimed that Hollowell quoted his victim as saying he 'woke up naked and pissing in a corner'."

Kekoa scrunched his forehead. "What the hell does that mean?"

"No goddamn idea," said DJ. *Meth-heads ain't exactly known for their clever communication skills.*

"Whatever" answered Kekoa. "Let's take a hard look at Mr. Hollowell, just in case he actually had something to do with Pernell's death. And what about this guy who's all over TV claiming to be Pernell's best friend? What's his name?"

"Frank Dorrington," said DJ. "He's on my shortlist for a conversation."

Kekoa nodded. "He seems to have known Pernell better than anyone else. Set up a chat with him and remember to look him directly in the eyes DJ".

"Tough to do on FaceTime, Captain. I also need to re-interview Pernell's boss, talk to his HR department, and hopefully meet some of his co-workers. I need to know more about Pernell and his habits."

Sharpe spoke. "Good luck getting near any Tucker employees. You can expect their HR department to be present at any and all conversations."

"DJ, you gotta go talk with all of these people."

Do my ears deceive me? "Say what, Captain? Are you authorizing me to travel to the East Coast on departmental business?"

"You heard me. This goddamned case has captured the nation's attention like nothing since OJ in the Bronco. The Commissioner has authorized all expenses. And we all know the best interviews are done in person."

"Agreed," said DJ

"Need you out there within two days. Levi will handle this end. Ask Marty Penderson in PR to assist you with booking travel."

"Aye aye, Captain. Gimme 24 hours to set up some interviews and let Liz know that I'll be away."

"I assume you remember your LEOFA training," said Kekoa, referencing the mandatory training each detective received concerning the carrying of firearms on domestic flights.

"Yessir boss" answered DJ. "First time I get to use that info." *Thought this day might never come!*

"Ok gentlemen, go forth and prosper. And bring me some goddam concrete results!"

Chapter 37

"Can you believe this shit?" Mia had reached Debbie via FaceTime.

Debbie leaned her iPhone up against her laptop screen and looked at Mia. "I'm buried in a project. What's up?"

"St. Joe's just sent an email to the choir. This Sunday is a Solo Sunday."

"So what, we've had Solo Sundays before. Day off for the choir," replied Debbie. "Who's the lucky soloist?"

"Katie Paine. But that's not the point. The whole month has been changed to solo Sundays. All group choir practices have been changed to solo practices!"

"Whaaaat? Do you think this has something to do with your situation? Who sent the email?"

"Of course, it's about Ray. The note is from Lynette Elmer and Father Keenan. They just froze me out!"

"Listen, Mia, you and I both know that Mrs. Elmer doesn't have a mean bone in her body."

"True."

"This smells like Father Keenan has decided that the things being said about Ray don't agree with his archaic view of the world, so the best way to keep you away is to cancel all full choir activities."

"Of course, he's behind this. No doubt he got plenty of input from some of our 'friends' in the choir. Remember that shit from the last rehearsal?"

"Yeah, but I'd hope that most of our friends don't feel that way."

"I should call Father Keenan," said Mia.

"Of course you should. If you don't, I will".

"Thanks, Debbie. I'll handle it. I only hope the facts are on my side."

"They are! You know in your heart that Ray wasn't keeping any secrets. Just ignore those weak-minded assholes who believe that gossip is gospel."

"You're good for my soul. I'll let you know how it goes."

"Give Father Keenan my best," said Debbie with a chuckle.

"Of course. I'm sure he loves you too."

————

"St Joseph's Parish. Sister Mary Jo speaking."

"Hi, Sister. It's Mia Pernell. I'm wondering if Father Keenan is available for a brief moment."

Mia heard Sister Mary Jo suck in her breath. "I think he's hearing confessions now, can he get back to you Mrs. Pernell?"

Glancing at the clock, Mia said "The window for confessions ended an hour ago. Could you please check to see if he's back in the rectory? This is important."

"I'll look around. Please hold".

After nearly two full minutes of silence, Mia finally heard "This is Father Keenan. To whom am I speaking?"

"Hi, Father. It's Mia Pernell". said Mia, knowing full well that those two minutes were spent discussing how best to deal with her.

"Hello, Mrs. Pernell. I pray that you are doing as well as humanly possible under the circumstances. We all miss Mr. Pernell so much."

Mia swallowed her anger. "I'm calling about the switch to solo Sundays for the foreseeable future. Why the big change with the choir?"

"I'm sorry Mrs. Pernell. I don't choose the soloists. That's the job of Mrs. Elmer."

"Father, we both know that I'm not soloist material. I also know that using only soloists eliminates our group choir practices. Why would you remove so many of us from singing on Sundays?"

Father Keenan sighed. "It seemed the only prudent action to take".

"This is about Ray, isn't it? Are you letting those stupid rumors affect your better judgment?"

"Mrs. Pernell, there was a groundswell of opinion among our parishioners. Many of them felt they couldn't endorse Mr. Pernell's apparent behavior."

"Why?" demanded Mia.

"They felt it wasn't in keeping with the tenets of our faith. I'm just trying to protect you and your family from any backlash."

Biting her tongue, Mia said "With all due respect Father, I do not need your protection. This is your parish, not theirs. Are you just gonna cave in to their nasty gossip?"

"Mrs. Pernell, you know the Catholic Church's stance on homosexuality. We welcome celibate gay members into the church, but we do not condone homosexual acts. They are intrinsically immoral and contrary to the natural law. We cannot condone that behavior."

Mia nearly lost her temper but managed to tensely squeeze out "Father Keenan. Please explain to me which part of being murdered with a bullet in the brain is a homosexual act?"

"I'm so sorry Mrs. Pernell. The fact that your husband unfortunately lost his life isn't the church's point here. It's what he was doing, or seeking to do, that is contrary to Catholic Church doctrine."

Mia's loud voice reflected her anger. "You realize that you are talking about my husband, don't you? The father of my children. I was there when they were conceived, I can vouch for his heterosexuality! I can't believe that the Catholic Church would choose to believe this destructive gossip. Where's your proof that he was behaving inappropriately?"

"I'm so sorry, Mrs. Pernell," said Father Keenan, sounding a bit shaky. "I've learned over many years of hearing confessions that people can keep some very deep secrets, even from their loved ones."

"Are you telling me that Ray confessed some deep, dark secrets to you, Father?"

"No, I am not. I'm simply saying that actions speak louder than words. And Mr. Pernell's actions that night in San Francisco strongly indicate some aberrant sexual behavior."

"Based on what?"

"His clothing. The late hour he was out. The neighborhood he was in. All of it."

Mia's anger was getting stronger. "Well then, the police can stop their investigation because Saint Joseph's parish has it all figured out!"

"I'm so sorry Mrs. Pernell. I've spoken to the Archbishop about this and I've prayed on it. This was the best decision we could make for the majority of people. You and your family are certainly welcome at St. Joseph's for mass and any other functions."

"That's precious!" yelled Mia. "Should we sit in the leper section, Father?"

"I'm so sorry that you feel that way, Mrs. Pernell. If the police investigation uncovers something that disproves Mr. Pernell's apparent misbehavior, then we'd be just as overjoyed as you and your family."

"I doubt that Father Keenan. This will be the last time we ever speak. You are not representative of my God. My church has taught me that a good Catholic doesn't listen to gossip and rumor. My country has taught me that a person is innocent until proven guilty. And I embrace the gay community. I'm tired of your ancient view of the world. You're a man with archaic values, and I'm happy to be rid of you. Good day, Father Keenan!"

Later that evening, Mia was making her nightly entry into her laptop journal. "Well, Ray, I really did it today. I blew up our relationship with St. Joe's. Father Keenan believes that your behavior was not appropriate for a good Catholic. I know in my heart that he's wrong. I just wish I knew what you were doing…..God, I wish I knew."

Chapter 38

"Aren't you Mr. Big Time Detective!" laughed Liz, as she handed her husband a bowl of steamed okra and garlic mashed potatoes. "I can't believe the Department is sending you across the country."

"It ain't no big deal, baby," said DJ. "I'll only be gone a couple nights. This case has blown up. Levi Sharpe is working with me on this now."

"Tell Levi I send my best to Louise. She was so wonderful during our struggles back in the day."

"Will do Baby. And if you need anything while I'm gone, feel free to reach out to either of them."

Liz laughed. "I think I can manage a couple of days on my own. I know you don't like to talk about your business, but this is the Tucker case, right?"

"Yeah. And the Captain's getting some serious pressure from above for us to wrap this up as soon as possible."

"I can understand that. Can't turn on the TV without seeing some sort of crazy story about what the Tucker guy was doing. TEM must be going nuts."

"You got that right Baby. Tucker and the Commissioner are pushing us. That's why Kahuna's sending me out east. He believes face-to-face conversations are more revealing."

"I get that."

"I'm with that too. I love to watch the eyes and body language of someone I'm interviewing. There's so much to see." *And I like to watch 'em squirm.*

"Yeah. Talking through a laptop screen just isn't the same."

"No, it ain't. That's why I'm heading out east. I'll set up interviews tomorrow and hopefully leave the next day."

"Flying first class?" asked Liz, with a sly smile.

DJ laughed. "Good one baby. The department's got a budget, you know." *I'll be lucky if I'm not in the damn baggage compartment.*

"Poor baby, don't worry about me while you're jet-setting around the country. I'll just be back here with the rest of the great unwashed, trying to scrape by."

DJ chuckled. "You're a regular Wanda Sykes! You should be doing standup down at The Punch Line".

"I don't suppose you'd like to do a girl a favor and help her try to get pregnant before you fly off to paradise. Or is that beneath a world traveler like yourself?"

DJ stood up, walked around the table, wrapped his arms around Liz, gently kissing her neck. He whispered "I'm a public servant. Never let it be said that I didn't serve the will of the people." *Your will be done!*

————

"Watch out for the hookers in Times Square" laughed Marty Penderson.

"You slay me" mocked DJ. "I think they cleaned that shit up years ago. But thanks for the warning. Am I good?"

"Yessir. You leave Wednesday at 6:20 am."

"Geeezus. You couldn't get the 4 am flight?"

Marty laughed again. "If there was a 4 am flight, and it was cheaper, you'd be on it, per departmental policy."

"You speak the truth, my friend!"

"Anyway, you fly to LaGuardia on Wednesday and you depart from Hartford on Friday afternoon."

"Are we booked with hotels and a car?"

"Yes, Boss. Wednesday night is at the SoHo Grand Hotel. It's near the Tucker offices. Thursday night, You're at the Downtown Hyatt in Hartford. Pick up your rental car at LaGuardia and return it at Bradley Airport in Connecticut. You've got a compact car."

"No problem. It ain't the size of the car that a man drives, it's the ….." DJ paused and then said, "Aw hell, I got nuthin'."

They both laughed.

"Thanks, Marty."

———

DJ built his interview list for the two-plus days he'd have on the East Coast:

-Sharon Dillard and Tucker's HR representative

-Ray's co-workers

-Mia Pernell & family

-Debbie Slater

-Vera Eden at Hudson PD

-Frank Dorrington

DJ was certain that Tucker wouldn't allow their employees to talk to him without a Human Resources rep being present. He also knew that people tend to clam up when HR is present. It might cost him a round of drinks, but he had a way around that problem.

DJ retrieved the card that Carlos Madrigan had given him back at the Smythville hotel and punched up the number.

"This is Carlos."

"Mr. Madrigan, it's Detective Harland, from the San Francisco police department. Got a minute?"

"Oh, hey Detective. Sure, I'm just on the train. How goes the investigation? Man, Ray's homicide is all over TV."

"It sure is. Look, I'm coming out east tomorrow. I'm gonna meet with Sharon Dillard, and probably someone from Tucker's HR team."

"Wow, Detective. Maybe I'll see you around the office."

"I definitely want to talk to you again Carlos, and hopefully a few of Ray's closest friends. But I find that these types of conversations are better held outside the office." *In a bar, with no HR!*

"You mean, away from Human Resources, don't you Detective?"

"Bingo. It's just that people tend to be more open when the company watchdog is not in the room."

"Human nature my friend. How can I help?"

"Do you and Ray's pals have a favorite location where you may occasionally hold an after-work board meeting?"

Carlos laughed. "Oh yeah. We go to O'Finsky's, where we've solved many of the world's problems."

"I'm meeting with Dillard at around five o'clock. Any chance I could get some time with you and a few of Ray's pals after work, like maybe 6:30ish? I'm happy to buy the first round at O'Finsky's." *I'm on an expense account!*

"No prob. I'll round up the gang. We'd love to know how your investigation is going."

"Thanks, Carlos. See you then. And keep this on the down-low at work."

"You got it, Detective. See you tomorrow."

Following those meetings in New York, DJ planned to drive to Connecticut on Thursday morning where he'd meet with Mia, her parents, and, at Mia's suggestion, Debbie Slater. He also intended to talk with Vera Eden later that day, hopefully at the Hudson Police Station.

DJ had saved Friday morning for a meeting with Debbie Slater's ex, Frank Dorrington, the attorney who was all over the media defending his 'best friend'. DJ wasn't yet sure what this guy's angle might be.

DJ hoped that he'd return home with a clearer understanding of Ray Pernell, his motivations, and his lifestyle choices.

Chapter 39

Mia was balancing 5 cups of Earl Grey tea on a serving tray.

"Here we go. The lemon is for Vera and Debbie. Mom and Dad, your tea is unspoiled."

Vera Eden and Debbie Slater were sharing Mia's favorite couch. Mia's mother, Myoko was seated in the matching leather chair with her husband, Hiroshi, standing nearby.

Mia sat down on the hard back chair, at the end of the coffee table. "So Vera, what's on your mind?"

"Nothing dramatic" responded Vera Eden, the sole Grief Counselor for the Hudson Police Department. "Just wanted to check in with everyone."

"Any problem getting through the media outside?" asked Debbie.

"Not really," said Eden. "They were more interested in the protesters."

"Protesters?" exclaimed Mia, walking to the window to take a look.

"Yes," said Eden. "It looks like the LGBTQ community is viewing Ray's murder as a hate crime. Their signs are about 'Loincloth justice'. These protests are popping up all over the country."

"This is a nightmare," said Mia.

Eden continued. "They are demanding stricter federal laws against hate crimes. So they go where the cameras are."

Mia's frustration surfaced. "Media, protestors, and now Ray is a poster boy for the LGBTQ community. I feel like I'm living in 'bizarro world'!"

Eden spoke softly. "I can't begin to imagine the pain of your loss, and then to have all this craziness thrown at you."

"I've learned who my real friends are, that's for sure. I've heard from a few, but not many."

Myoko said. "Mia honey, maybe you should chat with Father Keenan."

"No Mom. He and I have talked, and I'm done with St. Joseph's."

"What are you talking about? He's been our priest for years. You can't just quit."

"Yes I can, Mom. I'm done with St. Joseph's, and I mean it. Father Keenan has never really been a progressive thinker anyway."

Debbie laughed out loud, then apologized. "Oops, sorry. I've never been a big fan."

"Me neither," said Mia. "Ray and I love some of our friends at St. Joe's, and I'll stay in touch with them, but I'm not going back there."

"You can't just quit the Catholic Church," said Myoko.

"I'm not leaving the church, Mom. Just that parish. We'll be fine at St. Patrick's."

Eden spoke. "Mia, how're your boys doing?"

Mia thought for a moment. "Ricky's been pretty stoic. His life consists of school, wrestling, and video games. He gets fired up when he wrestles. Ray said that 'Ricky wrestles angry', whatever that means."

"What about Karl?" asked Eden.

"Weird thing. When Karl came home from school yesterday, he asked me if his Daddy wore diapers."

"What the hell?" said Debbie.

"Some kid at school told him that. It must've come from that awful photograph."

"Maybe that kid overheard his idiot parents speculating about the picture" answered Debbie.

"Probably," said Eden. "How did Karl react to that comment?"

"We talked about how name-calling can be harmful. I think he's okay. But every day brings a new pile of crap. I'm so done with all this."

Eden spoke. "Tell me how Phoebe's doing."

Mia glanced downward. "She's barely eating anything. She sees criticism of her father on social media. She claims that some of her so-called friends have turned the other way."

"Certainly, not all of Phoebe's friends are being mean to her," said Eden.

"Of course not," said Mia. "She mostly hangs with her friend, Amy. But it only takes a couple of cruel comments on social media to blow up a teenager's life."

Eden frowned. "No kidding. They don't realize how damaging their comments can be. Is Phoebe still using self-harming phrases?"

Mia's voice tightened. "Well, she keeps saying that her life is over. And she continues to believe that Ray and I were keeping some great secret from her."

Eden looked directly at Mia. "Even though she seems to be rejecting you, Phoebe needs your love right now, more than she ever has."

Mia started to sob. "Damn…..I need your help, Vera. I think Phoebe is cutting herself. I noticed four slashes inside her forearm and asked her what it was. She told me it was nothing and stormed away. I had to look it up online. I'd never heard of cutting before." Tears were running down Mia's cheeks. "I'm so worried."

Hiroshi handed the tissue box to Mia.

Eden said, "She needs immediate attention from a professional."

"What's cutting?" asked Myoko.

"It's the actual cutting of the skin with sharp objects like razor blades, drawing blood, and leaving scars. It's generally done to draw attention or to evoke fear and distress in others."

"Pretty damn effective. I'm distressed." sobbed Mia.

"It's mainly done by adolescents, almost exclusively by females," added Eden. "Studies have shown that cutting may actually help to relieve anxiety in some cases. But, while it's not necessarily a precursor to a suicide attempt, it should be addressed immediately."

"It's a cry for help" offered Hiroshi.

"Yes, it is Mr. Higoru. Phoebe's facing some uniquely difficult challenges."

"I just don't know what to do with her" sobbed Mia.

Looking at Mia, Eden continued "Phoebe needs a therapist, someone she can trust to talk to about her father's passing."

"What about you, Vera?"

Eden shook her head. "That's against departmental policy. And she needs someone who specializes in teen trauma. Someone younger, likely a woman, with whom she can grow comfortable enough to share her true feelings."

"I'll get right on that," said Mia. "Appreciate any recommendations."

"No prob, I'll send you a couple of names as soon as I get home. Maybe you could get Phoebe involved in the selection process."

"Thanks, Vera. But, I doubt she'll even agree to talk to anyone."

"What about you Mia?" asked Eden.

"What about me?"

"How are you doing?"

"I'd like to say I'm doing well. But It's so difficult."

Myoko spoke. "Honey, you're doing great. You are handling the loss of your husband with dignity and grace."

"Love you Mom, but I don't feel like that." Mia dabbed her eyes with a now-soaked tissue. "It's such a mess. Lies on social media, news crews and protestors on my sidewalk, my church freezing me out, my kids unsure about their parents….." Mia exhaled.

"Screw the media" offered Debbie.

Mia brushed aside a tear. "And on top of all that, Tucker's holding up Ray's life insurance and his benefits. They want to know if he violated their damn morals clause."

Debbie spoke angrily. "Mia! You and I both know that Ray wasn't hiding any secrets from you guys. And I'm so sorry that my moron ex-husband is doing everything he can to fan those flames."

Eden spoke. "Thanks, Miss Slater for bringing him up. Were Mr. Dorrington and Mr. Pernell as close as he is claiming?"

Mia cut Debbie off with "NO!" Glancing around the room, she pleaded. "Ray and Frank had only met three or four times, ever! They played golf once. Ray didn't like his cocky attitude. Frank is fulla shit!"

Debbie answered. "I'm so sorry that I ever brought that bastard into our lives."

Eden asked. "So why's Dorington doing this?"

Debbie replied. "For fame, which he hopes will mean more clients and more money. He's got some big debts."

Eden seemed perplexed. "But he's an attorney, he's gotta know that he's opening himself up to a lawsuit."

Debbie answered. "Frank is great at baiting the hook, then encouraging others to make the wild statements. Such an asshole! Oops, sorry Mr. and Mrs. Higoru."

Hiroshi laughed. "You should hear the language I've heard from my students, in both English and Japanese!"

Eden had another question. "What about Dorrington's claim that he intends to push for tougher hate-crime laws in Connecticut?"

Debbie laughed derisively. "Self-serving baloney. I guarantee you Frank hasn't written a single word of his 'proposed legislation'. He only cares about crimes that are profitable for him."

"I feel like my kids and I are being targeted for something we didn't do," said a pensive Mia.

Eden added, "Totally unfair, Mia. You should probably retain an attorney to deal with both TEM and Dorrington."

"I already called Ken Samantis," said Mia.

"Isn't that Amy's Dad?" asked Debbie.

"Yes," said Mia. "We've known Ken for years. He's already in touch with Tucker and he's taking a hard look at what Frank is doing."

"That's excellent" interjected Hiro.

"I hope he nails Frank's ass to the wall" shouted Debbie.

Eden placed her tea cup on the tray. "I've got to go. Thanks, everyone, for your time. Mia, I'll send you the contact info for a couple of therapists that might work for Phoebe. Please keep a close eye on her."

Wiping her eyes with a fresh tissue, Mia said "Thanks, Vera. I appreciate you so much. You've been wonderful."

Chapter 40

"We'll be on the ground at New York LaGuardia in about 15 minutes".

The pilot's announcement shook DJ from his nap. He wanted to stretch, but the folks on either side of him had long since claimed their space and most of his. *I gotta remember to thank Marty for the middle seat.*

A text from Carlos Madrigan stated that a group of Ray's friends would be at O'Finsky's at 6:30 pm. DJ responded with a thumbs-up emoji.

After collecting his bag and weapon, DJ picked up his rental car and headed into the city. His GPS told him the drive would take twenty-eight minutes. An hour later, DJ arrived at the Soho Grand Hotel. The desk clerk inquired, "How was your trip in, Mr. Harland?" DJ simply replied, "Fine". *Except for my ungodly early flight, the cramped middle seat, and my tiny rental car with a GPS that was programmed by a chimpanzee.*

Those thoughts evaporated as DJ entered the elegant Soho Grand Bar and Lounge. The long space was lined on both sides by clusters of turquoise leather winged-back chairs, traditional leather couches, and overstuffed ottomans. The two-story windows lining one side of the room offered views of West Broadway, Canal St., and Soho beyond. Giant plants resided in front of each window, perched on sturdy wrought-iron, glass-topped tables. Hanging from the high ceiling were the largest lampshades he'd ever seen. *Hello, Smythville East!*

Arriving in his room, DJ tossed his roller bag on the bed, and unpacked his SIG Sauer P229, holstering it under his suit coat. Grabbing a cab, he arrived at the Tucker Entertainment Media offices 10 minutes early for his meeting with Sharon Dillard.

TEM Security had his day-pass credential ready, complete with a lanyard. It read "Detective DJ Harland - San Francisco Police Dept." That text was on top of an embossed TEM logo. Even the lanyard had the TEM logo stamped repeatedly on it. *Beats the hell out of our hand-written paper passes back at the shop.*

The Security guard asked, "Are you carrying sir?"

"Yes" replied DJ, revealing the holster under his jacket. "And, as always, I'm carrying cuffs and zip-ties"

"Thank you. Police officers certainly have that right here at Tucker."

No shit. Thank you for your permission!

"We ask that your weapon is unchambered with the safety on."

"Oddly enough, that's exactly how I'm carrying per police regulations." *God, I freakin' hate it when toy cops try to big-time me.*

"Fantastic, let's get you up to the Executive floor".

DJ was greeted as the elevator door opened. "Hello Detective, I'm Patti, Sharon Dillard's assistant. She's expecting you in her office."

Patti escorted DJ into Dillard's corner office. He saw floor-to-ceiling glass on two sides, a comfortable conversation area in one corner, a small kitchenette along the far wall, and a glass-fronted conference room on the opposite side. *Damn, our entire homicide department would fit in here!* In the corner, ensconced by glass on both sides, was an enormous wooden desk. *Serious desk envy!* Sharon Dillard stood up from behind the desk. "Detective Harland, so nice to finally meet you in person."

Noting Dillard's tightly wrapped gray hair and oh-so-perfect business suit, DJ simply replied "Hi Ms. Dillard."

"Please, call me Sharon" Then a quick aside to her assistant. "Patti, please let Mr. Weller know that Detective Harland is here."

DJ didn't have to ask who Mr Weller might be. Human Resources would want to be present at all conversations DJ had in the TEM offices.

"Anything to drink, Detective?"

"Maybe a bottle of water."

Reaching into the fridge, Sharon handed DJ a chilled bottle of water. "Ice?"

"I'm good. Take my water neat."

"Hi Sharon, hope I didn't hold you up." Richard Weller, TEM's VP of Human Resources entered the office. DJ eyed the short, squat man in his corporate uniform of grey suit and striped tie, sporting a flattop haircut and half-lens reading glasses perched on the end of his broad nose.

After introducing the two men, Sharon said "Why don't we step into the conference room so we won't be disturbed."

Once they were seated, Dillard triggered a device on the tabletop which instantly frosted the glass wall, creating total privacy.

Wow! Gotta get that for my cubicle!

"So Detective, how can we be of help?"

DJ produced his digital recorder. "You guys have any objection to me recording our discussion?"

Sharon looked immediately at Weller who nodded. "Of course not, Detective."

No doubt this room is wired for sound and probably video, too.

"We covered some of this stuff on the phone earlier, so I might repeat a thing or two."

"Of course, Detective," said Weller. "We are aware of the details exchanged earlier, and are comfortable with them".

"Well, thank you so much Mr. Weller," said DJ, stifling the urge to giggle. "No need to be officious. I'm just trying to gather background on a murder victim, a man in your employ, who was killed on my beat.

"Understood, Detective."

"I'm looking for facts that might help us further our investigation. I don't care about any of that crazy media speculation. Cool?"

"Very good Detective," said Weller, straightening the readers on the end of his nose. "Anything we can do to help. At Tucker, our people are our number one resource."

"Yes, I believe I've heard that before. Very admirable." *Good grief, they must have the damn company mission statement tattooed on their asses.* "First off, thanks again for expediting Mr. Pernell's fingerprints to us."

"No problem" answered Weller.

"Yes, no problem" echoed Dillard, a bit meekly.

DJ noticed palpable tension between Weller and Dillard. *HR must've hammered her for speaking to me earlier without them being present.*

Looking directly at Sharon Dillard, DJ asked "Any further thoughts on Mr. Pernell's celebratory habits after completing business projects?"

The answer came in Weller's voice. "No Detective. What Ms. Dillard told you earlier was accurate. He was the type of fellow who celebrated his achievements with joy but always gave the appearance of a man in full control. As a company, we cannot be responsible for unforeseen individual actions."

There's the old cover-your-ass corporate "not responsible" line. This is going nowhere fast. "Thanks again, Mr. Weller".

DJ tried Dillard again. "Sharon, do you have any names to add to your list of Mr. Pernell's closest co-workers?"

After a furtive glance in Weller's direction, Dillard found her voice. "No other names, Detective. The list you have is accurate."

After another glance at Weller, Dillard continued with a clearly rehearsed line. "You should know that Ray worked across departments, with many people. He had numerous acquaintances both inside and out of TEM. And we clearly cannot be responsible for any of Ray's associates who were not employees of Tucker."

Another corporate "not responsible" line. These two must've been up all night rehearsing! "How would you characterize the stress level of Mr. Pernell's daily job responsibilities?"

Dillard seemed caught a bit off-guard as if HR hadn't briefed her on this subject. "Well, just the regular amount of stress that comes with his job, I guess. He always seemed to handle it very well."

"Would you be surprised if Mr. Pernell had been seeking counseling to deal with work-related stress?"

Weller spoke up. "Detective, we have no knowledge of that and I'd prefer that Ms. Dillard not speculate."

You'd clearly prefer that Ms. Dillard not speak at all. Ignoring Weller, DJ asked, "Sharon, did large sums of money pass through Mr. Pernell to vendors and other creative partners?"

Weller interrupted again. "What's your point here Detective? Are you looking for some sort of financial motivation for Ray's behavior?"

What a pain in the ass this guy is! DJ spoke sternly. "Mr. Weller. We may not have the same agenda here. But I need to ask all relevant questions. And when it comes to homicide, nothing's off the table, especially large sums of money. So I ask again, was Mr. Pernell responsible for large sums of money?"

Dillard spoke carefully while eyeballing Weller. "Ray negotiated contracts involving large sums of money ranging from a couple hundred thousand into seven figures. But he was never directly involved in the exchange of funds. Tucker's Accounting and Legal Departments take care of those things."

"What were those contracts for?"

"Some were relative to music rights. Some were about studio and location set construction. But the majority of Ray's deals centered around design and animation packages."

"Would ThickBrickk qualify as one of those vendors?"

"Yes. Along with many others."

"Thank you, Sharon."

Weller jumped in. "Detective, we have redundancies in place that track all financial transactions with our vendors. I'm confident that nothing relating to Tucker's finances would be involved in Mr. Pernell's unfortunate demise."

"I'm sure you are correct Mr. Weller." *That was just me screwing with you, and enjoying it.* "Again, I must explore all avenues. Sharon, you told me earlier that you had no knowledge of Mr. Pernell belonging to any organizations that might promote unusual activities. Is that still your opinion?"

Dillard glanced down at the table as Richard Weller answered in a robotic tone. "Yes Detective, we have no opinion on any outside organizations to which Mr. Pernell belonged. That is none of our business, nor our responsibility."

That's three "no responsibilities"! The corporate trifecta!

DJ stared at Weller. "Mr. Weller, the less you help me, the longer Tucker will continue to receive negative publicity. I'm guessing your senior management is not enjoying all this public speculation."

Weller stared at DJ for a moment. "Again Detective, any organizations that Mr. Pernell belonged to outside of TEM, are none of our business."

Could you be more of a dick? "As you wish, Mr. Weller. Sharon told me recently that the Pernells would occasionally visit the Connecticut casinos. I'm curious about Ray's gambling habits."

Weller answered again. "What Ms. Dillard told you is that Mia and Ray Pernell attended a concert or two at Mohegan Sun, but that Ray was not a regular gambler, to her knowledge."

"Yes, so she did" answered DJ. "Thanks for confirming that for me, Mr. Weller." *No doubt you had your ass kicked regularly in high school.*

Staring at Weller's 1950's flattop crew cut, DJ said "One more thing and I'll get out of your hair. I'm curious to know if Mr. Pernell was taking advantage of the wonderful employee counseling that Tucker offers. Certainly, HR would know if Mr. Pernell was utilizing a company-supplied counselor."

Weller's voice remained flat. "Not true, Detective. Employees don't notify management. Their decision to seek counseling is kept in the strictest confidence."

"I don't suppose that I could get a list of those available counselors?" asked DJ.

"No Detective. That is against company policy."

"Just thought I'd ask." *Here's a little something to chew on.* "There's always the option of a court order."

Weller frowned.

"Anyway, thanks, Mr. Weller. And thank you, Sharon. Do either of you have any questions for me?"

Dillard asked. "How's the investigation going?"

"Nothing to share yet." Then staring at Weller, DJ added "We've made inroads in some areas where we've found cooperative people willing to tell us what they know." *Unlike you corporate shills.*

Weller's face puckered as if he'd bit into a lemon. Pulling himself together, Weller said, "Detective, this isn't a question so much as an iteration of Tucker policy."

"What else do you need to tell me, Mr. Weller?" *Do you know I'm carrying a gun?*

"The list of five Tucker employees which you received from Ms. Dillard is strictly confidential."

"Of course" replied DJ.

"And company policy dictates that a member of Tucker HR must be present if and when you interview any of those employees."

"Understood," said DJ, rising to his feet and glancing at his watch. "If there's nothing else, I've gotta get going. Thanks again for your time." *Don't want to be late to meet the five people you just told me not to meet.*

Dillard said "Bye Detective" while Weller said "Thank you, Detective. Security will escort you to the elevator."

Glancing at his watch, DJ saw that he only had 15 minutes until he was due at O'Finsky's where he would meet with Pernell's five pals.

But first, he had a phone call to make.

Chapter 41

"Proof of Aliens Locked Away in White House!" Frank Dorrington was reviewing the cover of "Dishing Dirt", a grocery store tabloid with whom he'd recently done a Zoom interview. The shadowy image of an "alien" filled the front page.

Just below the alien headline, in a smaller box, Frank read the words "TEM Loincloth Murder: Gay-Bashing?".

"Dammit! I'm supposed to be the lead story!"

Opening the tabloid to page four, Frank smiled. He saw a two-page spread with an "Exclusive" banner slashed across the top left corner. The giant headline read "TEM Exec. Murdered in Bizarre Loincloth Hate Crime!" The entire two-page spread was printed over a ghosted background of the now-infamous photo.

Racing through the copy, Frank found himself referenced several times, always with a different title. He was referred to as Ray's "close friend, best pal, golf buddy" and his personal favorite: "confidential cohort".

Frank hoped that additional media outlets would continue to seek his input, now that he was identified as Ray's "confidential cohort". He desperately needed the money to keep Stanley at bay and was planning on tripling his interview fee.

The tabloid article was filled with carefully worded statements about what Ray "may have" been doing and what type of secrets that Ray "must have" been keeping. Reading the final paragraph, Frank was amazed by the copy: "According to Dorrington, Pernell's confidential cohort, the victim had many quirks, which he kept secret from his family and his bosses at TEM. Those quirks may have included an affinity for opioids and alcohol, a secret lifestyle which included dressing in bizarre outfits, and a constant seeking of sexual gratification."

Frank mused out loud. "I didn't say that. These guys have zero regard for the truth. But they said it, I didn't. Perfect!"

Tossing the tabloid on the coffee table, he picked up a food container, and dug into some vegetable fried rice.

His cellphone chirped, signifying an incoming call to his law office. Frank answered using an altered voice. "You've reached the law offices of Frank Dorrington. How may I direct your call?"

"Hello. This is Detective DJ Harland with the San Francisco police department. Is Frank Dorrington available?"

"One moment please," said Frank in his fake voice, putting the call on hold.

After a professional length pause of about 30 seconds, Frank returned to the line and spoke more assertively. "This is Frank Dorrington. To whom am I speaking?"

"Hello, Mr. Dorrington." *And your fake assistant.* "This is Detective Harland, with the San Francisco police department. I'm investigating the Ray Pernell homicide and I'd like to spend a few minutes with you to gather some background. Would you be available for a conversation with me this Friday, any time before 3 p.m. Eastern time."

"Hello Detective. Of course, I want to help in any possible way. Such an awful thing that happened to Ray. Gimme a second to check with my assistant on my schedule for Friday."

"Sure," answered DJ. *Go talk to yourself.*

Frank again placed the call on hold, this time for a full 60 seconds. Reconnecting, he said "We were able to move a couple things around Detective. I can be available for 30 minutes at 1:30 Eastern. Does that work for you?"

"Yes, it does."

"How do you want to do this Detective? FaceTime, Skype, Zoom?"

"None of the above. How about if I come to your office?"

Frank tried to hide the surprise in his voice. "In person? Are you on the East Coast, Detective?"

Giving away nothing, DJ said. "Just verify the address for me and I'll be at your office at 1:30."

"Unfortunately, we are currently refurbishing our offices" stammered Frank. "Why don't we meet for lunch somewhere near the courthouse?"

"Too bad your office isn't available." *Or is it fake, like your assistant?* "But a restaurant doesn't work for me. How about if I book a conference room at the Hartford Police Department's downtown headquarters?"

Frank had nothing else to offer. "Excellent idea Detective. It's not far from the courthouse. I'll be there at 1:30 on Friday. I apologize for having to rush out at 2 o'clock."

"No problem. Just check with the Desk Sergeant when you arrive. We'll only make a minimal impact on your busy schedule." *Ambulance chasing can be so time-consuming.*

"Appreciate that Detective. I'll see you then."

"Thanks, Mr. Dorrington."

DJ began the short walk to O'Finsky's where he hoped to get some honest input. Neither the TEM executives nor Frank Dorrington had exactly oozed with sincerity.

Chapter 42

Carlos Madrigan was chatting with his co-workers at O'Finsky's. The circular table in the "Sinatra" booth was dotted with four tall mugs of Guinness and a chilled glass of Chardonnay.

"Are you sure this is okay?" asked Tim O'Shea. "HR doesn't want us talking to anyone about Ray."

"I hear you," said Carlos. "But we're not at work and we're not breaking any laws by having a confidential conversation with a Detective. If anyone wants to leave, I'd understand."

No one moved.

"What's he like?" asked Leigh Grayson.

"He's a straight shooter. He's all about the facts, no bullshit."

"Sounds like Jack Webb in Dragnet," said Tim O'Shea.

"Hardly," said Carlos. "Well, maybe if you put Sergeant Friday in a jacket and jeans, changed his skin color, injected some compassion and understanding, and gave him a personality."

Their laughter was interrupted by the Irish brogue of Shauna O'Rourke, a red-haired, green-eyed longtime employee at O'Finsky's. "Everyone, this is Detective Harland."

"Detective! Good to see you again," said Carlos extending his hand.

"You too," said DJ, shaking hands, then grabbing a chair and seating himself on the outer curve of the booth.

"Can I get you something Detective?" asked Shauna.

"The Guinness looks good," said DJ. "And the next round is on me."

"Thanks, Detective," said Carlos. "This is Leigh Grayson and her husband Bill."

DJ nodded "Good to meet you".

"And Tim O'Shea and Mitchell Claudino."

"Thanks for coming."

Carlos continued. "I saw you on the eighth floor this afternoon. I thought I should keep my distance."

"Good call, Carlos," said DJ as he placed his digital recorder on the table. "Does anyone mind that I'm recording this conversation? I'm a lousy note-taker." Heads nodded all around the table. "Okay, cool."

Carlos spoke. "Detective, we're all a bit concerned about speaking with you. As you probably know, HR has asked us not to talk to anyone about Ray."

"Understood," said DJ. *Don't you know that people are the number one resource at Tucker?* "Nothing said here will be attributed to any of you without your prior consent. If you are uncomfortable, please feel free to not participate."

"Thanks, Detective," said Carlos.

"So how was your meeting with Sharon and Richard Weller?" asked O'Shea. "Did they take you into the cone of silence?"

DJ laughed. "Oh yeah. They're all about protecting the TEM brand. Mr. Weller, and his snazzy crew cut, made that clear." Everyone around the table laughed.

Carlos asked. "Any progress on the investigation?"

"We've made some progress, but I can't share any of the details."

Mitchell Claudino spoke. "We just want to understand what the hell happened to our friend."

DJ nodded. "I get it. I think we'll eventually ID the killer. But we gotta understand the motives involved." *I hope you guys could help me with one of those.*

"Motives, plural?" questioned Claudino.

"We're working on the killer's motive," said DJ. "But, I'd love to know Ray's motive."

"Meaning what, Detective?" asked Carlos.

"I'd like to know why Ray left his hotel room, at 3 am, dressed in a loincloth, with no money, phone, or ID."

"We were a bit hammered. But I expected Ray to show up in the lobby on time like he always does." Carlos stared wistfully into his Guinness. "What the hell happened? One minute we're celebrating, the next minute Ray's gone. I just don't get it."

The booth went silent for a few seconds.

DJ broke the silence. "Answering those questions is why I'm here. I need to know more about Mr. Pernell's likes, dislikes, ambitions, and personality traits. That kind of knowledge is essential." *C'mon, you guys gotta have something!*

"Wouldn't Mia be the best source for that kinda stuff?" asked Carlos.

"I'm meeting with her tomorrow. But Mr. Pernell spent a lotta time at work, with all of you. It's not that unusual for someone to be a different person at work than they are at home."

"Unless you work with your spouse" offered Bill Grayson, nodding toward Leigh. "Can't get away with anything!"

"Real funny," said Leigh. "I'll show you a different person when we get home."

DJ pressed on. "Aside from the rare case where spouses work together." *Don't know how you guys do it.* "It's human nature that we behave differently around co-workers than we do with our families. Carlos, let's try again."

"Whadda ya mean?"

"Think back on that night. Did Ray have any conversations with any strangers? Maybe he talked to a server, a bartender, or even a doorman?" *Drug dealers, pimps, whores?*

"I don't remember Ray talking to anyone else, but he could've talked to someone in the men's room or at a bar. I just don't know."

"Did Ray smoke cigarettes?"

"Wow, didn't see that coming," said Carlos. "Not to my knowledge. Any of you guys ever see Ray smoke a cigarette?"

As everyone shook their heads from side to side, Tim O'Shea said "Cigarettes, no. I do know that he once was a pot smoker, if that matters"

"Everything matters until it doesn't" said DJ. "Ok, so we now know that he didn't leave his room to get a pack of smokes. But speaking of weed, could he have hooked up with someone earlier that night and was going back to score?"

"I don't think so," said Carlos. "His pot-smoking days were long gone. Maybe he wanted more alcohol."

"Was Mr. Pernell an aggressive drinker?" DJ asked the group.

"Ray wasn't an aggressive guy" offered Mitchell Claudino. "But if you mean, did he pursue his alcohol aggressively, I'd say that he never turned down a shot or two after having a few beers. Like most of us, he was 'overserved' every once in a while."

DJ had heard that phrase many times. *Overserved....why do drunks always blame the servers?* "How did Mr. Pernell behave when he was, uh, overserved?"

"That's just it," said Carlos. "No matter how much we drank, Ray always seemed to be the most sober."

O'Shea spoke up. "Ray was always our designated driver. He seemed to handle his liquor very well."

DJ resisted the urge to laugh. *Hello! A designated driver is supposed to be a person who is actually sober, not the "least drunk".* Instead, he said, "Is it possible Mr. Pernell thought that he wasn't drunk enough that night, and he left the hotel to go find more booze."

"Possible," said Carlos. "We were both pretty buzzed when we got back to the hotel. But why the outfit?"

"That's the million-dollar question," said DJ. "I'm guessing none of you have ever seen him dress that way."

All 5 heads nodded in agreement.

"Did he belong to any organizations that might have encouraged him to dress like that?"

Carlos chuckled. "Not unless you think St. Joseph's Parish or the Hudson Country Club are unusual groups. Mia will know."

"No doubt. What about work? Did he get along with Sharon Dillard?"

Tim O'Shea answered. "Ray was a great buffer between us and Sharon."

"Ditto," said Bill Grayson, as the others grunted in agreement.

"Any of you ever go to the casino with Mr. Pernell?" asked DJ.

The Graysons looked at each other, then Leigh said. "We did. We went with Ray and Mia to a Bruno Mars show at Mohegan Sun."

"Did Mr. Pernell gamble at all?"

Bill nodded. "Yes. Before the show, Ray and I played 'Let It Ride' for about an hour. Ray quit playing after he lost $200. He said that he worked too hard for his money and didn't want to give any more of it away."

Mitchell Claudino interrupted. "Do you think that Ray's death could be connected to gambling?"

"No idea. People keep secrets and those secrets can sometimes lead us to a solution. How well do you guys know the Pernell family? Anything I might need to know before meeting Mia tomorrow?"

The group fell silent. Finally, Carlos spoke. "Damn Detective, I kinda looked at the Pernells as one of those 'All-American' families."

Tim O'Shea cleared his throat. "Ray and I spent 3 weeks together in South Africa last year. We had plenty of downtime to talk between shoots, over a few beers. He and Mia were not without issues. But it just seemed like normal family stuff. He was thinking about seeing one of those counselors that Tucker provides."

Carlos was surprised. "Was he seeing a counselor?"

"I don't think he ever did" answered Tim.

Everyone looked at DJ, who said "Do any of you know if Mr. Pernell met with a counselor?"

Silence.

DJ turned to O'Shea and asked "What kind of issues did Mr. Pernell have?"

"Family stuff" answered O'Shea. "He regretted that Mia's career had ended once they had Karl. I think Phoebe was struggling in high school."

"What else?"

"Well, I think his biggest issue was the pain of watching his Mom losing her battle with Alzheimer's. That was tough on him."

Bill Grayson offered "For sure. Brutal."

"Round two!" Shauna O'Rourke arrived with more beers and chardonnay for the table.

"I got this round," said DJ handing Shauna a credit card. *Kahuna will love seeing a bar tab on my expense report.*

Looking at O'Shea, DJ said, "Did Ray mention anything else about counseling?" *Like perhaps a counselor's name and number?*

"Not that I can think of."

DJ changed the subject. "Do you guys know Frank Dorrington, Ray's best friend?"

Carlos laughed. "They were far from best friends."

"Say what?"

"Dorrington was married to Mia's best friend, Debbie. So Ray and Frank certainly must've met a couple of times"

"Do you know Dorrington?"

"No. And I don't think Ray knew him very well either. I can't recall Ray ever mentioning his name."

"Why would Dorrington pretend that he and Ray were close?"

Carlos shook his head. "Hell, if I know. Fame, fortune, notoriety? He's a lawyer."

"Sounds like he has an agenda" offered Leigh.

DJ, decided not to share the fact that he would be interviewing Frank on Friday. "If he's lying, it'll catch up with him at some point."

"Sure hope so," said Carlos. "All that bullshit in the media about Ray looking for drugs or sex is a straight-up lie. I knew Ray. Not sure that Dorrington did."

"Understood," said DJ. *Friday's meeting with Dorrington just got more interesting.* "Do any of you know if Mr. Dorrington has been successful in his legal career?" *He sounded like a loser on the phone!*

"Not sure," said Carlos. "But if you're meeting with Mia tomorrow, maybe you should include Debbie Slater. She's the connection between Ray and Frank."

"Gotcha, thanks Carlos," said DJ, not sharing that Slater was already invited.

The conversation at the table then evolved into stories about Ray and all of the work they had done together over the last couple of decades. After a few minutes of wonderful memories, Mitchell Claudino said "Anyone up for a third round?"

"Not me, thanks," said DJ. "Gotta grab dinner and get some sleep. I'm driving up to Hudson tomorrow morning."

"Good grief," said Carlos, "enjoy rush hour on I-95. There's a reason we take the train"

"Yeah. Heard about that mess."

DJ then surprised the group with one last query. "So y'all knew Mr. Pernell better than almost anyone. Bottom line. What do you guys think happened to him that night?"

After a few knowing glances around the table, Leigh answered. "We've talked about this constantly since everything happened. We don't buy the crap that's all over the media. Maybe someone with bad intent was waiting in his room. Maybe he was forced to dress that way to humiliate him. Or maybe he was forced to exit the hotel at gunpoint. We just can't believe that Ray, no matter how drunk he was, would choose to be in public dressed like that."

Sounds of agreement came from around the table.

"Heard that," said DJ, grabbing his recorder and rising to leave. "Thank you all for your time. And, of course, as far as Tucker HR is concerned, this conversation never happened."

Fuck you, Richard Weller!

Chapter 43

Peering out her kitchen window, Mia was pleased to see that the media and protestors were gone, hopefully forever. She poured a tall glass of chardonnay and began assembling dinner. Karl and Ricky were opening a bag of chips. "How many times do I have to tell you two, no snacks before dinner!"

The loud sound surprised her. Her tired senses didn't immediately register what she'd heard. Phoebe burst into the kitchen screaming "Someone's shooting through the window!" Mia yelled at her kids to "get down, under the table!", and she joined them there. Reaching up to the surface of the table, she grabbed her cellphone and punched in 911….after what seemed like two interminable rings, the call was answered: "911, what's your emergency?" Mia shouted; "someone is shooting into our house!" The operator confirmed the address and told her to stay on the line while waiting for the help that was already on the way.

After about 30 seconds of waiting, Mia handed the phone to Phoebe and told all three kids "Stay here. If anything happens, tell the Operator".

"I'm going with you," said Ricky. "Nobody does this to our house."

Despite Mia's protest, Ricky was right behind her as she crept, on all fours, out of the kitchen into the living room. They immediately saw a sizable hole in the front window, encircled by a spider web of cracked glass. On the floor, Mia spotted a baseball-sized rock with a folded piece of paper secured to it by black electrical tape. She inched her way across the shards of shattered glass and grabbed the rock. Mia removed the tape and was horrified to read the contents of the note: "Freaks are not welcome here. Get out or we will get you out"

Ricky exploded. "Those cocksuckers! I will smash anyone who comes near my family! I'm gonna find out who the hell did this and make 'em pay!"

"Ok Ricky," said Mia trying her best to sound calm. "The jerk that did this is long gone. The cops should be here shortly. Go back in the kitchen while I talk to the police."

"I wanna stay here."

"Go!"

A few minutes later, two Hudson police officers arrived, immediately demanding Mia's ID. Once they had determined that she was the homeowner and the originator of the 911 call, they introduced themselves as officers Cavanaugh and Brandt of the Hudson Police Department.

While Officer Cavanaugh talked with Mia, Officer Brandt searched outside the house, finding nothing of significance. Brandt spoke to Mia. "Look, Mrs. Pernell, this was probably just some dumb kids pulling a prank. If anything else happens, please give us a call."

"With all due respect officers, this isn't just a prank. It's an act of intimidation. It's a freakin' attack on my home and my family."

Officer Cavanaugh spoke. "I suggest that you keep your security system engaged at all times. Look, Mrs Pernell, this type of vandalism is usually done by a kid who has some sort of issue with the targeted family. Maybe one of your children had an argument at school."

However, the officers were well aware of the "loincloth murder". Everyone in this zip code, and beyond, knew about it. Speculation about the hidden secrets of Ray Pernell had become all the local rage. Standing outside, leaning against their cruiser, the officers were discussing the case.

Mia stepped outside to look at the damaged window and overheard the two cops chuckling. "..... maybe he was secretly a fashion critic, you know loincloths are coming back in style this year".

Mia's rage boiled over as she ran over and lashed out at the officers. "With no due respect! You don't know shit! How dare you make jokes about my husband and my family! I'm gonna report you two assholes to your Captain!"

"Look, Mrs. Pernell," said Officer Cavanaugh, "We're pretty sure this was an isolated act of vandalism, but please give us a call if anything else occurs." The cops retreated to their patrol car.

Unfortunately, Mia didn't have any good answers to all of the damaging comments, jokes, and assumptions. Sobbing, she covered her face with her hands. "Dammit Ray. What the hell happened to you?"

Chapter 44

Carlos had managed to catch the last express train from Grand Central Station to New Haven. The express travel time was significantly less than the "locals" which included multiple stops along the way.

He flopped into an empty row. The familiar swaying of the car and the clackety-clack of the wheels below felt soothing. Looking down to his right, he suddenly felt sick in the pit of his stomach. Staring up at him from the adjacent seat was a discarded copy of "Dishing Dirt". It had been folded open to page four and Carlos could see the first part of a giant headline: "TEM Exec Murdered......" He shoved the tabloid to the floor and kicked it under the seat in front of him.

Staring aimlessly out the window, Carlos had a thought that brightened his mood. Scrolling through his recent calls, he found Debbie Slater's number. He sent a text.

"Hey, Debbie. We met with Detective Harland, from San Francisco, this evening. He's meeting with Mia tomorrow. Maybe you should be there. He had a few questions about Dorrington.

-Carlos"

Checking his watch, he saw it was a little after 10p. "Oh shit, she's probably sleeping," thought Carlos.

Less than a minute later, Carlos' phone chirped.

"Carlos. Good to hear from you. I'll be there tomorrow when Detective Harland visits. So will Mia's parents. Thanks for the heads up. Hope everything is well for you."

"Damn," thought Carlos. "She must think I'm an idiot. Of course, she'd be there." Carlos suddenly had an urge. He sucked in his breath and texted: "Maybe we could get together over coffee soon and talk this through. Love to hear your take on everything that has happened."

As soon as he sent the text, Carlos felt that little heart flutter that comes with asking someone for a first date. No doubt a polite rejection would soon be forthcoming. His phone chirped and he picked it up, fully expecting a "no" from Debbie. He saw only three words:

"I'd like that".

Closing his eyes, Carlos smiled and whispered "I'd like that too."

Chapter 45

DJ was creeping along the gridlocked Cross Bronx Expressway, hoping to soon connect with I-95 to Connecticut. *Weren't we supposed to be flying around on jetpacks by now?* His iPhone buzzed in its holder showing "Levi Sharpe" on the screen.

"Damn Levi, you're up early. Ain't it like 5am back there?" *Did Louise finally kick your ass out?*

"Not up early my brother. Still up! Been up all night."

"Why? What the hell you been up to?"

"Couldn't sleep last night. I thought I'd give your Smythville Hotel back alley a try."

"My man! Any luck?"

"I didn't find any eyewitnesses to the Pernell homicide, but I've got two new sources for 'gently used' MD 20/20 and a standing offer to walk my dog in exchange for a bottle of tequila."

DJ laughed. "Quite a group of dudes hanging out back there. I still think one of them might've seen something that night." *And you ain't got a damn dog!*

"That's a possibility," said Sharpe. "But, I wanted to get with you this morning about a couple other things."

"Hit me."

"First, The Smythville wants us to release the Pernell room. You got any reason to hang on to it?"

"Good question. I've been thinking about our greasy snitch, Johnny G."

"He's a guest at County now," said Sharpe. "Couldn't make bail."

"He didn't bullshit us about 'Capone's' claim that he was gonna off somebody the next day, right?"

"True"

"And Capone, aka Lester Hollowell, got himself killed trying to do exactly that. So should we consider anything else Johnny said to be true?" *Even though the source is a professional liar.*

"Like what?"

DJ thought for a second. "Maybe his statement that Hollowell killed a gay man, who claimed to have 'woke up naked pissing in a corner', is actually true."

"Gotcha. And you want Pernell's room to be checked for urine in the corners, right?"

"Couldn't hurt. If we find any traces, then we'll at least know that Johnny G was sharing what he thought to be true."

"And we'll also know that Hollowell was speaking truth, and may actually be our murderer."

"Exactly," said DJ. "Too bad Hollowell's brains are splattered all over that car. It may be a reach, but I want the car searched for any signs of Pernell. Blood, hair, urine, anything."

"Of course," said Sharpe. "Oakland PD still has it. Gotta be a disgusting mess."

"Let's have them search it." *Better them than us.*

"Roger that. I'll have Chris Hardy reach out to Oakland PD."

"Cool."

"And I'll let the Smythville know that we need the room for another forty-eight. That'll give us time to check the corners for Pernell's urine."

"Thanks, man. What else you got?"

"Amal Ahmadi called me about that caption that was added to our victim's photo online."

"No kiddin'?" said DJ, recalling the 'TEM Exec Freak. - Hate Crime?' wording that was added to Wes Bell's photo of Pernell, and posted on noTrace. "Who did it?" *I wanna talk to him!*

"It ain't about who, more like where," said Sharpe. "He hasn't isolated an individual. The phone call to the Hudson High newspaper was a dead end. A burner phone. But he was able to narrow the geographic location of the noTrace source through whatever back-channel magic those IT guys use."

"Where'd it come from?" *Betting on New York or Connecticut.*

"The southern New England area. Either Connecticut, Rhode Island, or the southern half of Massachusetts. Ahmad said he'll keep trying to narrow it down."

"Damn. Ain't that interesting? How lucky am I that I just happen to be heading into that exact area right now." *If this goddamn traffic ever gets moving!*

"I thought you might like that little nugget."

"It could be a coincidence, but I'm not a big believer in coincidence."

"Police work 101," said Sharpe

"It could be an unhappy ex-TEM employee who decided to shit on their shiny reputation. Or someone who's got a bone to pick with Pernell. Let's keep this little detail between us."

"You got it," said Sharpe. "Not even sure it means anything to our investigation."

We gotta figure that out. "Thanks for the download. Go home and get some rest. Appreciate you."

"You too brother. Keep me in the loop."

Chapter 46

"Those are the exact measurements of the window." Mia was on the phone with a local contractor, inquiring about replacing her smashed front window. "Sure, we'll be here. Okay, thanks. Bye."

Hiroshi and Myoko had been with Mia all morning. "Are they coming out today?" asked Hiroshi.

"Sometime in the next few hours, Dad. Hopefully, they can replace it soon. That duct tape is ugly and just reminds me of the hatred that smashed its way through the glass."

"Hopefully, they can fix it quickly. They're lucky there's no reporters outside to bother them."

"Hope they're gone forever," said Mia. Her phone buzzed. "Hi Debbie. When are you coming over?"

"I'll be there soon, Mia. Have you seen what's going on at Bushnell Park in Hartford?"

"No."

"Turn on the local news. Channel 30."

" Mom, turn on the TV. Channel 30."

Debbie continued. "It's a demonstration by 'All Loves Matter', the LGBTQ rights group. They are demanding tougher penalties for hate crimes. They even mentioned the so-called 'Loincloth Murder'."

"What? That's crazy, but it explains where the media went," said Mia. "We'll take a look. C'mon over when you're ready."

"On the way."

Mia and her parents watched the ALM speaker passionately delivering her message. The on-screen graphic identified her as "Belinda Benson - Activist / All Loves Matter".

"When will the hatred stop? Why must we be victimized because of who we love? The Loincloth Murder is yet another example of unjustified violence based on hateful prejudice. The penalties must be tougher for all hate crimes against minorities, immigrants, members of the LGBTQ+ community, religious groups, and all the other victims of the outrageous prejudices that are surfacing in America. Today's event is just one small part of our nationwide movement to bring these hideous hate crimes out into the bright light of national scrutiny."

The crowd chanted: "All Loves Matter, All Loves Matter, All Loves Matter!"

The TV station cut back to the anchors in the studio. "You've been watching the 'live' All Loves Matter rally from Hartford's Bushnell Park. The San Francisco murder of TEM Executive Ray Pernell, a resident of Hudson, has brought new focus to the increasing number of hate crimes here in Connecticut and beyond."

Mia muted the sound on the TV. "I just don't know what to say or think anymore."

Hiroshi spoke. "Hate crimes should be punished severely. We've experienced our share of prejudice since we came to America. Sometimes it is subtle, sometimes not so much."

"Those moments are so hurtful" echoed Myoko.

"I understand that totally, Mom," said Mia. "I've had my share of Asian abuse. There's a lotta jerks out there. And I'm totally good with tougher penalties for hate crimes. But today, I'm more concerned with how Ray is being portrayed all over the country!"

"You shouldn't pay attention to that stuff dear," said Myoko.

"Can't help it, Mom."

Mia grabbed the remote and flicked off the TV.

Chapter 47

"Turn right, then your destination is on your right."

DJ's GPS had finally delivered him to the Pernell home in Hudson. *Nice neighborhood. Damn, I'm in the wrong business.* He parked behind three other vehicles in the double-wide driveway.

DJ noted all the trappings of an upscale Connecticut neighborhood. His eyes swept across a plush green lawn, framed on one side by perfectly trimmed shrubs and on the other by a long rock wall, the area anchored by a huge maple tree. An antique trellis draped with hanging vines was centered in a wildly colorful flower garden fronting the large brick home. DJ noted the regulation basketball hoop, accompanied by a shorter Nerf hoop, just off to the side of the three-car garage. His attention quickly moved to the crisscrossed duct tape patch on the front bay window, ringed by a haphazard pattern of cracks. He started to walk along the curved brick path when the front door opened and a pretty woman he recognized as Mia greeted him. "Detective Harland, please come in."

DJ extended his hand. "Nice to meet you, Mrs. Pernell."

Mia grasped DJ's hand. "Please, call me Mia." She introduced DJ to her parents and Debbie Slater.

"Can I get you anything Detective?" asked Myoko.

"Water would be great. Thanks." DJ removed his digital recorder from his pocket. "Does anyone mind if I record our conversation?" Hearing no protests, DJ placed his recorder on the coffee table. "Sorry if I'm a bit late. I-95 is packed from New York to New Haven."

"Parking lot," said Hiroshi.

"Sure is" said DJ, looking around the room and making eye contact with each person. "I just first want to tell all of you how sorry I am for your loss. I appreciate your time today."

"Thanks, Detective," said Mia. "It's been difficult, but we're hoping that you can help bring us some closure."

"Unfortunately, closure isn't possible today. The good news is that we are moving forward with the investigation. But, I gotta ask, what happened to your front window?" *Storm damage? Errant baseball?*

"Hate damage."

"Say again?"

"Some idiots decided to try to frighten me and my family. They sent their message by throwing a rock through my window with a threatening note attached."

"You call the Police?"

"Sure did. They came out, asked their questions, then dismissed it as the act of some misguided kids."

"So, no suspects?"

Mia laughed derisively. "Not unless you include the two officers."

"What does that mean?"

"It means, Detective, that not all cops are as genuine as you. I overheard those two officers mocking Ray and the entire "loincloth" situation."

"I hope you called them out." *Assholes!*

"I did. But they just played it off and left in a hurry. Hudson has a small police department and they, no doubt, look out for one another."

DJ shook his head. "No good cops would approve of that behavior, Mia." *That'd be an instant trip to the Captain's office back home.*

"My entire world is ridiculous these days" lamented Mia. "Do you know about the protests in downtown Hartford today?"

"No, fill me in."

"An LGBTQ group called 'All Loves Matter' is holding a rally there today."

"And….?"

"They are rallying in support of stronger legislation against hate crimes. They're using Ray's death as one example."

"I know that group, All Loves Matter," said DJ. "They're based in San Francisco. They're crusaders for LGBTQ+ rights. Do you know if Belinda Benson was speaking?"

"We only saw her name once, but I believe that is correct. Tall woman, wild salt and pepper curly hair?"

"That's her," said DJ. "She was a big-time DA in San Francisco until she took up this cause." *Wouldn't ever want to be on her bad side!*

"That's all good," said Mia. "But they are saying that Ray was killed simply because someone thought he was gay."

"You can't take that personally, Mia." *The gay community's gotta be fed up with this shit!*

"It sure feels personal."

Glancing at the damaged front window, DJ asked "How are your friends taking all this?"

Debbie answered. "Many of them are being silent. But their silence is deafening."

Mia added "Our closest friends are still good. But, I've gotten some anonymous hateful texts and messages. We've had reporters and protestors in front of our house every day this week. They must all be at that rally today."

"This anti-hate-crime movement is nationwide," said DJ. "Your husband's case is only the latest on their list." *Wish I knew if it actually belonged there.*

Mia nodded. "I'll support any hate crime legislation, but I want to know what happened to Ray, hate crime or not."

"So do we." *Which is why I'm here.*

"So how's your investigation going?"

DJ slowly unscrewed the cap on his bottle of water. "I'm confident that we'll eventually ID whoever did this to your husband. We're working several leads. But the motives may be tougher to determine."

"You said 'motives', plural" noted Hiroshi.

"Exactly, Mr. Higoru. Most of America seems to think that Mr. Pernell was targeted because the killer thought he was seeking gay companionship."

"Not possible," said Mia.

"Understood, Mia. But the killer's motivation doesn't need to be based on truth. Seeing your husband dressed like that could've been all the motivation a violent gay basher would need." *Wouldn't be the first time.*

"Makes sense," said Hiroshi. "What is the second motivation?"

DJ looked into Mia's eyes. "The second motivation pertains to your husband. It's important to know what motivated him to exit the hotel while dressed like that." *Not a smart fashion choice….*

"Someone else must've forced him to do that" interjected Debbie.

"Possible," said DJ. "But we know that Mr. Pernell was sleeping, or at least trying to sleep, in his room for 18 minutes. His CPAP machine gave us that info."

"Oh God, he loved that thing," said Mia. "Before he got that machine, he couldn't get a decent night's sleep. He got tested, and was diagnosed with moderate sleep apnea."

"Mia" asked DJ. "Do you recall if his sleep apnea was worse on nights when he consumed alcohol?"

"Not sure. Why?"

"We'd like to understand why he removed his CPAP mask after only 18 minutes. If having a lot of alcohol in his system made wearing the mask more difficult, then that could explain why he took it off."

"I want to help Detective, but I don't know how to answer that."

"Any history with Mr. Pernell of confusion or forgetfulness when he was inebriated?"

Mia paused, then said, "Not to my knowledge".

DJ noticed a brief, nearly imperceptible wince in Mia's face. *She's holding something back.* Scanning the room, DJ said "Most of America thinks Mr. Pernell was killed because of how he was dressed and what he was looking for. What do you guys think?"

"That bullshit has been pushed by my ex, Frank Dorrington," said Debbie. "He doesn't care who he hurts. He's using Ray's death to gain fame and money."

"I'll get to him," said DJ. "But for the moment, let's stick to what you guys think might have happened."

Hiroshi spoke. "I believe he was killed because he had a disagreement with someone that night and it resulted in a late-night confrontation. He was probably forced into that clothing."

DJ nodded. "Definitely a possibility." *But when and why?*

Mia spoke. "Ray would never leave his room without his phone or wallet. That's just not him. Someone must have come to his door and caused all of this to happen."

"I agree with Mia," said Myoko. "Someone must've forced him into this horrible situation."

"Yes, that's another possibility we're considering," said DJ. "What about you Miss Slater? Any thoughts"

"I agree with All Loves Matter," said Debbie.

"What are you talking about?" asked Mia. "They're saying Ray was killed by some gay-hating idiot!"

"Think about it," said Debbie. "if some gay-basher saw a 50-ish man in a loincloth, on the streets at 3 am, it's not a stretch to think that some hate-driven violence could occur."

"No doubt," said DJ. *You've just described Hollowell!*

"So what are you thinking?" asked Mia.

"We're making progress, but nothing I can share with you at this time." Turning to Debbie, DJ asked, "Can you fill me in on Frank Dorrington?"

"It's clear he's doing his best to make money off Ray's death, and doesn't care that he is screwing Mia and her family while he's doing it."

DJ nodded. "How about if you start from the beginning?"

"Sorry Detective. Frank and I started dating in college. He was very ambitious. I didn't have much money, but I supported him in every other way while he was going through law school. We got married just before his graduation. His dream was to open his own firm, hire a bunch of terrific lawyers, and live happily ever after, apparently with me and several children to be named later."

"Was his firm successful?" *Highly doubtful.*

"For the first couple of years, Frank nearly made ends meet. He invested a lot of money, but it never really got going. He had to go back to the bank for more money on at least two occasions. After a while, the financial hole just got too deep."

"Did the bank call in their loans?"

"Frank did his best to hold them off. But he wasn't even making payroll. He started going to the casinos to try to get caught up. Instead, he got further behind. We were basically living on my income as a graphic designer."

"Do you know if he is still in financial trouble?" *Gotta be his motivation.*

"No doubt. The last straw for me was a phone call from a man named Stanley who said that Frank owed him big money. Stanley was not shy about causing some serious physical problems for Frank if he didn't pay up."

DJ was listening intently. "Do you have any idea how much money Frank owes this Stanley? *Loan sharks don't generally use a variable interest rate!*

"I don't. But when I asked him who Stanley was, he got angry and told me to mind my own business. I left him right after that and filed for divorce."

"So what's his deal now?"

"I think he does some low-level legal work, but he can't possibly have paid off his debts."

"How close were he and Mr. Pernell?"

Mia spoke up. "That's just it Detective. They weren't close!"

Debbie concurred. "To my knowledge Detective, they met three or four times. Three of those times were when the four of us got together. He didn't seem to click with Ray real well."

"Ray played golf with Frank once," said Mia. "I remember Ray saying 'never again'."

One round is probably all anyone could stand with this jerk. "If that's true, then Mr. Dorrington is lying about how close he was with Mr. Pernell. Why?"

Debbie spoke angrily. "Of course, he's lying. To make the money he desperately needs. And fame has always appealed to him."

"Isn't he afraid of a libel or slander suit?" *Can a law degree disguise stupidity?*

"He's been very careful with his words. He never says the bad stuff about Ray, but he makes suggestive comments which the press then runs with."

"Duly noted," said DJ.

Debbie continued. "And when someone pins him down on something specific about Ray, he falls back on the 'confidential conversation' excuse."

"To your knowledge, has Dorrington ever had any business or social ties in San Francisco?"

Wrinkling her brow, Debbie thought for a second. "Nothing I can think of."

Looking at Mia, DJ asked, "Is there any chance that your husband and Mr. Dorrington were closer friends than you knew?"

"Absolutely not!" said Mia defiantly. "'Ray and Frank just didn't mix well."

Hiroshi had been listening intently. "Will you talk to Mr. Dorrington, Detective?"

Hell yes! "Mr. Dorrington isn't currently a suspect in this case. My job is to find the person who committed the murder. But, Dorrington's claims about Mr. Pernell having hidden "quirks" may be important for us to understand."

"Then you'll talk to Frank?" asked Debbie.

Totally looking forward to tomorrow's conversation! "Probably. Any unusual or secretive behavior by Mr. Pernell that Dorrington can describe may help us understand Mr. Pernell's motive."

"Ray didn't have any unusual behaviors," said Mia.

"Fair enough. But that claim gives me license to talk with Mr. Dorrington, and maybe understand his destructive behavior." *Fear of getting your legs broken by a loan shark is a helluva motivation.*

"Hope you nail his ass to the wall," said Debbie.

Looking at Mia, DJ asked "What are you hearing from Tucker? Are they taking care of you?"

"Exactly the opposite. They're waiting for your investigation to finish before they decide whether or not Ray has violated their goddam morals clause."

"Par for the course. Hope you've got a good attorney."

"We do," said Mia. "It's important to me that Tucker acknowledges that Ray died while working for them."

"Understood," said DJ. "How well do you know Mr. Pernell's co-workers from TEM? Specifically Carlos Madrigan and Sharon Dillard."

"I know them both. Carlos is a close friend. I've met Sharon a few times at TEM functions."

"Any professional rivalry among the three of them?"

"No way. Carlos and Ray were very close. And they respected Sharon as their boss."

"Seems to be the case," said DJ. "I've spoken with Mr. Madrigan, who has a ton of respect for your husband. Seems like a good guy."

"Yes, he is" interjected Debbie, drawing a curious glance from Mia followed by a brief moment of awkward silence.

DJ Placed two of his business cards on the low table and picked up his recorder. "Gotta go. It's been a pleasure to meet all of you."

"Thank you, Detective," said Mia, rising to walk DJ to the door.

Outside, DJ asked "Mia, is there anything else you can think of that might help us figure this out? Anything you may have forgotten to tell me?"

DJ saw a bit of tension in Mia's face as she said "Not that I can think of Detective. But I'll call you if anything comes to mind."

Reaching his hands out to grasp Mia's, DJ replied "Of course. I'll be in touch."

DJ trudged down the front walk. Before getting into his car, he picked up a Nerf basketball and dunked it through the 4-foot hoop. *Lebron's got nothin' on me!*

Chapter 48

The All Loves Matter demonstration in Hartford had Frank Dorrington riveted to his television. He decided against going to Bushnell Park. He didn't want anyone to ask him about his proposal for new hate-crime legislation in Connecticut since he'd written nothing.

Flipping channels, Frank saw news footage of a group of picketers in front of TEM headquarters in New York City. The group was carrying signs including "TEM: trust lost!" and "Not my kids!" One sign featured a drawing of a loincloth.

The Loincloth Murder story was everywhere. The apparently outlandish behavior of a high-profile Tucker Executive had polarized the entire country. TEM was receiving heavy criticism for employing such an "unstable" executive.

Frank's appearance on the nationally syndicated Hammy B show "legitimized" him as an "expert" on the innermost secrets of Ray Pernell. He desperately needed to capitalize on that publicity to generate some significant income.

Stanley's recent text was clearly threatening. "Good to see you on TV. It's great that you'll soon be paying off all of your debts and medical bills." It didn't take a genius to understand the threat inherent in Stanley's mention of "medical bills." Frank knew his time was running short with Stanley, but he didn't have anywhere near 150k. The Emerson Bank of Connecticut (EBC) was also chasing Frank about his two overdue business loans.

Frank noted an email from Dishing Dirt, the first tabloid to interview him about Ray Pernell. It was from Linda Piper, the Editor-in-Chief at DD, who had originated the "Loincloth Murder" label.

"Mr. Dorrington,

Your interview with us ignited national interest in the Loincloth Murder. Now is the time to share everything you know about your friend's innermost quirks. The light of scrutiny can only help others who face similar issues. We're offering you twenty thousand dollars for any new factual insight into Mr. Pernell.

Please respond asap. Stories like these tend to quickly fall out of favor with the public. If you talk to us today, we can get the story into Monday's print edition.

Best,

Linda Piper

Editor in Chief - Dishing Dirt "

Frank's eyes kept returning to two words: "twenty thousand". He briefly felt his conscience tugging at him, somewhere deep in the back of his mind. But hadn't Linda Piper just written that he "could only help others who face similar issues"? That thought was accompanied by a mental image of Stanley, and the opportunity to appease him with a quick 20k.

Frank immediately replied to Piper, demanding 30k in exchange for additional "exclusive information".

After sending that email, Frank walked to his refrigerator to grab a beer. Hearing his apartment door open, he spun around to see the outline of Stanley standing in the doorway.

"How did you?.... That door was locked" stammered Frank.

"Oops, guess I must have a key. I'm here for your overdue payment. I know you've been making some bank. Saw you on Hammy B, Frank. You're an excellent liar on TV, but I don't believe a fucking word you say."

Frank rushed toward his bedroom door and received a shoulder in his midsection which sent him skidding across his coffee table, crashing onto the floor.

Stepping forward, Stanley jammed a polished, size thirteen, black wing-tip shoe onto Frank's neck. "Don't be an idiot. Cash now!"

Gasping for air, with both hands wrapped around Stanley's ankle, Frank managed to push out a few words. "Have some now….big payday….today."

Stanley lifted his foot. "Talk!"

Frank pulled himself up into a sitting position against the front of his well-worn couch. Rubbing his neck, he said "I can write you a check for five thousand now. I'm earning another twenty thousand this evening."

"How?"

"Got an interview with Dishing Dirt. They are paying me 20 thousand. I'll get it in a couple days."

Stanley laughed. "My favorite newspaper! If only I could believe you, Frank. You'd sell your goddam soul to the devil if he didn't already have it."

"It's true. I can show you the email!"

"Tell you what Frank. Write me that check for five thousand. Make it out to 'cash'. That'll cover your interest for this week. I'll be expecting that twenty-thousand within two days. Then we'll discuss the additional hundred-thirty grand that you owe me."

Frank slowly pulled himself to his feet and shuffled to his kitchen with Stanley carefully eyeing him. He pulled open the silverware drawer, reached under the tray, and removed his checkbook.

"Nice hiding place. Guess you can't be too careful. Lotta bad elements hanging out in this shitty neighborhood."

Frank wrote the check and reached out to hand it to Stanley, who grabbed the check, and then snatched Frank's left arm and quickly pivoted, now holding Frank's arm pinned under his own.

"What're you doing?" yelled Frank.

"This five thousand at-a-time bullshit ain't gonna fly Frank. I expect twenty thousand within two days, and the hundred-thirty grand soon after. I told you not to fuck me on this." Stanley grabbed the little finger on Frank's trapped hand and yanked it. There was an audible pop and a cracking sound as Frank's finger and ligaments were torn apart.

Frank howled in pain. "Fuck, fuck, fuck!" Holding up his hand, he saw his little finger pointing out from his hand at a ninety-degree angle. "Dammit! Fuck!"

Stanley spoke in a low calm tone. "Just a little something to remind you that I ain't kidding, Frank. Next time it'll be much more than a finger. Now go make some money." Stanley calmly turned and walked out the door.

Moaning loudly, Frank kicked the door closed behind Stanley and headed to the freezer for ice.

Chapter 49

 Linda Piper stood up from her desk in Las Vegas and stepped onto her balcony overlooking Fremont Street. Directly above her, the blocks-long LED ceiling screen was running some of its perpetual motion, and four zip-liners zoomed by. To her right, she could see the gleaming Circa Hotel anchoring the end of the block. Piper's eyes swept across the remaining hotels on pedestrian-filled Fremont. The Golden Gate, Golden Nugget, and Four Queens stood proudly as reminders of the rat-pack glory days in old-world Vegas.

Piper was joined on the balcony by Gordon Dempster, her long-time pal and trusted Senior Editor.

"What's up, boss?"

"This Dorrington idiot thinks he's holding us up for a huge ransom on the Loincloth Story," said Piper

"What'd he ask for?"

"Thirty thousand."

"Guess he doesn't realize we've paid three times that for stories like his."

"Exactly Gordie. And we're gonna keep it that way."

"Of course. He got anything new?"

"If he doesn't, he'll make it up."

"SOP. As long as he says it, we have someone to attribute it to."

"Exactly," said Piper. "Hold Monday's front page until we talk to him."

"Website too?"

"Yes. And if he gives us some new stuff, we'll drop a few nuggets on the website before blasting it out in print on Monday."

"Gotcha boss. I'll have Spike work up some fresh artwork for both print and online."

"Great. Wanna join me when I talk to Dorrington?"

"Love to. You expecting big things?"

"Hopefully. He sounds desperate. I want to blow this thing out if he gives us anything new."

"Roger boss."

Piper quickly sent a "final" offer of 25k to Frank Dorrington, contingent on a conversation before the end of the day.

———-

Despite the throbbing pain in his swollen hand, Frank was thrilled. 25k! He couldn't believe they folded so easily. He would've done it for less. Frank reviewed the attached standard release form, then electronically signed and returned it.

He added "Done deal. I can do 8 pm ET tonight. Send me the video conference info."

Chapter 50

Following Detective Harland's departure, Mia rejoined her parents and Debbie in the living room. "Well, whatta you think?"

Her Dad spoke first. "Detective Harland seems confident that he'll find the killer."

"Sounds like it, Dad. I just wish I knew what he was thinking."

"The police never want anyone to know what they're thinking until they've gathered all the facts and made the correct assessment of the situation."

"Oh Hiro," said Myoko. "I think you watch too many police dramas on TV."

Mia laughed. "Good one Mom."

"We've gotta run a few errands," said Myoko. "Okay if we come back later, after the kids get home? We can bring dinner."

"Sure Mom. You know what they like."

"Great. Back soon."

Debbie was following Mia's parents to the door when Mia hooked her by the arm saying "Not so fast my friend".

"Sorry, I really can't stay," said Debbie. "I've got some work that's due by the end of the day."

"I'm sure you do, but first you need to spill."

"About what?"

"I noticed how quick you were to compliment Carlos when we were talking to Detective Harland. What's the deal?"

"No deal. Remember, it was Carlos who called me when Ray first went missing. And I was the one who told him the awful news."

"And?" asked Mia

"And nothing."

"Bullshit. Tell me what's going on. C'mon Debbie, this is me. I'm the one who thought you guys would make a good couple. Spread a little joy into my life, will ya?"

"Okay, but it's really nothing."

"Did you talk to him at the funeral?"

"No, But I certainly did notice how handsome and stylish he is."

"Exactly! I knew you'd like his look. I mean, who dresses like that for a funeral and pulls it off?" said Mia, referring to Carlos' perfectly pressed linen jacket, collarless dress shirt, and khakis.

"Of course I noticed. He dresses like I would dress if I were a guy, if that makes any sense. And he's handsome."

"He sure is."

"But it was more than that. I loved the way he spoke about his relationship with Ray, and how well they worked together."

Mia sighed. "They were a great team. But let's get back to you. Have you been spending time with Carlos?"

"Uh no, not quite. But he did invite me to join him for a cup of coffee to talk about all that has happened."

"I knew it! You two are so perfect for each other!"

"Whoa! Pump the brakes, Mia. It's just coffee."

"When are you two having 'coffee'?" asked Mia, making air quotes for the word "coffee".

"Sometime in the next couple of days. Don't get too excited. It's just a casual conversation."

"Sure it is. Next time it'll be happy hour cocktails. Then an elegant dinner. Then maybe a weekend at some fancy getaway on Block Island."

Debbie laughed. "Geez. You've got it all figured out! I don't have to do anything."

"Just be you. There's not a man alive that could resist your beauty, charms, and intelligence."

"You oughtta be my agent. OK, you've browbeaten a confession out of me. Can I go now? I do have a project to finish within the next couple of hours."

"Sorry. I'm just so excited for you. Let me know how the coffee conversation goes. I know it'll be great."

"Keep your expectations realistic," said Debbie, as she headed out the door. Mia thought she noticed a little extra spring in Debbie's steps.

Chapter 51

Vera Eden and Detective Harland exchanged greetings at the Hudson Police Department.

"Can I get you anything?" asked Eden.

"I'm good. I'll keep this brief."

Steering DJ into a conference room, Eden said "I'm not sure that I can be of much help, Detective. But, I'm willing to try."

"Great. So walk me through your connection with the Pernells."

"Once your department had made the positive ID of Mr. Pernell, we were sent to the Pernell house to deliver the news."

"Tough gig."

"I was sent with Officer Nate McKane. As soon as Mia Pernell opened the door, she collapsed and vomited. She knew why we were there. Officer McKane finished his official notification inside the home, then left."

"Anyone else home?"

"Mia's friend, Debbie Slater, arrived right after we did."

"Did Mrs. Pernell's reaction feel genuine?"

"Absolutely, Detective. I'd stake my career on it."

"Have you seen much of her since then?"

"A few times. This case came with some unique challenges."

"Like?"

"All the crazy public speculation about what Mr. Pernell may have been doing that night."

"How's Mia handling all this?" *Besides lying to me a few minutes ago.*

"It's been tough. Mia's house has been vandalized, she gets threats, and some of her friends have disappeared."

"That sucks."

"She's also had a falling out with her church, and her kids are getting some kickback at school. Her oldest, Phoebe, is really struggling. And that awful man, Frank Dorrington, has been stirring the pot."

DJ nodded. "Debbie Slater's ex-husband."

"Yeah. He thinks he's clever. He doesn't care about the pain he's causing Mia's family."

Not clever enough. "Guys like that eventually get what's coming to them. What about Ray Pernell? Any insight into his character?"

"He was a loving husband and father who was also a highly respected executive at Tucker."

"Apparently, he enjoyed his alcohol."

"Yes, that seems to be the case. Mia told me that her husband was always careful about his drinking. As you know, they rented a limo on the night of his death."

Why does everyone keep telling me that? Does St. Peter give free passes to limo riders at the pearly gates? "It seems like he went to great measures to protect his drinking."

"Agreed. But it's difficult to extrapolate much from that" said Eden.

"Give it a shot."

"Ray was very detail oriented, perhaps even a bit anal, so planning the details of his drinking was inherent in his personality. It doesn't necessarily indicate a deeper problem."

Doesn't rule it out, either. "Fair enough. What about Mia? Does she drink?"

"I would have to say that a glass of wine is never too far from her reach."

"What about drugs?"

"None that I'm aware of."

DJ looked into Eden's eyes. "What do you think happened to Ray Pernell?"

"I think he probably ran into some bad people that night, and that somehow came back to him in an awful way. Maybe his killers dressed him in that outfit just to embarrass him or send some kind of message."

"Thanks, Vera. Can I ask you a confidential question?"

"Of course, Detective".

"Has Mia mentioned the misbehavior of the two cops who investigated the window vandalism at her home?" *Morons!*

"Yes, she has. Embarrassing."

"Has anything been done about it?"

"Well, now it's time for me to ask for your confidentiality."

"Sure, go ahead," said DJ. *My fingers are crossed, just in case.*

"After Mia told me about the comments from those two cops, I decided to inform our Chief."

"Go on." *I like where this is going....*

"The Chief promised that disciplinary action would be taken, but that it wouldn't necessarily be visible to anyone else in the department. I can't become known as a snitch".

"You trust the Chief?"

"Guess I gotta. I sleep with him."

DJ raised an eyebrow. *If I'd done that, I'd be Commissioner by now!*

Eden smiled. "He's my husband."

"Oh, makes sense."

"Everyone on the force knows we are married, but I certainly don't want it to get out that I told him about Brandt and Cavanaugh."

"You did the right thing. Your secret is safe with me."

"Thanks, Detective. If you need anything else, please reach out."

"Will do."

Chapter 52

Adjusting to the 9th grade hadn't been easy for Ricky Pernell. Moving from his cozy public middle school to the much larger Grant Prep high school was a challenge. He'd developed a circle of friends, mainly from the wrestling team.

Since his father's death, school had become uncomfortable for Ricky. There were so many social media posts. Many expressed condolences, but more than a few were mocking his father's appearance in that viral photo. Ricky heard the whispers and felt the lingering glances from his classmates. Wrestling practice became his comfort zone. He thought Coach D was sometimes too intense, but better too excessive than not tough enough. Wrestling is not for the weak.

Ricky had excelled in middle school at his weight class of 145 pounds. His parents were proud when he received a partial wrestling scholarship to Grant Prep. His Mom attended his meets whenever possible, and his Dad managed to get to a few when he was not traveling.

After their initial period of stretching, Coach D announced: "We're doing some mixed matches today". It wasn't unusual for kids to practice against teammates who wrestled at a weight a few pounds above or below their own. There was merit in those types of challenges. Coach D barked: "Pernell get in there. Cormier, you join him."

Christopher Cormier, a senior and the defending state champion at 195 pounds answered. "You sure coach? 50 pounds is a lotta difference."

Coach D barked: "Can that shit Chris. Referee's position, Pernell on all fours. And if I get a sense that anyone is not trying their hardest to destroy their opponent, you'll all be running laps until midnight!"

Ricky gave it his best, but Cormier quickly overpowered him and pinned him with vigor. As Ricky pulled himself to his knees, he lashed out, "What the hell was that Coach? What's the fucking point?"

Coach D responded "No one talks to me like that! Bull in the Ring!" Ricky had heard about Bull in the Ring but had never actually seen it. He had to remain in the center of the mat, encircled by his teammates, while the Coach called out individual names. As each individual was called, they had to charge at Ricky with their full effort and most destructive moves, then depart as the next guy attacked. At first, Coach D paused a few seconds between names, but then sped it up and started calling names more quickly. Ricky was in self-defense mode, turtled up, trying to absorb each hit as his teammates came at him in rapid succession. After a couple of interminable minutes, Coach D called it off and sent the wrestlers to their normal workout positions in the gym.

Ricky hurt all over and wanted to cry. But he refused to give Coach D the satisfaction. He lifted himself off the mat and dragged his aching body over to his practice mat where his teammates whispered their apologies.

Coach D's assistant came running from the wrestling office. "What the hell was that all about? You know that shit's illegal….are you trying to get us fired?"

Coach replied: "He'll be fine….Just trying to make sure that he doesn't go down the same faggot path as his old man."

Chapter 53

DJ flicked on the hotel room TV to catch the local news. He saw the familiar face of Belinda Benson speaking at the "All Loves Matter" rally. The news anchor said, "The rally concludes tomorrow with appearances by some of our nation's most prominent proponents of stricter federal hate-crime laws, including Connecticut's own Governor."

DJ tapped "Levi Sharpe" on his phone. "What's up, my friend? How's the East Coast treating you?"

"All good" answered DJ. "What's new on the home front?"

"I think Louise called Liz and they are planning to get dinner together this evening."

"That's great. Thank Louise for me. I don't like leaving Liz home alone." *She'd kick my ass if she ever heard me say that.*

"Will do. Anything new out there?" asked Sharpe.

"Looks like Pernell was a solid dude or a great actor. The idea that he was looking for sex or drugs just doesn't seem to fit, but we can't rule that stuff out."

"Drunk people don't always make sense. It could've been a one-time thing."

"Yeah, of course."

Sharpe thought for a couple of seconds. "But let's assume that he didn't do that. What are we left with?"

"We're left with a good dude whose biggest known issue was that he occasionally enjoyed his booze."

"And?"

"And….on that night, he met some bad people who saw fit to put those rags on him and end his life."

"I hear ya. I think that makes the most sense. How was his family?"

"Devastated and confused." *And under siege…*

"No doubt."

"But I think his wife might be holding something back. She flashed me a couple of nervous tells. I tried again later, but no luck."

"Damn DJ!" said Sharpe proudly "Kahuna would love to hear that. You know how he is about in-person interviews."

"Yeah, I do." *That's why he sent me here!* "How's he holding up?"

"Commissioner Francis is really pushing hard. Captain's doing his best to shield us. But his nuts are in a vise. And it's clear that Tucker has the ear of the Commish."

"TEM is trying to screw Pernell's widow out of her husband's benefits by invoking their morals clause."

"That sucks" answered Sharpe "They don't even know if he willfully violated their damn rules."

"Well, let's just say they are laying the groundwork. They're just waiting for the outcome of our investigation." *That damn Richard Weller seems awfully anxious to screw Ray's family to protect Tucker's image.*

"That sucks," said Sharpe.

"Heard that. Hey, any results from our urine search in the corners of Pernell's hotel room?"

"Our guys were there this morning. It'll be a while before we hear back from Chris Hardy. He said you can only imagine the things that might show up in the analysis of a hotel room."

"Good Lord, I can't begin to imagine," *Gross!*

"Agreed." said Sharpe "We've released the Pernell room back to the hotel. All evidence has been bagged."

"Thanks, man. Gotta make another call. Stay close."

"Talk later."

DJ disconnected and then placed another call.

"Hartford Police. How may I direct your call?"

"Detective Harland for Sergeant Stephan."

"One moment please"

After hearing 10 seconds of some God-awful elevator music, DJ heard a deep, sandpaper voice that could've only been developed by decades of inhaling unfiltered cigarettes. "This is Sergeant Stephan."

"It's Detective Harland from San Francisco PD again." *How about a throat lozenge?*

"Hey, Detective. You're all set for tomorrow. Come in through the High Street entrance. I'll be at the desk. You've got the interview room from 1-2:30"

"Roger, thanks."

"Quick word of warning, Detective. We've got another rally in Bushnell Park tomorrow. The streets may be locked up."

"Thanks for the tip. I'll be walking over. You guys securing the park?" *Overtime for uniforms!*

Stephan answered "Yeah. Shouldn't be too big of a deal, but we may have a shitload of pedestrians in the area."

"Understood. Appreciate you, Sergeant." *How about some hot chicken soup for that throat?*

Chapter 54

Walking down the hallway, Mia saw a backpack on Phoebe's bed with some clothes scattered around. Tapping on the doorframe, Mia asked: "Are you going somewhere?"

Phoebe looked at Mia, her eyes red and cheeks moist. "Not tonight. I'm going to Amy's after school tomorrow to stay with her for the weekend. I'll be home Sunday night or Monday after school."

"Are her parents good with you staying a couple nights?"

"Geez, Mom. We do sleepovers all the time. What's the big freakin' deal? Call 'em if you don't believe me."

"Of course I believe you honey. It'll be good for you to hang out with Amy and talk things through."

Phoebe said "Yeah, sure" and continued stuffing her backpack.

"I know you probably don't want to hear this, but Vera Eden has recommended a young woman for you to talk to. Someone who might bring a fresh point of view to all the shit that's been happening. Her name is Shelby Moseley and her office is…"

Phoebe interrupted in a loud voice. "You think a damn shrink is going to help make all of this go away? Why the hell would I share anything important with someone I've never met? That's the stupidest thing I ever heard!"

"Honey, I just want to help. I know it seems like your world is crashing down, but I promise you that this is only temporary. There is light at the end of the tunnel. I just want you….."

"You want me to do what? Cheer up? OK, I'm happy! See me smiling? Now please leave me alone!"

"Damn it Phoebs! You need to understand that your future is long and bright. As bad as things feel now, this stuff will pass."

"Fine!" snapped Phoebe. "If it'll make you leave me alone, you can book me to see your shrink friend next week." She then stalked past her Mom and into the hallway bathroom, slamming the door behind her.

Thinking better of pursuing the conversation any further, Mia headed downstairs. Plopping onto the couch, she flicked on the TV. She saw more coverage of the rally that took place in Bushnell Park earlier that day.

She heard the refrigerator door close in the kitchen. "Is that you Ricky? I didn't hear you come in."

"Yes, it's me. You didn't hear me come in because you and Phoebe were screaming at each other upstairs."

Walking into the kitchen, Mia said "We weren't screaming, we were just……what the hell happened to you?"

Ricky was applying an ice pack to the left side of his face and eye.

"Nothing Mom. Wrestling is a tough sport. Sometimes we get banged up."

"Let me see." Mia pulled the icepack away from Ricky's face. "That's some pretty nasty swelling around your eye. Can you see ok?"

"Yes, Mom. I'm fine. It'll be fine. Everything's fine!"

"That's a lot of 'fines' Ricky. Maybe we should have Doctor Berman take a look at that eye."

"No Mom! I'm not a baby. I can handle it!" Ricky rushed out of the kitchen and headed up to his room, leaving Mia alone in the kitchen with her thoughts.

Chapter 55

The throbbing was killing Frank. He'd spent the last couple of hours icing his mangled little finger which he'd taped to his ring finger.

Frank knew that he had to "reveal" something new about Ray to earn his cash and land on the front page of Dishing Dirt. He knew the creative minds at DD would extrapolate whatever they wanted from his words, while he retained plausible deniability.

Purposely opening his laptop 5 minutes late, he sat in front of his seldom-used collection of law books. Joining the video conference, he saw two other participants on the screen.

"Hello, Mr. Dorrington. May we call you Frank?" asked Linda Piper.

"Of course. And what should I call you two?"

"I'm Linda Piper, Editor-in-Chief at Dishing Dirt. Please call me Linda. And you can see Gordon Dempster, our Senior Editor. He answers to Gordie."

"OK great, Linda and Gordie. Sorry, I'm late. Got tied up with a deposition this afternoon."

"No problem Frank," said Piper.

Frank nodded. "I just need to know that you're good with my electronic signature on the release".

"All good," said Piper. "I've returned a fully executed copy to you via email. After this interview, our accounting department will deposit $25,000 directly into your account, assuming you give us something newsworthy."

"Great. I also want you to know that I'm recording this interview" lied Frank.

He wasn't surprised to hear Gordie Dempster respond with "So are we".

Piper began. "So Frank, let's start with the big question that America would like to have answered. What was Ray Pernell doing on the streets of San Francisco, at that hour, dressed in that loincloth?"

"Geez Linda. That's the million-dollar question. No one knows the answer to that."

"Tell me what you think."

"It's such a bizarre circumstance. That behavior is not consistent with the Ray that I knew. Maybe his counselor could help us unravel Ray's thought process."

Piper asked "Are you confirming that Pernell was seeing a counselor? Can you share that person's name with us?"

"I believe he was. And no, I don't know her name. But Ray did say she was very helpful. He had a few demons that I don't believe he shared with his family or other friends."

"Like what?"

"Look, I didn't intend to share Ray's issues with anyone. But, as you suggested, maybe somebody with similar problems can benefit by understanding that they are not alone in their battle with depression and drugs."

"Of course," said Piper.

"So Ray was suffering from depression?" asked Dempster.

"Yes. At least that's what he called it."

"What kind of drugs was he using to treat his depression?"

"I don't know if he was taking drugs for depression."

"Okay. So tell us about the drugs you just mentioned."

Frank had carefully prepped for this question. "When we'd hang out, he would occasionally pop a pill into his mouth and put the vial back in his jacket pocket. He told me that it was a prescription for depression. Once, when he'd left his jacket on the back of the barstool while he went to the men's room, I sneaked a peak. It was OxyCodone."

Piper leaned in closer. "OxyCodone is not typically prescribed for depression. Where was he getting it?"

"I'm not sure. But the prescription bottle was full of pills."

"How long was Ray using Oxy?"

Frank had prepped for this question. "Ray tore up his knee on a ski trip to New Hampshire a few years ago. I think he received some Oxy for the pain. Apparently, that never stopped."

"So you're saying he was addicted to opiates?" asked Piper.

"Ray certainly seemed to function normally. But if taking Oxy daily is an addiction, then I guess you could describe it that way."

"Tell us about this counselor he was seeing," said Dempster.

"Don't know much, Gordie. TEM offers anonymous counseling to employees. But Ray did say, more than once, that the TEM counseling was a lifesaver."

"Are you sure that he never mentioned the counselor's name?"

"No, he didn't. It was a female, but that's all I know."

"How often did you and Ray get together?" asked Piper

"Maybe once every couple of weeks. Ray always had a lot on his mind."

"Like what?"

"Some of it work-related, some family stuff. But our best conversations were when we'd just shoot the shit and try to solve all of the problems in the world."

Piper spoke, "Did you guys have a special meeting place?"

"Usually in bars or restaurants, away from family and friends. We also played golf. I kinda felt like his alternate family, as if he were cheating on his wife and kids."

"What places did you guys frequent, Frank?"

"Well, one place was in Bristol.....called Preacher's. Kind of a pool hall type of place." lied Frank. "We always grabbed a booth in the back to stay as invisible as possible."

"Did you guys drink a lot when you got together?"

"I'm not sure how to define 'a lot', but we we sometimes had a couple shots with our beers. Ray would always outdo me on the shots."

"Would you say that Ray liked his booze?" asked Piper.

"Yes. He never was shy about ordering another round."

"Did either of you get a DUI after one of these episodes?"

"I never did. I can't speak for Ray, but he never mentioned one."

Piper changed the subject."Was Pernell happy at Tucker? Maybe their family image didn't allow for full, free creative expression."

Frank paused. "That could be true. But overall, I believe he was happy there."

Dempster asked the next question. "Did Ray belong to any groups that might encourage him to dress in bizarre outfits?"

"None that I know of."

"Frank," said Piper sternly. "I'm not sure you're giving me my money's worth here."

"I only know what I know."

Piper replied "America is trying to understand what Mr. Pernell was doing that night. Alcohol, Oxy, depression? All of those can cause aberrant behavior. But why dress like that? What the hell was he doing? There's gotta be more"

Frank had wrestled with whether or not to drop this next false bomb. He unconsciously stroked the makeshift splint on his throbbing left hand as he considered his desperate need for this 25 thousand dollars.

"I can only think of one other thing."

"What is it?" asked Piper.

"Just before he left for San Francisco, Ray was in Hartford on business and asked me if I was available to grab a couple beers. He suggested we meet at Pat's, a bar in West Hartford."

"So what did he want to discuss?"

"Mostly his upcoming trip to San Francisco."

"What am I missing here, Frank?" asked Piper.

"Well, It wasn't so much what he wanted to discuss, as where."

"Say again?"

"I didn't know it before arriving, but it only took about 5 seconds for me to realize that Pat's is a gay bar. It was happy hour, and crowded."

"Are you telling us Ray was gay? America already seems to think so."

"I never thought so. I asked him why he wanted to meet in this bar, of all places. He said that we'd be free from any prying eyes in there. I remember thinking that we could run into somebody one of us knows in Pat's just as easily as any other bar."

"Did you guys ever meet there again?"

"No. Just that one time. He talked a lot about his upcoming trip to San Francisco. He was also looking forward to seeing his friends from LA."

"Did anyone in Pat's come to your table to greet Ray?"

"No."

Piper asked, "Did you guys leave together?"

"We left at the same time and each headed our way. That was the last time I ever saw Ray."

Gordie spoke. "That day in Pat's, did you see any outfits resembling the loincloth outfit that Ray wore on his final night?"

"There were some wild outfits in there, but I don't recall seeing a loincloth. I'm just not sure."

"Thank you, Frank," said Linda. "We appreciate all that you've shared with us. You should receive your deposit by late tomorrow."

"OK, thank you both, gotta go," said Frank, who then reached for his bottle of cheap vodka, hoping to relieve the pain in his hand.

After downing two shots, Frank mentally reviewed all he had just said, determining that he had, again, cleverly promoted his agenda without any personal legal exposure. And he'd made twenty-five thousand dollars! Now he needed an emergency room to fix his finger, hoping they would accept his medical insurance card which had expired along with his law firm.

In Las Vegas, Gordon Dempster rushed into Linda Piper's office. "You don't need to say it. I'll send a couple of teaser nuggets to the online team, and we'll get busy on the front page through page three for Monday's paper."

"Exactly! Thanks, Gordie. Save the gay bar angle for the paper. Tease the other stuff on the website. And be sure I see an early layout before anything goes too far. This one should be splashy!"

Chapter 56

DJ opened one eye to see 9 am on his beeping bedside alarm clock. *Damn, it's only 6am at home.*

After showering, he settled down with the Hartford Courant newspaper. On the front page was a photo of the crowded Bushnell Park pavilion from yesterday's rally. The headline: "Anti-Hate Rally Concludes Today". DJ was impressed with the lineup of speakers for today's concluding session. Not only was Belinda Benson, from All Loves Matter, chairing again, but the speaker lineup also included a Connecticut Congressman, the Stop AAPI Hate group, the Connecticut Anti-Defamation League, and a recorded message from the Connecticut Governor.

After receiving his room-service breakfast. DJ settled on his bed to watch the local news.

———————

The performance pavilion in Bushnell Park, adjacent to the Connecticut State Capitol Building, was awash in sunshine. The raised pavilion buzzed with workers readying the sound system, large LED screens, and other technical gear for the day's events. The wooden lectern was located center stage, on top of a one-foot podium, backed by twenty chairs for the attending dignitaries. Ten rows of chairs were spread out directly in front of the stage, reserved for selected guests and friends. The vast majority of the crowd would be spread out across the grass utilizing folding chairs, blankets, tents, and whatever other creature comforts folks chose to bring. Facing the stage, about 100 feet back, was a long six-foot high riser for the media. Day two of the rally would be carried live on CPTV, Connecticut Public Television.

———————

DJ spent the remainder of his morning reviewing his recorded conversations at Tucker, O'Finsky's, the Pernell home, and the Hudson Police Department. Ray Pernell was apparently loved and respected by everyone in his life. *What am I missing?*

———

At 11 am, the event organizer stepped to the microphone in Bushnell Park. Her initial comments were about the safety and well-being of those in attendance. On-stage dignitaries were introduced. A video message was played from the Governor of Connecticut, who came out strongly in support of any legislation that would toughen the penalties for hate crimes.

The first speaker stepped to the podium.

———

On the other side of Bushnell Park, next to Lily Pond, a small group of men, dressed in a variety of camouflage clothing, sat chatting. Other men, similarly attired, arrived sporadically and began to form several small clusters. They talked quietly among themselves, drawing no attention to what could be a reunion of military buddies.

———

DJ continued to prep for his conversation with Frank Dorrington while watching the rally on TV. Haruna Higa, the representative from Stop Asian American / Pacific Islander Hate was delivering an impassioned speech about the ever-increasing numbers of hate crimes being perpetrated on Asian Americans, with women being the primary targets. DJ thought back to meeting Myoko and Hiroshi Higoru. They carried themselves with such dignity and grace. *No doubt those people have experienced plenty of anti-Asian prejudice. I can identify with racial abuse.*

———

Mia was watching the Bushnell Park rally on CPTV. She had been brought to tears by Haruna Higa's impassioned plea for tougher hate crime penalties. Mia knew that type of oppression. The side comments, knowing glances and implicit physical threats had always infused the fabric of her life as an Asian American. Lately, she felt things had gotten even worse as America seemed to be coarsening in many regards.

———

On the far side of Bushnell Park, the clusters of camouflaged men had congealed into one loose group of 30-plus. Speaking in low tones, the group's leader was giving instructions. "Once that dyke starts her speech, we'll start our walk. Jimmy and Marty will pull up in front of the Arch, and we'll offload our gear. If any civilian asks, we're a SWAT team being brought in for security. Then we move quickly and follow the plan. Don't point your weapons at anyone and do not discharge your weapon unless your life is in imminent danger, but keep moving forward. Use your batons for self-defense only. We are American patriots with every right to state our opinion, which I will be doing, loud and proud. If we disrupt this stupid rally, our mission will be successful. Each of you has your own departure route. Remember, God is on our side. He is blessing every one of us for doing his work here today. We're fighting for the natural order of human behavior, as he wants it!"

———

DJ cranked up the audio on his TV to hear Belinda Benson.

"I'm proud to be joined by so many like-minded proud Americans!" The crowd roared its approval. "All of us here today want the same thing: the end of hate crimes in America. We must make the punishment fit the transgression. Crimes motivated by misplaced hate because of who you love, where you are from, the color of your skin, or how you worship, are especially heinous, and need to be punished accordingly."

The crowd roared.

You tell 'em, sister! DJ left the hotel, hoping to maybe take in a few minutes of the rally on his walk to the police station.

———————

A loosely organized group of people, dressed mostly in military fatigues and hunting camouflage, was walking quietly by the Bushnell Carousel and toward the Soldiers and Sailors Memorial Arch. Stepping onto Trinity Street, closed for today's event, the group headed for a pickup truck parked on the Jewell Street side of the Arch. The members of the group quickly surrounded the truck and offloaded weapons, signs, communication devices, and a bullhorn. They swiftly formed into a wedge configuration and began to advance toward the rally at the pavilion. Some of their signs proclaimed them as the NOHB, the "Natural Order of Human Behavior", an anti-gay, white-supremacist organization known for their violent rhetoric. Other signs read: "Repent sinners!", "hands off my children", and "God sees you".

Benson was in mid-speech. "Hatred is taught. We're each born a blank slate, with no prejudices. We learn to hate from those around us. Hatred doesn't require any real facts. Our friend, Ray Pernell, a Tucker executive from right here in Connecticut, was brutally murdered in my hometown of San Francisco, possibly because someone THOUGHT he looked like he MIGHT be gay. Listen to me, people! Hate crimes require swift and severe punishment!" The crowd cheered wildly, but then was interrupted by a loud screeching noise from behind them.

An electronically modulated voice came from a piercing bullhorn at the back of the crowd. "God will send all you sinners directly to hell! The natural order of human behavior is for men and women to be together. All of you queer freaks who fuck each other, have sex with animals, and groom our innocent children…are going to burn in hell for all eternity!"

The entire crowd, and all the cameras on the media platform, spun around to see what the speakers on the stage could already see: a phalanx of camouflaged, helmeted individuals, some carrying signs, moving forward while they were spouting their hateful statements and condemning all the rally attendees to eternity in hell.

On stage, Belinda Benson was calling for calm. "Do not engage these people! They are looking for a reason to create violence!"

Most of the Hartford Cops assigned to this event were spread out around the perimeter of the park, handling traffic duty. Their radios all crackled simultaneously. "We've got a 10-76 in Bushnell Park. About thirty, armed. SWAT is being scrambled."

The bullhorn continued to blare away. "Have you no respect for the word of God? The time to repent is now. Stop behaving like animals and return to the human race."

From the stage, Belinda Benson was calm but firm. "Take a good look, my friends. This is what hate looks like! This is what we are here to eliminate."

———

DJ was a block away when people fleeing Bushnell Park came rushing by him. *Holy shit!* He immediately went into cop mode and started running in the direction of the disturbance, weaving through the frightened people trying their best to escape the park.

———

On her couch, Mia couldn't immediately process exactly what she was seeing. She was stunned when Benson mentioned Ray's name and then was further shocked at the appearance of the armed members of the NOHB. They seemed intent on wrecking this rally.

"Dear God, I hope nobody gets hurt!"

———

The bullhorn was continuing its loud assault. "The first step to your salvation is to accept the Lord Jesus Christ into your hearts. There is a cure for your sickness. It starts with God Almighty!"

Two men charged forward, attempting to pierce the human wedge and grab the bullhorn. They were overwhelmed, thrown to the ground, and stomped. More rally attendees started to crowd around the advancing NOHB group, shouting insults. A line of a half-dozen Hartford Police officers, nightsticks and tasers in hand, had quickly formed in the path of the walking wedge of hate. The advancing group stopped and the bullhorn blared "We American patriots and soldiers of God have every right to protest like any other American citizens!" The crowd continued to press inward as grabbing and pushing started breaking out on all sides of the NOHB formation.

The shape of the NOHB wedge was destroyed. Scuffles broke out all around. Fists and feet were flying as the frantic scrum intensified. Batons were brutally utilized by the NOHB members. The outnumbered police used tasers and handcuffs to neutralize those in the most intense fights. Each time calm had seemingly been restored, another scramble broke out.

Suddenly the bullhorn gave the word, and the still-mobile members of his group scattered in various directions, seeking their pre-planned routes of escape.

Arriving at the edge of Bushnell Park, DJ spotted two masked men in camouflage beating a man with their batons. "Hey assholes!" One of the men turned and leaped at DJ, receiving a fist so deep in the solar plexus that he crumbled to the ground, gasping for air. The second man swung his baton at DJ, yelling "Fuck you nig…." His sentence went unfinished as DJ's kick to the side of his head dropped him to the ground in an unconscious heap. Standing over the first man, who was on his knees vomiting, DJ pushed the barrel of his SIG Sauer P229 against the back of the man's head. "Don't move, asshole!" *You guys dress like soldiers, but you fight like pussies!*

A uniformed cop, with frightened dark eyes and ruddy cheeks, arrived as DJ affixed his gold badge to his lapel.

"I'm with San Francisco PD and these two assholes were assaulting this man over here. I'm happy to testify to that."

"So will I" echoed the victim of the assault, as he was rubbing his rib cage.

The cop quickly zip-tied DJ's two victims, then whistled that whistle of amazement. "Wow, my friend, I saw you take these two out. Nice job Detective…?

"Harland. DJ Harland."

"Thanks for your help, Detective Harland. I'll take them from here."

"Thanks, I'm heading over to your shop now, let me know if you need anything else." *Damn, that felt good!*

The Police, now supported by SWAT, were detaining and handcuffing as many of the combatants as possible. As the physical scramble finally subsided, the sounds of agitated screaming and crying continued to fill the air. Injured, bloodied people were moaning and cursing. Three unmoving bodies lay on the ground. One of the downed persons was an unconscious man in fatigues. When the other two were rolled over, both with bloody head wounds, it was discovered that one of the injured was a woman. Onlookers were screaming for help. EMTs arrived on site. The three unconscious combatants were quickly prepped to be conveyed to area hospitals.

————

Mia was in tears. She called Debbie who answered with "Holy shit! did you see that?"

"Oh my God! Yes, I did. I hope nobody was hurt. The violence started right after they mentioned Ray's name."

"Mia, stop it! This ain't your fault, or Ray's!"

"Oh my God! I just realized who they are….that NOHB. They picketed at the end of our driveway a couple of days ago. They keep sending me hateful messages."

"Listen to me, Mia! Pay no attention to those awful idiots!"

"I can't help it."

"Well, you need to try. Okay if I stop by later? I've got some work to finish, then I'll be over."

"Yeah, sure. Thanks."

"You sure you're good?"

"Yes, I'm fine. I just feel so bad for the people who went there in good faith and wound up in that mess."

"Me too," said Debbie. "Say a prayer for them. We'll talk soon."

————

Less than half the crowd remained in a now calm Bushnell Park. SWAT members were in evidence. Belinda Benson was speaking.

"I want to publicly thank the officers who so bravely stood strong against this hateful action. I also want all of you to join me in a moment of silence for the injured, no matter who they may be, that they may recover fully."

Benson bowed her head for 10 seconds. "People, what we saw here today was exactly why we came here. We saw violent hate in action. What kind of punishment might they receive? That remains to be seen, but if history is any indicator, it won't be commensurate with their actions. We cannot be deterred from our mission. Our motivation is now greater, our swords sharper, and our resolve is stronger than ever. Don't ever forget the hate crimes you witnessed here today. Please go in peace. Love and care for one another."

Chapter 57

The remainder of DJ's walk to the Hartford Police Station was on sidewalks filled with rally-goers, still stunned by the violence they had witnessed.

He was greeted by the desk cop whose round body was severely testing the limits of his uniform fabric. His dark eyes were set into a deeply lined face, topped by a thin layer of gray hair. Those eyes were affixed to DJ's gold shield.

"Good morning Sergeant Stephan. I'm Detective Harland. Rough day?"

The sandpaper voice of Stephan was unmistakable, "Just another perfect day in paradise."

"No shit, Sarge. That was a crazy scene out there."

"Yeah. Regular display of assholes on parade. We're busy entertaining several new guests. Just go through these doors. Then walk through Holding, which is no doubt currently standing room only. You'll see a door labeled conference-2. I'll buzz you when your guest arrives.'

"Thanks, Sarge. His name is Frank Dorrington."

"Roger"

The bench space in the crowded holding area was lined with combatants arrested at the rally brawl, each handcuffed to metal rings extending out from the benches. Many were dressed in camouflage and fatigues, and most were sporting bruises, blood, and bandages. DJ couldn't help himself as he passed by the wanna-be soldiers. "Tough day at the office boys?" He heard "fuck you cop" repeatedly muttered as he continued walking, a broad smile on his face. *Thanks, guys. It's asholes like you that keep me employed!*

———

Frank Dorrington spent the morning in the ER of St. Francis Hospital, getting his hand repaired. His new cast ran halfway up his left forearm. He was surprised that his now-defunct health insurance card had slipped by.

Dorrington intended to arrive at the police station 5 minutes late for his meeting. The crowded streets delayed him further and he arrived at 1:38.

After greeting Sergeant Stephan, Frank pretended to busy himself with paperwork. He soon heard "Frank Dorrington! I'm Detective Harland."

Frank looked up to see a handsome, fit, black man in jeans and a sports coat, with an impressive gold badge attached to his lapel. Frank stuffed his phony paperwork into his briefcase and stood quickly to grasp DJ's outstretched hand.

"Pleasure to meet you, Detective."

"You too. Follow me. Ignore the crowd in holding. Big rally gone wrong this morning."

"Yes. Such an ugly scene." Frank resisted the urge to hand his card to the many potential clients sitting handcuffed in the holding area.

In the conference room, Frank said "Sorry I'm late. The streets are crowded. Unfortunately, I still need to leave by 2 o'clock to get back to court, which gives me about 18 minutes. So, let's get to it. How can I be of service Detective?"

DJ produced his digital recorder. "I hate taking notes. The recorder is not an issue is it?"

"Not at all."

"Okay, cool. First, may I ask you what happened to your hand? You okay? That cast looks fresh." *Judging by the moist texture, it's less than a couple hours old.*

"Got it last night" lied Frank. "Slammed my pinkie finger in my car door. It hurt like hell. But I still had to be in court all morning. Anyway, I don't have much time. What can I do for you?"

"I'm gathering background on Ray Pernell. How would you characterize your relationship with him?"

"Ray and I were occasional drinking buddies. We sometimes got together in the evening when he got off the train from New York. We played golf together. We were pretty close."

"So you were good friends?"

"I guess you could say that."

Your ex-wife disagrees. "Where did you guys hang out?"

Frank expected this question and did his best to mirror the false information that he gave to Dishing Dirt so there'd be no conflict of information when the tabloid came out on Monday. He told DJ about the bars in Bristol and West Hartford, without mentioning that Pat's is a gay bar.

"Mia Pernell is surprised by your claims of spending time with her husband. Why do you suppose that Mr. Pernell never told his family how much time he was spending with you?" *Maybe because he hardly knew you?*

"I can't answer that for sure Detective. I don't think Mrs Pernell likes me very much. She hangs out with my ex, so you can imagine that Mia hasn't heard a lot of complimentary stuff about me."

"Makes sense." *Probably the first truth he has spoken.*

"Also, I think that Ray didn't want his family to know because, well, maybe they weren't listening at home, and I was."

DJ's internal lie detector was exploding. *Dude, for an attorney, you're a pretty shitty liar.* "What did you guys talk about?"

"Typical guy stuff most of the time. Work, sports, family life. That kind of stuff."

"On the Hammy B show, you said that Mr. Pernell might have been seeing a counselor. Is that a fact?"

Frank beamed slightly at the mention of his appearance on TV. "Yes, he was. But I don't know who it was other than it was a woman."

"Why'd he need a counselor?"

"I think he was having some marital issues. And sometimes he'd talk about problems at work. That's what we talked about the last time I saw him."

"When was that Frank?"

"Just before he left for San Francisco, at Pat's in West Hartford."

"What was his tone when talking about his family?"

"Tense. He loved Mia, but something was going on there. I'm not sure what."

Maybe a happy marriage? Something you wouldn't recognize! "Did Mr. Pernell ever tell you about any affairs he may have been having outside of his marriage?"

"Look Detective, if I knew something like that, I would have promised Ray that I would never share it with anyone, ever."

"You know I could make you share that under oath, correct?" *You pompous prick.*

"I understand the law, Detective."

DJ changed tact. "Did you guys drink a lot when you got together?"

Frank frowned. "Don't want to incriminate myself. But, yes, we may have had too much to drink once or twice."

"What was Mr. Pernell like after a few cocktails?"

"Ray had an outrageous sense of humor. The crazier the situation, the funnier he found it. Alcohol tended to magnify Ray's reactions."

"Did that outrageous sense of humor include dressing in bizarre outfits and running the streets?" *Like you want everyone to believe!*

"I never saw anything like that. But, Ray was the kind of guy who enjoyed the Jackass movies. He would do anything crazy for a laugh, especially if he'd had a few drinks."

So I've heard you say. "Did you ever meet up with Mr. Pernell outside of Connecticut?"

"Yes. His office is in New York City. Once or twice, we met for drinks there when I happened to be in town."

"Anywhere else?" asked DJ.

"Not that I can recall."

"Frank, have you ever had any clients from San Francisco?"

"No Detective. My business is primarily in the Connecticut - New York area. Anything else? I'm short on time."

"Why are you spending so much time talking to the media about Mr. Pernell?" *As if I didn't know.*

Frank put on a solemn face. "Someone has to stand up for Ray's reputation. He was a wonderful friend."

DJ had to bite his tongue. *Your fake sincerity disgusts me.* "That's very magnanimous of you. Tell me, as his close friend, did you ever see Mr. Pernell use drugs?"

"I can't answer that".

"Why not Frank? Are you afraid to incriminate yourself?"

"Absolutely not, Detective! I've signed a limited NDA with a newspaper that lasts for 3 more days. I can't discuss that subject until their issue comes out on Monday."

"Which newspaper would that be?"

"Dishing Dirt," said Frank sheepishly.

"Aaahh. That fine pillar of journalism. You understand that the tabloids aren't exactly known for factual accuracy, right Frank?" *Geeezus, they had a damn alien on the front page last week!*

"Nonetheless, my NDA is a legal document executed between two consenting entities."

"How much did they pay you for that information Frank?"

"That's my business."

"Doesn't it bother you to be profiting from the death of your friend?" *You clearly have no conscience.*

"That's not how I see it Detective. Shedding light on certain issues can be helpful to people who may have similar problems. Anyway, everything is legal. Anything else? I'm due back at the courthouse."

"Yes, sorry about delaying you from court." *They can't possibly survive minus one asshole.* "How's your law firm doing, Frank? Are you doing well financially?"

"That's none of your goddamed business, Detective."

Pretty darn sensitive Frank! "Okay, one last question. When did you first become aware of the photo of Mr. Pernell's body that circulated on the internet?

Frank hadn't expected that question and the slight tensing of his facial muscles was not lost on DJ. "Um, about the same time as everyone else, I guess. Couldn't believe it."

"Did you know it was him when you first saw the photo?"

"At first, I just thought it was another unfortunate victim, but as soon as I zoomed in, I knew it was him."

"So the photo had no caption when you first saw it**?"** *Here comes more bullshit.*

Frank tensed, clearly considering his answer as if in a court of law. "I don't recall seeing any text when I first became aware of the photo. I was surprised when I later saw the photo with the caption 'TuckerExecFreak – Hate Crime?."

"Yes, of course. Involving TEM certainly raises interest in this case. You had incredibly lucky timing to see that photo before the caption was added."

"Meaning?"

"It was only posted on CoCriRev for a couple hours before it was pulled down. But, someone who had exactly the same good timing as you, must've grabbed it, added the new text, and then reposted it to "unTrace" where it was initially found and then distributed by some Hudson High School students.

"You got a point?"

Looking directly into Dorrington's eyes, DJ said "The origin of that captioned photo has been traced to this very region. And amazingly, the Hudson High kids were anonymously tipped about it. Any idea who might want to do those things, Frank?" *Like you, for instance?*

Frank's face tightened. "Not sure, maybe an unhappy Tucker employee. Adding those words to the photo certainly made it a bigger deal to the average Joe. Everyone knows Tucker."

"You're right. It could've been someone who had an issue with Tucker. Guess we need to figure out who could most benefit from posting that photo." *Geez. Don't you own a mirror?*

Frank suddenly felt naked. He knew what DJ was implying, but declined to take the bait. "I'd like to help you further Detective, but I'm due in court. Gotta go."

"Of course, duty calls. Thanks for your time, Frank. I'll be in touch if I need anything further." *See you soon asshole.*

Chapter 58

Carlos and Debbie agreed to meet at the Hudson Diner for a 9 am breakfast. Debbie, dressed in jeans and a light blue sweater over a white blouse, arrived a few minutes early. She was disappointed when she saw the long line of hungry patrons.

She heard tapping on the diner window. Peering through the glass, she was surprised to see Carlos motioning for her to come inside.

Noting the faded Santana Abraxas t-shirt under his jean jacket, she asked "When did you….?" Carlos stood, reached out for her hand, and drew her toward him for a gentle hug. "So nice to see you."

"Nice to see you too," said Debbie, taking a seat across from Carlos in the booth. "I thought we said 9 am."

"We did. But it occurred to me that this place is so darn busy on weekend mornings that I might wanna get here early to grab a booth."

"That's so thoughtful. Thanks for doing that."

"Love this place. I used to tease Ray that this diner blew up his theory on achieving quality results."

"What theory is that?" asked Debbie while watching their server fill her coffee cup.

"When doing creative projects with clients, Ray would tell them to choose two of his three options. We can do things good, fast, or cheap. Pick any two, but we can't do all three."

As Debbie mulled that over, Carlos continued. "But this diner has all three. The food is good, the service is fast, and the prices are cheap."

Debbie laughed. She loved the ease with which Carlos had greeted her. "I guess that's why people don't mind standing in line here."

"Exactly."

"You know, I may steal that theory of Ray's for use with some of my clients. Especially those who want high-quality design work, overnight, at a bargain price. Can't have all three. Gotta pick two."

"Ray would be proud! I want to know about your design business, but first fill me in on Mia. How's she doing?"

Before Debbie could answer, their server arrived. "Are we ready? The usual for you, Carlos?"

"Sounds good Tibby, but ladies first. What would you like Debbie?"

"I'm not sure. What's your usual?"

Tibby answered. "Egg-white vegetarian omelet, all six veggies, feta cheese, side of fruit, and a grilled blueberry muffin."

"Sounds good. I'll have the same, minus the muffin. And a tall OJ."

Tibby smiled. "Let me know if you need anything else."

"So, how's Mia doing?" asked Carlos.

"I've known Mia since college. I don't have to tell you how deeply in love they were, so yeah, she's struggling."

"Totally get that."

"I can't help but wonder how different this would all be if Ray hadn't died under such weird circumstances. The media attention, the hatred, it has all become just too much."

"Just crazy. I have wracked my brain trying to figure out what happened that night in San Francisco. When Ray got off the elevator, I had no clue that I would never see him again. I wish I could've done something."

Debbie reached across the table to hold Carlos' hand in both of hers. "Not your fault. Whatever happened to Ray had nothing to do with you."

"It's just not fair. I loved that guy."

"Your beautiful tribute at Ray's service made it clear how you felt about him."

Looking directly into Debbie's eyes, Carlos felt his heart pounding as he said "Thank you. You're good for the soul Miss Slater."

Afraid she was blushing, Debbie changed the subject. "So where's home for you?"

"I've got a small place in West Haven."

"Near the water?"

"Yes, but very small. It's only me."

"Sounds nice. I'm here in Hudson. My spare bedroom is my office." Debbie sucked in her breath and shared further. "I've been living alone since my divorce."

"We've all got exes, I just didn't marry anyone. An ex is an ex, legal or not."

Their discussion turned to the creative business. Debbie provided Carlos with the history of ZTA and described some of her current projects. Carlos shared his employment history and some of his creative interests.

"Your job sounds tremendous," said Debbie. "TEM works with huge clients, I'm just a small shop".

"Design is design, the client's name doesn't matter. Was Mia a Designer when she worked with you?"

"No, a Producer. Mia wrote all our creative briefs and delivered our pitches. She was awesome on the client side."

"Do you think she'd ever consider returning?"

"I've tried. But she's not ready. She's still overwhelmed by everything that's going on."

"Heard that. I keep looking for a smoking gun that'll suddenly solve Ray's case."

"Find anything?"

"Nothing good. I found something on the Dishing Dirt website. You know, one of those grocery store tabloids."

"Oh God," said Debbie. "Was it Frank Dorrington again?"

"Afraid so."

"You know that Frank was my husband, right?"

"Not important."

"What are they saying?"

"It's a bunch of quotes under a headline of 'Insider Dish on Tucker Executive Ray Pernell'."

"Oh God. What did Frank say?"

"They quoted things like 'demons, depression and oxy'. They refer to Dorrington as 'Pernell's best pal'."

"That jerk," said Debbie, wanting to use harsher language.

"Were he and Ray really that close?"

"Absolutely not. Frank's just doing this crap to make money. God knows he needs it."

"Glad to hear that. Ray and I have traveled everywhere together, dined, and drank together dozens of times. He never once mentioned the name of Frank Dorrington. Not once!"

Debbie sighed. "I'm not surprised. They met maybe three times during our marriage. And I think they played golf once. Mia said that Ray refused to ever play golf with him again."

"So Dorrington is doing this crap for money? Is Mia considering suing him for slander or libel, whichever fits?"

"Yes. Mia's lawyer is building a case, but Frank is careful to never state a lie as fact. He just tosses stuff out there and lets the interviewer run with it."

"Guys like that mess up. We'll get him"

Two hours later, in the parking lot, Carlos said: "Thank you so much, Debbie. I enjoyed getting to know you. Maybe we could get dinner sometime?"

Debbie took Carlos' hands in hers, raised up on her tiptoes, and kissed him on the cheek. "You're a very special man Carlos. I'd love to see you again."

Chapter 59

"Morning Sugar, you gonna sleep all day? I didn't hear you come in last night."

DJ opened his eyes to Liz's lovely smile. She handed him his favorite oversized mug, filled with hot coffee.

DJ smiled. "Good morning angel. I tried not to wake you. How's everything?"

"I'm good. How was your trip?"

"All good. Gotta review everything today. You miss me?"

"Not at all!" Liz laughed. "Had dinner with Louise Sharpe while you were gone. It was great to catch up.

"What's goin' on with Louise?"

"She thinks that Levi is ready to retire. He's been talking about the nice weather in San Diego."

"He can't go right now. We need him too much. Anything new at work?"

"Nah. Until I'm pregnant, it's not worth discussing my future there."

"Speaking of that, you feeling okay?"

Liz smiled. "Yes, lover boy. We'll know in about 7 days if any of your early swimmers have miraculously hit the bullseye."

Placing his coffee on the end table, DJ reached up and pulled Liz down onto the bed. "What say we get busy sending more swimmers on this mission?"

Liz giggled as she kissed the tip of his nose. "Thought you'd never ask."

———

Debbie Slater answered her phone with "Hi Mia, what's up?"

"Morning. Did I wake you?"

"No, I've been up for hours. What's goin' on?"

"Couldn't sleep last night. Thinking about those people that were hurt at the riot. The news said that two of them are in critical condition".

"Mia, I get it. But their injuries are not your fault."

"I know. Just hope they're alright."

"Listen, Mia, that tabloid Dishing Dirt must've done another interview with Frank. It comes out Monday in their paper."

"Good Lord. What else can he possibly say?"

"Probably more of his bullshit lies. But I thought you should know." Hoping to change the mood, Debbie added "Carlos and I had breakfast together this morning."

"That's terrific! How was it? Are you going out again?"

"Whoa! It was only breakfast at the Hudson Diner. But you were right, he and I have a lot in common."

"I knew it!"

Debbie talked Mia through her breakfast with Carlos.

"Two hours? I just knew you two would hit it off. I'm so happy for both of you. We'll have to get together....." Mia stopped speaking, reality dousing her enthusiasm.

Debbie felt Mia's pain. "Yes, Mia. If Carlos and I start dating, we'll definitely get together with you and your family."

"I'm so happy for you both. Really, I am. That's so exciting."

"Don't go making wedding plans for me just yet!"

"No prob. I can wait a week or two."

Toweling off after a shower, DJ saw a text from Officer Ahmadi.

"Dishing Dirt is promoting a 'bombshell' in their Monday print edition. It's about Ray Pernell. Their 'inside source' is Frank Dorrington. Check DishingDirt.com."

DJ opened the Dishing Dirt website and saw the splashy presentation of quotes arrayed on top of a ghosted image of Pernell's body. The headline, "Insider Dirt on Tucker Executive Pernell" was big and bold. The page was populated by several buzzwords spurred by the conversation with Dorrington. "Demons", "Oxy", "Depression", and "Clandestine Meetings" were all floating on the page. On the lower screen was a large smoking volcano, in full eruptive motion, repeatedly spewing out the words: "See Monday's Dishing Dirt for an Explosive New Bombshell. On Newsstands everywhere!"

DJ groaned. *Geeeezus. These people will say anything!*

From the next room, Liz asked "What are you groaning at?"

"Just a bottomless shit-spewing sewer."

———

Mia's call to her attorney, Ken Samantis, hit voicemail. She considered calling Phoebe at Amy's to ask if Mr. Samantis was home, but she didn't want Phoebe to think that her Mom was checking up on her.

Opening the Dishing Dirt website, Mia saw the outlandish posting. She muttered, "I've had it with that asshole!"

She pulled up Frank Dorrington's info and hit "call".

"You've reached the law offices of Frank Dorrington. Please leave your name and number and we'll return your call as soon as possible."

Following the beep, Mia spoke. "Frank! It's Mia Pernell. You remember, the wife of your so-called best friend! What the hell are...."

"Hello, Mia? Mia? I'm here. Slow down!"

"Frank? Frank, what the hell are you doing? Why are you dragging me and my family through this crap?"

Frank tried to tone down the conversation. "First of all, Mia, I'm sorry for your loss."

"You've got a shitty way of showing it!"

"For real, Mia! I miss him too."

"Oh right, you miss your best friend that you never hung out with. Bullshit Frank! I'm gonna sue your ass until there's nothing left to sue!"

"I've done nothing wrong."

"Geez, Frank. I used to think that you were, at least, fairly intelligent. Now I know that you are just a selfish idiot, looking to make money off the death of my husband!"

"That's not it. I just….."

"Just what, Frank? Are you struggling financially?….good! Are you lonely with no friends?….good! I hope you rot in hell, you bastard!" Mia ended the call, then screamed "What a flaming asshole!".

Chapter 60

After spending most of his Saturday reviewing the material from his East Coast trip, DJ fell asleep on the couch. Waking at 8:15 pm, he found a note from Liz. "Out with work friends. No alcohol….just in case!"

He texted Liz. "Have fun. Going to work. Don't wait up."

Following a quick In-N-Out Burger, DJ drove to the Smythville Hotel. He wasn't halfway across the lobby when he heard the unmistakably shrill voice of Tim Bernard. "Hello Detective. What brings you here?"

Bernie was waving at DJ, purple stripe still boldly in place on top of his head. *Damn, that voice matches the wattage of his hair.* "Hey, Bernie. Which Smith brother is on duty tonight?"

"Freddie. I buzzed him as soon as I saw you. He'll be here in a second."

"Thanks, Bernie."

"It was so sad, about that Mr. Pernell, wasn't it?"

"Sure was."

"A few reporters have asked me about Mr. Pernell, but my boss told me not to talk to them."

"You've got a smart boss."

"What's up, Detective," said Freddie Smith.

"Hey Freddie. Let's go to that alley door in the service stairwell. Then you can go. I won't be coming back in that way."

"Anyone who chooses to breathe the air in that alley is a better man than I. Let's go".

Ray thought the service stairwell seemed even more dank and moist than it had on his last visit. Smith pounded the metal bar on the alley door and it creaked open. The smell of ripe garbage immediately filled their nostrils.

Smith pinched his nose. "Sure is fragrant on the weekends. They empty those dumpsters on Mondays."

"Stinks like hell." *Note to self. Only come here on Tuesdays.*

"Anything else you need, Detective? Flashlight?"

"I'm good."

"Roger. Watch out for 'rodents of unusual size'" laughed Freddie.

DJ chuckled at Freddie's reference to 'The Princess Bride', one of Liz's favorite movies. "Oh yeah, the Fire-Swamp! Good one, Freddie."

Hearing some low voices ahead, DJ walked to the now familiar small space with the sawed-off trashcan. The glowing fire in the can illuminated at least three bodies on the ground.

"I'm a cop. Not here to roust you guys. Just looking for a little help".

No one spoke.

"Any of you regulars at this location?' Anyone speak English?

A voice said "C'mon man, we've ain't bothering nobody. Just trying to stay warm."

Another voice spoke up. "Shut up Oscar. I'm on parole."

"Don't give a shit" said DJ. "Just got one question. Did any of you guys recently see a white dude, who might have been naked except for a small towel over his junk, come through here late at night?"

"Nope." said one voice.

"Holy shit, he's talking about Tarzan!" said another voice.

"Shut up Oscar!"

DJ removed the digital recorder from his pocket and hit 'record'. "Oscar, I need to talk to you. There could be twenty bucks in it for you."

"I'm sorry officer. I must have been mistaken."

DJ hovered over "Oscar". "Listen, my friend, we gotta talk or none of you will get to enjoy this fire tonight." *Ain't no fires in jail!*

The man struggled to his knees, then slowly rose to his feet.

Standing before DJ was a short, filthy-headed bald man, with bloodshot eyes, a patchy beard, wearing a heavy, ragged thing that might once have been a woolen dress coat.

"Is Oscar your real name?" *Holy shit, I thought the dumpsters smelled bad!*

"Yeah".

"Well Oscar, tell me about this Tarzan you mentioned".

"I made up the name. Don't know who he is".

"When did you see him?"

"I dunno. Maybe a couple weeks ago. Only saw him once."

"Was he living on the street, like you guys?"

"He wasn't one of us."

"How do you know that?"

Oscar looked up at DJ. "When do I get that twenty?"

"When and if you tell me everything you know about this Tarzan. And don't try to play me."

"There's not much to tell. I was trying to get some sleep, right here by this can, when some guy started jabbering at me."

"What was he saying?"

"He offered me a hundred dollars for my coat. But I knew he didn't have the money. So I said no."

"How did you know he didn't have the money?"

"He didn't have any pockets. He was naked except for a little cloth in the front, like Tarzan"

DJ's heart rate ticked up a notch. *Holy shit!* "Can you describe him?"

"It was dark, but he was a white dude with short hair. That's all I can remember."

"Any tattoos or marks?"

"C'mon cop, it was dark."

"Was anyone else here with you?"

"Don't remember."

"Did this Tarzan seem like he was drunk?"

"Maybe. Seemed excited. How about that twenty dollars?"

DJ stared at Oscar. "Where did he go after you refused his offer?"

Lifting an arm coated in a shabby sleeve, Oscar pointed down the alley toward Lund Avenue. "He went that way."

"Was there anyone else in the alley that you saw?"

"Not sure. Sometimes there are cars parked at the end of the alley. Dealers or pimps, I think. We stay clear of 'em."

"Oscar, I'm gonna need to know how to find you again. You got an address?"

"Oscar, stop talking!"

DJ glared at the man who'd shouted. "Shut the fuck up, asshole. One more word outta you and your parole will cease to exist!"

Oscar nearly whispered. "I ain't got no damn address. But I stay at the homeless shelter on Quarry Road every Sunday. Money please."

"You got a last name?"

"It used to be Avery, but I don't use it no more."

DJ pulled out a twenty-dollar bill. Handing it to Oscar, he asked "Did this Tarzan guy say anything else?"

"He was talkin' crazy. Said he wanted my coat because he 'woke up naked pissing in a corner'" said Oscar while carefully folding the twenty-dollar bill and stuffing it in his sock.

"What?" exclaimed DJ, feeling an adrenaline rush. *No way!*

"The dude was nuts or maybe high as a kite."

"You sure he said 'woke up naked pissing in a corner'?" *We've heard that phrase before!*

"Yup. He said that shit more than once. Really weird."

Handing Oscar his card, DJ said "Thanks, Mr. Avery. Tuck my card into your sock and reach me if you remember anything else about that night. "

"Nothing else to tell, but okay," said Oscar.

"Sleep well, Oscar. I'll find you at the Quarry Road shelter if I need you again."

Walking the remainder of the alley, DJ was excited by what Oscar had said. "Woke up naked pissing in a corner" was the exact phrase the snitch, Johnny G, had used in their interview. Maybe Hollowell had actually told Johnny the truth when describing how he'd killed that "gay man".

Gotta call Levi!

Chapter 61

Levi Sharpe picked up his phone. "Welcome back weary traveler".

"What's goin' on?" asked DJ.

"All's well. I didn't want to bother you yesterday since you got in so late on Friday night."

"Appreciate that." *We were busy making a baby anyway!*

"Were you anywhere near that disturbance in Hartford?"

"I was, but no harm done. That NOHB needs to be shut down."

"Heard that. Any progress on the East Coast?"

"Informative for sure. We can get into that at work tomorrow. But I went back to our Smythville alley last night." *My stanky home away from home.*

"And?" asked Sharpe.

"And I think I may have found our guy." *My new best friend, Oscar!*

"Someone saw Pernell out there?"

"Sure seems like it. One of the regulars in the alley claimed to have seen a dude he nicknamed Tarzan because of how the guy was dressed in a loincloth!"

"No shit?"

DJ walked Levi through his conversation with Oscar, including "Tarzan's" quote: 'Woke up naked pissing in a corner'. "I recorded the entire conversation."

"Excellent job, DJ. Holy crap, that's the same phrase that our snitch, Johnny G, used!"

"Exactly!" *A direct bullseye!*

"So that slippery bastard might have been telling us the truth about his conversation with Hollowell at their little meth party?"

"Sure seems like it partner. I also remember Johnny giving us two other claims from Hollowell."

"Remind me," said Sharpe.

"He said that Hollowell was planning to settle a jailhouse feud the next day. We know that was true, although it didn't go so well. He got his ass slaughtered in his car in Oakland."

"Roger that".

DJ's voice was excited. "And he shared Hollowell's story about shooting a gay man".

"Yes, he did."

"Well damn. Is it fair for us to think that everything Hollowell told Johnny that night was true?" *That would make things a lot easier….*

"Course not," said Sharpe. "But it's certainly worth digging deeper."

"To that end, have you heard back from Chris Hardy or Oakland PD about Hollowell's stolen car? Any signs of Pernell in that mess?"

"Not yet. I'll give them a buzz tomorrow".

"We should also check the security cameras on Lund Avenue from that night to see if we can track Hollowell's car."

"Already made that request partner. They're checking Lund, from the Smythville area, all the way down to the parking lot in Hollis."

"Thanks for that," said DJ. "I gotta give this some more thought."

"Cool. See ya in the morning."

DJ stared at his reflection in his iPhone. *What am I missing? There's gotta be something here that explains Pernell's clothing.*

Chapter 62

"Samantis residence".

"Hi, Ken. It's Mia Pernell. Have you got a minute?"

"Sure Mia. What's on your mind?"

"I'm a little freaked out by the violence at Bushnell Park. Would it help things if I said something to the media?"

"Look Mia, attracting additional attention is not a good idea. You're better off just putting out a statement condemning hate crimes. I'll compose an initial draft."

"I already can't go outside without being accosted by someone with a camera. I've been offered money to divulge all of Ray's so-called 'quirks and secrets'!"

"That's awful. But you're doing great. It should get better soon."

"Funny, I don't feel so great".

"What else is on your mind?" asked Samantis.

"TEM is still dragging its feet on Ray's benefits. I'm fine financially, but damn it, Ray died while traveling on behalf of Tucker."

"Mia, I've met with Tucker Legal. This is a complex issue. Their primary concern is their corporate image. They want to know what Ray was doing when he was killed."

"But we might never know the exact details."

"Maybe not. Their morals clause, included in Ray's contract, contains the phrase 'reprehensible behavior or conduct that may negatively impact the company'."

"But no one knows if he was doing anything reprehensible" complained Mia.

"That's why Tucker is dragging their feet, waiting for the final police report. Then they'll spin their PR depending on that report."

"If they don't pay us, I want to sue them."

"That should only be our last resort. And Mia, a Tucker Executive on the streets of San Francisco, late at night, dressed like Ray was, certainly doesn't fit their image".

"That sucks. We both know that Ray would never choose to do that."

"Don't worry about that for now. No matter what the police discover, we'll likely be negotiating Ray's settlement, quietly and out of the public eye."

"For real?"

"Tucker doesn't want a highly publicized court case."

"Thank you so much, Ken. I appreciate your hard work." Mia changed the subject. "Detective Harland, from San Francisco, was here Thursday".

"No kidding? I guess the national interest in this thing has ratcheted up the investigation. Anything new?"

"Nothing that he would reveal. But I think he's on to something."

"Did he want anything specific from you?"

"He had questions for me about our lifestyle, friends, finances, social habits…..that type of thing."

"Sounds normal".

"He also talked to my parents, my friend Debbie Slater, and Vera Eden, the Hudson Police grief counselor. He was also going to talk to Frank Dorrington."

Samantis groaned. "Oh yeah, that guy. What a creep."

"Pardon my French, but Frank Dorrington is a low-life asshole. He keeps claiming that he and Ray were very close friends. They weren't. You can't believe anything he says."

"That seems clear."

"He just did another interview with Dishing Dirt. Apparently, more of his lies will be published in their Monday edition. Isn't there anything legal we can do to shut him up?"

"Not yet Mia. I've got one of my assistants on full-time Frank watch. She's collecting all of his television appearances, radio interviews, podcasts, and every time that he is quoted in print and online. "

"That's awesome!"

"We're building a case for defamation."

"Thanks, Ken. That jerk would sell his soul for profit. He's causing my family a whole lotta problems."

"I hear you loud and clear," said Samantis. "How are your kids handling all this talk about their Dad?"

"Not great. Both boys are struggling in their own ways, but I'm most worried about Phoebe. How is she today?"

"What? Why are you asking me about Phoebe? I haven't seen her with Amy lately."

"You've probably seen her more than I have. She's been staying at your house with Amy the last two nights, hasn't she?"

"I didn't know that. I guess it's possible. But I haven't seen her. Gimme a second to see if Amy is here."

Mia started feeling a sense of dread.

"I'm with Amy in her room and she's concerned about Phoebe."

"What's going on? Where's Phoebe?" asked Mia.

"Hello? Mrs. Pernell?" Amy sounded nervous.

"Amy! Where's Phoebe? She was supposed to be staying with you this weekend."

"I'm sorry. I had no idea. I thought she was at home. But I'm worried about her."

"So am I! Well, where is she?"

"I really don't know Mrs. Pernell."

Ken Samantis spoke to his daughter. "Amy! If you know where Phoebe is, you need to tell us right now!"

"I really don't know Dad. Phoebe hasn't texted me in forever. And she's deleted all her social media. Snap, Instagram, TikTok. There's nothing out there. It's like she has erased herself from the world."

"Oh my God", said Mia. "I've gotta call the police. Bye." She hung up and dialed the Hudson Police.

After a frantic twenty minutes of providing the HPD with full information about Phoebe, Mia called Vera Eden to ask for help.

Chapter 63

Mia's sense of despair was growing stronger. She was praying for some positive news, but was beginning to think the very worst. She texted Debbie Slater "Phoebe's missing." Debbie immediately called.

"Oh my God, Mia. What's going on with Phoebe?"

"She was supposed to be at Amy's house this weekend, but never went there. I don't know where she is. I've contacted the police and asked Vera Eden for her help. I don't know what else to do. Please God, let my baby be safe."

"I'm on my way. See you in a few minutes."

Mia curled up in a ball on her couch, her breathing rapid and feeling paralyzed. "Dear God in heaven, I can't lose my baby too."

Within minutes, Debbie rushed in and wrapped Mia in a hug. "Have you heard anything?"

Mia could only shake her head from side to side. "No."

———

After two desperate hours of praying and waiting, Mia's phone lit up with "Vera Eden."

"Vera! Have you heard anything?"

"We found her."

"Oh my God. Where? What happened?"

"She's at Saint Francis Hospital in the trauma center."

Mia could barely get the words out. "Is…. she….okay?"

Eden spoke evenly. "She has lost a lot of blood and they are doing everything possible to stabilize her."

"No!" screamed Mia. "What happened to my baby?"

"She was found in Hampshire Park, bleeding from what appeared to be self-inflicted cuts on her wrist. A passerby noticed her on a park bench and called 911."

"Self-inflicted? Oh dear God in heaven, please save my baby. I'm on my way! Debbie, can you watch the kids?"

"As long as you need."

Chapter 64

Levi Sharpe poured DJ a cup of coffee in the break room before their Monday morning case review meeting with Captain Kekoa.

"I think this stuff might be left over from Friday afternoon," said Sharpe.

"It's usually got a three-day shelf life." laughed DJ.

"I took a look at the Dishing Dirt website about an hour ago. Nothing new on there yet."

"Probably won't be until later today or tomorrow. They won't give anything away on their website until they've sold every last damn paper."

"Of course, makes sense."

"Morning Detectives." Amal Ahmadi walked into the break room, newspapers tucked under his arm.

"Hey Amal," said DJ. "What's up?"

"Thought you might like to see this. Pretty crazy stuff" said Ahmadi, handing a copy of Dishing Dirt to each Detective. "Take a look at these."

"Damn, you read our minds!" said Sharpe.

"Geee-zus!" exclaimed DJ. The front page again featured the photo of Pernell's body with a screaming headline: "Tucker Exec: Clandestine Gay Bar Meetings!"

"Where do they get this shit?" asked Sharpe.

That question was immediately answered when both Detectives turned the front page to reveal a two-page spread, which included another headline saying "Depression, Oxy, Loincloth!". That was pasted over a montage of the Tucker logo, multiple Tucker movie titles, a tight image of the word "FREAK" on Pernell's chest, and a small insert photo of Frank Dorrington.

"It's freakin' Frank Dorrington again," said Sharpe.

"Of course," said DJ. "He refused to talk about this with me because he had a non-disclosure agreement with Dishing Dirt." *A lying piece of shit attorney and a tabloid rag that survives on lies! They deserve each other.*

"You think any of this stuff is true?" asked Sharpe.

"Highly doubtful" said DJ. "Dorrington doesn't exactly drip with sincerity." More of a habitual liar....

"Why's he doing this?" asked Ahmadi.

"No doubt, for profit. Dorrington is apparently in debt to his bank and a private investor of the shark variety."

Sharpe and Ahmadi chuckled.

"According to everyone I met last week, Dorrington and Pernell weren't close friends at all."

Sharpe spoke. "So partner, do you think this guy had anything to do with Pernell's death?"

"The thought has crossed my mind, repeatedly. But there's nothing to indicate that, other than the fact that he is doing his best to profit from Pernell's death."

"Roger that. So he's just a lowlife prick who has figured out a way to make money from the death of an acquaintance?"

"Looks that way." *And that low-life prick doesn't care about any collateral damage.*

"If that's Dorrington's only involvement in this mess, then he's not our concern. Our job is to identify the killer and hopefully a motive."

"Roger that," said DJ. "But that asshole is torturing the Pernell family and TEM with his bullshit. Tucker can fight their own battles, but Pernell's family doesn't deserve this crap."

Sharpe stared at DJ. "Eyes on the prize, partner. Our job is to solve this murder, not get involved in anything else."

Chapter 65

At 10am, Mia was fighting off sleep after sitting overnight in the waiting room at St. Francis Hospital. Phoebe looked pale and weak when Mia was allowed to briefly see her last night. The ER nurses had kept her appraised of Phoebe's condition, which seemed to be, at least, stable. Mia was texting with her Mom, who had replaced Debbie at home.

"Mrs. Pernell? I'm Doctor Bellefleur."

"Yes. I'm Mia."

"Phoebe is out of danger and doing well. We've stabilized her condition and given her multiple units of blood to replace what she has lost."

"Is she gonna be okay?'"

"Physically, yes. She is awake and conversational. In cases of self-harm like this, we strongly recommend a full psychological evaluation, followed by extensive counseling. Later today, she will meet here with our in-house counselor for an initial evaluation and she should be strong enough to go home tomorrow."

"Yes, of course. You have my full cooperation."

Doctor Bellefleur nodded her head. "You will need to provide her with a counselor going forward. We will share our psychological evaluation with that person."

"Thank you so much for all you've done. Life has been so tough for Phoebe lately."

Doctor Bellefleur reached out for Mia's hand. "Look, I won't pretend to not know what may have brought this on for Phoebe. I'm so sorry for the loss of your husband and for the wild stories that are circulating in the media. It's easy to see how all that publicity could affect your family. Phoebe needs your love and strength, in addition to some strong professional help."

"Understood, Doctor. We'll do our best. May I see her now?"

"Yes, but be brief. She needs rest. We should be able to release her late tomorrow morning."

———-

"Phoebe it's Mom."

Phoebe turned her head and opened her sleepy eyes. "Hi Mom."

Mia was happy to see some color in Phoebe's face and reached for her hand, noting the bandage wrapped around her left wrist. "Oh my baby! Are you okay?"

"I'm sorry I lied, Mom."

"I don't care. I just want to know that you are alright. You get some rest and I'll be back to bring you home tomorrow. We can talk later."

Chapter 66

Opening her door, Debbie greeted Carlos with a kiss on the cheek. "What's in the bag?"

"As requested. A sumptuous serving of bagels, muffins, and a large box 'o Joe. Only the finest for you."

"Thanks, Carlos. I love having breakfast delivered to my door. And I really need the coffee. I was up late last night, working on a project." Debbie had agreed with Mia to not share the news of Phoebe's attempted suicide with anyone outside the family. "You sure they aren't missing you at work?"

"Nah. The boss wants us to work from home the next few days and check in nightly in our Zoom meeting."

"Lucky you. My boss is much tougher."

"But you're self-employed."

"Exactly. I know me. I've gotta hold myself to a strict standard or I will ignore work on a regular basis."

Carlos laughed. "Guess you gotta know your personnel. Hey, I grabbed a couple copies of Dishing Dirt. Your ex has really crossed the line this time."

"Oh no. What did that lying bastard say now?"

Carlos held up the newspaper. Debbie was appalled at the garish headline. "Damn you, Frank!"

"I'm so sorry Debbie. How can I help?"

"Do you know a good leg-breaker?"

"Not off hand. But there's got to be another way for someone to make him stop spewing these damn lies all over the place."

Glancing through the article, Debbie couldn't believe some of the stuff she was reading. "What bullshit! A counselor, oxy, gay bars!…. Frank must've been hallucinating!"

"These tabloids will take just one or two keywords from an interview and build a narrative around them."

"That's exactly what Frank is counting on. He thinks he's being legally clever by dropping key words and letting someone else fill in the false details. He went too far this time!"

Carlos put down his blueberry muffin. "I know that bar, Preacher's. My first job in the business was in Bristol, and I used to play in a pool league there after work."

"You hung out there?"

"Occasionally. Got to know the owner fairly well. Wonder if he has any recollection of Dorrington and Pernell hanging out there?"

"Long shot," said Debbie. "But I guess it couldn't hurt to ask. Ever heard of this other bar, Pat's, the gay bar in West Hartford?"

"I don't know it, but according to this article, Dorrington and Pernell met there the week before Ray went to San Francisco."

"Damn. Frank's bullshit is killing Mia and her family. It needs to stop, now!"

Carlos picked up the tabloid. "You're right. They don't deserve this crap."

"Couldn't agree more."

"We've got to find a way to make Frank stop this bullshit."

Debbie put her arms around Carlos' neck. "Thank you for caring so much. I'm really happy that you've come into my life."

Carlos stared into Debbie's sparkling green eyes. He wanted to speak, but no words felt adequate to express his rush of emotion. He pulled her to him and kissed her deeply. They fell into a long, warm, silent embrace.

Chapter 67

DJ and Levi Sharpe were walking to the Captain's office.

"Heard a rumor you are thinking about retiring." *Say it ain't so.*

Sharpe smiled. "There ain't no secrets around here. Look, I'm just trying to get to the finish line with minimal damage. Not sure when that might be."

"Better not be soon my friend." *I need you right now more than Louise does!*

Sharpe's phone beeped with an incoming text. He silenced the beeping as they entered Kekoa's office.

"Morning Detectives," said Captain Kekoa in an officious manner.

Wow, Kahuna has his game face on early this morning!

Kekoa continued. "We gotta push hard on the Pernell case. Ignore all the outside noise. Our job is to find a murderer and a motive. All that other crap in the media ain't for us."

"Yessir" answered both Detectives.

"I've read DJ's most recent report. But first, tell me about your East Coast trip."

DJ reviewed the meetings in New York at TEM and O'Finsky's. He also reviewed the discussions with the Pernell family, Vera Eden, and lastly, Frank Dorrington.

"Quite a character, that Dorrington," said Kekoa. "Were you in Hartford during the disturbance at the Hate Crimes rally?"

"Yes," said DJ. "It was pretty ugly." *I had an enjoyable personal experience with two of those racist bastards!*

"Glad to see you're okay." said Kekoa. "Anything else to add?"

"I returned to the alley behind the Smythville Hotel Saturday night and had an interesting encounter."

"What happened?"

"I encountered a homeless man named Oscar who claims to have met a man fitting Pernell's description. Oscar nicknamed him Tarzan because the man was wearing just a small cloth covering his junk, a loincloth, like Tarzan wore."

"Did you record your conversation?"

"Of course" answered DJ. *C'mon Chief, ain't my first rodeo.*

"Excellent. Make sure I get a dub of that. Did this Oscar talk to the man?"

"Oscar claims the man tried to buy his coat for $100, but Oscar turned him down because the man clearly had no money."

"Makes sense," said Kekoa.

"Oscar said the man repeated the phrase: 'woke up naked pissing in a corner', which exactly matches the phrase used by our snitch, Johnny G., when relating the story told to him by Lester Hollowell."

"No shit?" said Kekoa.

While DJ was talking, Sharpe peeked at the text he'd just received. "I knew it!" he said out loud.

Kekoa asked, "What's up, Levi?"

"This text is from Chris Hardy. They traced the path of Hollowell's stolen car utilizing the traffic security cameras."

"And?"

"This is weird. The stolen car, presumably driven by Lester Hollowell, was seen traveling south on Lund at 12:45 am. It disappeared on the block between Seminole and Pine St. It wasn't seen again until 3:15 am on Lund crossing at the Pine intersection just south of the Smythville."

"So why would that car take two and a half hours to travel one block? asked Kekoa, sounding like a teacher administering a test.

"Only one explanation," said DJ. "The alley that goes behind the Smythville Hotel meets Lund on that block. We now know that dealers sometimes park their cars at the end of that alley to do their business. That's gotta be where Hollowell was parked."

"And that's the alley where we've placed Mr. Pernell thanks to DJ's new homeless friend, Oscar," added Sharpe. "So it seems likely that Mr. Pernell encountered Hollowell in that alley and things went bad, with Hollowell driving to the Hollis area at around 3:15 am, presumably to dump Pernell's body."

Kekoa asked "Any passengers visible in the car?"

"No mention of that" answered Sharpe.

DJ asked "Any evidence placing Pernell in that car?" *That would be mighty handy to know.*

"Nothing yet," said Sharpe. "That's some grisly work going through that gross mess of splattered body parts. Oakland PD will let us know if they find anything."

"This new information fits well with our scenario," said Kekoa. "I've reviewed your notes on the entire case. So let's see if I've got this straight. Your victim, Ray Pernell who was wearing only rags, was seen in the alley behind the Smythville late, on the night of his murder."

"Yes," said DJ.

"He tried to buy a coat from Oscar, to cover his near nakedness. He used the phrase 'woke up naked pissing in a corner.' And that phrase was repeated the next night, by Lester Hollowell, at a Meth house, while bragging about killing a 'gay man'."

"Correct Captain."

"And you know this because your snitch, Johnny G, was in the Meth house when Hollowell was bragging about killing the 'gay man'. And the snitch told you about this because he was trying to lighten a possession charge."

DJ beamed. "Exactly Captain." *Damn, nice to know that someone actually reads my reports!*

"How much do you trust this snitch?"

"Normally, not at all,"said DJ. *He's a desperate meth-head!* "But hearing our homeless guy, Oscar, repeat that exact phrase was definitely enough for us to revisit Johnny G's testimony. He also told us the truth about Mr. Hollowell's plans to end a personal feud the next day. But, Hollowell was shot up in his stolen car."

"Understood, Detective. Hollowell's street name was Capone, if I recall your notes."

"Exactly," said DJ. *Damn, the captain is laser focused!*

"So it's not a stretch if we believe testimony from both a homeless man and a snitch, to place Mr. Pernell in that alley late that night."

"No, it's not" echoed Sharpe.

Kekoa folded his arms across his broad chest. "It's also not a huge stretch to imagine that Pernell encountered Mr. Hollowell near the end of the alley, following his encounter with Oscar."

"That's kinda where we're at." said DJ "What we don't know is why he was in the alley, dressed in rags, in the first place. Did Hollowell, or someone else, previously force him into those clothes? Or was he really out looking for some type of action involving sex or drugs?"

"Tell me about the phrase, 'pissing in a corner'."

Sharpe answered. "As you read in DJ's report, we had all the corners in Pernell's hotel room checked for his urine. No luck."

DJ spoke. "We also think that if he accidentally locked himself out of his room, he would've gone downstairs to the lobby for help, not outside in the alley."

"Makes sense," said Kekoa. "Mr. Pernell was drunk when he returned to the hotel, correct?"

"Absolutely," said DJ. *More like totally hammered!* "And Pernell's wife got defensive when I asked about their alcohol consumption. She might've been holding something back."

Kekoa leaned forward and stared directly into DJ's eyes for a few seconds. "I suggest that you try again with Mrs. Pernell. Maybe you can pull out whatever she's hiding."

"I'll give it another shot," said DJ, returning Kekoa's stare. *Damn, please blink so I know you're human!*

Kekoa leaned back. "What else you got?"

DJ rubbed his temples. "Let's go back to the phrase 'woke up naked pissing in a corner'. Now that we have corroboration on that phrase, at least we think we do, let's go find the corner he was talking about."

"You mean outside his hotel room?" asked Sharpe.

"Yes."

"But he said 'woke up naked pissing in a corner'. His CPAP machine verifies that he used it for 18 minutes before he woke up."

"Maybe that's not exactly the case," said DJ.

"What the hell are you talking about?" asked Sharpe

"Not sure, but I've got a feeling that we're missing something that's right in front of us." *Just not exactly sure what it is.*

"Uh oh," said Sharpe. "DJ's got one of his feelings! Stand back!"

"Very funny. I wanna try something. Levi, have your team expand their urine search. Let's check all the corners outside his hotel room within 50 feet. Can you get that done within two days?"

"Will do, partner. The piss patrol shall return to the scene!"

"I'll talk again with the widow. Maybe dig a little deeper." *I know she was holding something back.*

"Sounds like a plan," said Captain Kekoa.

DJ and Sharpe nodded.

"Well, what are you waiting for? Get the hell out of my office and go do some goddam police work!"

Chapter 68

While making breakfast for the kids, Mia noticed an overnight text from Detective Harland, requesting a FaceTime conversation at noon, eastern time.

"Morning Mom," said Ricky as he and Karl walked into the kitchen.

"Morning boys. You're running late. Oatmeal is on the stove and bagels are in the toaster."

"Where's Phoebe?" asked Ricky.

"She stayed another night at Amy's" lied Mia, not really sure what to share with her two sons. "She'll be home later today."

Ten minutes later, Mia walked Karl out to the school bus, ignoring the shouted questions from reporters camped at the end of her driveway.

Returning to the kitchen, Mia saw Ricky shoveling the final spoonfuls of oatmeal into his mouth. "Do you have your lunch?"

"No Mom, I'll get one at school. Don't sweat it, Tuesday is salad day in the cafeteria."

A single beep of the horn signaled that the Grant Prep van was outside for Ricky. He grabbed his backpack and headed for the door. "See ya Mom."

"Love you. Don't talk to any of those people out there!"

Within minutes, Mia was driving to St. Francis Hospital to pick up Phoebe.

———

DJ Harland arrived at the office at 8 am, hoping to get some work done before his day got busy. Approaching his cubicle, he saw the top of the cleanly shaved head that he knew belonged to Levi Sharpe.

"Morning Levi."

"Where you been DJ?" said Sharpe in a mocking tone. "I've been waiting here for hours."

"Nice try. You're late. I'm just returning from my lunch break."

Sharpe laughed, stood, and embraced DJ. "How goes the battle?"

"It is what it is. Went shopping for baby furniture last night."

"You guys pregnant?"

"Not that we know of. Just getting ahead of the game. What brings you here at this early hour? Any news on your piss-seeking mission?"

Sharpe smiled. "No urine results yet, though we've got a team checking every corner within sight of Pernell's room."

"God bless 'em." *Should be a special bonus for the urine patrol.*

"But I do have some good news and bad news."

"Bad first," said DJ.

"The bad news is that Forensics has given up on trying to identify any of Pernell's blood inside Hollowell's stolen car. It is just too splattered with Hollowell's blood, brains, and all the other shredded pieces of his body."

"Not a surprise. So we still don't know if Pernell was even in that car. What's the good news?"

Sharpe smiled broadly. "They did turn up a few fibers, some of which match the fibers from the loincloth Pernell was wearing that night."

"No shit?" *Please don't be yanking my chain!*

"For real, my friend. We've placed him in the vehicle."

DJ smiled. "Sonafabitch! Seems like Hollowell was telling the truth about running into a 'gay man' when he met up with Ray Pernell."

"And putting a nine-mil slug in his head."

"Yup. Apparently, he did."

Sharpe rubbed his chin. "So Johnny G. was telling us what he actually believed to be true."

"Seems like it. Who knew a professional snitch would use the truth to get himself off the hook?" *What are the odds?*

"We've still got some loose ends, partner," said Sharpe. "Like when did Pernell first encounter Hollowell? Was it earlier in the evening when they were out partying, or did they meet for the first time in the hotel or even the alley?"

"Good question."

"And why was Pernell dressed like that, and what the hell was he doing on the streets at that hour?"

"Roger that, and let's not forget his quote of 'woke up naked pissing in a corner', which right now seems a whole lot more valid after talking to my new homeless friend, Oscar."

"Small steps, partner," said Sharpe. "Let's try to piece this thing together and come up with a plausible, if not factual, timeline explanation. The Captain, not to mention the Commissioner and the bigwigs at Tucker, would be down with that."

"And so would the Pernell family." *They've suffered enough.*

Chapter 69

At 9 am PT, DJ reached out to Mia Pernell via FaceTime. He saw her pretty face appear on his phone.

"Hi Mrs. Pernell, you're looking well."

"The magic of makeup. And please, call me Mia."

"Looks like you're in your car. Did I catch you at a bad time?"

Mia, parked in the hospital parking lot, decided not to share Phoebe's suicide attempt with DJ. "No. Just out running errands." She quickly changed the subject. "Were you still here when the Hate Crimes rally blew up in Hartford?"

"Yeah. I was on my way downtown to talk to Frank Dorrington when it got a little crazy out there."

"You okay?"

"All good." *Better than those two morons I met.*

"It sure looked awful. There are still two people in intensive care. How'd your talk go with Frank? Did you see his latest bullshit about Ray in the Dishing Dirt?"

"Sure did. You gotta be getting close to filing a lawsuit at this point."

"My attorney is on it. How was your talk with Frank?"

"He seems less than sincere."

"Not exactly breaking news Detective."

"Heard that. Are you still being harassed by the press?"

"Yes. They're still camped outside. My lawyer doesn't want me to speak to them."

"Good advice."

"C'mon Detective, any progress on your investigation? We'd love some answers."

"I don't want to speculate on anything." DJ saw his opportunity. "But you can help us move this along. That's why I wanted to speak with you." *Time to come clean Mia!*

"I can't imagine what's left that we haven't already discussed."

"Well Mia, I wanted to ask you again about your husband's drinking habits."

"Haven't we covered this already?"

"When I asked you about this, outside your home last week, you didn't seem to be sharing everything when you answered."

"I didn't tell you any lies, Detective."

Same shit I used to say to my parents. "Fair enough. But what did you leave out?"

Mia paused, clearly turning something over in her mind.

"Mia, I'm not looking to indict you or harm your husband's memory. But I must have all the facts to sort everything out."

"Well, Detective. There is one little thing that I may have left out. But only because I was trying to protect Ray's reputation and didn't think it was important."

"What is it, Mia?" *If you wanna put this misery to bed, you gotta come clean!*

"Do you remember when I told you that Ray injured his knee on a ski trip to New Hampshire?"

"Yeah."

"Well, he did injure his knee on that trip. But, I may have allowed you to think that his injury happened on the slopes when it didn't."

"How'd it happen?" *Line dancing, musical chairs, hopscotch?*

"We were staying on the mountain, in one of those two-level ski-out condos. We walked down the slope one evening to grab dinner, drinks and enjoy some live music in the lodge. It happened to be sake night, and we may have drank a bit too much."

"And?" *There's that evil sake again....*

"And…. the walk back up the slope to our condo was a little challenging. I don't remember much else, except that I crashed upstairs, in the bedroom, fully clothed."

"Did your husband make it upstairs to bed?"

"I'm not sure. But the next thing I knew, I heard Ray yelling my name. It took me a second to roll out of bed and regain my senses."

"Where was Ray?"

"I found him sprawled on the stairs in an ugly position. His right leg was bent the wrong way."

"What'd he say?"

"He was yelling for me to help him. His leg looked awful in that position. I asked him what happened. He said 'I don't know, I just suddenly felt a huge pain in my leg, and realized I was here on the stairs.'"

"So he had no recollection of falling on the stairs?"

"Apparently not, Detective. I didn't want you to think less of Ray because this happened. It probably happens to most of us at one time or another."

"Mia, I'm not interested in judging anyone. I just need to know about these kinds of things."

"I know. I'm sorry. It's just that the whole country already thinks Ray was looking for booze, drugs, or sex. I just can't take it anymore."

"Mia, did anything like this ever happen to your husband, before or after the ski trip?"

"Not sure. I mean there were mornings when we both might have been a bit foggy on some details from the night before, but we were always extra careful on nights that we might have drank more than usual" Mia suddenly realized how incredibly self-serving that statement sounded. "I mean that we…..aw hell, I don't know what I'm saying."

"Relax Mia. You're fine. Thanks for sharing these thoughts with me."

"Does this change anything about your investigation?"

"An investigation is built on many pieces of information, which eventually form a trend that leads us to a conclusion. You got anything to add?" *Any more secrets you might have 'forgotten'?*

"No. Sorry, I held it back, Detective."

"Better late than never, Mia."

"Thanks, Detective." After disconnecting the call, Mia exhaled a big sigh of relief and headed into the hospital to bring her daughter home.

Chapter 70

Frank Dorrington was showering with a plastic bag wrapped around his hand. The constant painful throbbing reminded him how badly he needed to get Stanley out of his life.

Throwing on gym shorts and a faded NY Giants t-shirt, he made a cup of coffee and opened his banking app. Frank felt thrilled to see that twenty-five thousand dollars had been added to his account. The check from Dishing Dirt had been deposited, as promised. He hoped this new equity would help persuade the banks to reconsider his loan request.

Frank received a text from a New York City area code that read "Give me a call at your convenience." It was from Jungle Jane, the Producer of the Hammy B show. After considering his options, Frank decided he had nothing to lose by returning Jungle Jane's call.

"Hammy B Productions. How may I direct your call?"

Frank suddenly felt odd saying "Uhh, Jungle Jane please."

"What is this in reference to?"

"This is Frank Dorrington. Returning her call."

"Please hold."

Frank had a fleeting urge to hang up, fearing that Jane was going to chastise him for sharing so much more information with Dishing Dirt than he had shared with Hammy. He would argue that DD had paid so much more.

"Hi, Frank. How are you?"Jane's warm tone immediately disarmed Frank.

"Hi Miss, uhh Jungle Jane. How goes it?"

"Call me Jane. I'll get right to the point. The Pernell case continues to dominate the national conversation. And you, my friend, have come out with some new revelations about him."

"Yes, I have. But those things were….."

Jane interrupted. "Don't care about that Frank. What we care about here is that you share those new revelations on national TV. We reach millions more people than that tabloid rag."

"Are you asking me to be on your show again?"

"Yes, Frank. We have an opening next Wednesday, a week from tomorrow. That show will air two days later, on Friday of next week."

"I'll consider it. You should know that my appearance fee has gone up."

"Shocking," said Jane flatly. "What are we talking about?"

"Fifty thousand, with ten thousand upfront upon execution of our agreement."

"Don't be ridiculous Frank. I'll go right to our top offer. Twenty-five thousand with nothing guaranteed upfront. You won't find a better offer on TV anywhere. Nothing even close."

Frank couldn't believe this windfall but needed to keep his cool. "Make it 30k and you've got a deal. The money needs to be deposited directly into my account."

"Listen, Frank, that's above budget for me. What can you guarantee you'll deliver that day? I need to justify this to my bosses."

"Everything you read in Dishing Dirt and then some."

"There's gotta be more. We aren't paying for recycled news, Frank."

Frank's desperate need for money overcame his common sense. "I'm pretty sure I know what Ray was looking for that night." lied Frank. "I can share that with Hammy on air."

"OK Frank. I'll convey that to management. Let's say we have an agreement in principle, and I'll get back to you later today with confirmation and our release form".

"Great, thanks, bye." Frank began pondering how he could stretch his lies about Ray without putting himself in legal jeopardy. But, that 30k would certainly help keep Stanley at bay.

His cell phone pinged, showing the name "Debbie." . Against his better judgment, he answered the call from his ex-wife. "Are you going to hang up on me again?"

"Hi Frank. No. I just want to nicely try to appeal to the man I once thought I loved."

"Nicely? That's hilarious. What do you want Debbie?"

"Listen, Frank, maybe you haven't carefully considered this, but the things you are saying about Ray are hurting Mia and kids." Debbie so wanted to share Phoebe's suicide attempt with Frank, but Mia had sworn her to secrecy.

"I'm not telling any lies, Debbie. I just say what I know to be true. It's the media that never lets the facts get in the way of a good story."

"Clandestine gay bar meetings? Really Frank?"

"I never used the word 'clandestine'. "

"So you and Ray met regularly in gay bars?"

"No, I said that we once got together for a beer at Pat's in West Hartford, which happens to be primarily a gay bar."

"Do you know how hard it is to believe that, on top of your other bullshit about Ray seeing a counselor and being hooked on Oxy? Yet, no one else, including Mia, knew anything about those things?"

"Look Debbie, you don't know those things to NOT be true."

Debbie so wanted to share Phoebe's suicide attempt with Frank, but Mia had sworn her to secrecy. "Don't play lawyer with me, Frank! I thought I would try one last time to appeal to whatever shred of decency you might still have. But I see now that you are too far gone."

"That's your opinion."

"No, that's a fact. You'll keep selling this horseshit, trying to squeeze every last dollar out of your lies. But, soon you'll be an afterthought, forgotten by all."

Frank was angry, trying to think of something to hurt Debbie. He blurted out "You ain't seen nothing yet. Catch me on Hammy B next week when I reveal it all!"

Ending the call, Debbie shouted, "You're an asshole Frank!"

Chapter 71

The ride home with Phoebe was quiet. The bandage on her left wrist had been reduced to a couple of flesh-colored band-aids which were covered by a long sleeved blouse. Mia met with Doctor Bellefleur who said Phoebe's initial session with a hospital staff counselor had been productive. The Doctor suggested another day of rest for Phoebe followed by a re-immersion into her daily routine on Monday. Continued counseling for her would start as soon as possible.

"I'm tired. I want to go to bed."

Mia was happy just to hear her daughter's voice. "Of course. It'll be quiet. Your brothers won't be home for a couple hours."

Phoebe grunted her acknowledgement.

As Phoebe was slipping into bed, Mia said "Please tell me what was going on in your head this weekend at Hampshire Park."

"I needed some time alone to think stuff through."

"I hear you. We all need that kind of time once in a while. And deleting all your social media might actually have been a positive step. Who needs that crap?"

"I don't know Mom. I'm just over it. All of it. I feel like a freak."

"Sweetheart, look at me. You are not a freak! You're a beautiful, intelligent sensitive young woman with an incredibly bright future."

"Please Mom. No pep talks."

"It's true. Your future is very bright."

"If only, Mom. My life is ruined. It's all about Dad's weirdo behavior and the secrets that you both kept from me."

"That's not true!"

"I'm so sick of all the texts, posts, and insta messages. I hear the whispering in the halls at school."

"All the crap you're hearing is just hurtful gossip. It's not true"

"Really Mom? Then why don't you tell me what 'normal' thing Dad was doing dressed like that on the streets, in the middle of the night?"

"We don't know yet. Whoever killed him may have had a lot to do with that stuff. But you know your Dad would never choose to do anything like that."

"Do I Mom? I don't know anything anymore about you guys."

Frustrated, Mia tried a different approach. "You must have some friends who refuse to believe this bullshit."

"Amy still hangs out with me, although I don't know why. A few others still talk to me, but it's not like we're close."

"It's good to know that some of your friends are showing some character and loyalty."

"Not really Mom. They're just waiting for the truth to come out about Dad's freakish lifestyle."

"Phoebe, honey. None of that is worth losing your life."

"Why not? My life is ruined. I'm the laughingstock of Hudson High. That awful picture of Dad in his party outfit is all over TV and the internet."

Mia tried to sound calm. "So what? We know your Dad wouldn't choose to look like that."

"Then why is Dad's friend telling the whole world all about his weirdness? Why is Dad's murder being called a gay hate crime? Why was our house attacked? Why did you pull us out of St. Joe's? Are you embarrassed too?"

"Geez Phoebe, I don't know where to begin with all of that, except to tell you that none of that bullshit is……"

"Stop lying, Mom! Of course, it's true, or the whole world wouldn't be talking about it. I wanted to get rid of all the pain. I literally have no reason to live."

Tears streamed down Mia's cheeks. "Phoebe, please listen to me! You've got to understand that this is a temporary situation that will pass with time. I know you are hurting…..a lot. But your solution is permanent, and it can't be undone."

"Gotta be better than this."

"No, it isn't. We love you so much. Please tell me if there is anything I can do to help you feel better."

" I don't know, Mom. I'm tired. Can I please go to sleep now?"

"Okay, honey. We can talk later. Can I hug you?"

Mia leaned over the bed and put her arms around Phoebe, hugging her tight. She didn't feel much of a hug in return, but at least she wasn't pushed away.

"Please Phoebe, please talk to me if you ever feel that way again. We love you so much."

Phoebe rolled over, burying her face in the pillow. "Bye Mom."

Chapter 72

Frank Dorrington was staring at an oversized oak desk in the ostentatious office of his Bank Manager, Seth Benjamin, who was currently across the hall, consulting with his team of loan specialists. Frank had been banking at Emerson Bank of Connecticut (EBC) since his graduation from law school. Mr. Benjamin had approved both of Frank's business loans from EBC. Unfortunately for Frank, despite the shuttering of his law firm, he still held those notes. Now, he was seeking more money, hoping that the twenty-five thousand in his account would serve as collateral for receiving a loan of 150k. He intended to use that money to pay off Stanley and make him go away.

Returning to his office, Seth Benjamin didn't mince words. "I'm sorry Mr. Dorrington, you don't qualify for another loan from us at this time."

"Why not?"

"You're still in arrears on both of your current loans. If you can bring those payments up to date, and share your plan for generating future income, then we could maybe explore a high-interest, short-term loan."

"But I have some equity in my checking account that can serve as collateral."

"Yes, I see," said Benjamin. "Twenty-five thousand, eight hundred and six dollars, to be exact."

"Doesn't that count for something?"

"Mr. Dorrington, you'd be much better off using that money to address your outstanding debt on your two active loans with EBC."

"I can't do that right now. But why can't I borrow against it?"

"We won't do that at EBC. I'm very sorry Mr. Dorrington. Is there anything else we can do for you?"

"No thanks. I'll take my business elsewhere."

"As is your prerogative, sir."

———

DJ was in Kekoa's office, sharing the details of his conversation with Mia Pernell.

The Captain smiled. "Love that you used your interviewing skills to get Mrs. Pernell to share her little secret. Good info."

"Thanks, Kahuna."

"But now that we've placed Pernell in Hollowell's car, we still need an explanation of how those two got together, and if anyone else was involved."

"Getting close on that, Captain."

"Good. Also, we still don't know what the hell Pernell's intentions were, or what that loincloth was all about."

"On that too, Cap'n." *Rome wasn't built in a day!*

"I know you are," said Kekoa. "The Commissioner, and his pal at Tucker, are very interested in Pernell's intentions that night."

"No doubt, Kahuna. It seems that Tucker hasn't yet decided if Pernell is a bad actor or a sympathetic victim."

"Exactly, DJ. That's why they are publicly playing both sides of the fence until our investigation plays out."

"The fact that Pernell asked our homeless friend, Oscar, for his coat tells me that he didn't choose to dress in that outfit."

"Makes sense," said the Captain.

"That leads us to the question of who or what caused him to dress like that."

Detective Sharpe appeared in the doorway to Kekoa's office.

"Come on in, Levi".

"Sorry, I'm late. Did I miss anything?"

"We're just reviewing some of the case details. Any luck on your urine search?"

"No luck. Our team has checked every corner within 50 feet of room 407. Nothing. Housecleaning vacuums the halls daily and washes the walls every month."

"Sometimes not finding something is as important as finding it," said DJ.

"What do you mean?" asked Kekoa

"Not sure, Captain. Gotta think this through." *There might be one more thing to check.*

"You do that, DJ," said Kekoa. "Now, both of you, get out. I gotta update the Commish."

––––––––––––

Frank Dorrington pulled his ancient car into his designated parking space outside his apartment building. The engine continued to knock for a few seconds after he killed the ignition switch. "Piece of shit.".

Keying the door and entering his apartment, Dorrington froze in his steps.

"Hello, Frank. Welcome home" Stanley's broad body, clad in his usual black suit and white shirt, was sprawled across the tattered couch, sipping a beer liberated from Frank's refrigerator. His slicked-back black hair appeared painted onto his skull.

Frank did his best to swallow his shock, while unconsciously reaching for the cast on his left hand. "How did you…?"

"Really Frank? I own you. And I own this crappy apartment too. You need to step up your game, Counselor."

"Just give me a chance. Things are shaping up."

"I'm here for the twenty grand you promised me."

"I've got it. I'll write you a check for cash right now."

Stanley smiled. "Your checkbook is right there on the table. I already removed it from your hiding place in the kitchen."

Frank grabbed the checkbook and began to write. Stanley's large, bony hand suddenly enveloped Frank's right hand.

"What are you doing? I'm writing the check!"

"You've been a naughty boy, Frank." Stanley was twisting Frank's hand. "Make the check for twenty-five thousand."

"Stop! Dammit! I won't be able to write any checks if you break that hand too!"

"I told you not to fuck me, Frank. Yet you keep insisting on screwing me anyway. You deposited twenty-five thousand at EBC, not the twenty thousand that you told me you were getting." Stanley twisted Frank's hand further.

"Fuck! Stop! I need something to live on while I make more money for you."

Stanley let go of the hand. "Write it for twenty-five thousand, you lying prick." Slapping Frank on the side of the head, he added "There's still another eight hundred dollars in there for your damn groceries."

"Geeezus, man. I can only do so much."

"Shoulda thought of that when you came begging for my money."

Pocketing the check, Stanley said "This little interest payment will buy you a few days. Better get busy on finding the other 125k."

Frank knew better than to again point out that he had only borrowed 100k in the first place. "I've got another payday coming up. Doing Hammy B again next week."

"Love that angry bastard!" said Stanley. "How much are they paying you, Frank? And you might want to tell me the truth this time."

"We're still negotiating. Probably another twenty-five thousand. It's all yours when I get it."

"Damn, straight it is." Moving quickly, Stanley grabbed Frank by the throat, pushing his thumbs in deep enough to cut off Franks's ability to breathe. Staring directly into Frank's frightened eyes, Stanley's voice was devoid of emotion. "For your sake, I hope you're done fucking me. I'm tired of this game. My people want me to terminate this situation, but I'm giving you another chance. Don't make me regret it."

Pulling his hands away, Stanley stalked out the door.

Dropping to his hands and knees, Frank gasped, trying to regain his breath.

Chapter 73

"This might be the best grilled-fish sandwich I've ever had," said Debbie Slater. She and Carlos Madrigan were enjoying lunch on Carlos' modest balcony.

"Glad you like it. Got it at Harry's Halibut House. It was swimming a couple hours ago."

"Delicious. The ocean view makes it extra special."

"That's one of the charming things about West Haven. Thanks again for driving down here for lunch."

"Short trip for such a wonderful reward. And the food is good too."

Carlos wondered if he was blushing. "You're sweet, please stay as long as you want."

"I will. Maybe next time, I'll pack a bag, and we can do brunch."

Now Carlos was sure he was blushing. He managed to say "Of course, anytime." Changing the subject, he asked, "You heard from Mia lately?"

"No. But I need to fill her in on a chat I had with my ex yesterday."

"Who called who?"

"Like an idiot, I came up with the idea that I could maybe somehow appeal to Frank's sense of decency."

"And?"

"No shot. He's in too deep to stop now. He's going back on the Hammy B show next week, probably to spew new lies in return for some more blood money."

"Hammy B? I worked on their original animation and graphics package back when they launched years ago."

"Really?"

"Yeah. I don't know if you've seen that show, but the green-haired Producer that Hammy calls 'Jungle Jane' was an AP with us, back when I was working in Hartford."

"No kidding?"

"For sure. I didn't hang on the newsroom side very often, but I remember her well enough. Except her real name wasn't Jane….It's Tiffany. Last name is Raye, I think, and her hair wasn't green."

"Did you guys work together?"

"Not really. But her dad worked over in PR. Matthew Raye. He and I collaborated a few times before I moved on."

"Wow, small world. She sure seems to have done well for herself."

"For sure. She's got the right kind of personality for that role. I think they shoot Hammy B in the old theater at Penn Station."

Debbie sighed. "Unfortunately, that show always goes for the garish headlines. Hammy is like a video version of those grocery store tabloids."

"Couldn't agree more."

"No doubt, Frank is cooking up some fresh bullshit about Ray to entertain Hammy and his leering audience."

Carlos shook his head. "Sooner or later, that fool is gonna be exposed for the lying jerk that he is."

"If there's any justice in this world" added Debbie.

———

Officer Amal Ahmadi couldn't help himself. "Damn, I'm good!". Picking up his phone, he called Detective Harland.

"Hey Amal, what's up?"

"Remember that I told you the TuckerExecFreak photo originated somewhere in southern New England?"

"Sure do."

"I reached out to a couple of my contacts deep in the IT world and they were able to pinpoint the source of the original posting to the noTrace website.

"No kidding? What'd you find?"

"How does this sound Detective? 'Law Offices of Frank Dorrington PLLC', a law firm registered in Waterbury, Connecticut."

"Not a shock." *That slippery bastard nearly vomited on himself when I asked him about the text being added to the original photo.*

"Hope this was helpful, Detective."

"Even though Dorrington isn't a suspect at this time, this information may interest the folks at Tucker. Thanks again, Amal. You're the best."

Chapter 74

"Hello, Mr. Dorrington. My name is Analyse Boyle, legal counsel for the Hammy B Production Group."

"Morning."

"We're prepared to meet your request for thirty thousand dollars as compensation for your appearance on the Hammy B program, to be recorded five days from now, on Wednesday, in the New York City studios of Hammy B Productions."

"Happy to hear that."

"The show will air via our syndicated network two days later, on Friday. Specific dates and times are in the release. Payment will be made via direct deposit into the account of your specification, immediately after the program airs."

"Sorry, I prefer to be compensated immediately following the recording of the show. No need to wait the 48 hours until it airs."

"Mr. Dorrington, you're being compensated for your appearance on a nationally syndicated television program, not for the recording of that show. Until that show airs, the recording holds no equity for us. This concept is ironclad and has been tested in the district court of New York."

"But you set a precedent when I was compensated immediately following my studio appearance the last time I appeared on the show."

"Understood Mr. Dorrington. That was a minimal cash payment that didn't meet the threshold you've surpassed with your thirty-thousand-dollar compensation fee. If this payment schedule is a problem, sir, we are happy to move on and schedule another guest."

Frank wanted to blast this holier-than-thou, two-bit attorney right out of her patent-leather pumps. He pictured a pimply-faced, recent law school grad, whose only job offer came from a sleazy group like Hammy B. But he desperately needed this 30k and swallowed his anger.

"Not a perfect scenario for me, Ms. Boyle. But let's move on. I need to understand your expectations for my appearance on your program."

"I believe you shared your intentions with our Producer, and she is comfortable with those promises. We outlined our expectations in the release."

"Care to give me a preview?"

"In essence, it states that you will reveal something specific as to the intentions of Ray Pernell on the night he was murdered. Additionally, you will be asked to expound upon any previous public statements you have made, in all media, about Mr. Pernell and your relationship with him."

"Sounds right. You can send me the release."

"Thank you, Mr. Dorrington. Please be expedient with your response as we normally schedule guests at least a week out."

"Yeah, yeah. Just send it along Ms. Boyle."

————

DJ Harland was in his "think tank", otherwise known as a hot shower. His mind was racing with thoughts about the Pernell case.

Something's missing. The key is in the phrase "woke up naked and pissing in a corner". We can't find evidence of urine in any corner of Pernell's hotel room, and even all corners within 50 feet outside of the room. What corner was he talking about? Or was he just confused? We know his CPAP stopped running at 3:08 am." That gives us a record of when he woke up....or does it? A fresh thought flashed through DJ's mind. Holy shit! It might be right there in front of us. I've gotta think about this and consult an expert.

DJ was able to arrange an end-of-day phone call with Judy Catellano, the SFPD Forensic Psychologist. After listening to DJ's description of the events surrounding Pernell's death, Catellano said "fascinating stuff Detective Harland, I do believe you are on to something. Your theory fits well with all of the evidence you've presented to me. I'm guessing you'll have Detective Sharpe reassemble his urine-search team."

DJ sent a text to both Levi Sharpe and Captain Kekoa. "Can we do a Zoom meeting tomorrow at 10 am? I know it's Saturday, but I think I've got something that may explain Pernell's behavior that night.

Damn, I hope I'm on the right track.

––––––––––

Carlos Madrigan sat back and patted his stomach."Wow, Debbie. That was awesome. I haven't had a homemade stir-fry like that in …..well, never actually."

"No kidding? Stir-fry is easy."

"Great choice. I grew up on meat and potatoes……repeatedly."

"Well, then you gotta keep coming here to my private bistro. You'll find more variety on my menu."

"I can't wait," said Carlos as he walked around the table to wrap Debbie in a tight embrace.

Following a long, slow exploratory kiss, Debbie said "Why don't we have an after-dinner drink in front of the fireplace?"

Carlos raised an eyebrow.

"Oh right," said Debbie, smiling. "I don't have a fireplace. It just sounded romantic. How about the couch?"

"That'll do."

Their conversation over wine was easy and free-flowing. They talked about their common backgrounds in the design and production business. They discussed their relationships with Ray and Mia.

"Someone needs to shut Frank down. He is killing Mia's family with his crap. Our HR department at Tucker is notorious for defending our almighty image. This could cost Mia a ton of money if they refuse to pay Ray's benefits."

"Short of threatening, beating, or shooting Frank, there's no way to stop him from spreading his half-truths and flat-out lies."

"There's gotta be a way to stop him," said Carlos. "I'll keep thinking about this until I come up with something."

Now feeling the warmth that comes from a good meal, fine wine, and the company of a loving partner, Debbie put her arms around Carlos' neck, pulled him close, and whispered in his ear: "Whatta ya say we table all that angst for now and focus on us?"

"My pleasure."

"Do you have anywhere else to be tonight?"

"No."

"Good."

They shared a deeply passionate, unrestrained kiss that was a precursor of things to come. Carlos was again lost in Debbie's deep, green eyes. He tucked her hair behind her ear and stroked her face. Debbie savored his touch which felt both arousing and comforting. She kicked off her shoes and pulled Carlos down on top of her. He couldn't believe how delicious she smelled. He kissed the nape of her neck, wanting to consume her. She reached under his shirt and ran her hands across his bare chest. He couldn't remember the last time he felt so alive with so much desire for a woman.

Carlos said "This couch is so small. Bedroom?"

"Yes".

Handing Debbie the two wine glasses, Carlos carefully picked her up from the couch and carried her into her bedroom. Their heated lovemaking was wonderfully intimate and deliciously satisfying. They eventually fell asleep, in each others' arms, coated in the cool sweat of pleasure, feeling that unmatchable glow of newfound love and intimacy

Chapter 75

At 5 am, Frank Dorrington surrendered to his insomnia and rose to make a cup of coffee. The throbbing in his left hand was constant, and it was feeling itchy inside the cast.

Checking for messages, Frank smiled at an email from Analyse Boyle, the attorney from Hammy B Productions. They had approved his 30k fee.

The release form clearly stated that he would not get paid until the show aired, two days after the recording. Frank hoped that Stanley would have 48 hours' worth of patience. The document outlined the information Frank had agreed to discuss, including revealing Ray Pernell's "specific motivation to dress in a loincloth and walk the streets of San Francisco on the night of his murder."

Frank thought that this might be one of the stranger attachments to a release form that he'd ever read, but the wording accurately captured his promises. Frank attached his electronic signature to the forms and sent them back to Ms Boyle.

———

Lying in bed, Debbie was feeling great, staring at Carlos, listening to the steady rhythm of his breathing. His eyes fluttered open and he said "Good morning beautiful."

'Morning."

"I'm so happy that wasn't a dream, though it would have been the best dream ever. So happy that you are here, next to me."

Debbie snuggled up close. "I'm happy too. Last night was wonderful. How do you feel about coffee and bagels?"

"Breakfast sounds great, but I'd rather have you first."

"Smart man. I'm calorie-free." Debbie slid her still-naked body on top of Carlos.

The loud bell-ringing tone of her phone suddenly filled the room. Reaching over to turn it off, she saw "Mia" on the screen. Looking at Carlos, she said "I just can't ignore Mia's calls these days. It'll only be a minute."

"No prob, honey."

Debbie brought the phone to her ear, whispering "Hi Mia, is Phoebe okay?"

"Yes. We're hanging in there. Did you hear the latest about the Bushnell Park riot?"

"No. What?"

"A woman who was injured in the riot passed away last night. Massive head injuries."

Debbie sat straight up in bed. "Oh no. That's terrible. Who was she?" Carlos looked at her quizzically.

"Don't recall her name, but she was a school teacher from Canton."

"God bless her and her family," said Debbie. "Now don't go thinking that this had anything to do with Ray's situation."

"I know," said Mia. "But I can certainly identify with the pain of losing someone. I feel for her family, and her students."

"Maybe there'll be a GoFundMe page or some sort of charity to which we can contribute."

"Hope so," said Mia. "You sound groggy. You sure I didn't wake you?"

"Nah, we were already up." as soon as those words slipped out, Debbie knew what was coming next.

"We? Carlos, right?"

"Yes, Mia. You were right. Carlos and I are getting along really well." Debbie winked at Carlos.

"Tell me everything."

Debbie chuckled. "Mia, I'm not exactly in a position to talk right now. I'll call you later."

"Oh yes, of course. My best to Carlos. Call me later. I am so very happy for you two. Love you, Debbie."

"Love you too, Mia. Talk later."

"Everything OK?" asked Carlos.

"One of the victims of the Bushnell riot has passed."

"That's awful."

"Agreed, but I don't want to discuss that now." Flopping back on the pillow, Debbie looked into Carlos' dark eyes. "Did you know that Mia had ideas about us getting together for a long time?"

"No clue. Ray never said anything. Wish he had."

"Me too. At first, I didn't want to say anything to Mia, in case this didn't work out."

Carlos gently stroked Debbie's cheek. "I guess Mia now knows we're together." Looking deep into Debbie's green eyes, he asked "We are together, aren't we?"

Turning on her side under the sheets, Debbie pressed her body against Carlos' tall frame."Yes, we're together."

He quickly rolled over, now propped up on his arms over her slender naked body, planting delicate kisses on her warm flesh. "You are so beautiful. Getting together seems like a great idea right now.

Chapter 76

Sitting at the kitchen table, DJ put in his earbuds and logged into Zoom. Soon he saw Levi Sharpe and Captain Kekoa appear on his screen.

"Thanks for getting up on a Saturday morning. I thought it was important that we're all on the same page."

He saw both heads nodding.

"Great. First, I'm not sure how relevant this is to our investigation, but we now know that Frank Dorrington, the self-proclaimed close friend of Pernell's, was the person who created and posted the TuckerExecFreak graphic, using the original photo of Pernell's body."

Kekoa scoffed. "That guy is a profit-seeking asshole."

"Clearly," said DJ. "The dude has an agenda. But he doesn't appear to be relevant to this homicide. Are we in agreement that he is not currently a suspect?"

"Roger" said Sharpe.

"Okay, let's eliminate him from our homicide discussion," said DJ. "Let's just review a few details about Pernell's death."

"Go ahead" said Kekoa.

"Thanks, Stop me if any of these observations are incorrect.

-Pernell's CPAP machine ran for 18 minutes on the night of his death.

-Pernell's wife confirmed that he sometimes slept in the nude.

-Pernell's room was found in an orderly condition."

No one disagreed with anything yet, so DJ continued.

"-Pernell was verifiably intoxicated when he returned to the hotel.

-the rags and duct tape Pernell wore came from the utility cart on the 7th-floor landing of the service stairwell.

-Pernell's only possible exit from the hotel was the metal door at the bottom of the service stairwell, that opens into the back alley.

-We've placed Pernell in that alley, based on testimony from a homeless man.

-We have reason to believe that Lester Hollowell, aka Capone, was parked at the end of that alley, near Lund Ave.

-We've placed Pernell in Hollowell's stolen vehicle utilizing forensic fiber matching.

-We know that vehicle traveled from the Smythville area to Hollis at a time that fits our scenario.

-We have testimony stating that Hollowell bragged about killing a 'gay man' with a nine-millimeter gun.

-Pernell's cause of death was a nine-millimeter bullet in his head."

"With you so far," said Kekoa.

"DJ continued. "On some of those things, the corroboration is stronger than others."

"True," said Sharpe. "But it all fits together so far."

"Okay," said DJ. "It doesn't take a genius to track Pernell, beginning in the alley, where he ran into 'Oscar', who refused to sell Pernell his coat. Pernell then likely went further down the alley, eventually encountering Hollowell, who we believe was parked at the end of the alley where it meets Lund Ave. And, due to the fiber match, we know that Pernell was in Hollowell's car at some point. The traffic security cameras tracked that car to the Hollis area . While we aren't sure when Pernell was shot, we do know that his body was left in the lot in Hollis......with a nine-millimeter bullet in his head, and "FREAK" scrawled on his chest."

"Roger that DJ, we're with you on those points," said Captain Kekoa. "We've likely identified our murderer. Hollowell gave a full "confession" to your snitch, Johnny G, in the crank house that night. What we don't know, and what the folks at Tucker desperately want to know, is Pernell's motivation for being in the alley at that hour, dressed like he was."

"Understood," said DJ. "We still need to know if anyone else may have been involved."

"Exactly," said Sharpe. "It's not like Pernell was just taking a normal late-night stroll down a dark alley, wearing only a freakin' loincloth. Who forced him to do that?"

"Good question," said DJ. "Levi, do you think that you could re-enlist your forensic 'piss search' team and do one more thing to satisfy my curiosity?" *Those guys must be loving us right about now.*

Sharpe said. "Sure DJ. But I'm not sure what else we can do."

"Great. I've got an idea about that. I'm fairly confident I know what happened. The key is the twice quoted phrase: 'Woke up naked pissing in a corner'. Here, let me spell it out for you and get your take."

Five minutes later, DJ finished his explanation with "and Detective Sharpe's forensics team will hopefully verify that for us."

Captain Kekoa said "Tremendous work, DJ. I think you are definitely on to something here. Send me your outline. Pending what Levi's urine search team discovers, I'm good to fly this up the flagpole with the Commissioner."

DJ said, "Let's wait to be sure that we're on the right path." *Damn, I hope so. Got nothing else.*

Sharpe spoke excitedly. "We'll get on it immediately. If this pans out, there's gonna be a whole lotta people with egg on their faces."

"Deservedly so," said Kekoa. "Great job, DJ. That's some damn fine Detective work. What triggered you to go in that direction?"

"It just occurred to me that we were focusing a whole lot on the "pissing in a corner quote" without addressing how the words "woke up naked" should be considered. Then boom….it just came to me."

"Tremendous!" said Sharpe.

"Let's not get ahead of ourselves," said Kekoa. "Levi, get your team on this ASAP. I'll see you both Monday morning in my office. I'd love to have an airtight scenario for the Commissioner by then."

Chapter 77

Mia, Ricky, and Karl had just returned from Sunday mass at St. Patrick's after picking up breakfast from their favorite deli on the way home.

Ricky asked. "Why didn't Phoebs come to church with us? Is she sick?"

"She's catching up on some sleep," said Mia.

"I wanna do that next Sunday," said Ricky.

"Me too!" echoed Karl.

Mia's phone chirped. "Ricky, pour your brother a glass of juice. I gotta take this."

"Hi, Debbie. Saved by the bell!"

"Glad to help. What did I do?" asked Debbie Slater.

"Not important. So tell me all about you and Carlos."

"Things are going great. He went home to feed his fish."

"So, overnight guest? That's fantastic. I just knew it!"

"Don't go overboard, Mia. We just started seeing each other. The newness has yet to wear off."

"Honey, if the relationship is meant to be, you'll know it."

"I do have to admit that he is every bit the gentleman. And we have so much in common."

"That's tremendous. I'm so happy for you guys."

"Thanks!"

"Oh, I almost forgot" said Mia, "I wanted to pass along something from Detective Harland."

"What's up?"

"The police have proof that it was Frank who created that awful TuckerExecFreak graphic. Did he have something against Ray? Or against Tucker?"

"Not sure. Maybe he was jealous of Ray's professional success or pissed at him for not being his friend. Either way, that bastard created this media storm, and now he's doing his best to get rich from it."

The pain in Mia's voice was evident. "What did we ever do to him?"

"It's not you Mia. He's a selfish asshole! I can't believe I ever got involved with him."

"Things were different then. But, hey, you've got a brand new romance in your life. To hell with Frank."

"Yeah, but I hate that he's screwing you and the kids."

"This might all end soon. I think Detective Harland is getting close to the finish line."

"Hopefully, that'll help. Frank needs to be stopped."

"That would be a relief. Gotta go. Love you. Best to Carlos."

"Love you too."

Before returning to the kitchen, Mia grabbed her laptop journal and entered: "Debbie and Carlos are definitely an item. Wish you were here to see it Ray. Miss you."

———

Frank Dorrington needed one big salacious nugget about his "friend" Ray Pernell, that would justify his exorbitant appearance fee on the Hammy B show. Frank reviewed his list.

1-Sex: going to see a secret girlfriend.

2-Sex: going to see a secret boyfriend.

3-Sex: seeking companionship at one of SF's gay bars.

4-drugs: needed to feed his opiate addiction with Oxycodone

5-drugs: had a secret heroin habit

6-alcohol: Ray was seeking more booze. He could never drink enough."

Frank decided that options 1 and 2 weren't flashy enough. Option 3 seemed to make the most sense. Ray's loincloth outfit might be considered appropriate for seeking companionship at a gay bar. And if option 3 wasn't outrageous enough for Hammy and his studio audience, he could blend in option 4. He'd already lied about finding Oxy in Ray's jacket, so this would just be corroboration of his lie.

If Hammy and his adoring fans needed more, Frank could always mention heroin, and maybe the fictional syringe that he claimed to have found in Ray's pocket. The mere mention of heroin would fire up that studio audience. Frank thought he could skirt any legal jeopardy if he carefully worded his "revelations".

For a brief moment, Frank wondered exactly what Ray Pernell had REALLY been up to that night. He decided it must've been sex because Ray was no druggie.

Frank's phone chirped with a text from Stanley. "Good luck on Hammy B. Should be an enriching experience." Frank understood that "enriching" was the keyword. He also knew that thirty thousand wasn't going to satisfy Stanley. He needed big money.

His thoughts turned to the Connecticut casinos. Two of the world's largest casinos were only an hour away. Tomorrow, he would empty his checking account of the remaining $800, and take it to the casino to multiply it many times over.

————

DJ was rinsing dishes. Liz had made a killer eggplant lasagna for dinner.

"Tremendous meal, baby. I'm stuffed."

"Got something to tell you, Sugar."

DJ spoke over his shoulder. "What is it, Baby?"

"I'm late."

"Late for what? Where you gotta be on a Sunday evening?"

"No Sugar. The big late!"

DJ slowly turned around. "You mean late for your period?"

Liz flashed a huge smile. "Yes, Sugar. But before you go all crazy on me, I'm only a day late. The doc said not to even bother her unless I'm four or five days late."

Hands dripping, DJ wrapped Liz in a huge hug. "Look, Baby, we're ready for this, aren't we?"

"I think so. But let's not assume anything. I'm gonna buy a home pregnancy test."

"Good idea. I just know it'll be positive!"

"Maybe Sugar. But let's give this a couple more days before we start handing out cigars."

"Hear you loud and clear, Baby." DJ hugged Liz again. "Love you so much. I just know this is gonna be our time."

Five minutes later, as he was wiping down the stovetop, DJ's phone buzzed.

"Hey Levi. Ain't it past your bedtime?"

"Fat chance, my friend."

"What's the word?"

"The word is 'good'. As in, you are very good, my friend".

"They found a urine match?" *Holy shit!*

"Yessir. Exactly where you had predicted."

"Damn. That makes everything else we outlined fit together perfectly. Are we all comfortable with this scenario?"

Levi was excited. "You nailed it, partner. There's no other way this could have gone down. It's amazing how the words 'woke up naked' kinda slipped by us while we focused on 'pissing in a corner.' Kahuna was thrilled to hear about this."

So am I! "You already talked to him?"

"Oh yeah. Called him right after Forensics matched it. He's freakin' delighted. He wants the complete case scenario from you as soon as possible. He wants to push it to the Commissioner."

"This is so freakin' amazing." *Kahuna must be doing cartwheels!*

"Damn straight" said Sharpe. "You knocked this case out of the park."

"Group effort, my friend." Send me those urine-search results and I'll add them to my document and send it over to Kahuna." *Love it when a plan comes together!*

"On the way," said Sharpe. "Kahuna reminded me that we have a 9 am in his office."

"Let's get together at my desk at 8:45 for a quick prelim. See you then."

"Sleep well, my brother."

"I'll try." *No chance!*

Chapter 78

Frank Dorrington arrived at Emerson Bank at 9:02 am to withdraw eight hundred dollars from his checking account. The teller asked, "How would you like this?" She then waved at Seth Benjamin, imploring him to approve this cash transaction.

Benjamin arrived at the window. "Morning Mr. Dorrington. How nice to see you again."

"Yeah sure," said Frank.

"Mr. Dorrington, do you realize that this withdrawal leaves you with only six dollars in your account?"

"Good to know," said Frank, noting to himself that Stanley hadn't wasted a moment cashing the twenty-five thousand dollar check.

"That's below our minimum balance threshold of one hundred dollars," said Benjamin. "A thirty-five dollar penalty will be assessed to your account at the end of the month if the balance isn't back above a hundred dollars."

"I'll be sure it is."

Benjamin nodded at the Teller and she counted out eight one-hundred dollar bills, placing them in an envelope for Frank. He grabbed the envelope and headed out the door, sure that he could feel the eyes of Seth Benjamin burning a hole in his back.

———

Arriving at his SFPD desk at 8:30, DJ again reread the case scenario document he'd created. A thought occurred to him that he wanted to take up with Levi, the Captain, and maybe the DA.

The baritone voice of Levi Sharpe flowed over the divider of DJ's cubicle. "Morning, Deej. Sleep well?"

"Not much. I kept trying to poke holes in our scenario. But it feels pretty solid."

"Indeed it is my friend."

"Just had a thought, Levi. Despite his meth arrest and his revolting appearance, Johnny G was straight up with us. Should we revisit his deal?" *Hope he showered by now.*

"Makes sense. Let's take it up with Kahuna."

After grabbing some coffee, the Detectives arrived at the Captain's office a few minutes early.

"Morning guys. Beautiful day ain't it?"

"Morning Kahuna!" said Sharpe. "All things good in the neighborhood?"

"It would seem so. Already heard back from the commissioner. He's good with what we've put together. DJ's idea for the final urine search clinched it."

"What's next, boss?" asked DJ. *How about two weeks vacation?*

"The Commish will get with the DA this morning for a full review. If there are no holes shot through our conclusions, he'll hold a press conference on Wednesday."

"Well, hot damn!" said Sharpe

"Hell yes" answered Kekoa. "The Commissioner wants us to send a courtesy emissary to Tucker's offices in New York to personally walk their HR and PR teams through the results of our investigation."

"Wow," said DJ. "That's some fine corporate service for his buddy at Tucker."

"I'm glad you think so DJ. Cause you're gonna be my emissary."

"Lucky me!" *Oh yay....another session with those knuckleheads in their corporate "cone of silence".*

"Atta boy!" said Kekoa. "Just talk them through your conclusions. And remind them to keep it confidential until after our Wednesday morning press conference."

Sharpe spoke. "Captain, how about if we cut some slack to our informant, Johnny G, who actually gave us some straight truth?"

"Fair enough, Levi. You wanna help him out?"

"We did agree to help him if he told us the truth. I don't think either of us expected a slippery snitch like Johnny to be honest."

Kekoa laughed. "The truth will set you free! What're you thinking?"

"The least we can do is run it by the DA," said Sharpe. "Johnny was truthful about Hollowell's claims of shooting a 'gay man', and the 'pissing' quote Johnny gave us from Hollowell was confirmed by Oscar.

"True enough."

"He even knew the murder weapon was a 9-mil" added DJ.

"Yeah. Beyond coincidence, at that point," said Kekoa. "Even for a professional liar like Johnny. Let's see what the DA thinks. I guess we owe him that much."

"While I'm out east, shouldn't I run all of this by Pernell's widow?" asked DJ. *She deserves to hear it directly from us after all the harassment she's been through.*

"Good thought, DJ," said Kekoa. "Remind her that this is top secret until after the Commissioner's presser."

"Roger. She'll be relieved to know that Ray wasn't into any of that crazy shit that's been said about him." *Frank Dorrington's not gonna like this!*

"Stay two nights if you need to. Just take care of business and get your ass back here. We've got a huge backlog of cases."

"Thanks, Kahuna."

"Now go pack your bags. I want you on the redeye tonight and in Tucker's offices tomorrow."

———

Frank Dorrington reached out and placed full odds behind his bet on the pass line, then said "Gimme twenty-five on hard eight and hard six." Frank knew that playing craps when you're desperate for money is a bad idea. Yet, he hoped that his luck might run hot for a while, and he could quickly accumulate a few grand.

"Seven out," said the stickman. Everyone around the table moaned.

Frank's bets were all wiped off the table. "Color out," said Frank, pushing his chips forward.

Frank had quickly transformed his eight hundred dollars into about five hundred and fifty. "Damn!"

———

After thanking Marty Penderson for booking him a window seat, DJ placed his packed suitcase by the door and started making a sandwich. He heard Liz key the door.

"Sugar? You home?"

"Yeah, Baby. In the kitchen."

"Why the suitcase? You leaving me?" asked Liz facetiously as she walked into the kitchen and shared a warm hug with her husband.

You ain't that lucky. "No, I'll be back in a couple days."

"Where you going?"

"Back to the East Coast. We've wrapped the Tucker case and the boss wants me to personally walk the Tucker bigwigs through everything."

"No kidding? Who killed him?"

"You know I can't talk about that Baby. Mum's the word until the Commissioner holds his press conference Wednesday morning. Let's talk about you. How you feeling? Any morning sickness?"

"No dear. But, happily, still no period. I think I'll pick up a home test kit tomorrow."

"I feel it in my bones. We're starting our family!"

"Slow down mister. First, let me take a home test. If we get a positive, then I'll stop in to see Doctor Manier. She'll let us know for sure."

"Damn Baby. If you get a positive while I'm gone, please let me know. Don't keep me in suspense."

"Okay, Sugar."

———

A half-hour at the Blackjack table had reduced Frank's stake to about two hundred dollars.

Frank tried all three of his credit cards at the cashier's cage. All were rejected. After a fruitless thirty-minute battle with the cashier, Frank walked away with his same $200.

Five quick hands at the Ultimate Texas Hold 'em table left him with next to nothing.

Thirty minutes later, while driving on Route 2 towards Hartford, Frank's failure to raise funds, and the looming figure of Stanley, had brought him to a dark place. For a moment, he considered slamming his car into the guardrail, flipping it, and just going to sleep.

———

At 10:30 PM, DJ boarded his red-eye flight from San Francisco to LaGuardia. The meeting at TEM Corporate had been set up for 10 am Eastern time. DJ texted Mia Pernell, asking if she was available tomorrow afternoon. *Hopefully, this will bring some closure and relief to Mia.*

Chapter 79

After reacquainting himself with Security, DJ was escorted to the 8th floor at Tucker's corporate headquarters.

"Good flight, Detective?" asked Sharon Dillard.

"Fine, for a red-eye."

"Oh gosh. Every time I book a red-eye, it seems like a great idea. But it never feels that way after flying overnight. Coffee Detective?"

"Thanks, light and sweet." Two men entered Dillard's office. DJ recognized Richard Weller but had never before seen the tall, angular man with piercing dark eyes and perfectly gray temples.

Dillard spoke. "You already know Mr Weller, Detective."

DJ nodded. *Truly an unforgettable, humorless prick.*

And this is Mark Lodge, our Executive VP of Corporate Relations." Greetings were exchanged all around and Dillard directed them into her secure conference room.

"Welcome to Tucker, Detective," said Lodge. "We appreciate this courtesy call."

"Not a problem." *Not like I had a choice.*

"Okay Detective," said Dillard, the floor is yours. Can you fill us in on your investigation?"

"I can, and will," said DJ, placing his digital recorder on the table. "But first, I need your absolute cooperation on one point."

"What's that Detective?" asked Weller, peering at DJ through his half-moon readers, still permanently perched on the end of his stubby nose.

"I need your absolute assurances that what I tell you today does not go any further than this room until after tomorrow's 9 am Pacific press conference. By 12:30, eastern time, you should be good to share your reaction to our investigation. Our conclusions are being reviewed by the DA and others. Until we get their sign-off, everything I'm about to tell you is off the record. Also, we are not notifying the news media about the press conference until early morning, just in case the DA shoots any holes in our conclusions."

"Understood" said Lodge.

"Okay," said DJ. "What if I told you that Ray Pernell went to bed that night in room 407, but didn't wake up in that room?"

Seeing quizzical looks all around, DJ launched into his detailed description of the night's events.

Fifteen minutes later, DJ concluded with "So that's why we're certain we've identified the murderer, his motive, and the circumstances surrounding Mr. Pernell's outfit and motivation.

"It all makes sense," said Weller.

DJ stared silently at Weller. *Thanks for your opinion, douchebag.*

"Damn," said Lodge. "Tucker's reputation has taken a beating. But according to you, Pernell did nothing outlandish that night."

"Yes. Those are our conclusions," said DJ.

"So why is his friend telling us otherwise?" asked Lodge.

"Mr. Dorrington's claims had no bearing on our investigation. Our only concern was solving the homicide of Ray Pernell. Commissioner Francis plans to share our conclusions with the world tomorrow morning." *Dorrington will get his.*

Dillard spoke. "If this is all true, it means that Ray truly was the victim of a hate crime, even though he wasn't what his killer took him to be."

"That would seem to be the case" added Weller.

"Wouldn't be the first case of mistaken identity that resulted in murder" said DJ. "Wrong place, wrong time."

"And wrong clothing" added Dillard, dabbing her eyes with a tissue.

"I'll prepare a statement for our PR team," said Lodge.

"Just don't share it with anyone before tomorrow's press conference," said DJ.

"Of course not, Detective".

"Also, the statement I just shared may be altered before the Commissioner reads it tomorrow. Please listen carefully in the morning before sending out any public reaction."

"Understood," said Lodge. "We can't thank you enough for this private preview. Please forward our sincere thanks to Commissioner Francis for his gracious collaboration with Tucker."

"I'll be sure to do that," said DJ. *Next time he invites me for tea!*

———

Awakening after a night of fitful sleep, Frank Dorrington remembered that he'd soon be earning thirty thousand dollars for his appearance on Hammy B. He felt good about that for a split second before reality hit. That money would be going to Stanley to pay back a debt that was likely gonna cost him twice as much as he borrowed, not to mention his hand injury and whatever other horrors awaited him. Last night's failed trip to the casino came rushing back to him.

Frank read another cryptic text from Stanley. "Good luck at the Hammy show. Be careful in NYC. Such a dangerous place."

"This sucks!" yelled Frank. "I gotta get Stanley off my fucking back."

Frank started going through his drawers and hiding places, scraping up some cash for his trip to the City.

———

Liz Harland was keeping busy, but her eyes kept moving to the paper bag sitting on the corner of her desk. She'd purchased an at-home pregnancy test, and that little bag kept calling to her.

She'd promised herself that she would wait until lunch break to take the test. By 11:30, her curiosity got the best of her. She grabbed the bag and headed to the ladies room.

Only a few minutes later, she was staring at a positive test result in her shaking hand. Looking at her image in the mirror, she said "Dear God in heaven, please bless this baby". As she walked back to her desk, Liz felt like she was glowing. Grabbing her cell phone, she hit a now familiar contact number. "Hello, this is Liz Harland. I'd like to make an appointment to see Dr. Manier as soon as possible."

———

While waiting for his car, DJ saw a text from Mia Pernell. "I'll be home all afternoon. Shall I ask my attorney to be present?"

"Your attorney is welcome. No one else. This needs to be a confidential conversation. Should be there around 2p."

DJ tipped the valet, jumped in his rental, and headed out of New York City, hoping that this trip to Connecticut would bring some understanding and closure to the Pernell family.

Chapter 80

Just before 2 pm, Mia greeted DJ at the front door.

"Hi, Mia. Good to see the media has disappeared."

"Hopefully they'll stay away."

"Let's hope so".

"This is Ken Samantis, our attorney and a long-time family friend."

Standing before DJ in a golf shirt and khakis was a man with blonde hair, bright blue eyes, and a healthy complexion. DJ shook his hand. "Mr. Samantis, good to meet you."

"Likewise Detective."

Mia was anxious. "Have you got something new to tell us?"

"I do, but first I have some ground rules."

"Go ahead Detective," said Samantis.

"Everything I tell you today cannot be shared with anyone until after 12:30 pm local time tomorrow. I mean family, friends, co-workers, neighbors……nobody."

"Why the specific time?" asked Samantis.

"Commissioner Francis will hold a press conference tomorrow at 9 am Pacific. By 12:30 Connecticut time, the Commissioner will have delivered a carefully worded version of the information that I am about to share with you. The press release is still being reviewed by our legal experts in San Francisco. The content could change between now and then, so please watch the press conference to be sure that nothing I tell you here today has changed."

Samantis said: "Understood Detective. We're good with that agreement. Do you mind if I record this conversation?"

"Not at all. I'll join you," said DJ, placing his digital recorder on the table. "Just so you understand, every step of this scenario has been corroborated by eyewitnesses or participants, including Mr. Pernell."

Mia asked. "What? How can Ray give corroboration?"

"I'll get to that. Let me run through this, then you can ask your questions."

"Go ahead Detective," said Mia nervously.

"Mr. Pernell and Carlos Madrigan were intoxicated when they returned to the Smythville after their night out with their LA buddies. They spoke briefly with the desk clerk and went to the elevator. Your husband got off on the fourth floor, stumbling and dropping the bottle of sake he had been carrying. He picked up the bottle and headed to his room. Mr. Madrigan proceeded to the seventh floor and exited the elevator, going to bed.

Before going to bed, Ray tossed the sake bottle into the bathroom wastebasket, then prepped for bed, removing and folding all his clothes."

"That's exactly what he always did!" offered Mia. "Ray was neat like that."

"After setting the alarm on his cellphone, a now naked Mr. Pernell climbed into bed at 2:50 am and put on his CPAP mask. Exactly 18 minutes later, at 3:08 am, Mr. Pernell removed his mask."

"Did someone wake him up?" asked Mia.

DJ looked at Mia. "This is where your input was so valuable, Mia. No, no one woke him up."

"You just said he removed his mask. Please explain, Detective" said Samantis.

"This is something that we were already strongly considering. Then Mia told us about how Ray had injured his knee on a stairwell in New Hampshire after a night of heavy drinking but had no recollection of how he arrived there. That event was important."

"So you're talking about an AUD, correct Detective?" asked Samantis.

"Exactly. There is significant precedent for this type of behavior."

"What the hell is an AUD?" asked Mia.

DJ answered, "AUD is a broad term covering several conditions that fall under the category of Alcohol Use Disorders."

"Ray didn't have any disorders! He was fine!" exclaimed Mia.

"Mia, your husband apparently had a susceptibility to alcohol-induced blackouts, as he displayed in New Hampshire. People who blackout can engage in complex behaviors that they cannot recall once the blackout has concluded."

Mia was dabbing her eyes with a tissue. "Ray was sleepwalking?"

"No," said DJ. "Sleepwalking is quite different and can be caused by many factors. After consultation with our experts, we are terming your husband's condition as an alcohol-induced blackout."

"How do you know that?" asked Mia.

"Let me finish walking you through this, and then we can revisit some of these details. When Ray removed his CPAP mask at 3:08 am, he was functioning in an alcoholic blackout. His blackout ended when he actually 'woke up' on the fourth-floor landing of the service stairwell in the back of the hotel, still naked."

Mia sobbed. "What? How did he get there?"

"He exited his room, naked, while in a blackout, walked down the hall, through double doors, around a corner, through another door, and out onto the service stairwell where he came out of his blackout while urinating there."

"Were there no security cameras in the hallways?" asked Samantis.

"None. Security cameras in California hotel hallways are currently the subject of a lawsuit being considered by the California Supreme Court."

"Oh yeah" answered Samantis. "I'm aware of that case, it's made some national headlines."

"I don't get it Detective. How do you know that Ray was in the stairwell?" asked Mia.

"At first, we didn.'t" answered DJ. "But your husband was quoted by two individuals as saying that he 'woke up naked pissing in a corner'."

"Wait. Two people spoke with Ray? Why didn't they help him?" asked a sobbing Mia.

"I'll get to that. It was the phrase 'woke up naked pissing in a corner' that had us perplexed. We checked all the corners in and around his room for evidence of his urine but found nothing. Our original assumption was that the only place he could wake up was in his room, but as I've just described, he actually 'woke up' from his blackout in the service stairwell. Once we ascertained that he could have "woke up" outside his room, all the pieces fell into place. We found a match to his urine there, on the 4th-floor stairwell landing."

"Oh my God" sobbed Mia.

"So you placed him there, presumably naked and urinating. What happened subsequent to that?" asked Samantis.

"Of course, he would've tried to reenter the hotel, but those service stairwell doors are locked on the stairwell side. He probably pounded on the door, but no one in the far-away guest rooms would've heard anything, we tested that. Unable to reenter the hotel from the service stairwell, he looked for 2-things: something to cover his nakedness and a way to reenter the hotel."

"Oh my poor Ray!" sobbed Mia. Samantis put his arm around her.

"You okay Mia?" asked DJ

"Yes. Please go on."

"Searching the service stairwell, Mr. Pernell found a janitor's cart parked on the 7th floor. He found duct tape and cleaning rags that he used to create his 'loincloth' to, at least, cover his private parts."

"Wait. What?" said Mia "So Ray put those rags on himself, just to cover his nakedness?"

"Exactly right Mia."

"All that public bullshit about why he was dressed that way and looking for drugs or sex, was just…..bullshit?" Mia started weeping. "The pain we've endured. My daughter tried to take her life….."

DJ was shocked. "What? Is she okay?"

"Yes. Barely."

DJ spoke. "So very sorry to hear that Mia. The world will know the truth tomorrow."

"Incredible, Detective." said Samantis, "Please continue."

"Mr. Pernell saw only one way to return to his room. That was to exit the building at the ground level of the service stairwell and walk around the building to the main entrance. He exited through the door, which opens into a back alley that's often populated overnight by some of San Francisco's homeless. In the alley, Mr. Pernell encountered a homeless man named Oscar. He offered a hundred dollars for Oscar's coat. Oscar refused, seeing that your husband clearly had no money on him. Oscar described Mr. Pernell as excited, perhaps confused, and supplied us with the quote "woke up naked, pissing in a corner"."

"Why didn't this Oscar guy do something to help Ray?"

"Unlikely, Mia," said Samantis. "The homeless see all kinds of crazy stuff on the streets, and they don't get involved."

"You got that right, Counselor," said DJ. "After Oscar's refusal, Mr. Pernell continued down the alley, hoping to turn the corner and find the entrance back into the hotel. It was near the end of that alley that he encountered a man named Lester Hollowell, who was parked there, likely involved in the drug trade. We're not sure if Ray asked him for assistance, or if Hollowell approached him, but we are sure that Ray wound up in Hollowell's car and he was driven to the lot in Hollis where his body was later found."

"You've placed Ray in Hollowell's car?" asked Samantis.

"Yes, through forensic fiber matching with the cloth he was wearing."

Mia was sobbing. "What issue did this Hollowell have with my husband?"

"Hollowell had recently been released from prison. He had a long history of violence toward gays and minorities. Hollowell likely thought Ray was gay, based on his unusual appearance. He probably took Ray's life for that reason."

"How do you know that?" asked Samantis. "Has he confessed?"

"Not to us," said DJ. "He was killed two days later in a street ambush. But Hollowell had bragged the details of his murdering a 'gay man' to another witness the night before he died."

"You and I both know that's not enough, Detective."

"Understood. We felt the same way, until our homeless friend, Oscar, quoted Ray using the same exact phrase 'woke up naked, pissing in a corner' that Hollowell used when talking about his gay victim."

"Hollowell used that phrase too?"

"Yes. Word for word. Additionally, Hollowell bragged to a druggie friend about killing a 'gay' man with a nine-millimeter, which is exactly the type of slug removed from Mr. Pernell's body."

"Dear God. He must've been terrified. I hope he didn't suffer." sobbed Mia.

"Was the weapon recovered?" asked Samantis.

"It disappeared when Hollowell was ambushed."

"So let me get this straight," said Samantis. "After Ray regained his senses in the stairwell, he found the materials to make a loincloth to hide his nakedness and then left the hotel through a back alley door to find a way back into the hotel. He encountered this 'Oscar', then Mr. Hollowell who, at some point, killed him, likely because Ray's skimpy attire caused Hollowell to think he was gay. Hollowell drove Pernell to the Hollis area and left his body in a parking lot."

"Oh my poor Ray." sobbed Mia.

"You've hit the major points there," said DJ. "We don't have to prove these details to a jury. There won't be any trial. We only need to have a fact-based understanding of who the murderer was, and the events of that night, in order to close our investigation. We're very confident that we've accomplished that."

"Remarkable," said Samantis. "So all the wild talk about Ray's 'aberrant behavior' was speculative and incorrect. Yet, this likely was a hate crime. Hollowell apparently killed Ray because he thought he was gay."

"I'd agree with that assessment, sir."

"Who took the photo of Ray's body that was so hot on the internet?"

"That photo was taken by a young man who had no agenda other than to seek fame as a crime photographer. As you guys know, it was Frank Dorrington who added the TuckerExecFreak wording and pushed it out to the world."

Mia straightened up, wiping her eyes. "What can we do about that son of a bitch? Franks's been exploiting these lies about Ray since day one."

DJ looked at Samantis. "Counselor?"

"His fifteen minutes of fame are nearly up. We're putting together a libel and slander suit that should bring this all to an end."

"Excellent," said DJ. *Hope you nail that piece of shit to the wall!* "Remember to keep this information to yourselves until 12:30et tomorrow. You guys will probably think of many more questions. Text me or give me a call. And don't forget to watch the Commissioner tomorrow."

"We'll be riveted!" said Samantis.

Ten minutes later, Mia picked up her cell phone. "Hi, Debbie. There's something you need to know, but it has to be kept secret….."

Chapter 81

Wednesday 8am PT / 11am ET

A press release issued by Officer Marty Penderson of the San Francisco Police Public Relations Department notified the media that SFPD Commissioner Lorenzo P. Francis had scheduled a press conference for 9 am regarding the "SFPD's specific findings relative to the homicide of Tucker Entertainment Media executive Ray Pernell". Local TV and radio stations quickly notified their affiliated news networks and crews were scrambled to be in place by 9 am local time.

————

At 11 am ET, Frank Dorrington walked through the doors at the Penn Station studios of Hammy B Productions, anxious to earn some cash.

Recognizing the makeup artist, Frank said "Hey Kathleen. Any idea when I can talk to Jungle Jane?"

"How about right now?" Jungle Jane's voice filled the little makeup room as she swept in the door, green hair and all. "How are you, Mr. Dorrington?"

"Just fine."

"You ready to give us all that you promised?"

"Yes, of course. Am I in the Hammy Rant segment again?"

"Mr. Dorrington, you're the lead story. If you're compelling enough, we could do the whole hour with you. We're hoping that your new information will be of great interest to our audience."

"In that case, I'd like to renegotiate my rate."

"Good one, Mr. Dorrington! You've already broken the bank. Hope your info is commensurate with your asking price."

————

Liz Harland woke and showered early. Her excitement about the positive pregnancy test made sleep challenging. Her appointment with Doctor Manier was not until tomorrow at 1 pm.

Liz thought about sharing the news with DJ. The painful disappointment of their previous miscarriage suddenly entered her mind. She decided to wait until she received confirmation from Dr. Manier before telling DJ.

————

In his Hartford hotel room, DJ rose after a much-needed night of sleep. He flicked on the TV in anticipation of the Commissioner's presser. *This oughtta be fun!*

————

9 am PT / Noon ET

"Good morning ladies and gentlemen. I'm Officer Marty Penderson, with the SFPD Public Relations team. Thank you very much for joining us today as we share our findings on the homicide of TEM Executive Ray Pernell. Police Commissioner Lorenzo Francis will read a prepared statement. Following that statement, Captain Tehaki Kekoa of the Narcotics and Vice Department, whose group headed this investigation, will be available to answer your questions. Our goal here today is to provide the facts about this case, as we have discovered them to be. Now first, here are a few ground rules….."

————

"In three, two, one" The opening animation and music of the Hammy B show started playing, the studio audience quickly came to their feet and started clapping in unison. Their slick-haired, wiry hero, in his trademark jeans and sport coat, scooted out from behind the scenery and onto the set. His usual frantic energy seemed ramped up a bit more than usual as he ran along the edge of his audience, slapping high fives with everyone in the front row.

After 30 seconds of simultaneously creating and consuming the energy in the studio, Hammy waved his arms and his audience quickly settled down.

"Greetings everyone. Whether you are here in the studio or watching at home, you won't soon forget today's show. Our guest today is Frank Dorrington, close friend of Ray Pernell, the Tucker Executive who was recently killed in San Francisco. There has been much national speculation about what this TEM Senior Executive was doing at 3 am that night, wearing a loincloth and running the streets."

Watching the monitor behind the scenery, Frank Dorrington was getting pumped up. He was feeling the pressure to deliver some fresh misinformation that would befit the moment.

———

In San Francisco, Commissioner Francis was beginning his message. "I want to thank Captain Kekoa and his team for their fine investigative work. Their careful diligence has provided us with a solid explanation of the events of that night. I will now read our synopsis of those events. Please hold your questions until I'm finished."

The full media in attendance fell silent.

"Ray Pernell, Vice President of Creative Services at Tucker Entertainment Media, utilized a limo to go to dinner and celebrate the completion of a project here in San Francisco. Joining Pernell in the limo were Carlos Madrigan of TEM and two West Coast business partners…….."

———

Hammy B was wrapping his introductory remarks.

"And now, right here in our studio, Mr. Pernell's close friend, Frank Dorrington, a Connecticut Attorney, is going to divulge all he knows about Pernell's personal habits. Mr. Dorrington was with us once earlier, but he may have been holding back a couple of things to protect his friend's reputation. Let's see what he has for us today."

As Frank walked out from behind the scenery, the audience, led by the Stage Manager started chanting "Frank! Frank! Frank!".

Adrenaline was coursing through Frank's body as he walked to his chair, sat for a moment, stood up again to acknowledge the audience with a wave, and then sat down.

Hammy quieted the crowd and jumped right in with his usual directness. "So Frank, what have you come here to tell us?"

'Well, Hammy, when I came here the first time, I held back a couple of things out of respect for Ray's privacy and his family."

"Very thoughtful, Frank. So why the change?"

"I just think that people need to know the truth about these types of challenges. There are, undoubtedly, many people just like Ray out there who face the same struggles and suffer in silence. Hopefully, someone can benefit from some light being shed on those issues."

"Since you were last here Frank, you've been quoted as saying that you and Mr. Pernell hung out in gay bars and that he had an OxyCodone addiction."

"Yes. I mentioned those things. Although to be accurate, we got together in various places and only once in a gay bar."

"Right," said Hammy. "You guys met the one time in the gay bar just before his trip to San Francisco, correct?"

"Yes."

"Not a big deal, you guys can meet wherever you want. But, let's get right to it, Frank. America wants to know. What was Ray Pernell doing the night he was killed?"

Frank paused. "Well, as you know, I wasn't there with him. But going to gay bars to seek companionship was something Ray had done before."

"He told you that?"

"Yes." lied Frank. "It was something he had done several times. Probably one of the reasons he was seeing a counselor."

"Let's get this out of the way. Are you saying Pernell was gay?"

"I'll let his actions speak to that, Hammy"

"You know, being gay isn't a crime Frank. We love our gay community."

"I'm totally with you. That's why I've been defending Ray. But it was his drug and alcohol addictions that caused him to do things he'd never do when sober."

————

In San Francisco, Commissioner Francis was continuing his description of the events from the night of the Pernell murder.

"Once we knew that Mr. Pernell was on the fourth-floor landing of the service stairwell when he regained his senses, or 'woke up' as he put it, we were able to ascertain his steps from there. Seeking to cover his nakedness, Mr. Pernell found a janitor's cart on the seventh-floor landing and created his 'loincloth' from some duct tape and two old cleaning rags. Unable to reenter the hotel from the stairwell, he returned to the ground floor level, and exited into the alley where he encountered a homeless man who later quoted Pernell as saying he "woke up naked 'urinating' in a corner." He offered the man a hundred dollars for his coat, but the offer was refused because Pernell was clearly not carrying any money. From there, Pernell headed down the alley where....."

———

Frank was warming to the task, feeling the rapt attention of Hammy's studio audience. "Ray's use of OxyCodone was not something we spoke about. But it was seriously evident."

"How evident, Frank?"

Frank had rehearsed this answer. "Whenever Ray and I would get together after work, he was almost always tense, verging on the edge of angst. But after an hour or two, Ray was anything but edgy, actually kinda out of it."

"You guys were drinking, right? Couldn't it have been the alcohol?"

"The alcohol might have loosened Ray a bit, but he often seemed way more than drunk."

Hammy stood up and walked toward his adoring studio audience, preaching at them. "So you are saying, Frank Dorrington, that your buddy Ray Pernell was often out seeking sex with strangers, and was toting an OxyCodone addiction around with him as well?"

"Well, yes, but I don't know how often. It didn't seem as terrible back then as it sounds now."

Continuing to face his audience, Hammy took off his sport coat, tossed it aside, and preached, "Then I gotta ask the world, how could Tucker Entertainment Media, with all their resources and executive training, not know they had this giant problem in their midst? Would you want this man creating content for your kids to consume? What might he teach them? That OxyCodone is good? That sex with strangers is okay?"

Under the orchestration of the Stage Manager, the studio audience began chanting "Tucker Sucks! Tucker Sucks!".

After reveling in that noise for a few seconds, Hammy waved his arms and the chanting ceased. Turning to face Frank, he asked "Is there anything else about Mr. Pernell that you might have 'forgotten' to tell us?"

———

In San Francisco, Commissioner Francis was wrapping up his description of the events of that night. "Utilizing forensic evidence to place Mr. Pernell inside Mr. Hollowell's stolen vehicle was a key piece of detective work. We traced the movement of Mr. Hollowell's vehicle from the block where the Smythville is located, directly to the lot in Hollis where Mr. Pernell's body was found. That is the basic breakdown of the events of that night. I know you have many questions about the 'hows and whys'. Captain Kekoa will field those questions now. Thank you very much."

As Kekoa stepped to the podium, he faced a rising crescendo of shouted questions. "One at a time please."

———

Hammy was standing with one foot on his chair, leaning over Frank. "What else are you holding back Frank? You're past the point of protecting your friend. It's time to clean all the garbage off your side of the street."

Frank carefully considered this answer, not wanting to say anything that could put him in legal jeopardy. "Geez Hammy, I wasn't ever going to tell anyone about this, but I guess it's time to just come clean."

"Go ahead Frank" encouraged Hammy.

"As you know, I found that vial of OxyCodone in Ray's jacket. After that, my curiosity got the best of me, and I would sometimes do a quick check of his pockets when he'd run to the men's room since he often left his jacket on his barstool."

"What'd you find, Frank?"

"Usually nothing. But once, and only once, I found a syringe. I don't know what was or wasn't in it, or what it may have been used for. But that scared me."

"Did you ask him, Frank?"

"Of course not. If he knew that I was going through his pockets, that would've ended our friendship."

"Wow, Frank. That's some heavy truth you've just shared. It must be painful for you to talk about Pernell like this."

Frank lowered his eyes. "Ain't easy. Ray was my friend."

Hammy paused. The studio was silent.

Seeing an off-camera thumbs-up from Jungle Jane, Hammy nodded and then spoke. "Well Frank, maybe this video will help enlighten us. Everyone watch the monitors".

The studio lights dimmed, and the multiple monitors located around the studio were suddenly filled with the image and voice of San Francisco Police Commissioner Lorenzo P. Francis.

"Ray Pernell, Vice President of Creative Services at Tucker Entertainment Media, utilized a limo to go to dinner and celebrate the completion of a project here in San Francisco. Joining Pernell in the limo were Carlos Madrigan of TEM and two West Coast business partners…….."

Everyone in Hammy's studio was silent, except for a quietly audible "What the fuck?" which tumbled from Frank Dorrington's lips. Several minutes later, following the Commissioner's detailed description of the factual events of that night, the press conference playback ended.

The lights came on in Hammy's studio. Frank was sitting in stunned silence, not sure if he should leave the set. Immediately, the studio audience started booing and yelling insults at Frank. Hammy waved his arms to quiet them. Four uniformed security officers entered the studio. "Everyone please behave. These officers will deal with anyone who gets out of line."

Hammy gestured towards Frank saying. "We shouldn't instantly condemn Mr. Dorrington here. He wasn't present the night his friend was killed. He never claimed to know the exact behavior of his friend that night. He has only given us background on Mr. Pernell's personality, based on their experiences together in Connecticut. Right Frank?"

Frank, still in shock, saw the off-ramp that Hammy was offering him. "Exactly" said Frank. "That's the main reason that I didn't previously share a lot of these experiences I've had with Ray. I had no idea if they came into play on the night of his death."

"What's your reaction to what we just heard?" asked Hammy.

"I feel awful to hear how it happened. It's crazy to know that Ray was killed for the way he was dressed when he was only dressed that way to cover himself up."

Facing his audience, Hammy said, "Life takes some weird turns doesn't it?" Then spinning around to face his guest. "So Frank, just to remove any doubts that America may have about your character after hearing this description of your friend's unfortunate death, let's prove your honesty to them?"

"Huh? Yeah, sure. I've told no lies"

"Did you know the police have determined that it was you who created the TuckerExecFreak graphic that's become the cause of so much wild speculation?"

"I never denied that. I was just trying to…"

"Trying to what, Frank? Create a controversy where there was none, perhaps so you could profit from it?"

"But I….."

"Moving on" interrupted Hammy. "You told Detective Harland that you were a bit late to your meeting with him because you were in court when you were actually at the hospital getting your cast. And, court records from that day show that you had zero cases that morning, and did not appear in court at all that day."

"The days run together….what are you doing Hammy?"

"Just checking on your history of honesty, Frank. So everyone will know what a stand-up guy you are."

Frank noticed that two of the four uniformed officers were now positioned on either side of the set, just off camera.

"Well, at least the state of Connecticut will benefit from the anti-hate crime bill you've proposed. How's that bill coming, Frank?"

Frank gripped the arms of the chair. "Good….well, in process…not quite done."

"Shocking" replied Hammy. After looking to the heavens for apparent inspiration, Hammy stared directly into Dorrington's eyes. "Frank, I know we're paying you a large appearance fee to talk about Ray Pernell. Just how much money have you made off the death of your friend?"

Frank squirmed. "What? No. What do you mean? I loved…."

"Are you in financial trouble, Frank?" interrupted Hammy. "As far as we can ascertain, you are underwater on two business loans, and you are also indebted to a, shall we say, unconventional loan source. The type that doesn't take no for an answer?"

Frank was shocked. "How did you….? Geezus! What's going on here? What are you doing?"

"We're just trying to help you prove what an honest up-front friend you were to your buddy, Ray Pernell. You've said that you met with Mr. Pernell at a bar called Preacher's in Bristol, right Frank?"

"Yes, that's true," mumbled Frank, head hanging down.

"You said that you sat in the booths in the back, right?"

"Yeah, so?"

"Well, let me go to another source, for that, Frank." Turning to his audience, Hammy said "Is our special guest in the studio?"

The cameras spun around and a tall, handsome man rose to his feet. "Sir, may I have your name?" asked Hammy.

Taking a stick mic from the Stage Manager, the man said "My name is Carlos Madrigan."

"What's your connection to Mr. Dorrington?"

"None. But I was Ray Pernell's closest friend at Tucker. I was with him on the night he was killed."

"Of course, the Commissioner mentioned your name. What do you have to offer us, Mr. Madrigan."

"First of all, there are no 'back booths' at Preacher's in Bristol. I played in a pool league there for a couple of years. Secondly, the owner of Preacher's offered us access to his security footage of the bar entrance, which lives on the cloud in a one-year loop. We hired a private investigator to review all of the footage for the last year, using his facial recognition software, and it seems that neither Ray Pernell nor Frank Dorrington came through that door in the last twelve months."

The Hammy B studio was filled with boos from the audience.

Hammy quieted the crowd. "Ouch, Frank. Sounds like you may have made a mistake there".

Frank started to rise from his chair, considered his options, and sat back down. Running wouldn't help his cause. He was now concerned about being disbarred in Connecticut

Looking at Frank, Hammy said, "Well at least you didn't mislead us with that one meeting you had with Mr. Pernell in the gay bar.....it was called Pat's, wasn't it Frank?"

"What about it?" snarled Frank.

Hammy B again turned to Carlos. "The floor is yours, sir."

"This one was easy," said Carlos. "I drove to Pat's in West Hartford. It was closed for renovations. It took only one phone call to discover that Pat's had been undergoing renovations for more than seven weeks. That means that Pat's had already been closed for about a month at the specific time Mr. Dorrington claimed to have met Ray there for drinks."

"Ouch, again, Frank. I'm having a hard time defending you here" said Hammy."One more question Frank. Does the name Stanley mean anything to you?"

Frank was horrified. "I have nothing to say. Talk to my attorney".

"Aren't you an attorney?" asked Hammy. "Although I'm thinking that your future in that business may be in doubt at this point."

Turning to Carlos, Hammy said "Thank you, sir. It appears that we may have found Ray Pernell's actual best friend."

"Yes I was," said Carlos. "Frank Dorrington has done his best to make money off the death of a man he hardly knew, a man I loved and respected. He's brought unnecessary heartache and pain to the Pernell family." Staring at Ray, Carlos added, "You, Frank, are a lying, grifting piece of shit."

"The studio audience began chanting "Lying Frank! Lying Frank! Lying Frank!"

Frank stood up, ripped off his mic, and stormed off the set, followed by two of the uniformed officers. Rushing by Jungle Jane on his way out, he yelled "You set me up, you bitch!".

"You told the lies, sir!" answered Jane.

Frank then heard a familiar voice. "You're such a piece of shit!" Spinning to his left, he saw Debbie Slater step out of the shadows, arms folded, dismissively shaking her head from side to side.

"You! I should've known you were behind this! Why did you do this to me?"

"That's rich Frank. You did this to yourself. And you didn't give a rat's ass about who you hurt in the process."

"Fucking bitch!" screamed Frank as he stormed away.

"My best to Stanley!" yelled Debbie at the retreating Frank.

Still on the set, Hammy was energetically conducting his studio audience in the "Lying Frank!" chant when he suddenly silenced them with a wave and preached his final "Hammy Rant."

"Mr. Ray Pernell, by all honest accounts, a very decent man, suffered a horrific end to his life. And this incredibly selfish person, Frank Dorrington, sought to profit from Pernell's death, with no thought given to the harm he was causing so many others. I thank you all for helping us expose this lying sonofabitch. He has earned whatever fate awaits him." Picking up his jacket and twirling it in front of his adoring fans, Hammy delivered his signature sign-off: "I'm Hammy B - Talk later!" He then hustled out of the studio, leaving the audience chanting "Hammy! Hammy!"

As the closing show music ended, Jungle Jane grabbed a mic to address the studio audience. "Thanks so much for being here and sharing your energy. This program will air coast-to-coast Friday at 11 am Eastern time. Be sure to tune in to see the incredible moments you guys helped create. Spread the word!"

The crowd began to disperse as Jungle Jane found Carlos Madrigan standing with Debbie Slater. "That was tremendous television, Carlos! Thanks for the heads up."

"Thank you so much, Tiffany."

"Feels strange to hear my real name here" laughed Jungle Jane, aka Tiffany Raye. "And thanks for suggesting that we record the San Francisco press conference. How did you know about that before it was even announced?"

Debbie answered. "Through a friend of a friend in the Police Department. We didn't specifically know what the Commissioner was going to say, but we had a tip that we needed to record it."

"Worked out great for us," said Tiffany.

"Ray was my closest friend" said Carlos. "I knew in my heart that America was wrong. He would never do any of those things."

"Who would know better than you?" said Tiffany.

"Please thank your Dad for me. This might not have happened if he hadn't been able to put us in touch. I'm so happy to be able to expose Frank's lies."

"Me too," said Tiffany. "Dorrington stunk of dishonesty on his first visit. I admit we often push the envelope on this show, but airing straight-up lies for profit ain't what we're about, either."

"Good to know and great to see you," said Carlos, hugging Tiffany. "Many thanks and best of luck in your career."

Reaching out to hug Debbie, Tiffany said "Right back atcha, Carlos. Pleasure to meet you, Debbie. You guys make a great team"

"Yes, I believe we do," said Carlos, putting his arm around Debbie.

Tiffany added "I'm so sorry about Mr. Pernell. Sounds like he was a great guy."

"He sure as hell was…."

Chapter 82

"Good stuff, Carlos," said DJ. "That must've been a crazy scene in the Hammy studio. Friday's show is gonna be great! Thanks for the call." *I'll be watching that with Liz at home!*

Before heading to the airport, DJ placed another call. "Hi Mia, how'd you enjoy the Commissioner's press conference?"

"It was great. He laid out the facts for all the world to hear."

"How'd your family take it?"

"We all loved it. It was incredible to hear Phoebe say she was sorry that she'd ever doubted her Dad, and me."

"That's cool."

"I'm just so happy that she knows the truth about her Dad."

"She'll be alright. How about the boys?"

"Ricky was relieved too, although he now wants to strangle Frank Dorrington. I'm not sure that Karl understood much, he just misses his Daddy."

"So happy for your family."

"Appreciate that. You got any kids?"

"Working on it." *Might have one in the oven!*

"Congrats in advance. I know you'll be a good Daddy, like Ray."

"Thanks, Mia."

"I wanted to let you know that my friend, Debbie was in the studio for today's Hammy B show. Frank Dorrington was the featured guest and was busted for all his lies!"

"So I've heard from Mr. Madrigan," said DJ.

"Carlos? Excellent. So you already know. After that show is broadcast on Friday, America will know the truth about that lying bastard."

"We'll all be watching." *Absolute appointment viewing!*

"Thanks for everything, Detective. Safe trip home."

"Thanks, Mia."

———

Frank Dorrington's train ride to New Haven was spent in the bar car, pounding beers with tequila chasers. The drive home was challenging. Once home, Frank stewed in his anger, while slamming down the first four beers of a six-pack. He pounded a number on his phone.

"Hammy B Productions. How may I direct your call?

"Frank Dorrington for Analyse Boyle."

"Please hold."

"Hello, Mr. Dorrington. How may I help you?"

"Did you know what they were planning to do to me today?"

"I'm sorry sir. I work in the Legal Department. I have nothing to do with content" lied Boyle. Today's entire potential Hammy B scenario had been carefully reviewed by the Legal Department prior to the recording of the show.

"I don't believe that." slurred Frank.

"Mr. Dorrington, if you are calling to check on your thirty-thousand dollar appearance fee, it will be paid, as contractually agreed upon, immediately following the airing of this program at 11 am Eastern time Friday, the day after tomorrow."

The mention of his fee caught Frank off guard. He absolutely had to have that money for Stanley. But if Stanley heard his name mentioned on the show, Frank was as good as dead. "I'm calling to demand that this show not air. I was deceived as to the content of this program. I was unfairly and illegally blindsided."

"Please feel free to pursue that notion through legal channels, Mr. Dorrington. But you should also note, as clearly outlined in our release form, any legal action taken in an attempt to alter the content, or to delay the airing of this program shall result in the immediate withholding and potential forfeiture of any agreed-upon appearance fee."

"Thanks for nothing" growled Frank, disconnecting the call while opening beer number five. Frank's confused, drunken mind was buzzing with desperate scenarios. He now knew he couldn't take legal action against the Hammy people because he wouldn't get paid. That would be unacceptable. But maybe if Mia demanded that Hammy B cancel the show, he could still collect his fee.

––––––––––

Two hours later, DJ was at the ticket counter in Hartford's Bradley Airport. His phone again buzzed with "Mia Pernell."

"Hi, Mia."

"Detective, I'm sorry to bother you again, but I need your advice."

"What's up?"

"Frank Dorrington just called me. He sounded pissed off and drunk."

"Did he threaten you?" *His fifteen minutes are up!*

"No. But he wanted me to call the Legal Department at Hammy B and tell them that they cannot televise today's program on Friday."

"Why you?"

"He apparently thinks that I could stop the program. I'm not interested in doing that."

"Thanks for calling me Mia. Don't worry about it. I'll talk to him."

DJ blew off his flight, left the airport, and headed to Frank's home.

––––––––––

"Who is it?" demanded Frank Dorrington from behind his locked door.

"Police"

"Bullshit," said Dorrington. "Go away. I ain't talking to nobody."

"Mr. Dorrington. It's Detective Harland of the San Francisco Police Department. I'd like to speak with you." *Unless you prefer I kick your ass.*

Frank opened the door a crack."What the hell are you doing here?"

DJ stared into Frank's glassy eyes. "You okay Frank?" *Besides being shitfaced!*

"State your goddamn business, Detective. Ain't you a bit out of your juris…jurish…jurishdiction?"

"I'm here to be sure that you are thinking clearly and making the right choices. I'm aware of what went down at Hammy today." *They pulled your pants down!*

"Then you know everything. Go away."

"Listen, man. You got busted for a lot of dishonesty today. You know better than I if any of that was illegal." *If being an asshole is illegal, you're already guilty!*

"Go away!"

"Frank. Don't let your emotions get the best of you. Be careful about how you react to all this. Do not contact Mia Pernell ever again."

"Great advice. Bye." Frank tried to close the door, but DJ blocked him.

"The police can help you with the other thing. The debt you owe to the loan shark, Stanley."

"No idea what you are talking about."

"Frank, those kinds of debts are never fully paid. He will just milk you until you can no longer keep up. Then you become dispensable." *And very likely disposed of…..*

For a fleeting second, Frank wanted to yell "help!", but he knew that no one could possibly help him.

"Get the fuck away from me!" screamed Frank, as he finally managed to slam the door.

Returning to his rental car, DJ texted Captain Kekoa and Marty Penderson, telling them that he needed one more day here in Connecticut.

This asshole might do something stupid.

Chapter 83

After getting the kids off to school, Mia opened her laptop. She reviewed her most recent entry. "We now know what happened to you, Ray. It must've been so scary. I pray you are in a better place."

Mia's phone buzzed. She felt a chill when she saw "Frank Dorrington" on the screen.

"Stop calling me Frank! There's nothing to discuss."

Frank Dorrington spoke in slow, slurred words. "You have to tell the Hammy people to cancel that show. They'll listen to Ray's widow."

"Are you shitting me? You sound drunk, Frank. I can't wait to see that show. You're the goddamn attorney. You figure it out!"

Frank sounded angry. "I can't do that. Mia, you gotta do this! It's a matter of ….."

"A matter of what, Frank?"

"Fuck!"

"Do you know the pain you've caused me and my family? You're a lying asshole. You need to go away and leave us alone!"

"Mia, if you don't do this I'll….."

"You'll what? Are you threatening me?"

Frank disconnected the call.

Mia reached for her laptop and entered "Frank Dorrington called at 8:15 am. He was drunk. Demanded that I try to stop the Hammy show from airing tomorrow. Scared me."

DJ woke in his hotel room. *Oh yeah, still here.*

Checking his phone for any messages from Liz, he found only a text from Mia. "Frank Dorrington called this morning. Very drunk. Still wants me to cancel the Hammy show."

DJ texted Mia. "I'm still in Connecticut. I'll go talk to Dorrington again. Then I'll stop by your place."

———

Arriving at Dorrington's apartment, DJ got no response at Frank's door despite his loud pounding. *He's either passed out or heading out of town.* A call to Frank's phone went unanswered. DJ headed back to his car.

———

Mia heard a knock on her door. "Be right there Detective." As soon as she opened the door, she tried to slam it shut. Frank Dorrington forced his way in.

"Get out of here right now Frank!" screamed Mia, reaching for her phone.

Frank swiped at her hands, knocking the phone away. "Listen to me Mia" slurred Frank in a husky voice. "You gotta talk to the Hammy people and cancel that show."

"You're crazy! And drunk!" said Mia, backing slowly away. Frank grabbed her by her arm, and forced her onto the couch, "Sit!".

"Frank don't do this! Walk away now and no one will know."

Frank leaned over Mia, his drunken breath assaulting her nostrils. "You know, I always liked Ray. Why didn't he like me? I tried so hard. He always dodged me. He acted like I was beneath him."

Mia tried to calm things down. "Frank, he liked you fine. He just had a whole other life with his work. We didn't see him that much either."

"Fucking Ray had it all. Beautiful wife. Family. Great job. Money." Frank was growing more agitated. "My goddamn wife left me. My law firm tanked. Why did life fuck me? Who said Ray could live my life?

"Stop it, Frank!"

"You should've been my wife, not that bitch Debbie!"

"You're crazy! shouted Mia. She jumped up, running toward the door. Frank tackled her. Rolling over in his grasp, Mia yelled "Let me go!" She twisted the fingers jutting out from the cast on Frank's left hand. Frank howled. Struggling to her feet, Mia tried to break free, but Frank's strength was too much. He pinned her arms to her body and tossed her toward the couch. Mia's body landed on the couch, but her head slammed against the end table and she went limp.

"Get up, Mia!" demanded Frank. Mia remained motionless. Frank crept closer. "C'mon Mia, I know you're faking." Seeing blood trickling from Mia's ear, Frank reached out to nudge her head. It rolled off the table as if her neck were made of rubber, and Mia's body crashed to the floor.

"Oh no! Fuck! Fuck!" Frank turned and ran out the front door……slamming directly into a bear hug from Detective Harland.

"Whoa! What's your rush Frank?" said DJ as he drove Frank face-first into the turf and cuffed his hands behind his back. Standing Frank up, DJ marched him back into the house where he spotted Mia's motionless body.

"She was like that when I got here! I swear it!"

"Shut-up asshole!" DJ slammed Frank to the floor and quickly dialed 911, requesting an ambulance and police assistance.

Seeing the awkward position of Mia's neck, DJ did not want to move her. He whispered in her ear "Mia, can you hear me? Mia? Mia?"

There was no response.

Chapter 84

"Oh my God, Sugar. Are you ok?" exclaimed Liz Harland from her office desk. DJ had just described the morning's events on the East Coast.

"I'm good," said DJ, from just outside the waiting room at Hartford Hospital's Bone and Joint Institute. "Mia's still in surgery. Dorrington's under arrest. He'll be charged with felony assault and possibly attempted murder. If Mrs. Pernell doesn't survive, those charges will change."

"That's awful. Her poor family. How long will you be out there, Sugar?"

"Until tomorrow. I'll be home late night. Sorry about this, Baby. What's going on at home?"

"I'm seeing Dr. Manier today. She'll let us know our status."

"What status?"

"I had a positive test Tuesday."

"What? That's super! How you feeling? Any sickness? This is great!"

"Slow down, Sugar. The doctor has to confirm our pregnancy. Those home tests aren't always accurate."

"Okay. But, damn! This is so cool. You sure you don't wanna know the sex of our baby?"

"We'll talk about that later. Gotta get back to work. I'll let you know when I know."

"It'll be good news, Baby. Call me as soon as you know."

———

"Is Mommy ok, Oji?" asked Karl Pernell.

"Yes, the doctors are fixing her up right now," said his Grandfather. "But she might be away for a few days." Looking at Phoebe and Ricky, he added "And when she comes home, she'll need your help to keep things running around here."

"I want to be at the hospital with Mom," said Phoebe.

"Me too" added Ricky.

"We can't do anything there right now. Let's just pray for your Mom's full recovery," said Myoko Higoru.

Phoebe spoke "I know, Oba. But I just want to be near her."

"I know sweetheart."

————

DJ Harland returned to the waiting room, rejoining Carlos and Debbie.

"Thank God you got to Pernell's when you did," said Debbie. "Frank lost his freakin' mind."

"I only wish I could've been there sooner." *I should've broken HIS goddam neck.*

"How long are you sticking around?" asked Carlos.

"Hopefully out tomorrow evening."

A woman in surgical garb walked into the waiting room. "Pernell family?"

"Right here!" said Debbie.

"I'm Doctor Burns. Mrs. Pernell is out of surgery. She has suffered trauma to her C4 through C7 vertebrae. She is stabilized and will be in a halo for a while."

"Is she gonna be ok?" asked Carlos

"It'll be a long road, we may need to stabilize her neck with further surgery, but her prospect for a full recovery is good."

"Thank God," said Debbie. "Can we see her?"

"She is currently under sedation. Tomorrow afternoon would be better. She'll be in ICU, so immediate family only."

"Thank you so much, Doctor"

— — —

After returning to his hotel room, DJ was preparing a report summarizing the events of the day for Captain Kekoa.

His phone buzzed with a text message from Liz.

DJ stared at the message. "Just back from Dr. Manier's office. In a meeting for the next two hours, but I promised to tell you right away, so: CONGRATULATIONS DADDY!"

With a loud "Yeah Baby! I'm gonna be a Daddy!" Devante James Harland began dancing around his hotel room in Hartford Connecticut, 3,000 miles away from his precious Liz, but feeling closer than ever.

Chapter 85

Friday - 10:50 am ET

At the nurses' station, outside the ICU, DJ flashed his badge. "I was the officer on the scene when Mrs. Pernell was attacked. I must speak with her as soon as possible."

"Ok officer, but she may be sluggish. She is under significant sedation."

"Yes, of course".

Seeing Mia, with the halo screwed to her skull, was both disturbing and uplifting for DJ. She looked terribly uncomfortable, but he was so happy to see her alive. *Oh damn, that looks painful.*

"Mia?"

Mia's eyes slowly opened. Realizing she couldn't move her head, she did her best to survey the room. Her eyes settled on DJ. A look of recognition came over her face. She tried to speak, but only a raspy grunt escaped her throat.

"Hi, Mia. Don't try to talk. You look great! Do you remember Frank Dorrington coming to your home? Blink once if you do."

Mia slowly blinked once.

"He injured you. But you're going to be ok. Do you understand that?"

Mia blinked again.

"Excellent! Have I got a treat for you!" DJ reached up and pulled down an articulating arm which was dangling along the side of Mia's bed. The end of the arm held a small TV. DJ dialed up the correct station. Turning up the volume, he said "This is what it looks like when the good guys win."

Mia's eyes widened as the music and animation for the Hammy B show began to play on her TV.

———

At the Pernell house, the family was gathered around the TV.

"This is important for you all to see. Lying and dishonesty are never the correct choice" said Hiroshi.

————

Four of Ray Pernell's five direct reports were gathered in Sharon Dillard's office, in front of her giant flat-screen monitor. Tim O'Shea led the boos when Frank Dorrington first appeared on the screen.

————

Ray Pernell's fifth direct report, Carlos Madrigan, had his arm around Debbie Slater as they reclined on her couch in Connecticut.

"I've never been a big Hammy B fan, but I wouldn't miss this for the world!"

————

Sitting in his jail cell, a despondent Frank Dorrington heard the Hammy B music playing from a TV at the guard's station. "Turn that shit off!" yelled Dorrington.

"Fuck you prisoner" was the response. "Been looking forward to this."

————

Captain Tehaki Kekoa and Detective Levi Sharpe had agreed to meet at 8 am PT in Kekoa's office to watch the Hammy B show.

"Damn! Shoulda brought some popcorn" said Sharpe.

————

The Hammy B program reached the point when the Commissioner's press conference was played. That was followed by Hammy and Carlos Madrigan calling out Frank on his series of lies about Ray.

In the ICU, Mia squeezed DJ's hand.

"I know. Ain't this great? Frank's bullshit gets exposed on national TV. You and your family are due an awful lot of apologies."

————

Ricky Pernell was yelling at the TV. "I'd love to get my hands on you Dorrington, I would make it hurt!"

"Easy my Grandson. If there's any justice in this world, that man will never walk the streets again."

———

Debbie turned to Carlos. "Your five minutes of fame are coming up!"

Carlos smiled. "I can't wait to see the look on his face when he gets outed. I couldn't see him clearly from my spot in the audience."

"His reaction is precious!"

———

"Oh, that was a good one!" laughed Detective Sharpe. "Dorrington's getting burned so much, he needs gauze pads."

"So sad," said Captain Kekoa. "This bastard of a human being caused so much needless pain for the family of a man who was murdered. Gotta be a special place in hell for him."

———

In Sharon Dillard's office, the hooting and hollering began when Carlos made his appearance on Hammy. "Our man!" yelled Leigh Grayson.

"You tell him!" shouted Mitchell Claudino.

"Love it when justice prevails" added Bill Grayson.

———

Sitting on the edge of his aluminum bed with his hands over his ears, Frank yelled at the guard station. "Turn that shit off!"

"Shut up cocksucker! Wow, they really nailed your ass without lube!"

Frank kicked the breakfast tray that was sitting on his cell floor. He saw a folded piece of paper tumble free. Picking it up, he read "I told you not to fuck me. You won't last a day in the penitentiary."

Frank removed his shirt and used his teeth to start shredding it.

———

The Hammy B show ended.

In the Pernell house, Phoebe couldn't stop crying. "What an evil jerk! My life has been absolute hell because of him."

"He's an asshole," said Ricky. "I hope he gets what he deserves."

"Oh, he will," said Hiroshi. "Let's go to the hospital to see your Mom. They said she should be able to see immediate family this afternoon."

———

Captain Kekoa turned off his TV. "Now that was some quality television!"

Detective Sharpe shook his head "What an idiot. How the hell did he expect to get away with that shit?"

"Desperation knows no bounds."

"Ain't that the truth? Hey Captain, speaking of desperate dudes, should I let our snitch, Johnny G, know that the DA is about to shorten his bid because he did us a solid?"

"Yes, Levi. The DA's on board. What're you waiting for? Get on it. Then we've got a hundred more cases that need our attention!"

Sharpe threw a mock salute. "Yessir, Kahuna!"

———

"Wow, that was fun! Carlos deserves an Oscar," said Tim O'Shea. Everyone in Sharon Dillard's office excitedly voiced their agreement.

A silence settled over the room as the euphoria evaporated. The loss of Ray Pernell rushed back into the hearts and minds of his closest co-workers. Sharon Dillard spoke for everyone. "Damn, we all miss you, Ray."

———

Debbie turned off the TV and looked into Carlos' eyes.

"This doesn't happen without your hard work and your connection with Jungle Jane".

"I knew Tiffany would help us out if we could show her that Frank was lying about his friendship with Ray. But you provided the ultimate hammer: Stanley's name. That triggered Frank into panic mode."

Debbie's eyes moistened. "I think Ray would've loved what we did."

"For sure. We did the right thing."

"It took both of us. We make a great team!"

"Yes we do," said Carlos, wrapping his arms around Debbie. "There's no one I'd rather be teammates with."

———

Frank Dorrington tied the torn strips of his shirt together and wrapped his makeshift "rope" around his neck, twisting very tightly until he couldn't draw a breath. Laying on his bed, choking, he bound his neck securely to the aluminum bed. With a burst of energy, he rolled his body weight off his bed, creating a popping sound. Then nothing.

———

DJ assured Mia that Doctor Burns had just shared a very positive prognosis for her full recovery. *I'm sure that's what she would've told me if I had actually seen her this morning.*

Mia seemed to be drifting in and out of clarity. DJ said his goodbyes and promised to check in with her soon. Just before turning to leave, he said "Hey, did I tell you that I'm going to be a father?" Mia grasped his hand and tears welled up in her eyes.

She tried to speak.....she pushed the sounds out twice before DJ finally understood what her raspy voice was saying.

"Good Daddy....like Ray."

You got that right, sister!